Shadow Beneath the Bluffs

a novel

Ted Bolerjack

This book is a work of fiction. Any reference to historical events, real people, or real places are used fictitiously. Other names, characters, places and events are products of the author's imagination, and any resemblance to actual events, places or persons, living or dead, is entirely coincidental.

Copyright ©2024 by Ted Bolerjack

ISBN Print: 979-8-9915367-0-7
ISBN eBook: 979-8-9915367-1-4

All rights reserved. No part of this book may be used or reproduced in any manner whatsoever without written permission except in the case of brief quotations embodied in critical articles and reviews.

Chapter One

Luck came and luck went, and now it was nowhere to be found, leaving Algernon Crisp trapped. Ensnared in the tangled web of his own making, he searched desperately for a dignified exit as his schemes unraveled.

"Don't know what's worse—the cards in my hand or the whiskey in this glass," he commented flatly.

The dim atmosphere in the Pendergast saloon buzzed with a raw energy that harkened back to Kansas City's bygone days, a time only a decade earlier when the then-named City of Kansas was still considered a rowdy frontier boom town. That energy was still palpable in the winter of 1893 all along Ninth Street in a notorious stretch known as "The Wettest Block in the World", where the entire strip in a one block area was lined with an unbroken chain of saloons, each beckoning to the merry and downtrodden alike, each offering a respite from the sober demands of daytime society.

In the rear of the adjoined dance hall, on a small stage, three crib girls belted out *Ta-Ra-Ra-Boom-De-Ay* to the accompaniment of a piano that was out of tune. Their voices competed with a constant clinking and clattering of beer mugs delivered by topless waitresses to an eclectic crowd of top-hatted hustlers, freshly shaven cowboys, spruced-up country bumpkins, and professional gamblers dressed to the nines.

"Any more wagers?" the dealer asked, his hands hovering just above the cards.

Crisp, wholly absorbed in the cards, and trapped both in game and spirit, sat back from the baize-covered table, his hand held close and angled to avoid prying eyes. He'd been hoping for an eight or a king, but luck had abandoned him again. With his free hand, he rubbed the back of his neck. A cloak of gloom settled over his spirit, the weight of his failures, both in and out of the saloon, pressing down like the heavy air before a storm. Amidst the noisome racket of the barroom, his attention occasionally drifted to revelers and their rough shouts from the adjoining bar, yet he remained largely unfazed, his nerves hardened by years spent in the gambling dens and dance parlors of Kansas City's West Bottoms. He blithely ingested the sights and sounds surrounding him, puffing on his Peruvian cheroot, and pondered what to do next.

As he brought his arm down, his elbow brushed against his coat jingling the few remaining coins tucked in his breast pocket, and reminded him he had one or two hands of play at best to break even.

"Excuse me, sir, but do you mind moving the game along?" This sudden outburst was followed by an exaggerated, "hmph!"

Crisp looked up from his cards at the impudent son of a bitch sitting across from him. His eyes narrowed, a flash of irritation crossing his features, with a chill of disgust at the mere thought that someone so crass would dare challenge his tempo.

He assessed the gentleman opposite him who sported an impeccably tailored black suit, its sharp lines and custom fit complimenting a vest of maroon and gold brocade that bespoke of elegance. A black bow tie added a final touch of finesse. His slick hair, recently trimmed and perfumed, was parted from the left, and a thick, well-groomed mustache adorned his upper lip. The man's soft brown eyes, held a gentle gaze; a man at ease, with no hint of stress or despair, nor why should there be, when a large stack of chips, evident of his winnings, lay on display in front of him. All in all, the man exuded wealth and affluence, and if he thought his apparent prosperity would jar Crisp into action, well then, he may be damned!

Likewise, this fellow sized up Algernon Crisp in the same instant. He supposed correctly that Crisp was somewhere north of thirty, his unkempt hair and three-day old razor stubble speckled with grey suggested probably closer to forty. Puffy circles beneath a pair of blue eyes—slightly dilated and reddened—hinted at a recent lack of sleep and although he possessed an intelligent stare, his gaunt face and high forehead were etched with lines, alluding to a man beset with worry. A threadbare, wool suit hung on Crisp's lean frame and suggested a cut at least a decade out of style. Observed through the discerning eyes of a legal professional, indeed were he to describe Crisp to a jury, he would depict him as a gentleman recently, and most unfortunately, fallen on hard times.

In exasperation, Crisp displayed his cards on the table provoking snorts and chuckles from the surrounding players. The dealer, indifferent to the drama unfolding before him, efficiently raked the chips toward the ever-increasing pile of winnings in front of the well-dressed man.

Crisp tamped out the remains of his cheroot in a tin ashtray, and frugally stuffed the remaining inch-long butt into his breast pocket, throwing down the next ante in the same maneuver. He was tired of being broke, tired of being on the bottom rung of a ladder that had not been used in several months, and tired of trying to eke out a day-to-day existence from his meager winnings. He was all in on this last chance to avoid walking out empty handed, and dreaded the thought of having to ask his girl Cassie for another short-term advance.

The dealer paused while the others decided whether to stay in or retire, and Crisp held on to the hope of one more good hand. He'd played his cards well all afternoon, yet his target cards had never come. It dawned on him then: could one of these swindlers have pulled a fast one? Doubtful, but possible. Perhaps the house had rigged the deck. Crisp despised cheating, despised corruptness, and if either were true, what then would be his recourse?

A boisterous outburst of laughter from a nearby table momentarily diverted his focus. He recognized the two men at the center of attention. The first was Bill Haggan, a tough guy, a real delinquent. Fearless and impulsive, a hard drinker and hard gambler. The other man was Ed Findlay, a lothario, easy going, but gambler at heart. Both men worked for Boss Jim Pendergast, and although Crisp did not know in what capacity, everyone knew who worked for Pendergast; he was always surrounded by two or more men that were part of his ring, but no one knew what those men did, and truthfully, most people didn't care. They simply thought of "Big Jim" as a jovial man, a friend of the working class, someone who was there to help them out, and his ring of hangers-on was nothing more than a natural element to the man's persona.

Crisp played his hand, another loss. Luck had abandoned him again. There was always hope it was hiding on the backside of the next hand, so he motioned to be dealt just one more round. He looked around the saloon. All the tables but one held card games and frequent gamblers. These were not city slickers, nor travelers just off the train on Union Avenue, but the frequent cardsharps and plungers of The Bottoms. He recognized several players at other tables he had once faced: Silver Jim, Barnabas Bixby, Dazzling Jim Dare, and Blackjack Barrett to name a few. But he also caught sight of the most notorious man in the room, Boss Jim Pendergast.

Pendergast stood behind the bar alongside one of his cronies who distributed cash in exchange for paychecks deposited with his private bank. The last of the workers lined up to cash his check, pocketed a roll of greenbacks, and thanked Jim for his hospitality. Pendergast patted the man on the shoulder, "Remember, you don't have to spend your money here, but if you do, tell him the first beer is on me!"

"Thank you, Boss, you're too kind!" and with a large grin and pocket full of cash, the man proceeded directly to the bartender to funnel his hard-earned pay back into the Pendergast bank account.

With the weekly distributions paid out and a room full of happy customers, Pendergast made his rounds, greeting patrons by name, inquiring about their families, and listening to heartfelt stories of tragedy and sorrow that beset the working-class men of The West Bottoms. On more than one occasion, Crisp spied Pendergast reaching into his pocket to withdraw a handful of coins to share with down-trodden customers. Crisp knew these favors paid themselves back a hundred times over in the form of votes that kept Jim in power, for "Alderman Jim", another of his titles, controlled the First Ward—everything west of the Bluffs where the city proper stood—as democratic party leader. Political favors were the backbone of the Pendergast machine. Favors for the working man, favors for the police department, favors for other business men, all paid off in allowing Pendergast to run The West Bottoms from City Hall, and allowed Pendergast to keep things as they are.

Recent laws aimed at curbing betting and games of chance passed The Bottoms. Any attempt to discourage the vice that was the way of life in the district were also shrugged off by the Pendergast machine. The police were on his side, and while every morning they were there to sweep the streets clean of drunkards, they never threatened Jim's businesses that brought money into The Bottoms and kept it there.

Crisp despised corruption, despised politics of this nature, but he had to hand it to Jim; it was all handled behind a firm handshake and a wide smile. It all appeared on the up and up. There were no stories of corruption surrounding Boss Jim, but Crisp knew it was there. Power and corruption always went hand in hand. Jim was just good at hiding the corruption and flaunting his power.

The interruption came as a jolt. A young boy, ragged and earnest, tugged violently at Crisp's sleeve.

"Colonel, they just fished a barrel out of the river what contains a chopped-up body. Down in The Patch." The boy looked upon the table realizing his intrusion and turned back to Crisp, "I thought you would want to know."

The table fell silent at the boy's announcement, the momentary pause in the game marking the gravity of the news.

"Indeed? Thank you, Percy my boy," Crisp replied, handing the youth a few coins from his pocket. Recognizing the potential significance of this grim find, Crisp pushed back from the table, his mind already turning over the implications. "Gentlemen, I must take my leave," he announced, standing abruptly.

The other men at the table seemed to ignore the absurd interruption, all but the legal man across from Crisp whose brow was frozen upwards in an arch that did not hide his curiosity. The games and petty victories of the saloon suddenly seemed trivial against the backdrop of murder in the streets of Kansas City. As he left the haze of cigar smoke and the clatter of chips behind, Crisp stepped onto Ninth Street, his thoughts dark with the possibilities of what lay ahead.

Accompanied by the boy, he approached the intersection of Ninth and Genessee. The closeness of the icy Missouri River just a few blocks away cast an immediate chill through Crisp, mingling the cold of late winter with the dark foreboding that mirrored his own turbulent thoughts.

He inwardly urged himself forward despite the dread pooling

in his stomach. "Where exactly is this barrel you spoke of?" Crisp asked, urgency tightening his voice with curiosity.

"Just ahead, where the street ends at the river." The boy extended a thin arm toward the ignominious enclave known as The Patch, an area less than two blocks square; a cesspool of human misery, squeezed unceremoniously between the meatpacking plants of The West Bottoms.

The lowlands at the convergence of the Kansas and Missouri rivers were aptly named The West Bottoms due to the flat land that sat beneath the bluffs upon which the heart of the city was built. Originally settled by French fur trappers, the area blossomed in the years after the Civil War and became the industrial powerhouse of Kansas City, housing its railroads, stockyards, and dozens of factories and warehouses. And with the industrial boom came waves of European immigrants and transient workers who carved out a meager existence in the surrounding environs, including The Patch.

The dismal stretch was best described as one of the most wretched slums in America and a blight on the city's landscape. It was a place where the air hung heavy with the reek of sewage and the remains of dead animals strewn carelessly along its narrow and muddy footpaths. Tiny shanties were hastily thrown together on any barren spot of land. Scraps of rusty sheet metal, aged and weather-worn lumber, broken bricks, and even hollow logs, were assembled in every combination imaginable to make small homes for the people of The Patch.

"Over there, the place where the Croats sort through the renderings," the boy continued, his tone indicating a grim familiarity with the site.

They crossed a half-dozen sets of railroad tracks, avoided a passing steam locomotive shunting cars into a siding, and wound their way through a pile of brambles and thorny bushes that signified the river's edge. A crowd had already formed—a mix of curious onlookers and desperate scavengers—drawn to the grotesque spectacle of the barrel washed up on the riverbank.

Despite the cool breeze coming off the river, the stench of decay was overpowering, forcing Crisp to seize a handkerchief to fend off the assault on his senses. Offal from the nearby packing plants was routinely washed out to the river in long troughs, and on any given day, it was common to see recognizable animal parts floating amongst the rancid flotsam and lurid foam that gathered at the water's edge.

It was one of those days in the American plains where just twenty-four hours earlier the temperature had been forty degrees warmer. But today, the sun hid behind a grey cloak of shapeless clouds, and although a brisk west wind threatened to take away many a top hat, Crisp was thankful for the cool breezes near the riverfront. The river, swollen from upstream rain and snow melt, lapped at a barrel so ordinary, yet so ominously significant on this blustery day.

"Who discovered the barrel?" Crisp turned on a group of men standing nearest the waterline.

"I found it, washed up here," a mud-caked man emerged from the crowd, his Eastern European accent thick as he gestured towards the river's edge. "I opened it, but didn't touch nothing," he added defensively and stepped back to blend into the gathered mass.

Crisp edged forward, his detective instincts leaping into action as he peered into the barrel. The sight that greeted him was haunting: a human leg grotesquely flopped over the rim, swaying with the gentle push of the water. He moved closer to get a better view of the contents, withdrew a notepad from his coat pocket, and began to jot down his observations. Crisp, a self-employed, inquiry agent—a private detective—had been commissioned by the labor union representing the workers in the nearby packing plants. As he surveyed the carnage before him, he realized with a sinking heart that this brutal scene would bring that job to an abrupt end.

At that moment, the relative calm was shattered by the authoritative shouts. "You there, stay back! Everyone, go about your business!" Three lawmen arriving on the scene quickly pushed the crowd back. "This is police business. Move along there."

The command was clear, but Crisp, known for his tenacity and disdain for authority, especially when it masked incompetence, stayed put. Although the patrolmen looked nearly identical—they were dressed in double-breasted long coats adorned with brass buttons, and wearing tall derby-style hats—he recognized one of them as Dennis Crotty, a patrolman whose integrity had often been questioned in the whispers of The West Bottoms. The onlookers stepped back and a few even disbursed, but curiosity held most of them in place, including the boy Percy who peered out from behind a tall man in the crowd.

"That includes you too Crisp; we don't need your help here!" With a flick of his hand, Crisp dismissed the nightstick prodding his ribs and confronted Crotty, "I happen to be here on business." The recognition was mutual, and with a begrudging nod from another patrolman, Crisp was allowed a closer look. The officer next to Crotty, Detective John Halpin, was already ankle-deep in the muck, his eyes narrowing as he assessed the scene with a mix of fascination and revulsion. Together, they heaved the barrel onto the bank, tipping it to reveal its macabre contents. A body, dismembered and pale, tumbled out, each part a silent testament to a brutal end. Crisp, ever the observer, noted the distinctive scar running down the victim's face—a detail that confirmed his worst fears.

Halpin covered his mouth in disgust to avoid gagging. "We'll have to get the surgeon down here directly. It will be a tough job identifying this poor sod."

"I can tell you who it is." Halpin's head jerked up to look at Crisp. "Josef Bolinsky, union leader from the Dold plant. I've been hired to look into threats he'd received."

The revelation drew a snide remark from Crotty, "Seems like you failed the man."

Crisp ignored the jab, his focus narrowing as he pieced together the implications of Bolinsky's murder. This was no random act of violence, but a calculated message meant to sow fear among those who dared challenge the powers that be. Crisp looked on in derision as Halpin took statements and Crotty shooed the last of the onlookers away. Their lack of concern for the victim was apparent in their lingering conversation, dismissing Bolinsky as no one of significance in the city.

Crisp gestured to Percy to follow him up the riverbank. He glared back at the lawmen, confirming they were out of earshot and muttered, "Fools." He quickly dismissed them, his mind shifting to the real work that lay ahead, already mapping out the next steps in his investigation.

Three days after the grisly discovery, Crisp lay on a narrow bed he rented in the Meadows Boardinghouse, gazing at the ceiling of his modest room. A single window facing Ninth Street, fogged and forlorn, let in just enough light to reveal the sparse contents: an iron-framed bed centered on one wall, an uneven wooden chair leaning against a scratched dresser, faded and peeling wallpaper adorning the walls, and brown water stains mottled upon the ceiling. The austerity of the room held a quiet dignity, mirroring his own resilience.

The mystery of Bolinsky's murder had slipped from his grasp, and was now entangled in the slow, indifferent hands of the police. The lack of resolution gnawed at him; there would be no payment from the union, and more unsettling, likely no justice for the man either. The city detectives would question locals, inquire with coworkers from the Dold packing house, and soon hit the same dead ends Crisp had, and he knew from there the case would likely fade into another unsolved mystery.

"I was damned close to figuring this out," Crisp muttered with a tinge of frustration. "I'd narrowed it down to just a couple of rabble rousers in the plant who, when properly interrogated, would've confessed their sins against the poor man."

"Why don't you give their names to the police?" suggested

the soft voice beside him. Cassie Curtain, her head nestled against his shoulder, offered a semblance of comfort in the confined room. "They should know what you've uncovered."

"It irks me to think that I've done their work for them. But perhaps you're right, out of respect for Bolinsky, I should share what I've learned."

"Or—" she shifted slightly, her eyes searching his, "what if you finish it for them? Forge ahead, show them. Show them you can solve this mystery with your skills alone. Don't let Bolinsky's death be in vain."

"To what end? Show them what?"

"You have the ability to see through the lies, to piece together the truth from the smallest clues. You see patterns others miss. Use those skills now. Show them you're a good detective, Charlie."

Crisp glanced at her, his expression softening. He nodded slowly, considering her words, "Sometimes I wonder if it's all worth it, Cass. It doesn't matter how good I am, my reputation is shot in this town... it weighs on me." Pushing the covers back, he swung his legs out of bed and reached for his trousers. He moved to the dresser where *The Kansas City Star* lay folded alongside a porcelain platter holding a teapot and cup—a routine courtesy from his landlady, Beatrice Meadows.

The scent of Cassie's perfume lingered in the air, a silent testament to the night's company, which had not gone unnoticed by Meadows when she brought up his breakfast. Her boardinghouse on Genessee Street, just south of the city's most notorious block on Ninth, was known for its respectability—a rare virtue in The Bottoms. Unlike most of the brothels, listed as boardinghouses in the city's registers, Meadows maintained a "clean" establishment, catering to the hardworking men from the surrounding factories and stockyards. Crisp's relationship with Cassie, while not explicitly concealed, was tolerated with a discreet nod by Meadows, who never pressed for details so long as decorum was maintained under her roof.

Crisp picked up the newspaper, scanned the headlines, and sipped the last of his lukewarm tea.

"See, here's another one that'll go unsolved," he announced, his voice tinged with cynicism as he read aloud, 'Body Found Near Union Depot.'"

"Is that yesterday's paper?"

Nodding, Crisp set the paper down, reached into the pockets of his coat draped on the edge of the bed, and fished out three stubs of the Peruvian cheroots he favored. He meticulously unfurled each of the used cigarette butts dropping their unsmoked remains into a tiny jar.

"I guarantee we shall never hear of the poor victim or the cause of her death again. On the other hand, if her body had been discovered somewhere above the bluffs, or if she were someone of stature in this town, perhaps they'd muster some effort to investigate properly and find her killer."

"Killer? Maybe it were just an accident?" Her voice held a flicker of hope, betraying her naivety.

He paused, turning to look at her with a skeptical arch of his brow. "There are not many details here, but I'm certain it was no accident. The paper would declare it differently if it were." He returned to his task, mixing tobacco with a pinch of Walker's Paste—a mild opiate to ease the day's frustrations.

He moved into bed, paper in hand, where Cassie promptly snuggled against him.

"Can you close that window?" She burrowed further beneath a heavy blanket.

"In a moment." He lit a small wooden pipe inhaling deeply on the tobacco and opiate tincture. "Look at this one," he said exhaling a cloud upwards. He handed her the pipe still smoldering and as she drew on it, he read, "'City Behind the Times'." He skimmed the news story and set the paper down. She handed the pipe back to him and he started to draw again but realized the bowl was empty. He scooted out of bed, closed the window, and moved back to the dresser.

"They're raising hell again about unpaved streets and lack of sewers." He worked at preparing another bowl. "I guarantee they're alluding to the poor state of Union Avenue, but you watch, all their cosmetic efforts to glorify the city will be directed toward Quality Hill." He swept loose tobacco back into the palm of his hand and carefully emptied it into the jar. "You know damned well the members of 'the Commercial Club' as they call themselves dread the notion that the sordid atmosphere surrounding their cherished Union Depot, might tarnish the city's reputation."

Cassie, drifting into the comfort of an opiate haze, didn't respond. He looked over, his eyes lingering on her, the contours of her face softened by sleep, and her troubles momentarily eased. The covers had fallen from her shoulders revealing her firm white breasts. He admired her there in sleep. The syringe on the side table told him should would be out for some time. He climbed back into bed and brushed a lock of hair from her face before readjusting the pillow behind her head.

"You sweet girl, will you ever find peace?" He removed the makeshift tourniquet she had used and placed it on the side table. Cassie was a lady of the night, a vixen to her clients known affectionately as 'Cassie Diamond'. But to Crisp, she was his confidante and partner in a city that offered little kindness. She was the closest thing he had to a companion. She was his friend and lover.

He covered her with the blanket and laid beside her, his thoughts lingering on the headlines. With a sigh, he pondered on how he might investigate the murder near the incline if the case were his, and wondered too about the depths of indifference that allowed such tragedies to remain mysteries.

Chapter Two

Nestled just two blocks from the unending uproar of Union Avenue and the nearby Union Depot, The Philadelphia House saloon on the corner of Ninth and Hickory was a sanctuary for the serious gambler. It was a stark contrast to the clamorous stretch of saloons, policy shops, hotels, ticket offices, and all of the hullabaloo on Union Avenue, where a cacophony of hawker calls and enticements from lottery vendors, lured newly arrived visitors with promises of easy fortune and the coldest beer in town. But those familiar with Kansas City's tenderloin district bypassed such obvious traps and opted instead for the quiet discretion of saloons such as The Philadelphia.

Outside, the mercury had dipped once more, now skulking in the low teens; the air was heavy, laden with the imminent promise of snowfall, but inside The Philadelphia House, the air was thick with tobacco smoke and the faint scent of desperation.

"Ante up," the dealer's voice cut through the haze, prompting Crisp to push another silver dollar into the pot. His fingers lingered on the coin, betraying a moment's hesitation. The cards were dealt swiftly, two face down to each player, followed by a third face up. Crisp's eyes flickered across his initial hand, his mind racing through probabilities and outcomes, crafting a strategy as the game unfolded. His fortunes at the table mirrored the precarious nature of his life—twenty dollars deep and sinking fast. When he'd left the boardinghouse three hours earlier, he had quietly borrowed from Cassie, who lay lost in a morphine slumber. Now there would be no repayment; the borrowed sum meant to be his stake, intended to turn enough profit and perhaps generate a little extra to ease his woes. He'd left a note in place of the money, a promise inked with affection but borne from necessity.

The table was a microcosm of the city itself. To Crisp's immediate right, a Mexican immigrant, whom Crisp called Sancho, muttered prayers over his dwindling stack. Johnny Morris, a seasoned gambler and previous victim of Crisp's luck, now holding steady, sat adjacent to Sancho. To Crisp's left, the inscrutable businessman Crisp new only as Mr. Adams stared at his cards, grinning as his fortunes seemed as secure as the livestock he dealt in. Across from Crisp sat his recent adversary, the well-dressed gambler from Pendergast's Saloon, a man whose fortunes had flourished at Crisp's expense during their last encounter.

"I don't believe we were introduced properly in our last game," Crisp ventured, breaking the tension as everyone stared at their cards, directing his words toward the sophisticated man across from him.

"Moreland's the name; Marcus Moreland," the man said, his gaze never straying from his hand.

"Algernon Crisp," he replied.

"Colonel Crisp, is that right?" Moreland inquired, a hint of mockery in his tone that drew the attention of the table.

"No, that is just what the boy calls me," Crisp explained, brushing off the implied status with a mix of amusement and irritation. "I believe my accent has confused him in some manner."

Adams quickly interjected with a brief introduction to Moreland, followed by Morris who looked to Moreland and Adams. Sancho introduced himself to the table, proudly using his given name: Francisco Luis Rodriguez de Velasco. His introduction was spoken with such rapidity that the others caught no more than Francisco.

The game progressed, the stakes rising with each card that hit the table. Each man received another card face up and placed their bets. Moreland continued his conversation with Crisp. "You left so suddenly the other day; I didn't get to thank you for your generosity. There are times when I ask myself, I say, 'Moreland, what have you gotten yourself into'. But then along comes a winning day like that and my love for the game is rejuvenated. So, I say thank you." With that, Moreland tossed a silver dollar to Crisp.

"What's this for?"

"You left in such haste; you missed picking it up from the table."

Crisp twirled the coin in his fingers; his pride bristling with derision. "I'm afraid you're mistaken old boy. I'm quite sure I left nothing behind."

Before he could flip the coin back, Moreland interjected, "Keep it. I felt bad taking the rest of your money that day."

"I don't need your charity, sir, I'm doing quite alright," he asserted, tossing the coin back across the table, his pride stinging as sharply as the smack of the silver on the wooden table.

"Apologies, no offense intended."

"None taken, I just want to be clear where we stand." With this, Crisp pulled a Peruvian cheroot from his pocket and lit it with a match struck on the underside of the table. He inhaled deeply, feely the rich smoke swell inside his lungs. He held it there momentarily, his mind craving the oncoming rush, and exhaled a large cloud above the table. Moreland's idle banter faded into the background as play commenced, the dealer swiftly distributed a fourth card face up to each player, their calculations running silently through their minds. Morris raised, emboldened by a king and an ace, compelling the others to match his stakes. As cards continued to be revealed—eights, fives, and another six joined the table—the tension escalated sharply. Each man now bore four cards face-up, two secreted in the hole, with only one more to be dealt face down.

Anxiety surged as Morris, brandishing a promising pair of sixes, raised again. Crisp's own hand—a blend of potential straights and possible pairs—displayed a jack as its highest merit, his hopes pinned on the last secretive draw. Amidst the muted clatter of coins and the soft rustle of cards; the silent strategists sat poised on the brink of triumph or defeat. Adams' nervous fidgeting, Morris' darting glances, and the stoic calm of Moreland and Sancho, marked the final moments before the decisive turn.

"May I ask what you're smoking? It has a peculiar aroma." Moreland cut into Crisp's concentration like a slap in the face.

"Peruvian. I have them custom made." Crisp said proudly,

taking another puff from the cheroot dangling from his lips as he contemplated his next move. The dealer threw down the final cards, each face down. Crisp's hand was a bust; another bum hand. When the round ended, and all the cards had been flipped, Moreland took the pot with a full house of sixes and sevens, and he gathered his winnings without boasting.

As the dealer dispatched another round of cards, the atmosphere at the table thickened with suspense. Bets grew bolder, the air was infused with anticipation, and players focused intently as their hands were fortified or their hopes dashed with the turn of each card. The stakes escalated dramatically, with coins clinking and stacks growing. Each player's breath seemed to catch in his throat as the crucial decisions of folding or raising loomed, the silent tension evident in the smoke-laden air of the saloon.

Morris, once again, led the charge with a hefty raise, challenging the resolve of his opponents as they delved deeper into their reserves.

"Peruvian? That must be the strain, but do tell me, what else is mixed in there?" Moreland added.

Crisp was not about to show distraction. With either a seven or eight in the next deal he'd have a straight. "Well, if you must know, I have the chemist blend in a coca leaf extract."

Morris stared intently at his cards, oblivious to the conversation around him.

"Cocaine? Interesting. Do you find any long-term side effects? Loss of memory, inability to focus or rationalize thought patterns? Perhaps insomnia or paranoia?"

The dealer dropped the seventh and final card to each player face down. Crisp finally got the deal he needed.

"On the contrary. I find, in modest doses, it sharpens my wits and perception, gives me a hyper awareness of everything around me; a mental stimulation that often proves quite beneficial." This Crisp said triumphantly as he revealed a straight beating out a pair of eights for Morris, and Moreland's pair of queens.

"Well done," Moreland exclaimed.

"I'm out." Morris backed away from the table dejectedly. Sancho and Adams both withdrew in kind. Crisp gathered his meager winnings from the table. After he returned the twenty back to Cassie, he'd still have a few dollars left for himself. Not enough for another round today, he thought, but tomorrow always brings another opportunity.

"What's all this commotion outside?" Moreland asked looking toward the front facing window of the saloon. As the front door drifted shut with someone coming in off the street, both men caught a snippet of unintelligible shouting and hollering from a crowd amassed outside The Philadelphia. "Let's have a look," Moreland offered.

Outside, at least twenty women dressed in long black gowns and white blouses with exaggerated shoulders, wearing black hats perched primly on their heads, and tight gloves clasping their hands, gathered in the street. They carried banners and signs while shouting a chorus of slogans and chants aimed at the customers of the saloons and gambling houses along Ninth Street. One such banner displayed the large gold letters 'WCTU' emblazoned against a maroon background.

"What does that stand for?" Crisp asked.

"The Women's Christian Temperance Union. Very bad for business, I'd say," Moreland remarked, a note of disdain in his voice as the women's chants clashed with the crude heckles from local laborers.

Crisp cupped his hands together blowing warmth into his palms. "They sure picked a fine day for a parade."

A few patrolmen moved in, keeping the hecklers at bay. "That's enough. Let them have their say and they'll move on. Stand back now. You there, if I hear another foul word from your gob, I'm running you in. Stand back, d'y hear!"

In the bustling chaos along Ninth Street, the leader raised her voice, hopelessly attempting to pierce the din with a heartfelt plea against the depravities of the locals. Her words, however, dissolved into the air, scarcely grasped by the indifferent crowd. Undeterred, she summoned her inner conviction and led her contingent with a resolute chant, "No more gambling, no more drinks!" Their voices merged into a single, forceful echo, a clarion call for reform, that rippled down the street. With renewed vigor, the group marched toward the infamous 'Wettest Block in the World,' where the glow from saloon windows flickered like beacons of vice, promising confrontation with every step.

***

The next morning was a Thursday, and the echoes of the temperance parade still lingered in the air as Crisp accompanied by Moreland ventured onto Union Avenue. Their day started with a late breakfast at Blossom House, a spot conveniently located across from Union Depot. An hour later, they had yet to agree on their next port of call for gambling as they made their way down the bustling boardwalk, brimming with temptations and throngs of visitors newly arrived in town.

Crisp drew Moreland's attention to a neighboring policy shop whose owner promised a quick chance to win forty-to-one on one of his lottery games. "Let's see if luck is with me today." They entered through a brightly painted yellow door as Crisp fished in his coat pocket, waving to the owner with recognition. "If either of these tickets hit, I can recoup the twenty I lost to you."

"Games of chance don't interest me," Moreland frowned.

The man behind the counter quickly perceived Moreland's skepticism. "I see you're a man of higher standards," the clerk remarked to Moreland, trying to pivot his interest. "Perhaps you'd prefer horse betting, or a dog or cock fight?"

"No thank you, I prefer games of skill," Moreland declined politely.

"Oh, trust me, them mutts and cocks are quite skilled," the man retorted with a wry smile.

Stepping back onto the bustling streets of Union Avenue, Crisp's pockets were no richer than before. The two men were immediately enveloped by the clamor of commerce along the boardwalk. Carts and wagons lined the thoroughfare, horse-drawn railcars clattered down tracks laid in the middle of the street, and a diverse mob of pedestrians surged along the boardwalk around them.

"What say we leave this crowd behind? I know a little place on St. Louis Avenue," Moreland proposed, but his words were abruptly cut off by the urgent shouts of a young boy sprinting toward them.

"Colonel, Colonel!" the boy called out, his voice slicing through the clamor.

"Easy there, Percy," Crisp said, steadying the breathless boy with a gentle grip on his shoulders. "What's the urgency?"

"Colonel, there's a woman there," he gasped, pointing toward the Ninth Street incline, the elevated trolley trestle that connected The West Bottoms to the top of the bluffs. "She's in need of help!" His eyes, wide with concern, prompted Crisp and Moreland to follow quickly to the scene he described.

As they approached the shadow of the incline, a chilling sight awaited them—a woman's body crumpled near one of the supporting girders. Crisp's heart sank; the immediate thought of another murder victim flashed through his mind. They drew closer, observing the woman dressed in the same black and white garb as the temperance women from the previous day's parade, lying in disarray and vulnerable on the ground.

"I think she's still alive," Moreland exclaimed as he kneeled beside her, checking her vitals with uncertainty. He leaned in with his ear. "Still breathing," he confirmed, his voice steady amidst a growing crowd of onlookers.

"Shall we sit her up? Shall I fetch some water?" Crisp asked, ready to assist.

"No, no. Let's not move her until we assess her injuries," Moreland instructed.

"Do you think she fell?" Crisp asked, looking up at the towering incline overhead.

"I don't believe so," Moreland said pointing out reddish-blue splotches around the woman's throat just visible above her high collar. He gently adjusted her leg which was bent awkwardly beneath her, as Crisp helped to carefully extend it back to a natural position. Their assistance was soon interrupted by the familiar whistle of law enforcement as two officers closed in on the gathering crowd. The first was a stranger to Crisp, but the other held a familiar face filled with disdain.

Patrolman Dennis Crotty was a caricature of authority draped in ill-fitting garments. His round, boyish face, perpetually shadowed beneath the brim of a tall bowler hat, gave the impression of youth awkwardly assuming the guise of manhood. A bushy mustache framed his downturned mouth, adding an almost comical severity to his expression, though the effect was spoiled by the beady eyes that peered out with a perpetual sneer. Standing nearly six feet tall, Crotty's lean frame was swallowed up by his oversized uniform and boots. The sight of him—a lanky figure that might have passed for a pubescent teenager playing at adulthood—lent an air of unease to his patrols, as if even the uniform itself questioned the authority it was meant to represent.

"What are you up to Crisp? Another investigation gone wrong?" he accused, his tone sharp and dismissive.

"This woman needs help Crotty, and we—" Crisp's rebuttal was abruptly cut off as both policemen moved past him to intervene. The woman suddenly regained consciousness with a start, panic setting in as she recognized the uniforms and crowd of faces before her. Her attempts to speak were met with coughs and struggled breaths.

"There, there. Try to relax, take a deep breath," Moreland

reassured her, his voice a calm anchor in the surrounding tumult.

"What's this about? What happened here? Who did this?" demanded the other officer with a thick Irish accent, his barrage of questions overwhelming the distressed woman.

"Easy now," Moreland protested. "Let her catch her breath. Her health is the priority now; you can question her later."

"Can't you see she's been most cruelly treated!" Crisp said stating the obvious.

"We still need the details," Crotty insisted.

Moreland turned on him, "In due time, sir!" He bent closer to the nearer of the two officers, his voice hushed from the onlookers, "It appears she's been abused." He lifted the edge of her collar to display her neck.

"Alright, Crisp, stand back I said!" Crotty caught him unawares, grabbing Crisp by the shoulder and pulling him back with such force that Crisp stumbled on the loose rock and detritus beneath the incline. The spectators took further steps back after seeing Crotty's rage.

The patrolman who hunched near Moreland, barked an order to his partner, "Crotty, hurry now. Use the phone in the depot and call the station. Arrange to move this woman uptown."

As the officers coordinated her transport to the hospital, suspicion and concern hung heavily in the air, the severity of her condition underscored by the marks on her neck and her evident distress. Crisp lingered, unable to shake the feeling that the scene unfolding beneath the incline was more than an isolated incident; it was a harbinger of deeper troubles brewing in The West Bottoms.

———

Crisp and Moreland had dispersed with the other onlookers once the woman was loaded into the back of a police wagon, crossing Union Avenue to reconvene in the refined elegance of The New St. Paul Saloon. Unlike the boisterous taverns on St. Louis Avenue, this upscale establishment catered to a more distinguished clientele, its interior a spectacle of polished mahogany, gleaming brass fixtures, and plush, red velvet drapes that whispered of opulence. Here, out-of-town businessmen mingled over clinking glasses, the air rich with the scent of imported cigars and the low murmur of discreet conversations.

Knowing the injured woman was on her way to the safety of the city hospital perched on the respectable heights of Quality Hill, the two men sought to unwind. Yet, despite their efforts, their deep-seated worries refused to be dismissed, casting a pall over their attempts at relaxation.

"An assault in broad daylight," Moreland said, his voice heavy with disbelief as he sank into the chair opposite Crisp. "What is happening to this city?"

"What did you learn?"

"She's one of the temperance women from the parade," Moreland revealed, sharing what he'd overheard. "Crossed the street to avoid the chaos along the avenue, ventured too close to the incline viaduct, and that's when she was set upon."

"Were there any witnesses? Did they catch any details?" Crisp pressed, his urgency underscored by a relentless pursuit of justice in an increasingly unruly town.

"Little was gleaned before they rushed her to the hospital. She was quite distressed," Moreland replied with a sigh, his tone reflecting the inadequacy of the police response. "I had to assist them getting her into a carriage. Where did you get to anyway?"

"Crotty. He held me back from the scene until he'd been abruptly called away."

"What's the history between you two?"

"Crotty is a vindictive man, finds pleasure only in doling out misery, wielding his badge like a weapon," Crisp said, his voice tinged with bitterness.

"That much is clear, but it seems more personal. He's particularly malicious in your direction."

Crisp sighed, a mix of frustration and resignation crossing his face. "Some men thrive on power, and Crotty's no different. He's turned it into a personal vendetta though, using his authority to settle scores both real and imagined."

A waitress interrupted their discussion with two glasses of beer, and Crisp took the opportunity to light one of his Peruvians. The smoke curled around his thoughts as he reminisced, "I used to work for the railroad, The Kansas Pacific. Not directly, but as an investigator with Pinkerton's Agency. Crotty worked there too, an inspector for the K&P freight department. We crossed paths a lot, and he didn't like that I had more access than he did. There's history there... and not a good one."

"How long ago was this?"

"About ten years ago I guess?" he asked himself out loud.

"That's quite the grudge to hold all these years."

"It's not just that. His family lost a large sum in a bad investment with my uncle. He blames me for his misfortune however, since my uncle left the States."

Moreland, sensing Crisp's darkening mood, let the background with Crotty stop there.

Both men were quiet in their own reflections for some moments. Eventually Crisp broke the silence, "Tell me Marcus, what's your story? I know you are an attorney, and an astute gambler, but I know nothing beyond that."

Moreland smiled, "Nothing interesting. I grew up near Chicago. After law school, Northwestern, I practiced for a few years under the tutelage of an old curmudgeon named Bickerstaff, an old-world lawyer, set in his ways. Eventually, it was time for me to move on, and I chose to move south; the weather in Chicago can be quite brutal this time of year you know. I set up shop here about eight years ago, an office near Seventh and Main."

"I spent time in Chicago myself. My uncle brought me there, when we first came across from London. He was on the look to buy cheap property in the States. We weren't there long before we moved to a town out west, Victoria, Kansas." Crisp thought for a moment. "I went back to Chicago in eighty-two to get a fresh start."

"I left in eighty-two. Why did you leave Pinkerton's for Chicago?"

"Sorry, I should clarify. I was still with my uncle when I left for Chicago. It was in Chicago where I joined Pinkerton's Detectives, and eventually found my way back to Kansas."

"I see. And what happened there, at Pinkerton's?"

"A bullet, just here," he pointed to the pectoral area near his left shoulder. Couldn't be but a few inches from my heart I reckon?"

"Yes, you were lucky."

"After that, I mean once you have a close encounter with death, you tend to reevaluate your lot in life."

"But you are a private investigator now, are you not? Does that not also bring the same sort of dangers and threats?"

"To a certain degree. I can choose which clients to accept and the level of danger or risk they bring. Honestly, much of my work is nothing more than checking business references, proving or disproving infidelity, that sort of thing. Quite different from a police detective who is responsible for investigating crimes and associating with persons of lesser moral quality."

"Speaking of which, here comes one of our finest now."

Detective Hayes who'd been on the scene of the assaulted woman entered the saloon and immediately saw Moreland. "I hoped I'd find you here. The woman has been delivered to the hospital and is being treated for her ordeal. Do you have a minute to answer a few more questions?"

Marcus shrugged but agreed to help.

Crisp stood to leave. "Marcus, I'd be happy if you'd join me for dinner, if you're not predisposed that is."

"Afraid I can't this evening, but I'd enjoy another game of cards later this week."

Crisp stepped into the gusty afternoon, where Kansas City sprawled before him with all its grit and promise. The wind tugged at his coat as he subconsciously massaged his shoulder, his eyes drifting toward the bustling avenue. Beneath the towering incline, the weight of the recent assault lingered in his mind, but the city carried on, indifferent to the battles fought in its shadows.

The victim's plight had stirred old memories, pulling him back to a dire chapter ten years in the past. Back then, the railroads had been overwhelmed by a relentless wave of crime. Unable to stem the tide of robberies and violence along their tracks, the Pinkertons were called in, and Crisp among them, had been tasked with a particularly dangerous assignment. He'd been charged with guarding a significant shipment of bullion, the responsibility of Miss Jocelyn Evers, heiress to her father's burgeoning soap empire in Des Moines. She was on board a Denver-bound train, overseeing the transfer of assets from Kansas City to their new operations there, when the train was ambushed. Though Crisp and his fellow detectives secured the bullion, Miss Evers had not been so fortunate.

The failure to protect her still haunted him; a specter from his past that he could never quite shake off. His gunshot wound, a harsh souvenir from that fateful encounter, remained a painful reminder of his shortcomings. After a lengthy convalescence in Salina, Kansas, where physical activity eluded him for endless weeks, gambling had become his temporary solace. At the time, he'd recognized the futility of that life; it was an empty existence, devoid of purpose and promise. Driven by a need for redemption, and searching for a new start, he'd eventually drifted to Kansas City and took up work in his uncle's booming real estate business. That had ended poorly too.

As the wind tore down Union Avenue, its chill entwining with the ghosts of his past, he felt the heavy burden of history on his shoulders and recognized the arduous path that lay before him in his quest for atonement. What Crisp wanted was redemption—not just from his past misfortunes or from family entanglements that sullied his name—but a chance to right some of the wrongs that plagued this city. He yearned for a new start, an office downtown, away from the squalor of The West Bottoms, with new clientele, specifically customers above the bluffs who paid well, and paid frequently. Perhaps then he could shed the weight of his guilt over past failures, particularly the haunting memory of Miss Evers. This city needed him, not as a gambler or a washed-up Pinkerton, but as a beacon of hope for those caught in the shadows. Here, in the underbelly of the city, he would find his purpose, and perhaps, his redemption.

With nowhere to be, and no money quick at hand, his curiosity got the best of him and he sauntered over under the incline near the railyard where both the most recent assault and the previous murder had occurred. Surely there must be some clue that the police had overlooked. He doubted whether they would spend much time on either investigation. With today's attack, the woman had survived and once recuperated, she would likely move on with her life. As far as the body discovered just days ago, the papers subsequently revealed her to be a woman of disreputable character. Once the police detectives had realized she was not an out-of-town traveler, or prominent woman from above the bluffs, they had lost interest in finding her killer.

Crisp searched beneath the incline, but the rocks and mud didn't provide much; there were scant footprints, and only partial at that. Rail workers routinely passed through the area and he noted at least a half dozen sets of separate tracks that all came from an array of footwear. He spotted a man in overalls standing not more than fifty paces away, waiting to cross a set of tracks as a string of boxcars passed in front of him. As a car counter, the man's job was to write down the numbers painted on the sides of rail cars and report them to the freight office to confirm the whereabouts of specific cargo on the railroad.

After the last of the boxcars moved past, Crisp caught the man's attention, "Excuse me there, good man, I hope you may offer some assistance." After a short exchange, Crisp quickly surmised the rail man had seen nothing, nor had he even been in the area until just minutes before. No, he hadn't been in the vicinity on the day the previous body was discovered; yes, he frequently saw unauthorized people milling about the yards—vagrants roaming around, migrant workers looking for a lift, people cutting through the yards to get to Union Avenue.

Crisp moved to the east side of Union Depot that housed a large baggage room and freight dock. A cut of passenger and baggage cars sat on the tracks nearest Union Avenue, the third car extending all the way to the Ninth Street viaduct. He had no idea how long the cars had been there, nor could he recall if they were there earlier when he'd witnessed the distressed woman. Nonetheless, the baggage cars were the nearest obstacle of cover that a would-be assailant might take cover in. He decided to investigate, cautiously approaching the cut of cars from the south side where he would not be seen from Union Avenue.

As the afternoon drew on, shadows stretched like dark fingers across the ground, providing Crisp with a semblance of concealment he dearly hoped sufficient for his task. The bustling activity at the station, with porters loading luggage, and passengers hurrying to their platforms, ensured that countless eyes were present, any of which might spot an interloper if they looked closely. Yet, with the tumult of the nearby railyard as a backdrop, where workers shouted orders, steam engines hissed, and railcars squealed and banged together endlessly, he hoped to go unnoticed.

He knelt beside a stationary coach car, intently studying a lone set of footprints that trailed from the east—directly toward the looming incline. The prints were unmistakably those of a large man; placing his own foot beside one imprint, Crisp's boot was dwarfed in comparison. As he bent closer for a better look, the sudden crunch of gravel behind him sent a shiver up his spine. A dark shadow fell across him, cast ominously on the side of the baggage car in the waning light. Turning to identify his visitor, his world burst into a cascade of sparks. A sudden blow to the back of the head sent him spiraling into darkness, and as he collapsed to the ground, the mysteries of the footprints remained unsolved.

Regaining his senses and emerging from the murky depths of unconsciousness felt akin to climbing out of a black hole. How much time had elapsed, he could not tell. The back of his head throbbed as he struggled to lift himself, pushing up slowly, only to be met with a vicious kick to his ribs that sent him rolling onto his side in agony. Wiping mud from his face, Crisp tried to focus on the blurry figures looming over him.

"Stay down!" a gruff voice commanded. Ignoring the order, he attempted to sit up, only to fend off another blow from a hefty man standing menacingly over him. Another figure, restraining the aggressor momentarily, moved into Crisp's line of sight.

"You just don't know how to keep out of trouble do you Crisp. Get up!" Dennis Crotty barked with contempt. Crisp struggled to his feet, forcibly aided by two burly men who grabbed his arms, treating him roughly with indifference to his pain. "What do you think you're doing here?"

"Finishing the job you and your detectives have neglected," he said defiantly, as he spit mud from his mouth, which Crotty took as a personal slight. The backhand of Crotty's free hand across Crisp's cheek was swift, and his nightstick found its way to lay across Crisp's throat.

"You always thought you were better than me, Crisp. Eh? Well, look here," Crotty taunted, tapping the badge on his coat. "I'm the one with the authority now." Crotty's laughter echoed off the baggage cars, a sound devoid of any warmth. "The once high and mighty Crisp, the Pinkerton agent, now just a gutter crawler kept by a whore," he sneered. "That's right, I know all about you; who you lay with at night."

Struggling against the iron grip of Crotty's henchmen, Crisp gasped, "What do you want from me?"

Crotty delivered a jab to Crisp's gut with his nightstick. "What I want, is to see the Crisps reduced to nothing but lowlife scum. You and your uncle ruined me. At least seeing you down in the mud gives me some peace of mind." With a nod to his accomplices, Crotty walked away, his steps heavy and deliberate, leaving Crisp to the mercy of his goons.

"Now wait a minute fellas." Crisp's attempts to negotiate a peace fell to the ground, discarded like autumn leaves swept aside by an unforgiving wind. The beating resumed with even greater ferocity, each punch and kick driving Crisp further into despair and darkness. When the assault finally ceased, Crisp was a mere shell of himself. He was shoved around the side of the train car and thrown into the back of a waiting covered wagon. The pummeling had left him in agony, each blow a testament to Crotty's deep-seated malice, each causing a pain that resounded within him long after the fists had ceased. He rolled onto his knees and retched. When the wagon eventually stopped, he was dragged out onto the pavement, and up a series of steps, barely conscious, every footfall causing fresh agony. His swollen eyes caught only blurred glimpses of his surroundings—dim street lamps, harsh concrete steps, tiled floors, and finally, the unforgiving lumpy surface of a cot, where he was unceremoniously dumped.

As darkness enveloped him once again, his last coherent thought was a silent prayer for deliverance from Crotty's cycle of vindictiveness and retribution. But even that thought faded as he succumbed to the welcoming oblivion of sleep, with the echoes of Crotty's malicious laughter still ringing in his ears.

Chapter Three

Everything hurt. It hurt to move, it hurt to open his eyes, it hurt to breathe. Crisp regained consciousness slowly with every part of his body protesting in pain. He lay sprawled face down on a threadbare cot, his cheek pressed against a rough, wool blanket that barely softened the firm surface beneath him. As awareness seeped in, his senses were assaulted by a harsh yellow light beyond his room. He faintly recognized the distant echoes of footsteps and the jangle of keys; the mundane sounds of a police station, he realized somberly.

"Awake? I thought I heard you moaning." The voice was gruff, yet not without concern. Crisp squinted through swollen eyes, making out a pair of dark boots and navy-blue trousers—a police uniform standing ominously at his bedside. "I brought you a drink, only water." A tin cup appeared in his peripheral vision. "Can you sit up?" With rough, yet strangely careful hands that helped him into a sitting position, the cup was pressed into his hands. "Drink."

After a few sips, his vision cleared enough to recognize the retreating back of a police officer moving through an open cell door. His mind raced, trying to piece together the events leading to his current predicament. The last thing he remembered was the brutal beating under the shadows of the incline—a planned assault, no doubt. But by whom? And why? In a flash, it came to him—the demonic image of Crotty, looming large and menacing in his mind.

"Here's a clean towel," the officer returned, breaking into Crisp's troubled thoughts.

"Speers?" his voice was hoarse, disbelief coloring his tone as he recognized the Chief of Police, Thomas Speers, approaching with a basin of water. Speers set the bowl down and began gently cleaning the dried blood from Crisp's face.

"It's been a while, hasn't it?"

"Where am I? Downtown?"

"No, no. St. Louis Avenue station. I happened to be down here on business; found your name on the overnight roster," Speers explained, his tone casual. "What happened to you?"

Crisp hesitated, "Let's just say I had a run-in with your 'troops'."

Speers raised an eyebrow but pressed no further, and instead assisted Crisp to the front of the station where a potbelly stove radiated a welcoming warmth. Handing Crisp a cup of freshly brewed coffee, he instructed him to sit. "Tough times?" he inquired, watching as Crisp nursed the hot beverage with bruised hands trembling noticeably.

"Is it that obvious?"

"Are you still making a go of it as a private agent? How's that playing out?"

"Business has been slow," he admitted, rifling through his pockets in vain for a cheroot. His coat, hanging on a nearby peg, was empty as well, including the two bits he'd had in its breast pocket.

Speers leaned back, assessing Crisp with a mix of concern and curiosity that only an old friend could express. "You should consider working up top of the bluffs. Much more lucrative prospects I would think."

"You know it's all about connections, and mine are with the railroads and packing houses. Makes more sense for me to work here in The Bottoms." Crisp gently patted at his face assessing his wounds.

"Have you considered hiring back on with the Pinkertons, or maybe the railroads? They're always in need of good agents."

"I like working on my own now," he responded, his tone firm yet weary.

Speers hunched forward and nodded slowly; his gaze thoughtful. "Algernon, I'll be honest with you. I've felt I owed you a favor for many years and never paid off. Remember the De Soto heist?"

"Of course. That played out well for you," he said, the memory bittersweet.

"That was back in eighty-five, wasn't it?" Speers continued, a serious undertone to his voice.

The station door swung open, allowing the chill of St. Louis Avenue to seep into the warmth of the room; a patrolman entered, shaking off the cold. "Morning Chief, didn't realize you were coming down today," he remarked, moving to the stove to warm his numbed hands.

"I'm looking for Captain Weber. Have you seen him today?"

"No, sir, weren't here when I started my shift. Been over on Ninth most of the day," the officer replied, his gaze finally settling on Crisp with a flicker of suspicion. "A friend of yours, sir?"

"Indeed, a very dear friend," Speers answered, gesturing towards Crisp. "This is Algernon Crisp, private detective."

The introduction barely registered with patrolman Hartwell, who muttered something about retrieving gloves from the back room as he excused himself.

"You shouldn't have told him that, your boys aren't too fond of my title."

"Ah, horse stuff!" Speers dismissed the comment with a wave. "As I was saying, I do feel obliged to you. I'd like to help you regain your footing."

Crisp bristled slightly. "I appreciate the thought, Thomas, but I'm not in the market for charity. Things are slow, but they'll turn around."

"You're a stubborn man Crisp. You can sit here and scrape out an existence with the rest of the bottom dwellers in the, uh Bottoms—" Speers chuckled at his own unintended pun, "or you can take on real work for me. I'm talking investigations, on a contract basis. You wouldn't be on the city's books."

"And how exactly would that work?" Crisp asked, his tone laden with a wariness born of too many hard knocks. "Working for you, yet off the payroll?"

"A sort of consultant, a private contractor." Speers stood and paced with a thoughtful air. "I haven't ironed out the details yet... Do you think you're up to a visit downtown?"

"Looking like this?" Crisp's fingers gingerly touched the edge of his mouth.

"Let's see if we can get you cleaned up." Speers said, his voice carrying a decisive note, underscored by an urgency that made it clear this was more than a simple offer—it was a lifeline.

———

The normally harrowing trolley ride up the steep incline to Quality Hill paled in comparison to Crisp's recent trials in the murky bottoms of Kansas City. Seated beside Speers in a cable car that creaked and clattered its way uphill, Crisp tried to settle his nerves. Half a pot of coffee and two shots of bourbon from Speers' flask helped to set him back to rights. Despite his attempts to clean himself up, the remnants of mud on his knees and the battered visage he presented were less concerning to him than the thoughts swirling in his mind.

As dawn unfurled, its pale light hidden just beyond the eastern horizon, the precise hour remained unknown to Crisp; his pocket watch had been lost in the previous night's ordeal. The street lamps on Union Avenue still flickered behind them, while ahead, the lights on Quality Hill began to disappear one by one, surrendering to the encroaching day. Despite the physical pain, it was the stark divide between the city's prosperous heights and its desperate lows that etched deeper lines of worry across Crisp's brow. Beneath the steep grade of the incline, a scattering of lights twinkled from a haphazard arrangement of shacks and shanties that clung to the lower bluffs. Their modest glow was momentarily obscured from view as the cable car intersected a plume of smoke, exhaled by a steam engine chugging beneath them. Once the smoky veil dissipated, the car jolted forward, hesitating for a heartbeat, before resuming its ascent over the final stretch of the viaduct to reach solid footing.

Speers broke the silence as they transitioned from the clattering viaduct to the smoother streets atop the bluffs. "We're headed to my office at City Hall. There's something important I want to discuss with you." Crisp pondered the need for such secrecy. Why couldn't Speers just reveal the urgency? But he held his tongue. His head throbbed painfully, and each rattle of the cable car amplified the discomfort in his battered frame.

As they reached the top of the bluffs, the landscape shifted dramatically; Quality Hill basked in the morning sunlight rising above the city. Here, Ninth Street was lined with imposing brownstones flaunting proud facades that hinted at fortunes recently made in the rough-and-tumble world of frontier commerce. Their orderly lawns, trimmed to perfection, reflected the ambition and success of those who had quickly risen to wealth, each home standing as a testament to the bold entrepreneurs who had carved out their place in this thriving city. The meticulously clean streets of the neighborhood were bordered by tidy sidewalks and evenly spaced streetlamps, each casting a subtle elegance upon the neighborhood. This scene of urbane tranquility stood in sharp contrast to the rough-hewn life of The West Bottoms, where grit and grime marked the struggle of a different world.

At the intersection with Jefferson Street, the car paused momentarily as Crisp's gaze met that of two matronly women stepping onboard, their eyes probing him with scrutiny, mistaking him in his disheveled state for a miscreant being ushered to the city jail. The buried cable took over, tugging the trolley car further toward the vibrant heart of Main Street as the women moved past, taking up seats in the rear of the carriage.

Passing the imposing silhouette of the New York Life Building, Kansas City's pioneering ten-story skyscraper, Crisp knew they were nearing the usually bustling crossroads of Main and Delaware known as The Junction. Here, they would transfer carriages for a short jog north, and travel toward the oldest part of the city where City Hall and Police Headquarters awaited on their right, just four blocks from the river.

Once situated in Speers' office, the warm glow of a desk lamp did little to ease the chill that had seeped into Crisp's bones. He collapsed into a wooden chair, ignoring its discomfort and unyielding hardness.

Speers seemed hesitant, shuffling papers before settling into his own chair with a grave look. "My detectives are overwhelmed with high-profile cases," he began, his voice low. "And it's true, the tragedies in The Bottoms often don't get the attention they deserve. It's not right, but it's reality." Crisp listened, a twinge of disgust rising as Speers continued, revealing the bleak fate of a recent murder case—a prostitute found dead, her case swiftly closed once her occupation was discovered. "Once the detectives learned who she was, they lost interest. They figured whoever was responsible would end up in our hands sooner or later for some other crime, or just as likely end up dead themselves."

"That's quite the cynical outlook," Crisp remarked dryly, unable to mask his contempt.

"It's the hard truth of our resources and priorities," Speers admitted, his tone defensive yet resigned.

"So where do I fit in? Why bring me all the way to your office just to share what I already suspect?"

Speers stood, a sudden energy to his movements. "Come with me," he said, leading Crisp across the hall to a locked room. Inside, the walls of the cramped room were lined with photographs of known criminals, each meticulously measured and cataloged—representing Speers' adaptation of The Bertillon System, a method of identifying criminals by their physical measurements. Speers, proud and even enthusiastic, explained, "I've been using this approach to catalog criminals, not just to solve crimes, but to prevent them. My men keep a watch for these known offenders, and when they show up, we run them out of town before they can cause trouble. In some cases, we hold them overnight until we can arrange their transport."

Crisp browsed through the gallery of rogues, each face telling a story of a sinister side of the city. "And you think this can really make a difference?"

"It's a start. We're keeping the city safer, by apprehending one known criminal at a time."

Crisp spent a few minutes examining various photos in the collection. He made note of the details Speers had gathered, specific measurements including head length and breadth, length of middle finger, length of the left foot, and length of the arm from the elbow to the tip of the middle finger. Along with these details, Speers had captured a front and side photograph of each suspect's face. He was fascinated with the scientific measures employed by Speers, yet wondered about its efficacy. "All of these photos are of men. Do you not keep the same records on women?"

"I haven't been able to accurately apply the method to women, or children for that matter, as of yet. This system was mostly designed for men who have reached full maturity. I'm sure in time we will refine techniques for cataloging similar features for both."

Crisp nodded, showing his interest. The conversation shifted as they locked up the archive room. Crisp still couldn't see how he played a role in this, but figured Speers had more to reveal. "So, what else do we need to discuss?"

"In time. Let's grab breakfast; I'm starved," Speers suggested, changing the subject. Despite his frustration with Speers' aversion, he accompanied him to a nearby restaurant; the morning air felt heavy, laden with the unspoken realities of their city's struggles. Speers' proposal had opened a door, revealing a new chapter in his life, one where the distinctions between right and wrong were blurred, and every decision carried unforeseen consequences.

As they stepped into the bustling diner, the clatter of dishes and the hum of conversation enveloped them. Fending off gawking stares, Crisp felt the weight of impending choices settle heavily around him, a harsh reminder that a step forward through that door would lead to ever more complex and uncertain territory.

Three days later, on a bitterly cold Tuesday morning, Crisp found himself sitting in the waiting room inside the bustling

Union Depot, ensconced in the ebb and flow of city life, an observer on the cusp of action. The depot, a building reminiscent of a French chateau that seamlessly blended Gothic and Victorian architectural elements into a harmonious and striking edifice, stood on the aptly named Union Avenue in the heart of The West Bottoms. Stretching three hundred and eighty-four feet in length, its mansard roof was adorned with dormers, steeples, rooftop finials, and ornately decorated gables. This impressive structure left first-time visitors to the city in awe, despite local critics who scoffed at its original cost to build.

Multitudes of travelers navigated their way through the terminal, while Crisp sat tucked away on a wooden bench, strategically positioned to keep watch. His mission, as dubbed by Speers, was an 'experiment'—a chance for Crisp to test The Bertillon System first hand. He was to spot any of ten known criminals from their photographs he'd memorized, along with the details meticulously catalogued for each of the lawbreakers.

His thoughts were tinged with skepticism. He understood Speers' rationale: preemptively catching criminals based on their past transgressions would prevent future offenses by the same perpetrators. However, he held reservations about the morality and effectiveness of such an approach. He wholeheartedly believed that those who commit crimes should be punished, but the notion of taking measures against someone before the deed was committed struck him as a step too far. Not all who wander are lost, and not all who have sinned do so perpetually.

Yet here he sat, burdened with a method that indiscriminately cast a wide net, ensnaring both the repentant and the habitual offender alike. Crisp knew then that the path ahead would be fraught with moral and ethical dilemmas. Engaging deeper with the city's law enforcement could provide resources and access he needed to effect real change, but at what cost? Could he navigate this new alliance without becoming part of the system he had long criticized from the outside?

The atmosphere in the depot was charged with the excitement and chaos that only a major railway station can muster. As he surveyed the scene before him, he divided the masses of people into two groups: the seasoned city navigators coming and going in routine, versus the ones he deemed newcomers—wide-eyed and hesitant, their first impressions a confused mix of reverence and repulsion.

Thousands passed through Union Depot daily and for many, it was their first visit to Kansas City. New arrivals stepping out of the station were bludgeoned with the overwhelming stench from the nearby stockyards, a pungent welcome to the so-called 'Paris of the Plains'. Beyond the olfactory assault, the carnival-like frenzy of Union Avenue besieged them, with runners, barkers, shills, and cappers promising everything from ephemeral pleasures to permanent vices.

A young girl declared to her mother, "It stinks to the high heavens!" A capper grabbed the elbow of the woman, "Welcome madame, you don't want to miss the best food money can buy! Allow me to guide you to the Blossom House; I can secure a table for you and your children." Not far from the woman, a hawker stopped two young men, enticing them to come visit the 'Hell Dances' at The Lotus Flower dance hall just two blocks from the station. "What's a Hell Dance?" one of the men asked. "You never been to a Hell Dance son? Where you boys from?" the hawker asked in mock astonishment. "Peoria," one of them responded innocently. The hawker moved closer, and in a low voice added, "Imagine dancing ladies, wearing nothing but boots on their feet and blossoms in their hair! I guarantee you ain't never seen nothin' like that in Peoria!"

For those travelers with a more genteel interest in 'The City on the Hill', they chose to bypass Union Avenue and its vices, and instead proceeded directly to the elevated cable car incline. But first they had to navigate their way across a crowded street filled with mud and excrement, and succumb to clouds of effluvium and greasy smoke from the nearby packing houses, combined with soot and ash blown from the adjacent rail yards, all the while dodging massive rodents that lined the gutters of Union Avenue.

It was this overwhelming combination of profligacy and putrescence, the first impressions heaped upon the Kansas City visitor, that worried the mayor and his city council, the business men of the Commercial Club, and the ladies of the temperance movement. Collectively, they aspired to shed the town of its frontier status and endeavored to show the world how Kansas City had blossomed into a burgeoning metropolis poised on the doorstep of the twentieth century.

Crisp picked up a copy of *The Kansas City Star*, his attention drawn to a headline on the front page: "Senator Introduces Bill to Close Policy Shops". The consequences were both immediate and personal; Crisp often supplemented his income through games of chance. With potential new legislation, his already precarious financial situation could worsen, increasing his dependency on Cassie's intermittent support.

His contemplation was cut short when he saw a figure moving suspiciously through the crowd. Crisp studied him—though the man did not match any of the ten men he was looking for, he did recognize the man's face from a photograph in Speers' collection. The man exhibited a certain nervous energy typical of those with something to hide. Caught in a dilemma, he found himself torn between the practical application of The Bertillon System and its theoretical promise. He realized he could not rely solely on Speers' catalog of criminals; the real world was more complex, and justice was not served by photographs and measurements alone. As he kept his eyes on the man, the complexity of his own role in this new system solidified in his mind. Working with Speers under this new system would either be a path to redemption or a descent into moral compromise. The stakes were not just about catching criminals before they acted, but about defining the kind of man Crisp wanted to be in a city that teetered on the edge of the modern age.

———

His contemplations were abruptly shattered as a scruffy boy appeared by his side, his sudden presence jerking Crisp back to more pressing matters at hand.

"Hello, Colonel."

"Percy, my boy. How have you been?"

"Darn cold," the boy replied, shifting from one foot to the other. His youthful face was pinched from hours spent out in the biting wind, a blunt reminder to Crisp of the harsh realities faced by many in this booming city.

Their conversation quickly turned to the reason behind Percy's presence at the depot. The boy often came there to 'assist' travelers—seeking any insignificant job to earn a few coins. Crisp's heart twinged with a familiar pang of empathy; he too scraped by, his recent endeavors more about survival than prosperity.

"What are you doing here, sir?" Percy removed his oversized derby and pulled a cigarette butt from the headband inside, which he lit from a match in his pocket.

"Watching that man over there. The tall one."

"What's he about?"

"Perhaps nothing, but tell me, what do you see that makes him different from others in this hall?" Crisp challenged Percy to discern why the man looked suspicious, using this as a teaching moment.

The boy studied the man for several seconds. "He's looking for someone I'd say."

"Looking *for*, or looking *out* for?"

Percy took a closer second look. Then panned around the room. "I don't see anyone he needs to be afraid of. I think he's waitin' on someone." The boy's sharp, young mind quickly provided insights, but it was Crisp's seasoned eye that confirmed his suspicions about the man's nervous actions.

"See here now, watch his reaction." Crisp pointed toward a side door that opened as a policeman entered the station.

"Now he's nervous!"

This moment crystallized the harsh reality that came with

Crisp's journey: the city was a breeding ground for crime and despair, and his role in Speers' experiment thrust him directly into the vortex of potential danger and moral dilemmas. They watched as the policeman moved through the crowd on some other errand. When he had moved from their sight, their target man promptly exited the depot.

"Oh, I forgot to tell you. They found a body over by Dold's," Percy said flippantly.

"A body? Where? How long ago was this?"

"I can show you, but it'll cost you," he replied with a wink and a smile.

Crisp and the boy rushed westward along Union Avenue to where it angled onto Liberty Street, and as they approached the northwest corner of Liberty and Ninth, they found a crowd of people gathered on the opposite side of the elevated trolley tracks. They approached warily toward the scene where four policemen had cordoned off the area. Crisp threaded through the onlookers with care, relieved that Crotty was not among the uniforms, and there at the center of the throng, a familiar officer stood by a shrouded form on the ground. Crisp signaled Percy to hang back as he edged nearer the blanketed bundle.

"H'lo Ennis, I thought that was you. What have we here?"

The patrolman acknowledged Crisp with only a cursory nod, his eyes never leaving the notebook in which he fervently scribbled. It was only when his pencil snapped, the lead fracturing under the pressure of his thoughts, that he muttered, "Drat." He fumbled with the broken tip, scraping at it with his fingernail before looking up reluctantly. "I don't reckon this concerns you, Crisp," he said tersely.

"It may." He took a knee near the blanket. "Can I have a look-see?"

"Suit yourself. Just a quick look, from that side there. No need to startle these folks," he said gesturing to the crowd. "But Crisp, I should warn you—"

Too late—the shock of it hit Crisp like a slap in the face. He looked away, then forced himself to take another, closer look. He had braced himself for a corpse, there was no doubt of that, but nothing prepared him for the macabre spectacle beneath the grimy blanket. It was the body of a woman, that much clearly evident. In those few heartbeats of observation, he took in the devastating details of her condition. The woman, barely clothed, lay on her back, her blouse savagely torn to reveal her breasts. But what really got to him, what brought a tang of bile to the back of his throat, was the horrific condition of her face. At first glance, he thought she had been brutally beaten, but a second, longer look, told a more sinister story: her face, slashed with deep lines running from just below her eyes down to the corners of her mouth, was carved into a grisly mask.

"My God!"

"Exactly," Detective Ennis agreed.

He stood and wiped his forehead with a handkerchief. "Any idea who she is? Any witnesses?"

"Another bar girl who met her untimely demise. I've only talked to the watchmen over there so far; he's the one that came across the girl and covered her before we got here."

"How do you account for her appearance? She looks like she's been mauled by a bear."

Ennis scratched his head. "No, no bears around here," he said stoically.

"How do you know she's a bar girl, do you recognize her?"

"Look again, see what's she's wearing."

Crisp ventured another look at the risk of losing his breakfast. He lifted up the side of the blanket to get a better view of the woman's torso. That quick glance confirmed Ennis' suspicion. The woman's short skirt and ruffled blouse suggested the garish flash of a woman of the night.

"I suppose we'll need to inquire with the madams on this block as to whether they are missing one of theirs," Crisp suggested.

"Or, we can just wait until one of them reports a missing girl matching her description. Then we'll know what name to etch on her headstone."

"And then, end of case I suppose? Once she's in the ground, your work's through?"

"What are you getting at Crisp?"

"Aren't you the least bit interested in determining who the perpetrator of this gruesome crime is? There's a man out there who not only killed this young woman, but brutally slashed her in a fashion that is uncommonly macabre."

"I've seen worse." Crisp stared in disbelief as Ennis tried to clarify, "These types of women get mixed up with rowdies, or maybe they double cross one of their customers. He gets his revenge by leaving them like this as a warning to other girls."

"I wholeheartedly disagree Detective. I think you've got something far more sinister here. If this were the type of murder carried out in the heat of the moment by some rowdy or even a slighted customer as you postulate, the act would be committed by bare hands or a quick gunshot. The body would then be hidden somewhere with no risk of being found. The story itself of how the girl disappeared after some transgression had transpired between her and her employer or customer, would be enough to cause any other such girl to be more wary in her trade."

He watched as Ennis reflected on this and jotted down something in his notebook. For the detective, it was just another day's work—another unfortunate soul lost to the city's ruthless undercurrents. But Crisp saw something deeper; he perceived a more significant truth beneath the surface. The brutality of the murder spoke of not just a criminal act, but of a profound evil that had taken root in the city's soil.

In an epiphanous moment, his mission crystalized before him; it wasn't just about identifying criminals before they acted; it was about understanding the depth of darkness that could drive such acts, and about confronting the fact that he might be one of the few willing to delve into such depths to seek justice.

Chapter Four

Crisp spent the next four days lost in the thick veil of cigar smoke and the rhythmic clatter of poker chips, irresistibly drawn back to the gambling tables where each wager blurred into the next, erasing past losses and offering the seductive promise of a new hope. It was another unceremonious Saturday in the hazy back room of Sam's Place located in the 1700 block of Ninth Street. He shuffled a deck of cards with an absent-minded precision that betrayed his inner turmoil. Across from him, Moreland studied Crisp with a mixture of concern and curiosity.

"I must say, your eye is looking much better. The bruise has shifted from black and purple a few days ago to yellow on the edges there. That's a good sign."

"Nothing I haven't dealt with before," Crisp replied with cold detachment.

"What about your side, do you think the ribs were broken?"

"It doesn't hurt much when I breathe, just a little tender when I cough."

"You really should have consulted a physician right away. Very dangerous to let things fester."

Their conversation shifted as Crisp deftly cut the deck and

handed it back to Moreland. They were alone, playing a practice game, with no money at stake. Moreland had insisted on it, claiming it would keep their minds sharp.

"What have you been up to these past few days?" Moreland inquired as he dealt.

"Resting, mostly," Crisp responded, eyeing his hand before discarding two cards. "I'm a bit hard up at the moment, so I've avoided the expensive tables you frequent."

"I would've covered you," Moreland said, tossing two cards onto the discard pile.

Crisp shook his head, a smirk playing on his lips. "I have a feeling my luck is about to change."

"How's that?"

"I don't have the exact terms worked out yet, but the Chief of Police, Thomas Speers, has brought me on as a private examiner, separate from his force of detectives."

"That's wonderful news," Moreland replied, his eyes lighting up. "What will you be doing for him?"

Taking a deep breath, Crisp laid down his hand—eights and king high. "I'll be taking these investigations one step further than his detectives."

"Looks like three fives takes this round," Moreland said, revealing his winning hand. "What investigations are you referring to?"

"The recent beating of that woman beneath the incline, and a murdered prostitute found at the Dold Packing plant, among others."

"And they are somehow related?" Moreland queried, collecting the cards for another round.

"That's what I aim to reveal," Crisp said, his voice firm, revealing none of the uncertainty that simmered within him.

The cards dropped listlessly before him, and Moreland asked, "Ever work with Speers before?"

Crisp shuffled, his gaze distant. "I knew him back when I was with the Pinkertons. He was a well-known figure in law enforcement circles back then, everyone knew Speers." He hesitated, weighing whether to share more with Moreland, then chose to open up. "Remember I mentioned Crotty and the debacle with my uncle losing money?"

Moreland, rearranging his own hand, nodded without looking up.

Crisp continued, "I was embroiled in that mess too. My uncle—he was not the man I believed him to be." He tossed a card to the discard pile. "After I got laid up from Pinkerton's, I decided to relocate to Kansas City, and poured my savings into my uncle's business. Real estate. Thought I'd learn a legitimate trade, but I was blind to the illicit dealings he conducted behind closed doors. These deals entangled many of Kansas City's elite, and a few regular folks like Crotty. When the market crashed in '88, my uncle's schemes crumbled, investors were ruined, and he ended up in the penitentiary. As part-owner of the business, I got dragged into the aftermath. I claimed ignorance of his illegal activities during the trial, but the jury didn't buy it. Ended up serving six months for my indirect involvement." He watched Moreland closely, searching for a sign of judgment or a shift in demeanor from his newfound ally.

Moreland studied him, with a flicker of recognition in his eyes. "I thought you might be the same Crisp from those trials

I'd heard about. I'd kept an eye on that case during those months." Sensing his discomfort, Moreland tactfully shifted the conversation, "You say you're from England?"

"Yes, and so was my uncle. He was the one who took me out of the orphanage after my parents died. I was just a boy, staring down a bleak path. Then one day, a mysterious benefactor surfaced, secretly funding my education. That changed everything." He paused, the memories vivid and bittersweet. "I was sent to boarding school, and by fifteen, I'd landed an apprenticeship with a London import-export firm." His voice took on a reflective note. "It was there I began to hone my skills in investigation—tracking discrepancies and shortages in shipments, dealing with the dishonest shippers and unscrupulous customers we sometimes encountered." After a moment of introspection, he let out a held breath, "By '76, I'd scraped together enough to book passage to America. Attracted by ads looking for British immigrants, I eventually found my way to Victoria, Kansas, where I hired on as a security boss for a large cattle ranch." Moreland listened intently, drawn into the narrative of Crisp's complex past. "You know the rest," he concluded, his tone a mix of resignation and relief at sharing his story.

After further introspection, he continued, "It was only after reuniting with my uncle here that I discovered he was the benefactor who had changed my fate so many years earlier," he said, his voice tinged with a mixture of gratitude and confusion. "Sometimes, I still wonder... Did he come to Kansas City on his own, or was he following me?" His question hung in the air, a testament to the unresolved mysteries that still haunted his life.

Moreland focused intently on his cards, giving no outward reaction to Crisp's revelations. After a pause, he looked up, the game momentarily forgotten.

Crisp willingly resumed, "After I was released, I was penniless, my reputation in shambles. I figured the only path left was to strike out on my own, so I opened my private inquiry agency." He sighed deeply. "However, it seems my past clings to me; my name's been dragged through the mud, and it's been a constant struggle to attract the kind of clients that would make a difference." His gaze met Moreland's, searching for understanding, or perhaps a glimmer of encouragement in a world that had shown him little.

"These matters don't resolve themselves overnight," Moreland remarked. "It seems you've gained some ground with Speers' backing."

Crisp gave a slow nod; his expression grave. "True, but frankly, I'm weary of depending on others' generosity. I yearn to steer my own course." He paused, reflecting on Moreland's observation. "Yet, you may be right. Speers' support could well be exactly what I need at this juncture." He folded. "Marcus, can you just give me a few moments? Just need some fresh air," Crisp muttered, rising abruptly from his seat.

"You feeling alright?"

"Yes, yes. Just a couple minutes outside."

"Of course. I'll be waiting."

Crisp stepped out of Sam's place, flat broke, and headed

towards the policy shops, hoping for a quick windfall. The brisk afternoon teetered between snow and rain. Sleet pellets bounced off the brim of his bowler, and without looking back to see if Moreland watched, he blended into the crowd of drunks and working-class men that meandered the boardwalk along Ninth Street.

Just a few paces from Sam's, a green door in a quaint one-story building nestled snugly between the clamor of neighboring saloons, called out to Crisp. The door, once adorned with a rainbow arcing in bold contrasting colors above a pot of gold, now stood blurred and scarcely discernible under the wear of time. Yet, to the seasoned patrons who had crossed its threshold over the years, the promise of fortune within its walls remained undiminished. Without lifting his gaze from the puddled boardwalk, he reached for the door's handle, his steps measured, halting just short to avoid collision with the unyielding door.

Locked.

Peering through the tiny, clouded window inset in the door, he discerned the absence of any inviting light within. He shuffled further down the stretch of saloons, approached another policy shop, only to find its doors locked, the lights out, and the business emptier than his pockets. He let out a deep breath in exasperation, looking back and forth down the street indecisively. Drops of water fell from the brow of his derby as he moved still further down the block. He approached another nondescript door set within a brick facade, but was greeted with the same result: a door locked with no apparent occupants.

"What the devil is going on here?" he muttered, frustration

mounting. "You there, boy!" he called to a youth selling newspapers across the street.

The boy, nimble and quick, dodged puddles as he approached. "Mayor's closed all the policy shops on Sundays. Some've already closed for good," he informed Crisp, handing him the day's paper.

In what seemed like a cosmic nudge, Crisp felt a pull away from Ninth Street, a silent message that his fortune no longer lay in games of chance. He lingered there on the street corner, torn between his options. He desperately needed a quick win. Should he hurry back to his boardinghouse, plead with Cassie for a few dollars, and risk it all on a swift hand? Or should he approach Moreland for a modest advance on their next game, hoping to turn that into a gain? The weight of indecision held him fast, as each choice held its own peril and promise.

The warm glow of a lighted window nestled on the side street of Genessee caught his eye, offering a glimmer of hope. It was a discreet location, with an unassuming exterior and lights showing from within, suggesting the mayor's clutches had not reached every corner of The Bottoms. In that moment, his decision crystallized; the allure of a quick fix to his financial woes drew him in. Without hesitation, he descended upon the ticket shop, driven by a desperate need for a payout. He rummaged through his pockets looking for the tickets he'd purchased days earlier. The familiar thrill of potential winnings welled up inside him as he stepped across the threshold, relieved that the store was indeed open for business. Inside, the smell of cheap tobacco and desperation clung to the walls of the cramped shop.

"Greetings Bailey," Crisp declared as he closed the door. Arthur Bailey was the proprietor of one of the many such policy shops sprinkled not just throughout The West Bottoms, but situated across various quarters of the city, each nestled in close proximity to their brethren drinking establishments. Three other patrons were in the room, each evidently drawn by the same lure as Crisp.

Behind the counter, Bailey maintained a large chalkboard, segmented into days of the week and marked with the myriad lottery games he orchestrated. He disappeared behind a curtain separating the backroom. Crisp's pulse quickened while he sifted through his tickets and, with a surge of good fortune for a change, he identified a winner—twenty dollars, a rare but timely boon! His brief burst of elation, however, was swiftly disrupted by a stir at the rear of the shop.

Had Crisp not been so engrossed in the array of numbers before him, he might have noticed a fleeting shadow near the front window of the shop, or may have heard the soft click of a lock behind him at the front door after he'd entered. Perhaps even the faint tinkle of a bell from the back room might have caught his attention, the sort typically hung to announce the arrival of customers. Instead, with a victorious grin, he clutched his winning slip, and his mind raced through its possibilities: five dollars for Cassie, a small sum for cheroots, and meals for the day. Yet, with rent looming, prudence suggested reserving ten. His thoughts danced through various allocations, dividing his winnings into multiple potential budgets.

His attention shifted abruptly from the chalkboard to the curtain that veiled the back room. Voices, low and urgent, reached his ears. "But I don't understand," Bailey protested.

"This warrant's for selling tickets to minors. You can take it up with the judge," another voice responded, just before the unmistakable clink of handcuffs echoed through the shop. Crisp exchanged furtive glances with the other patrons who had also heard the commotion. Attempting to catch a glimpse of the unfolding drama, he peered through the curtain, but his view was suddenly obstructed by a hand whisking the curtain aside, revealing the all-too-familiar countenance of a certain policeman.

"Well, well. Look what we have here," Crotty sneered, his reptilian eyes locking onto Crisp's.

Nestled between Hickory and Mulberry on the north side of St. Louis Avenue, The Pendergast Hotel and Boardinghouse commanded the block with the air of an imperious warden overseeing its lesser neighbors. The four-story hotel sat prominently in the midst of smaller and narrower one and two-story structures, all scrunched together, and bookended by a saloon on each corner of the block. The hotel, morphed from the acquisition of The Old American House Hotel and The Climax Saloon, represented more than mere brick and mortar; it was the nucleus of Jim Pendergast's sprawling dominion over The West Bottoms; it was the nerve center for his intricate network of influence and control. While *Councilman* Pendergast officially ran the business of the First Ward—comprising all of The West Bottoms—from his office downtown, his influence extended well beyond the municipal governance scribbled into the city's ledgers. From his office and residence at his hotel in The Bottoms, *Boss* Pendergast steered local politics with a mix of charisma and iron fist, his presence as commanding as the bushy Bismarck mustache that adorned his round face.

Pendergast's office, spacious in the old manner, was adorned with heavy drapes and walls lined with dark wood paneling. A high ceiling presided over a long window on the south wall allowing ample light into the otherwise darkened space. Opposite the window, a compact potbelly stove huddled against the wall. Heavy chairs had etched scratches in the hardwood floors where they sat in front of a well-worn oak desk bearing the scars of countless meetings and decisions. Overall, it was a setting of pure utility—no frills, just the unembellished essence of business.

And in the center of it all, Pendergast loomed large over his desk. His broad shoulders and solid arms, ended in short, beefy hands which bore the telltale marks of a rugged youth filled with toil and brawls, and his sinews were hardened from countless battles fought and won. Today, he was dressed in his finest—a sharp black suit and matching vest, neatly offset by a white shirt and black bowtie, attire befitting a king in his court as he prepared for his afternoon audience at City Hall. This outfit stood in contrast to the more subdued brown suits and tieless shirts he normally wore when orchestrating his empire from his less conspicuous office here in The Bottoms.

The robust thud of Pendergast's fist against his desk punctuated the quiet of the room as he tossed aside *The Kansas*

City Star, its headlines declaring multiple stories in opposition to the policy shops that he controlled. The news was a harbinger of encroaching threats to his empire, which sprawled from the rough-and-tumble saloons and gambling dens in The Bottoms to the more respectable facades of downtown commerce.

"This is not good! By God, I'll do everything in my power to stop this."

Across the desk, Thomas Banwell, his attorney and chief strategist, maintained a calm demeanor. A middle-aged man dressed in a suit that whispered of silk and affluence, Banwell calmly suggested, "Even if this ordinance passes, it shouldn't hurt us that much. The shops can be converted, or even sold off, if necessary."

Pendergast's scowl deepened, his voice a low rumble of discontent. "Regan and Young are basically declaring victory already. If I cast my vote against theirs, it will surely paint me as a scoundrel in the eyes of the council."

Two other men seated across the desk listened intently, their faces tense with anticipation, each reluctant to interrupt. Finally, in an effort to dispel the silence that held them in suspense, Banwell interjected. "Don't worry, you're clean. They associate everything with Ed here." He tossed a smirk in Ed Findlay's direction causing the man to shift uncomfortably.

"Tom, you're missing the point. It's not just the policy shops. Once they succeed there, who knows where they'll stop. Today it's the tickets, tomorrow it's the saloons, and before you know it, they're going after the girls, and dice, and everything else we've built up."

With a gambler's daring in his eyes, Findlay, the youngest

of the gathered men, chimed in, "The cops won't touch us, Boss. They haven't before, and they won't start now." Findlay occupied the space between Banwell and another middle-aged man. Findlay was an image of meticulous grooming and sartorial elegance. He wore a double-breasted suit of the latest fashion, complemented by a striped silk necktie that added a dash of refined flair. A subtle hint of rich cologne lingered around him, evidence of his recent visit to the barber that had left his hair in a glossy, precise parting. His cheeks and jaw, freshly shaven, glowed with a healthy, rosy hue, while his mustache and chin beard were trimmed with exacting precision.

Reclining with casual grace, he clasped his fingers behind his head, projecting a brash confidence that belied his youth, particularly noticeable in contrast to the more seasoned figures flanking him. More than just a gambler, Findlay was the mastermind behind the lucrative games that thrived in the shadowy depths of Pendergast's saloons, overseeing the roll of dice and the silent exchange of fortunes with a vigilant eye.

"If we lose the policy shops, can you establish other games to make up the loss?" This was directed to Findlay.

"We've got the Ninth locked up; I suppose I could start more street games on Union. But don't worry Boss, the new shops back east will more than make up for the losses here."

"No, I want something more permanent, those stand-up games are great for attracting newcomers and getting the fever started, but I want places, out of sight mind you, where we can entice the greenhorns and rookies with low antes and easy money, and eventually graduate them up to our other more lucrative games. Talk to the owners of New Albany, The Adams,

The Kentucky, maybe The New England," Pendergast said counting these off on his left hand. "Start with the smaller places, don't worry about The Blossom, The Kansas City, or Traveler's. Let me know if you get any pushback." He grabbed the newspaper again, his face darkening. "And as far as the games back east, why the hell did you give them so much detail? I don't want anything in print without running it past Tom!" He pointed to *The Star* and shifted his view back to Banwell, "How did you let this slip?"

"It wasn't a slip, sir. All the details here give legitimacy to our businesses, and as I said it shifts ownership to Ed."

Pendergast's gaze flicked to Felix Wexler, his accountant, a man whose nervous demeanor belied his crucial role in the financial orchestrations of the Pendergast machine. "We may have to grease a few more palms at the precinct to keep things running smoothly."

Wexler looked up from his ledger, "Yes, of course," he said in a meek voice, and flipped through his journal scribbling notes in the margin of another page.

The stakes were clear: adapt or perish. As Pendergast contemplated his next move, the discussion was interrupted by the arrival of his valet Dermot Gallagher, who entered accompanied by another man who hung back just outside the doorway. Gallagher promptly reminded Pendergast of his upcoming civic duties—a luncheon uptown that served as a calculated display of Pendergast's influence and power, each guest carefully chosen, not just for their loyalty but for their potential usefulness in his schemes. Pendergast's overcoat was draped over his arm and he held a derby hat and black gloves in his other hand. "Will you be staying at the Main Street office the remainder of the day?"

"Thank you, Dermot. No, I've got a council meeting tonight, but first I'd like to spend the afternoon here, downstairs, conversing with my *friends*. There'll be plenty coming around by end of week on Friday, but no harm putting out a few dollars ahead of that." Friday meant payday for the thousands of workers from the packinghouses, warehouses, railroads, and other businesses in The Bottoms. Those who had recently lost confidence in the local banks knew they could assuredly cash their checks at one of Pendergast's saloons where he ran a sort of private bank, distributing hard-to-come-by greenbacks and silver specie in exchange for their paychecks, which Wexler later deposited at the National Bank downtown. Pendergast turned to Wexler, "Are we all set for payday?"

Wexler shifted uneasily, "I'll need to move funds, I want to make sure we don't run out like we did a few weeks ago."

"Yes of course. Get with Carnes, he'll safely escort you with that much cash on hand. Anything else?"

"Not at the moment, thank you." Taking a cue from Banwell, Wexler, followed by Findlay and Gallagher, left Pendergast and Banwell alone in the office. As the meeting adjourned, the tension in the room was distinct—a storm was brewing, and Pendergast was at its eye, determined to hold his ground against the winds of change.

He looked at the newspaper again, and in frustration shoved it toward Banwell. "Tom, things are changing faster than I can keep up." Banwell looked at the frontpage settling on two of the more relevant headlines of concern to his employer.

One declared 'Mothers Add a Protest', and the other read 'The Policy Shop Curse'. Pendergast let out a blast of air in exasperation, "We've got Glass and the other parks men coming at us from one side with their 'city beautiful movement', and now the church people are getting behind this policy movement."

"What do you intend to do Jim?"

"Now that we have a foothold uptown, I'll do my best to keep things in The Bottoms as they are, but for how long, that's the question."

Banwell nodded in agreement. "We should look further out. In another five years, The Bottoms will be all slums, Jim. You should invest now and move your businesses downtown, or out south. That's where our future lies."

"It will take time. Nothing is going to happen overnight, but you're right, our future in The Bottoms will not last forever. I worry Findlay has overstretched himself. Chicago? Cincinnati? Indianapolis?" He pointed again to the day's lead story. "He's got police from half a dozen cities listed here after him. And we don't know who runs those territories. He's stirring up something way bigger than we bargained for."

"Don't worry about that. I've got his back and have been in contact with the right people. We'll keep this under the rug."

In the lull that followed, the door to Pendergast's office swung abruptly open, admitting a man whose attire spoke of long and rough use rather than fashion. His suit, frayed at the edges, clung awkwardly to his bulky frame, and his large boots bore the scars of many an unpolished day. This was not a man of delicate tasks but of brute strength, the sort Pendergast kept at hand for the less savory operations required by his extensive enterprise.

"Dermot sent me to check if you're wanting for anything," the man stated in a tone that brooked more of command than query. Banwell's frustration at the interruption was apparent.

Pendergast directed his gaze toward the big man. "Colin, hitch up a wagon and head down to fetch a load of coal. Bag it neatly and have it outside the hotel by five. Throw one of those old campaign banners over the side, make sure it's clean and visible. You know how we do this. I'll join you out front to distribute the bags to the local folks who need them."

Colin Wyse stood silent, his presence in the room as imposing as a great ape.

"Be sure to check in with the missus, see if she needs anything." Pendergast continued, handing over an empty cigar box. "And fetch another box of these from Beaumont's. If they're out, try for the Gaucho's or La Carolina's instead. Can you remember that?" His tone slowed, a hint of caution threading through his words. "Shall I write it down so we avoid the sort of mix-up we had last time?" With a declining nod, Wyse exited, the door closing behind him with a resonant thud. His footsteps echoed heavily as they descended the back stairs.

Banwell asked annoyingly, "Really Jim, why must you employ these oafs?"

"You know damn well this Boss business is all about making friends and doing favors. His father is a dear friend of mine. Besides, who else can I get to do the dirty work..."

For four days, Algernon Crisp had lingered in the cage-like atmosphere of his boardinghouse room, with empty pockets and a shattered heart. The room, with its peeling wallpaper and creaking floorboards, seemed to close in on him, a cage he could neither escape nor afford to leave. The bed he shared with Cassie was a tangle of unwashed sheets and stale regret. He lay sprawled across it, staring at the cracked ceiling, his mind a whirl of shame and desperate calculation.

The greenbacks she'd slipped into his hand a week ago were long gone, swallowed by the pitiless tables that beckoned him with their false promises. He knew he could ask for more—she had never refused, her love for him as unwavering as his need. But the thought of her eyes, filled with disappointment yet again, stopped him cold. He couldn't look at her and instead turned over, burying his face in the pillow, trying to suffocate the voice in his head that whispered of one last chance, one final gamble, that could turn his luck around.

It wasn't long, and he found himself shrouded in the depths of night, walking the quiet streets under a starless sky. He veered into a narrow alley flanked by two weathered brick behemoths, seeking refuge from the cold that gripped the city. Outside the alley's mouth, gas lamps offered a warm, golden haze, spilling light that turned the main thoroughfare into a soft, amber dreamscape. But within the alley, darkness was sovereign, broken only by the rank stench of stagnant, forgotten waste. Unseen shapes lurked in the gloom there—ominous, dark masses, felt more than seen.

He clung to a brick wall just inside the alleyway, waiting, hiding. His breaths came in ragged gasps, and his chest heaved in a desperate rhythm as he tried to marshal his senses. Suddenly, a shadow began to shift, a specter seething and swirling like steam rising from hot pavement after a summer rain. The wraithlike form sent an icy chill racing through the alley, that clawed at Crisp with an ethereal hand. His throat constricted, his cries for help reduced to futile whispers swallowed by the oppressive fear bearing down upon him.

Instinctively, he ran, his boots slapping in the slick muck of the alleyway as he burst onto a well-lit street. To his dismay, it was eerily deserted, the usual vibrant life of the city having retreated into the inviting warmth of nearby buildings for the night. The unyielding chill pursued him, like a spectral predator in a desperate dash through the city's streets. Each lamp he passed flickered and died as the darkness, pronounced and relentless, advanced behind him.

Crisp's panic soared as he navigated street after empty street, his heart pounding a frenetic beat in his ears. The city seemed abandoned, each turn revealing only more desolation, more isolation. In a last-ditch effort, he dove into another shadow-laden alley, hoping to elude whatever phantom chased him. But it was in vain; the darkness seemed indifferent to light or shade, its icy tendrils ever encroaching, ever nearing. Gasping, his voice now just a choked whisper in the frosty air, he barely registered distant, muffled sounds pounding within his brain. Somewhere close, a faint voice called through the veil of his nightmare, "Mr. Crisp? Mr. Crisp? Are you alright?" But the murkiness was unyielding, smothering, pressing down on him, squeezing the very breath from his lungs.

Then, abruptly, his nightmare dissolved. Crisp awoke,

drenched in sweat, sitting bolt upright in the narrow bed of his modest room once again. Daylight seeped through the curtains, its weak light offering no clue as to the time of day, yet the rhythmic clatter of horse-drawn carriages in the streets below his window gradually dragged him from the depths of sleep back into the harsh light of the morning.

"Yes, just a moment," he called out, tucking his nightshirt into his trousers and combing his fingers through his disheveled hair. When he opened his bedroom door, his landlady, Beatrice Meadows, peered anxiously at him.

"Oh, Mr. Crisp, I heard you moaning in your sleep. Have you taken fever? Are you ill?" she asked, stepping into his room without waiting for invitation.

Crisp rubbed at his unkempt beard, messaging at his throat; he still felt the clutch of the phantom chill from his dream. "Just a night terror, nothing more," he reassured her, though the dark tendrils of fear lingered, and a cold, hard knot wrenched in his stomach.

His mind flashed back to the evening before. He had retired to his room with Cassie, they had shared a pipe which now was nowhere to be seen, and sometime in the middle of the night, she had left him alone with his opium-infused dreams. Before he could protest, Ms. Meadows fussed over his room, tidying up as she spoke of bringing him tea and porridge. She nonchalantly retrieved his chamber pot next to the bed, moved to the window, and launched its contents into the street below.

"Are you sure you're alright now?"

He nodded reassuringly.

"Good. A messenger called on you, not long ago, sounded

urgent," she began, her voice trailing as she tucked at his pillows and bedding.

"Messenger?" Crisp's mind sharpened instantly. He began wrestling with his boots. "Was he just a boy, about eleven, with a derby?"

"No, not a boy. A young man, sent by The Chief of Police no less," she clarified. "You've been summoned downtown, at once," she paused, her memory catching up. "He requests your presence immediately outside City Hall. It's urgent, you mustn't delay."

"Was that all he said?" Crisp asked, hurriedly exchanging his nightshirt for a fresh shirt she'd placed in his drawer the day before. He cleaned himself up swiftly in front of the mirror above his dresser, probing further as she tidied his room, "anything else at all?"

"That was the entirety. Struck me as peculiar, such urgency at City Hall on a Saturday no less."

"I see. It's nothing worrisome, ma'am. I've been working with the Chief as of late; perhaps he's eager to dive into our matters before the day's chaos ensues." Crisp patted his coat, securing three loose cheroots from his dresser and slotting them into his pocket. He moved toward the door, halting with a courteous pretext. "Ms. Meadows, I must depart—"

"Of course, go, urgent matters," she replied, bustling about. "Do you have your key? If not, remember the back door. Will you return for supper? Should I keep the stew warm?"

"No, thank you. My schedule is uncertain," he shouted over his shoulder as he raced down the back stairs from his room. He fitted his derby, popped his head back around the corner at the bottom of the steps, and offered a curt nod. "Good day, ma'am," he concluded, exiting the boardinghouse briskly.

Stepping into the cool morning air, Crisp headed towards City Hall, his mind flooded with questions. Among them, what did Speers want so urgently? The answer, he feared, might just tie back to the dark shadows of his night terror. Leaving Ms. Meadows' house behind on Genessee Street, he rushed to the Metropolitan trolley, shot up Eighth Street through the tunnel onto Washington Street, and made his way downtown. He jumped from the trolley near Fourth and Main and hastened toward City Hall by foot.

Crisp paused momentarily to behold the grand edifice of the new City Hall building, less than a year old, that occupied the entire block between Fourth and Fifth Streets between Main and Walnut. As he resumed his steps, Crisp noticed a group of men gathered on the lawn near Fifth, and recognizing Thomas Speers among them, he diverted his path to join the Chief.

The grass, still wet from overnight rain, held shallow puddles forcing Crisp to navigate carefully, and sucking his boots into the soft ground as he closed in. He made it over to Speers, who stood above a brown blanket spread on the ground, speaking to two workers standing at attention. At Crisp's approach, Speers looked up.

"Oh good, you received my caller." He dismissed the two men, and shifted his gaze back to the disturbing scene in front of him.

"What's this then?" Crisp asked, noticing a lumpy heap under the disheveled blanket.

"I wanted you here before my detectives," Speers said,

bending down. He beckoned Crisp closer, hesitating as he began to lift the blanket. "This is not a pretty sight." He pulled the blanket back, and Crisp caught his breath as the brutalized body of a young woman was revealed. Half-dressed, and body marked by violence, her limbs lay contorted unnaturally. Speers covered her again, and Crisp stood there, the severity of the scene etched in his expression.

"When did this happen?" Crisp looked around. It had started to sprinkle again. Although the streets were crowded with early morning businessmen bustling along under their umbrellas, they seemingly took no notice to the investigation underway. A dark patch of sky to the southwest rumbled with thunder.

"Sometime early this morning, before sunrise. I had just arrived across the street there when one of the custodians summoned me over."

"Where are your men?"

"On their way, but as I said, I summoned you first." Crisp looked dumfounded and began to inquire further but Speers handed him a piece of paper.

"What's this?" He turned it over in his hands, his features contorting in confusion that gradually shifted towards an inkling of understanding. He glanced at Speers, seeking confirmation.

"It was on top of the body," Speers murmured, his voice low and laden with a grave significance. "I believe we now have a clue that links these killings together."

Crisp turned his attention back to the handbill in his trembling hands. It was a promotional flyer for The Women's Temperance movement, identical to the numerous others thrust into his hands along Ninth Street and Union Avenue; each one vehemently condemning the sins of alcohol and gambling, denouncing the myriad vices that plagued The West Bottoms. As he stared at the flyer, a chilling connection began to form, casting a shadow over the simple piece of paper.

"There was this too," Speers said, handing a crumpled piece of newspaper to Crisp, "stuffed in her mouth."

Crisp slowly unfurled the paper, his expression a mix of confusion and dawning realization. "It was meant to silence the victim," he added menacingly. He handed it back to Speers. "What do you mean by *these killings*?" His voice betrayed a flicker of apprehension.

"That's what I've been meaning to talk with you about. There have been others," Speers responded gravely, "slayings of a very similar nature, starting late last year." As he spoke, a macabre slideshow of images flickered through Crisp's mind like a whirling zoetrope, accelerating his heartbeat. He envisioned the haunted face of the girl found in The Patch, the lifeless eyes of the woman discovered beneath the incline trestle, the hideously scarred face of the woman uncovered at Dold's, and now the tragic figure lying under the blanket before him. Each image, etched with the cruel imprint of violence, linking them in a gruesome chain of unspeakable acts.

Speers delved into his coat and produced a handwritten note. He pressed it into Crisp's palm. "Take a look. These are women murdered over the past year, all from The Bottoms. I need you to determine if there's a thread that ties them together."

Crisp pursed his lips in concentration as he scanned the list, shielding it with his free hand from the rain. He handed it back to Speers.

"I've got the case files, I can give you all the details," he continued, his voice low and urgent. "I want you on this, Crisp." Speers gestured towards the morbid scene under the blanket. "This requires dedicated attention, someone who can focus solely on these cases without other distractions. You know The Bottoms, Crisp. You're not just another cop; you understand that place, and its people."

"And why do you think this killer would be from The Bottoms?" Crisp asked, skepticism lacing his tone.

"That's for you to figure out," Speers replied. "The victims all worked there. Our killer might be lurking there too. And we can't afford a public spectacle, not with the crowds at the depot every day. If this gets into the papers, it'll scare away the city's visitors. We need this handled quietly, and efficiently."

"Your men already despise me. How will I get around them? Crotty for instance, what about him?"

"Don't worry, you'll have my full authority going forward. I can't guarantee you any respect from my men, but I'll guarantee no further harm. I'll order them to stay clear of you."

Crisp's mind was clouded with the looming threats of the task at hand, as he considered the perilous ramifications of accepting the offer, "With all due respect, sir—"

Speers headed off any doubts, "This is your chance to rebuild your reputation, a chance to set yourself up right, get a fresh start. Isn't that what you want?"

The distant skies rumbled ominously as Crisp, absorbed in thought, stared at the ground near the covered body. He noticed an indentation in the grass where a puddle had formed. "Look here, Chief, that seems to be a footprint," he observed, pointing it out.

Speers bent closer, inspecting the ground. "Yes, those as well," he replied, indicating more marks near the first.

"They seem to lead to and from the street. That might explain how the body got here. But you mentioned a custodian found the body, right? These may only be his prints. But we shouldn't discount them yet." Crisp aligned his own boot beside one of the impressions for a size comparison. "What's the next step for her?" he asked mournfully.

"My men will be here soon to gather details, and I'll bring in the surgeon to record everything officially."

As the rain-soaked ground reflected the muted light of dawn, Crisp noticed two uniformed patrolmen hastening towards them, their boots sloshing through shallow puddles. Detective John Hayes, a familiar face on Speers' force, was accompanied by another officer Crisp didn't know. Before they arrived, he asked abruptly, "Can I see that paper again, the newspaper? There might be something I missed."

With a knowing smile, Speers forcefully handed both papers and his handwritten note to Crisp. He watched Crisp's stare intensify, with a familiar spark of curiosity and analytical precision ignited in his eyes, a spark that Speers knew all too well. It was the look of a man on the cusp of unraveling a mystery.

"Crisp," Speers said, his voice steady, yet infused with compelling urgency under the dreary, rain-heavy sky, "you're going to help me find the killer."

Chapter Five

In the warmly lit interior of Pendergast's office, located at the rear of his hotel on St. Louis Avenue, the space was suffused with the unmistakable aroma of Bushmills Irish Whiskey, its rich notes subtly mingling with the modern hum of electric lamps—an innovation that lent the room an air of progress and intensity. Banwell, with the practiced ease of an old confidant, poured whiskey into two glasses; it had been a busy Monday, and as he handed a glass to Pendergast, he broached the subject of their mutual concern. "Findlay's asking for help against the mayor's new law."

Pendergast took a slow sip, savoring the warmth. The whiskey was not just any spirit; it had journeyed across the Atlantic on the maiden voyage of the *SS Bushmills*, marking the distillery's foray into the American market. Banwell had secured a case through a relative in Philadelphia, gifting it to Pendergast as a Christmas tribute. "Ed's got nothing to worry about. Speers' men won't touch him here. Cowherd's only reacting to that mess uptown where they found tickets sold near the high school. It wasn't even one of our shops."

"But it's given our opponents a foothold; the Republicans and the women's groups are rallying for a total ban on gambling, not just the tickets. Even the Baron's beginning to turn against us."

"Poppycock," Pendergast scoffed, his disdain evident. "Nelson and his *Star* play both sides. He's just drumming up scandal to sell papers."

"But it's damaging publicity all the same," Banwell insisted. "The more they talk, the more the people might follow."

"Bah," Pendergast grunted, his mind already moving to other matters. "Who's on the schedule this afternoon?"

Banwell consulted his notebook. "Father McClary from All Saints, Mr. Gavin Kavanagh, and a Mr. Novak."

"Kavanagh?" Pendergast raised an eyebrow. "Didn't we address his concerns before?"

"He requested an audience again; left an inquiry with Gallagher yesterday."

Pendergast's annoyance was clear. "Let him wait. And what about Novak, why do I know that name?"

"A worker from Jarboe's. He's downstairs now."

Pendergast nodded, reflecting back on his early days in Kansas City. "Have Gallagher send McClary up first. I don't want to keep him waiting." With that, Banwell left the office.

Alone, Pendergast finished his whiskey and set the glass aside. He tucked the bottle into his desk and quickly set about reorganizing the room, replacing Banwell's comfortable leather chair with more modest seating, to subtly remind his visitors who wields the power in this space. He positioned himself behind his desk, drew back the curtain revealing the rail yards in the distance, and allowed sunlight to flood the room, silhouetting him against its brightness. A gentle knock preceded

Gallagher at the door. "Father McClary to see you, sir."

Pendergast greeted the priest with a careful balance of respect and authority. Banwell entered the room behind McClary and busied himself on the far side of the room, but well within earshot of Pendergast.

"Dermot, fetch a fresh pot of coffee if you please."

"No thank you, I won't be long," McClary said.

Pendergast recognized the priest's demeanor signaling this was no time for small talk. "Please sit. How can I assist you today?"

McClary's concern was immediate and grave. He exhaled heavily, "It's been a harsh winter at the Bethlehem School. The sisters are struggling to provide for the growing number of needy families. Our flock is growing. Every time I visit, it seems there are another dozen or more women and children at the school than my previous visit." He paused sighing heavily. "I must say, it was most kind of you at Christmas, when you sent those wagons of stores to help during the holidays, but alas I fear the cupboards are nearly bare again, and the school is short on blankets and linens. Mr. Pendergast, could you see it in your heart to help the children once again?"

Pendergast nodded, his face a mask of civic duty. "Of course, Father. Another wagonload of supplies shall be arranged. We can't have the children suffering. What else can I provide? Do you need money?"

The sunlight behind Pendergast made it difficult for McClary to make eye contact, let alone read Pendergast's emotions, as he searched for his next words. "No, no, another wagon will be help enough. Once this weather eases in the spring, I suspect many of the women will return to their husbands with the children in tow."

"Consider it done, Father. I'll take care of it immediately!" He feigned a scribbled note to himself.

"You're a good man James Pendergast. Your beneficence has not gone unnoticed," McClary added glancing upwards, yet, his wrinkled brow hinted at other concerns.

"Is there something else, Father?"

The priest's relief was evident, but he hesitated before adding, "I don't wish to impose, but yes, there is another favor to ask." He cleared his throat. "The primary purpose of my visit today concerns my nephew, Denis Skahill. Do you know the man?"

"I'm afraid I do not. Is he in regular attendance at All Saints? Have I met him there?"

McClary shifted in his seat to avoid the sunlight. "No, I doubt you have met him before. Oh, he does frequent my parish, but he is a bashful soul. And I will admit, what the Lord giveth him in size and strength, the Lord did not provide in wisdom and judgement. He's not a bad man mind you, but when it comes to smarts, he is as slow as molasses in the winter. And then he also carries the burden of the pituitary enlargement. Are you familiar with the medical term acromegaly?"

Pendergast shook his head no.

"It's only a recently discovered condition. A glandular affliction that causes irregular growth in some parts of the body. 'Gigantism' it used to be termed. For you see, Denis is a very large man. Strong as an ox mind you."

"And how can I help your nephew? Is there some surgery or medicine he requires?"

"No, nothing like that. I only seek your help in employment. His size and simple nature make him the target of cruelty. He needs employment suited to his unique abilities. Something that keeps him away from harsher eyes."

Pendergast considered this, his mind calculating. "Why certainly a man of his strength would be most employable at dozens of jobs here in The Bottoms. The stockyards, the butcheries, perhaps a factory post. Would not those suit his purpose?"

"While his strength is certainly his dominant characteristic, it's no use. He has tried commonplace employment, but you see his peers and fellow workers are very hard on him. Their mockery and jeering play most cruelly upon his spirit. Compound that with his intellectual deficiencies, and the poor man has scarcely survived more than a few weeks at any such profession. No, I fear I seek your generosity once again. Is there any such use you may have for this man? He works well on his own mind you. Perhaps there is a position as man-servant, or some other simple tasks he can routinely perform?"

"Father, I understand the poor man's predicament, but honestly, I have a dozen or more men already in my employ. I have a valet and man-servant, Mr. Gallagher there," he motioned toward the doorway. "Most of my other men are educated in accounting, law, or political affairs you see." He read the distress in McClary's weary face. The priest had been a good ally. When the temperance women had tried to rally on Ninth Street recently, it was McClary who came to Pendergast's rescue by persuading the women to move their parade to Eighth Street near All Saints parish. "I'll tell you what, let me discuss this with my men. Maybe I can bring him on as assistant to my driver, or find him a place at the hotel; if nothing else, I'm sure I can find the man some form of service with my colleagues in the saloon business."

"I will say it again, you're a good man James Pendergast!"

"We'll find a place for him."

As Father McClary expressed his gratitude and departed, Pendergast summoned Ivan Novak. Once the priest had left, Banwell remained in the room with Pendergast taking up position next to the desk. When Gallagher ushered Novak into the room, Pendergast's face immediately lit up, and he rushed past Banwell to greet the man.

"Ivan my old friend. How are you?" He held the Croatian man by the elbow and helped him into the chair across from his desk.

"I am doing well Boss." His expression was infectious with joviality, its warm features radiating friendliness. "My crucible still holds the pig, but I am no bull ladle." Together they laughed heartily forcing Pendergast to explain to Banwell that Novak had worked alongside him at the Jarboe Foundry many years prior.

"Thomas, pour this man a glass of wine." Banwell turned toward the bookshelves shaking his head and muttering to himself, knowing there was no such bottle there to be found.

"Thank you, Boss, but no, I will not take too much of your time."

Banwell instead moved to a file cabinet on the far end of the room so that Pendergast did not see his expression.

"And how are the old Jarboes?"

"There are not so many left; many have gone on to God's pastures. The rest, the older ones, had to lay down their hammers." Novak shook his head. "The shinglers, the puddlers, the fillers; those are jobs for a young man." He squinted and nodded frequently in encouragement, always smiling as he spoke.

Pendergast nodded in agreement and sat quietly reflecting on his youthful days. He read concern in Novak's face. "You seem troubled. What can I help you with my old friend?"

Novak glanced over his shoulder at Banwell who seemingly ignored the man. He curled the brim of his hat in both hands and began hesitantly as his expression changed. "It is my sister Marija. Her husband, Damir, was a Jarboe man, a furnace man that started some months after you departed. He was a good man, my apprentice; I trained him well. The men still talked of 'Lucky Jim' in those days, and many men shared the story of your successes. It gave them hope that there was something more than spending all their days next to the furnace. Damir was aroused by these stories. He dreamed of one day owning his own factory, and bragged how he would take care of his workers. He believed so strongly in his dreams that he convinced me he would become a successful man like you Boss."

Pendergast nodded, showing Novak that he held his full attention.

"In those days, Marija used to bring lunch to the foundry. I would gather coins from the Jarboes, in turn she fetched pails of beer for us. Damir saw her one day, and before he even knew she was my sister, he told me in confidence, I am going to marry that girl one day. I believed in his dreams, so I made the introductions, and eventually it became true, he married Marija later that summer. They had four children: Darko, Antonija, Jelena, and Mirko." At the mention of his nephews and nieces, Novak's eyes brightened momentarily, but then the greyness returned. "But even though Damir had his dreams, as we say in the old country, what man devises, God determines, and it was not to be. He was killed at the foundry. The steamer blew one day, Damir was standing close, and was scorched most horribly. Within three days, he was gone leaving Marija to raise her family on her own." Novak wiped at his eye. "I have my own family and needs, but I do my best to give Marija food when we have extra; I don't want her to worry that my nieces and nephews will go hungry." He paused, his face becoming more forlorn. "But I come to you Boss, for help about her landlord. The man has raised her rent continuously since my brother-in-law has passed."

Pendergast, expecting Novak to ask for money—which he fully intended to provide—was surprised when Novak continued.

"Koppelman is his name; he knows without a husband he can press my sister and control her. He knows she can't make ends meet and even though he has enslaved her with taking care of his laundry and mending his clothes—her whole family must help with this—he continues to threaten her if she does not pay the increased rent. Even now, I think this man wants to force my sister to meet his demands in some other way."

Pendergast pondered on this. He was familiar with

Koppelman, a miserly landlord that owned multiple tenement flats not only in The West Bottoms, but in the Kansas City slum called The North End. "Where does your sister live? In which of Koppelman's buildings?"

"Just off State Line, near Tenth. Marija fears if she is evicted, she will have to live on the bluffs. She is proud, but stubborn like a mule. She does not want to live under my roof."

"Do you need money to move her to a new room? Surely there are other boardinghouses you can find?"

"Her friends live there in Koppelman's building, and it is close to her son's work. Marija too has jobs in the neighborhood. She does not wish to move. Boss Jim, I hope you can speak to Koppelman and convince him to let my sister stay." Novak said pleadingly.

Pendergast, his face expressionless, did not wish to give Novak any false hope. He stared blankly past Novak for many seconds and finally exhaled deeply. "I believe Koppelman is a good man. I am sure, once he understands your sister's misfortunes, he will have a change of heart. Do not worry my old friend. Do not let this trouble you anymore. Your sister will be able to stay."

Banwell turned from his filing duties and locked eyes with Pendergast behind Novak's back. Novak was promptly ushered out of Pendergast's office, but not before offering his thanks and wishing many blessings on Boss Jim and his family. As Pendergast returned to his desk, Banwell stood at the door. "Do you wish to see Kavanaugh now?"

"In due time. Let's wait for Ed."

"What do you want to do about this Koppelman?"

"Have Carnes and his men give him a talking to."

"Of course. And McClary?"

"What does he expect me to do with that idiot nephew of his? Have you seen the man? I declare, he must stand seven feet tall!"

"So, you do know him then? Is it true he's as strong as he says?"

"I don't know, I suppose." He let out a deep breath. "Send Colin round to fetch him. He can help around the hotel for starters, we'll find some errands for him."

"Someone of his size could be quite intimidating. Perhaps he should report to Carnes."

"No, let's keep him close to the vest to begin with until we determine what we can do with him."

Tucked away from the awe-struck gazes of visitors arriving at the heart of The West Bottoms on Union Avenue, Ninth Street between Bell Street and State Line, pulsated with a lively, untamed spirit of its own. This single stretch of road existed as a testament to vice and survival in The Bottoms, with twenty-two of its twenty-four aging structures housing saloons. The buildings, huddled together as if for protection, bore the scars of countless brawls and the wear of time. Every weathered doorway served as a portal to another world—each a shadowy realm steeped in harsh tobacco smoke, where the floors were sticky with spilled beer, and the rough murmur of voices intertwined with vibrant strains of fiddles and pianos, all engulfed by the clinking of glasses and the heavy thuds of boots on wooden floors.

Here, amid the flickering gaslights lining the muddy, unpaved streets, the night was always young and the next drink promised to erase the cares of a hard day's labor. In this rugged and chaotic landscape, Crisp found a gritty magnetism amongst the gamblers, the brawlers, and the disillusioned; here he felt the pulse of the city most acutely. The corruption and vice that fueled this quarter was as open and rampant as the liquor that flowed within its saloons. Yet, within this lawlessness, there lay a raw honesty—a stark, unvarnished display of humanity in its most unguarded form. Crisp, with his own past shadowed by complexities, was drawn to Ninth Street's unpretentious rawness. To him, this was the real Kansas City, far removed from the polished facades and manicured narratives above the bluffs. Here, on Ninth Street, the city bared its soul, and in its flawed, tumultuous rhythms, Crisp found a strange and compelling harmony.

Inside Sam's Place, Crisp sat before a green, baize-covered table, his fingers idly shuffling a deck of cards. His luck was as capricious as the weather outside. The night before, a balmy forty degrees had wrapped the city in a false sense of warmth. But as midnight passed, a ruthless chill descended, dragging the temperature to a bone-numbing ten below. The mercury fought valiantly throughout the day to edge above zero, but the relentless cold held sway. The sudden freeze gripped the city in a vice, seeping into bones and spirits alike, leaving everyone feeling brittle and dispirited—much like his fortunes of late, which kept him anchored to his seat with nothing gained and nothing lost.

Yet his mind, only partly focused on his cards, was occupied by the heavier gamble laid out by his new employer just two days earlier. Speers had hinted at a lucrative opportunity, a chance not just for steady income but to establish a reputable investigation business. Since his departure from Pinkerton's, Crisp had struggled to gain a foothold, his ambitions hampered by both the lack of a significant backer and the tarnished reputation that now clung to the name Crisp. A partnership with Speers could open doors uptown, connecting him with influential figures and profitable contracts.

"Two cards," Crisp muttered distractedly, accepting the dealt hand and folding two back into the pile. His mind churned as he pondered the disturbing nature of his new case—murders most foul, targeting the vulnerable women of The West Bottoms. It wasn't just the violence that puzzled him, but the dark intent behind it, a sinister thread woven through each crime scene. These were not typical crimes of passion, but something far more evil, and more malignant.

Crisp fumbled with his cards, his thoughts racing. The killer targeted the women of The Bottoms—the working girls, to be precise. He needed to begin his investigation there, delving into the lives of those who had fallen victim. He would need to ask questions, probing for enemies, searching for motives, any thread that could lead to the perpetrator. Yet the challenge seemed daunting; The Bottoms teemed with illicit women, from dance hall entertainers to full-time prostitutes living in boardinghouses and plying their trade in assignation houses. Where should he even begin in this labyrinth of lost souls? He needed an insider, someone who understood the shadows of

The Bottoms better than he did.

He would start with Cassie; her connections and history were the key to that underworld. She knew a great deal of the women on Ninth, and knew, or had worked with, many others in The Bottoms over the past few years. Although Crisp did not fully understand the depths of her involvement in the underground world of prostitution, he knew she could help him begin his inquiry. Despite the murkiness of her past and the obscurity of their complicated relationship, he trusted her insight.

The game resumed, and his lack of concentration cost him. Another round lost, another few dollars trickling away into the pot. He looked around the saloon, noting the familiar faces of Blackjack Barrett and Dazzling Jim Dare among others—hardened men of The Bottoms, unlike the transient gamblers from uptown.

"How's lady luck treating you?" The familiar voice of Moreland broke through his thoughts, announcing his arrival at the table.

"The same as ever," He folded his dismal hand and stood up, signaling Moreland to join him at a quieter spot in the room. They moved to an empty table, and Crisp ordered a round of beers.

"Where'd you get to the other day? I waited around for nearly an hour, then gave up."

"Sorry for that. I had a run-in with Crotty. Ran me in for a trumped-up charge; took me until the next morning to get out," Crisp explained.

Moreland noted the unease in Crisp's demeanor as they sat. "You're out of sorts today. What's on your mind?"

Crisp took a slow sip of his beer, his expression lightening. "It's settled, I'm officially working for Speers now."

"That's fantastic news, cheers!" Moreland responded; his voice filled with genuine enthusiasm. Yet he caught a hint of hesitation in Crisp's eyes. "It is good news, isn't it?"

"Yes, of course, it's just…"

"And money coming in for a change," he added jokingly.

"It's not just the money Marcus. It's different this time. I have to succeed," he said, his voice gravely earnest. "I can go a month or two without winning at cards, and sure it gets me down, and I think what good am I if my luck's gone? But then I land a good hand and I'm back on my feet again. I can feel like I'm not at rock bottom for a change. The money's important enough, sure but it's that feeling. You don't know what it's like losing and losing, over and over again. I need a win." He sat back pushing his beer away.

"Well now you have your chance with Speers; a chance to get luck back on your side."

Crisp paused, weighing his next words. "It's more complex than I initially thought. Speers showed me a list—victims dating back to last year. I have a hunch this goes deeper than anyone's suspected." His voice lowered, tinged with a grave concern. "Marcus, there's a malevolence at work here, a darkness more profound than anything I've faced before. And the troubling part is, our suspect could be anyone from The Bottoms, or anyone in the city for that matter." His gaze swept over the bar, shadowed by the thought that the killer might very well be listening in at that moment. "And the worst of it is, I haven't a clue where to begin. There's nothing solid, no clear leads to follow, nor a list of likely suspects."

Moreland edged nearer, his voice steady and encouraging. "But you've faced blind leads before, haven't you? How did you navigate those? Where did you start?"

Crisp let out a slow breath, his mind filtering through past cases. "Truth be told, the cases with the Pinkertons were more straightforward. They weren't so much about unmasking unknown culprits as they were about unravelling the background behind those situations. Sure, I've tackled complex cases before, but nothing of this dark magnitude. I have a few leads, a couple of notions, but it's all a jumble right now."

"Well then, what are you doing sitting here?" Moreland challenged, a smile playing at his lips. "You won't find your answers in the cards or at the bottom of a beer glass."

Crisp's gaze sharpened, a steely determination flickering in his eyes, as Moreland's words struck true. He needed to shake off the paralyzing doubt that had driven him to seek refuge in the indistinct corners of the saloon. It was time to step out into the fray and face whatever awaited him in the shadowy depths of The Bottoms. He knew deep down that hiding wasn't an option; action was the only path forward.

Two days later, the cold snap began to break. White flakes mixed with heavy drops of water as the chill of the impending winter clashed with a relentless downpour. Crisp stood resolute on the corner of Ninth and Jefferson in Quality Hill. The affluent neighborhood, usually basking in its seclusion from the grit of the city, stood today marred by a gruesome discovery. A woman's body, young and violated, lay covered under a tarpaulin on the lush front yard of the prominent liquor merchant, William C. Glass. A figure of stature, Glass stood on his porch clutching his wife, both of their faces etched with horror as they looked upon the dire spectacle and the detectives milling about in their front yard. Their home, a symbol of their life's work, had now became a backdrop to a macabre scene.

Crisp knelt, huddled under an umbrella at the curbside, his gaze fixed on a set of footprints that cut through the mud toward the street. They were detailed, clear, muddy imprints of a boot—too well-defined against his own, soon to be washed away by the cold rain and snow. This clue, however minor, was a tangible link to the culprit. Detective Halpin had introduced Crisp to the scene, the victim's state reminiscent yet distinct from others before her. The red-haired woman in her twenties, garbed only in a frilled blouse now soaked and stained, bore the brutal signature of her attacker. Her face, deeply slashed, presented a grotesque mask; her torso too, further marred by precise cuts, similarly revealed bone and sinew. But there was one outstanding difference from the others, a wicked atrocity committed upon the victim; both of her breasts had been removed with chilling exactitude. The nature of these wounds suggested a perverse precision, almost surgical, executed by someone with a disturbing familiarity of the human form.

The faint murmur of sobs from the porch drew his attention, where a policeman ushered Glass and his sobbing wife back inside, muttering, "You better take the missus out of the cold

Sir."

As two more patrolman arrived and began conferring with the detectives, Crisp lowered his gaze, avoiding the piercing look of one officer in particular. He turned his attention back to the edge of Jefferson Street where he now examined wheel tracks in the mud. He knelt down close to the tracks, and there alongside the refuse in the gutter, he found two piles of manure which piqued his interest. His meticulous focus, however, was abruptly jarred by a crass voice full of contempt and hatred. "Well, if it isn't the limey Crisp," Crotty sneered, his disdain for Crisp as tangible as the cold biting through their coats.

Crisp closed his eyes and exhaled. "What do you want Crotty?" he said without turning to face the man. With a stick, he poked at the dung, assessing its freshness, a mundane task that belied the tension of the moment.

"If you're hungry Crisp, maybe you should'na spent all your money last night gamblin' and whorin' on Ninth." This brought a series of chuckles from the other patrolmen accompanying Crotty.

Crisp maintained his composure, his voice steady. "If you're done with your juvenile remarks, I have real work to do here." His reply earned him a boot to the backside, forcing his palms to the ground with a thud that matched the heavy droplets of rain.

As he pushed himself up, the imposing figure of Thomas Speers, his authority unmistakable as he approached, stepped in between them. "That will do, Crotty," Speers commanded, his voice a low growl, barely audible over the rain.

The arrogance drained from Crotty's face as he wheeled

around to face his chief. "Yes, sir!" Saluting sharply, he said, "Just keeping this man in his place; interfering with police business he was, sir."

"Now get this straight Crotty, this man is here on my orders," Speers said, closing the gap between them with determined strides.

"Yes, sir. It's just that he was disrespecting the uniform, sir. Had to show him proper, what his place is!" Crotty insisted.

Speers' eyes hardened as he surveyed the officers standing rigid before him. "Let me be clear, with all of you: Crisp works for me. Whether in uniform or not, you will regard him as you would me. Is that clear?"

The three policemen responded in unison, "Yes, sir!"

Speers' voice took on a finality. "Perhaps you'd be more useful assisting Detective Halpin." With a dismissive nod from the Chief, the trio moved reluctantly towards the other detectives congregated in the yard. With the situation defused, he turned to Crisp, his expression somber. "Another one, same suspect, I figure. Any ideas?"

Crisp, wiped the mud from his hands and nodded. "I was thinking about the logistics just now. How did he get the body here? How did he get the bodies to those other places? He must have a wagon? A chaise of some sort? These wheel tracks might give us a lead."

Speers, following Crisp's line of thought, looked towards the tracks. "Yes, a cart or a wagon, likely. Something that wouldn't attract attention at dawn."

"Yes, and look here," Crisp continued, pointing to differing sets of manure and hoof prints along the curb. "I need to confer with someone more learned in the science of horses, but this may be something noteworthy. These prints, they're from a smaller horse, possibly a mule. Stopped here long enough to make multiple prints in the same spot."

Speers listened, his eyelids drawing close in thought. "So, he stops here, does the deed quickly, and moves on. It would take no more than a few minutes if he's hurried."

"Exactly. We should inquire about any unusual wagon activity last night or early this morning," Crisp suggested. "There must be dozens of carts, wagons, chaises, and coaches that traverse these streets every day." As if in confirmation, both men looked up as a horse drawn coach wheeled onto Jefferson Street causing them to take a step back as it passed. "But what type of wagon? This is a messy business. A coach would suffice, but a wagon is more likely. A wagon that is already dirty."

"Hmm. Go on," Speers said, hanging on Crisp's words.

"What type of wagon would be out at dawn? That is assuming, all of our victims are placed before the sun comes up. There aren't many coaches about at that hour." His words were consumed by the rain.

As they walked back towards the body, Crisp counted his steps, measuring the distance from the curb to where the tarp lay. "Ten, maybe twelve paces. It suggests he didn't want to carry her far. Quick and discreet."

Speers nodded. "Yes. Must be a big fella to carry a body any sort of distance, even say from the curbside." His thoughts were interrupted by one of the officers.

"Just getting ready to move the body, with your permission that is, sir." He motioned toward his companions standing next to a funerary wagon that had arrived.

"Has the surgeon been around yet?"

"No, but the homeowner is most anxious for us to remove it."

"Just another minute, if you please," Crisp insisted.

Glass watched from his window, a silent sentinel to the dark dealings that had encroached upon his doorstep as Crisp used a stick to lift the corner of the tarp, taking one last look at the victim. "The cuts, they're made after the victim is already deceased. Very little blood here. It's all been done elsewhere. He brings them here for us to find, a message or a display of some kind."

Speers grunted, acknowledging the deduction. "What's your next step?"

"Have your men inquire with the good folks of this street as to what coaches and wagons they normally see early in the day; especially ones drawn by a small, single horse, see if we can narrow down the specific make. It's a long shot, but it's all we have at the moment."

Once the surgeon arrived, he took note of the specifics, and the patrolmen loaded the cadaver into the wagon. As Crisp watched, there was something peculiar in their efforts that he couldn't place.

The rain intensified, as Crisp and Speers parted ways. Each step Crisp took was measured, his thoughts churning with possibilities; the cold seeped through his clothes yet he barely noticed. He was a man on a hunt, and every clue, every whisper of evidence brought him one step closer to the monster he sought. In the bleak landscape of crime and punishment, it was his keen eye and relentless pursuit that might just restore a semblance of peace to the shadowed streets of the city.

Chapter Six

Mist clung stubbornly to the streets of the city the next morning, as Crisp found himself aboard a trolley operated by The Kansas City Cable Railway, descending into the bowels of the Eighth Street tunnel. The clatter of the car along its tracks provided a rhythmic backdrop to his thoughts, clouded by the grim discovery the day before on Quality Hill. The brutal murder was more than just a killing; it was a message, though to whom and what it signified, he was still piecing together.

Exiting the cable car at St. Louis Avenue in The Bottoms, he made his way to The American Kitchen. The humble eatery, a haven for rail workers and tradesmen, offered no grand breakfast, but for a man counting his coins, a cup of coffee and a plate with a slice of bacon and toast would suffice. As he ate, he observed the patrons, a cross-section of the city's backbone, wondering which, if any, carried secrets connected to the horrors unfolding uptown. Thinking back on Speers' scientific methodologies, he took note of individuals with distinguishing features and vowed to look them up in Speers' inventory.

With his modest meal concluded, he ventured further down

the block to an open barn-like structure, displaying a sign that read J.A. Ondecker & Sons, Blacksmith. The clang of metal and the glow of a forge spilled out into the streets as he approached the shop. A heavy-set man in a soot-blackened apron met him within the confined interior of the barn.

"Mornin'. What can I do fer you?" His voice was as rough and gritty as the iron he hammered.

"Good morning. Do you make horseshoes here?" Crisp inquired, trying not to inhale too deeply the acrid tang of metal and sweat.

"Make, no. We get them already precast. D'you need your horse shod?" he inquired, looking past Crisp toward the street.

"Not at the moment, just a few questions about the process if you would."

"My boy is the farrier, let me fetch him for you." The smith called over his shoulder for his son, then gestured for Crisp to follow out back of the main building where a narrow corral housed three horses. Navigating around piles of manure and puddles of muddy water, Crisp treaded precariously through the adjoining alley.

Under a lean-to, the farrier, a younger version of his father but just as burly, finished up shoeing a horse that was tethered to the wall. Crisp surveyed the interior of the cramped shed, its walls a testament to the tradesman's craft, with every inch occupied by an assortment of tools: shovels and rakes hung alongside pokers; sledges and swages shared space with cutters and chisels. In a corner, a shoeing box lay open, revealing an orderly arrangement of knives, rasps, and files, each reflecting the faint light that filtered into the space.

"Be with you in a moment. You can put your horse in the pen there with the others."

Crisp closed the distance and stood watching the man work. "No horse, just a few questions if you don't mind." After a brief introduction, he got straight to the point. "Could you tell me about the shoes you use for different types of horses? I'm particularly interested in the sizes and any customization you might do."

The man looked up from his work, "No horse? You fixin' to buy one?"

"Yes," Crisp delayed, as he crafted a rebuke, "but before I do, I'd like some insight into the upkeep if you will. I hope you can educate me on what's involved with keeping them shod."

The farrier, wiping his forehead with the back of his hand, said, "This here's a standard size," holding up a precast shoe. "Fits most horses, but for draft horses or small breeds, we make adjustments. Heat 'em up and shape 'em to fit."

"So, tell me, when does a beast need shoes? Do not most horses spend their entire lives in the wild without shoes?"

"I don't figure there's any smiths in the wild, but if you're getting a city horse, then you pro'lly need shoes." The man hung his tools on the wall and stepped outside. Reaching into a pocket on his overalls, he pulled out a large wad of tobacco, and stuck it between his teeth and gums. "Have you never owned a horse before?"

"No, I'm afraid not. But might be needing one soon." Crisp looked to the horses penned up behind the man. "I see that one's smaller than the others, does he require smaller shoes?"

"That one there, no, his feet's same size as them others."

"And mules? Do they require a different type of shoe?"

"Mules's just like horses, mostly. Depends on the work they're doing," the farrier answered, growing curious about the line of questioning. He spat and wiped his mouth on the back of his hand. "In the city, if they's pulling wagons and working in the streets, horses and mules need shoes. Gives 'em traction and helps 'em be more surefooted in mud, ice, snow, loose rocks, you know."

"But they use the same shoes, or do you have different ones for mules and horses?"

"Same ones. Listen, once you pick out your horse, bring him back and I'll fix him up. Easier to look at the horse and tell you what you need done than playing guessin' games."

"Yes, yes, of course. Crisp nodded, absorbing the information. "Do you have many clients who drive wagons up to Quality Hill, particularly at night?"

The farrier shook his head, chomping on his tobacco. "Folks don't usually talk much about their comings and goings." He spit again. "But we shoe a lot of horses; some might be pulling wagons up there, night or day. All my customers are reglars, but I don't ask them about their business none."

Thanking the farrier, Crisp stepped out onto the sidewalk adjacent to St. Louis Avenue, his mind not quite satisfied but filled with new leads to follow. Just then, he noticed a group of boys huddled around a mouse maze, betting on the outcome.

"Hello, Colonel."

"Percy, I didn't see you there. How are you making out?"

"Just watching; I didn't have no money to bet."

Crisp fished two pennies from his pocket, "Will this do?"

Percy grabbed the coins in a flash and jumped into the huddle. "Put these on One-eye!"

The boys sorted their bets, the oldest acting as game boss, collected the money and started the race. He lifted a wooden slat in the box and the mice surged forward through the maze to the cheers of the boys. Within in moments, a collective groan rose from the huddle as the mouse known as Grey Ghost found his way to a morsel of food before his competitors.

Percy stepped back from the group and stood next to Crisp dejectedly. Crisp placed a hand on the boy's shoulder, "Tough luck. But tell me, do you not suppose a rodent would perform better with two eyes?"

"Oh no, sir. One-eye has a better nose!"

He drew Percy aside, away from prying ears, settling on a bench with the boy by his side. "I have a job for you; need you to watch for wagons or carriages pulled by a single horse. I'm particularly interested in those making early morning trips up to Quality Hill."

Percy's eyes sparkled with excitement

Crisp searched his pocket subconsciously, found a cheroot and lit it, inhaling deeply. "Tell me, how would you head up to Quality Hill with a horse and buggy from here?"

"From down here?" the boy paused, thinking through various routes. "If I weren't in a hurry, I'd go all the way to Toad-a-Loop—skirt the bluffs down that aways—and then back up the hill." Percy gave the question more consideration. "Directly through the gooseneck and up on Fourth is quicker though; only if the trains ain't blocking it."

"Yes, focus on that for me," Crisp instructed. "I need to

know about those wagons and carriages heading up that way, especially at night or in the early morning. And keep an eye out for any making regular deliveries, especially any drawn by a small horse, or maybe a mule."

Percy's eyes were alight with the thrill of the task. "Sure thing, Colonel. I'll keep my eyes peeled."

Crisp nodded, appreciating Percy's readiness. He reached into his pocket and pulled out a handful of coins, handing them over. "Here's something for you," he said, the metal clinking softly in the quiet. "I'm counting on your sharp eyes."

The boy pocketed the coins with a quick grin. "You won't be disappointed, sir. I'll find what you're looking for."

As Percy rejoined the other boys, Crisp's mind mulled over the information he'd learned from the farrier. The city was alive around him, the streets filling with the noise of daily toil, but beneath the surface, there lurked secrets that only the observant could discern.

———

The cold gusts sweeping across St. Louis Avenue later that afternoon seemed to cut straight to the bone, but Crisp was hardly aware of the chill. His mind was occupied with darker thoughts, ones that drew him inexorably towards the scene of his latest investigation. Lighting a cheroot to steady his nerves, he spotted a familiar figure approaching through the mist.

"Good afternoon, Algernon." Moreland's greeting carried a lightness that Crisp found dissonant with the grimness of his own thoughts.

"H'lo Marcus," he replied, his tone subdued. "Looks like it might rain again."

"Fancy a game?"

"Can't; business to attend to," Crisp replied curtly, his eyes scanning the horizon to read the clouds, searching for something more sinister hidden in the gloom. "What about you? Your afternoon clear?"

"My schedule is free today," he said, and sensing the weight of Crisp's mood, he offered, "Look at you, all business over pleasure now."

Crisp didn't smile. "Actually, you may be of some help. Walk with me, if you don't mind."

"Absolutely," Moreland matched Crisp stride for stride as they headed north on Liberty Street.

"I've told you about these murders," he began. "The perpetrator doesn't just kill; he's taken to slashing his victims in a gruesome display. The most recent women we've found have had deep gashes in their faces and torsos."

"Quite a lurid discovery I'd say."

"It's appalling," Crisp agreed, a distant look in his eyes. "I've seen many things in this world, but I must admit, I never get used to seeing a body in that state. How do you suppose a mortician or surgeon can deal with these things on a daily basis?"

"It's unimaginable, encountering such horror for the first time," Moreland said thoughtfully, "much less dealing with it daily."

"I must speak with the police surgeon who examined the victims; perhaps he's noticed something in his autopsies—some detail that could shed light on this fiend's motives or methods."

"Is that where you're going now?" Moreland inquired, catching the urgency in Crisp's step.

"No, I have another appointment with a former client," he revealed, pausing at a street crossing to let a horsecar lumber past. He gestured towards the industrial silhouette looming ahead. "That business with the body found in a barrel—I was investigating for Jacob Dold Packing at the time. I'm to meet Mr. Klein there today; he's one of their managers. He's the one who initially brought me in on the case of Josef Bolinsky."

"Bolinsky?"

"Yes, he was labor union leader at Dold's. Received threats from an unknown source before his death," Crisp explained, his gaze fixed on the plant's distant outline. "Klein suspected internal strife within his workforce was to blame. He brought me in to delve deeper, but they got to Bolinsky before I made much headway."

"Sounds like a complex case."

"It was, and still is. Bolinsky was a tough line boss, pushed his men hard. They elected him union leader hoping he'd use that same toughness against management for better conditions. Instead, he exploited his position to curry favors with the upper echelons, leaving his fellow workers in the lurch."

They approached the gates to the plant, their conversation dimming as Crisp prepared to revisit a case fraught with tangled loyalties and unfinished business.

"So, your meeting with Klein relates to that case then?"

Crisp displayed a wry smile. "In a way, yes. The gruesomeness of these murders got me thinking—perhaps the killer might be someone from the packinghouses, like Bolinsky's murderer, someone accustomed to blood, and skilled with large knives. I want Klein to show me around, let me observe the processing of the animals, the tools they use. It might shed some light on my case."

"That could prove quite insightful," Moreland noted with sparked interest.

"Care to join me? It'll certainly be enlightening."

"Do you think Klein will have any objections?"

"None at all," Crisp assured him as they approached the entrance. "I'll introduce you as my colleague. Klein won't mind."

Arriving at the offices of the Dold plant, their eyes scanned the neat brickwork and recently cleaned windows, and they both couldn't help sense that the office exuded an air of false cleanliness in contrast to the filth-stained factory buildings looming beyond, where the true nature of the operation lay hidden in the stench of slaughter.

After cursory introductions with Klein, Crisp and Moreland were escorted through the vast labyrinth of the Jacob Dold Packing plant. Their guide, a wiry young man who had spent the better part of a decade on the killing floor, narrated the grisly ballet of industry as they ascended a grimy staircase to the upper levels of the plant.

Inside the cavernous depths of the processing plant, the metallic tang of blood and the sickly-sweet stench of decay attached itself to everything. Modern machinery whirred and clanked relentlessly in a discordant symphony that echoed off the cold, damp walls. Workers, their aprons soaked with gore, moved like ghosts among the carcasses that hung from hooks like macabre decorations in a house of horrors.

The animals, led to the slaughter with eyes wide in the terror of impending death, bemoaned their last cries, a haunting lament, quickly silenced by the final, fatal stab. Each slice of the butcher's knife released a fresh spurt of blood, painting the worn wooden floors a deeper shade of crimson. Saws buzzed through bone and sinew with a terrifying efficiency, their teeth tearing through flesh still warm with life. Conveyors carried disjointed limbs and severed heads past the gaunt faces of the laborers, who were numb to the horror of their tasks.

In a dark corner of the plant, a young worker vomited, overwhelmed by the unyielding assault on his senses. Children, as young as ten, swept the killing floor, pooling blood and ooze into large drains, and picked up scraps with bare hands stained and filthy. But all the while, the machines did not stop; the assembly line of death and dismemberment continued unabated, feeding the insatiable appetite of the nation for fresh meat. Their tour ended in a warehouse where packed tins of meat were packaged and neatly stacked before being loaded into waiting boxcars destined for railyards across the country.

Emerging into the fresh air after an hour-long visit, Crisp and Moreland instinctively gulped down deep breaths, shedding the heavy scent of the slaughterhouse.

"Thank heavens for those aprons they gave us," Crisp remarked with a grimace, "otherwise we'd be in the market for a whole new wardrobe. Our boots might never forgive us, though," he added, scuffing his soles against a tuft of grass in a vain attempt to clean them.

"Nonetheless, it's a remarkable operation, I had no idea," Moreland mused, his tone mingling awe with a hint of revulsion. "To think, the entire disassembly line commences right at the top and works its way down, less than fifteen minutes from start to finish."

"It's staggering, truly staggering," Crisp agreed, "the efficiency in which they process each animal. Did you catch the number of hogs they handle daily?"

"Around five thousand, if I recall." Moreland tried to visualize the scale in his head. "If my figures are correct, that's nearly two million a year, operating non-stop! A formidable testament to industrial ingenuity, no doubt."

Crisp shuddered momentarily at the memory. "I'm fairly certain I'll be steering clear of pork for a while," he confessed. "However, the precision and swiftness with which those butchers work did catch my eye. It lends credence to my theory about Bolinsky's demise, as well as the skills of our other culprit. A butcher with such adeptness, whether from this facility or another in the vicinity, could have methodically dismantled Bolinsky's body, and brutally sliced up those women."

Moreland nodded in agreement, yet added a note of caution, "True, the expertise required to handle a blade that size does suggest a professional. But, Algernon, isn't it possible that skilled butchers exist outside these industrial confines? We saw that little butcher shop on Liberty Street enroute here. Surely, someone from such a place might also possess the necessary skill to carve—" he hesitated, "to carve a body with such precision."

Crisp considered this for a moment. "There's no direct motive or link connecting local butchers to Bolinsky, though.

Are you implying that a butcher might be the murderer or that someone employed one for the dissection?"

"Not exactly," Moreland clarified, "I'm simply suggesting that the ability to wield a blade with such finesse isn't exclusive to factory butchers."

"True," Crisp conceded, "but without a specific murder weapon, like a cleaver or another such tool used in the crime, tracing it back to its origins and thus to a potential suspect proves difficult. For now, I still believe the key to Bolinsky's murder lies within these factory walls. If only we had more tangible evidence."

"Don't you feel compelled to solve his case?"

"I wasn't hired to find Bolinsky's killer," Crisp's voice carried a note of resignation as he continued, "I was merely tasked with identifying who threatened the poor man and his kin. The case of his murder is now in the hands of the police, though I hold little hope they'll solve it. There's a certain level of dedication that an investigation like this requires—something the police force often lacks unless the victim is of high societal standing."

Moreland interjected, visibly troubled by the implication, "but shouldn't they exhaust all avenues to catch Bolinsky's killer? Doesn't every victim deserve that?"

Crisp sighed, a mixture of cynicism and realism tinting his words. "Ideally, yes. But pragmatism often paints a different picture. If Bolinsky had been a prominent politician or a business magnate from Quality Hill, then sure, Speers' detectives would scour the earth for clues. As it stands, they likely consider his death a trivial matter, perhaps the unfortunate end to a sensical squabble amongst the laborers of these factories." Seeing Moreland's discontent, he added, "I share your frustration, Marcus. If it brings you any comfort, I'll speak to Speers to gauge whether his detectives are still on the case. However, much like my own current inquiries, I suspect they've moved on to matters they deem more pressing or profitable." His words, while blunt, reflected the harsh realities of their world.

In the hushed grandeur of City Hall's hallowed council chambers, Jim Pendergast meticulously scribbled a list titled "Parks Men" on a piece of paper, underlining names of key influencers: Bullene, Hammerslough, Glass, Van Brundt, Armour, and Meyer. Each name a pillar in the complex edifice of Kansas City's elite, each with a stake in the unfolding drama.

Seated at a modest desk within a semicircle arrangement, it allowed him an unobstructed view of the podium where Peter H. Tiernan, the President of the Upper House, and John Fitzpatrick, speaker of the Lower House, conducted the day's proceedings. Behind the house speakers, perched a large oak desk raised on another boxed platform, where a high-backed chair sat reserved for Mayor William Cowherd. Around this formation, half a dozen other chairs and narrow tables had been crowded together—all in all, seventeen out of twenty City Council members attended the afternoon session.

The room, steeped in the rich scent of mahogany and the muted whispers of the city's most influential men, buzzed with the tension of impending decisions. Behind the ornately, carved, courtroom bar, the public gallery was speckled with individuals of note, among them, three reporters from Kansas City's leading newspapers—*The Star*, *The Journal*, and *The Times*—huddled in conversation, their pens poised to capture the day's events. Nearby, Chief of Police Thomas Speers sat with a stoic expression, his mind perhaps on the darker corners of the city he patrolled. To his right, muted words passed between August Meyer, recently appointed President of the Parks Board, and a young lawyer.

Next to Meyer's name, Pendergast scribbled the name Haff. He made a mental note that he must find out more about Meyer's young legal assistant.

The council had yet to reconvene after a short recess, in which the remainder of the chamber's gallery had been cleared of citizens, primarily a large contingency of women who were in attendance to support the Women's Christian Temperance movement. In the hushed aftermath, Pendergast lingered in his seat, his expression unreadable, observing the departure of the women whose applause and cheers had filled the room just moments before.

Their passionate outcries had been in support of Florence Williams, a staunch leader among them, who had boldly proposed a new citywide ordinance. Her aim: to staunch the flow of vice by closing saloons and other liquor-serving establishments on The Sabbath. The mere mention of such a proposition stirred a visceral unease in Pendergast. His mind raced back to a previous session when Williams had successfully spearheaded the shutdown of all policy shops on

Sundays. That move alone had rippled unfavorably through his intricate network, influencing the city's underbelly in ways that threatened his dominion. Now, the potential of her latest campaign pressed on his nerves with a sharp intensity. Mayor Cowherd and a majority of the City Council had previously aligned with Williams, a fact that had cost Pendergast both in influence and in finances.

As the chamber settled into a tense silence awaiting the reconvening of the council, Pendergast's mind worked feverishly. His jaw tightened imperceptibly as he contemplated his next move. The battle lines had been drawn clearer with each of Williams' words, and with each applause from her supporters that echoed her sentiments. In the quiet of the now seemingly empty gallery, the weight of impending decisions pressed heavily upon him. This was no mere skirmish over public morality; it was an assault on his livelihood, and he felt the cold grip of challenge tighten around the future of his operations. As the council members filtered back into the room, his determination grew firm. Whatever it took, the outcome of this proposal would not mirror the last.

Many of the councilmen had returned to their seats; a few still huddled around a tiny table that held a pitcher of water debating the merits of Williams' proposal. Mayor Cowherd approached his desk, and with practiced authority, and three raps from his gavel, he called for order. "Gentlemen, if you will return to your seats, please, we still have a number of items on the agenda that I'd like to get through today," he announced, his voice resonating off the high ceilings.

The session resumed with August Meyer presenting a

visionary project conceived by esteemed landscape architect George Kessler, employed by the Parks Board. Meyer's face was distinguished by a high forehead and elongated sideburns that traced the contours of his narrow jawline. A pronounced moustache and a sharply, defined, cleft chin further accentuated his visage. However, it was his piercing, sagacious eyes that captured and held the attention of all present.

Meyer stood confidently before this audience, prepared to articulate the revolutionary vision for the city's landscape. After introductions, he began, "Our little river town has blossomed remarkably, doubling its population in just the last decade alone," he paused, seeking affirmation from Mayor Cowherd. "Each day, twenty thousand visitors traverse Union Depot, drawn by commerce and leisure. Yet, their first impressions are marred by the unsightly shanties and billboards defacing our bluffs."

Unfurling detailed renderings, Meyer outlined a transformative plan for Quality Hill's west slopes—a bold vision that created an inviting gateway to the city. His presentation, both grand in scope and meticulous in detail, painted a future of urban elegance and public enjoyment, aimed at erasing the blight of hovels and advertising boards marring the city's entrance on the west bluffs.

He continued, detailing the proposal laid before the Council. "Mr. Kessler, with his renowned expertise in landscape design, has reimagined these bluffs, not as scars of urban sprawl, but as potential havens of natural beauty. Our plan," he gestured towards the displayed blueprints and drawings, "proposes eradicating these eyesores. We envision terraced walls that curb erosion and beautify the slopes and muddy paths, transforming them into verdant walkways." Meyer pointed out further enhancements on the diagrams. "The plan maintains our vital trolley inclines ascending the bluffs but introduces staircases to ease pedestrian access as well. Moreover, we propose an elegant gateway for the Eighth Street incline, replacing the current dismal entrance. Here, atop the bluffs, palisades will ensure safety, and create a serene overlook where families may enjoy the same vistas admired once by Lewis and Clark on their historic journey."

His speech dragged on for several minutes, meticulously rehashing his key points, much to the dismay of Pendergast, but finally, completing a slow, deliberate turn to address each council member personally, Meyer concluded, "We've laid out a comprehensive strategy to enhance our parks and boulevards, anticipating the needs of both today and tomorrow. The immediate challenge, however, lies in clearing the bluffs of transient encampments—a task that requires your decisive action. This development hinges on preparing the site for its promising future, a responsibility that falls to this esteemed council."

He closed his presentation with a heartfelt plea. "Gentlemen, my board has been charged with developing a plan that not only meets the needs of the present, but one that addresses the concerns of the future. The development on the bluffs is but one part of our entire parks and boulevards recommendation. And while the cost of the glorious design you see here rolls into the overall plan's budget, the effort to begin that development is fully the responsibility of this council. Before this project can move forward, the area must be prepared for its eventual future, and that is what I seek from your jurisdiction."

Yet, as Meyer concluded, a heated debate erupted among the council members. The costs of such beautification, the displacement of the hill's poorer residents, and the prioritization of aesthetic improvements over more pressing civic needs were hotly contested. Pendergast, ever the strategist, listened intently, his mind sifting through the implications of Meyer's plans not just for the city's landscape, but for its political and social order. Recognizing the potential shifts in power and public opinion that such a project could precipitate, he weighed his intervention carefully.

When the debate veered into the logistics of funding and the potential impact on The Bottoms' factories and stockyards, Pendergast seized the moment. Rising with a gravitas that quieted the room, he addressed the council with a blend of passion and pragmatism. "Why should we prioritize parklands and boulevards while ignoring the plight of those whose labors power our city? Are we to sweep away the least among us like so much refuse in our quest for beautification?" His voice, deep and resonant, underscored a profound challenge to his peers—to reconcile the city's ambitions with its responsibilities. "I say, let them build parks out in the woods on the edge of town." This prompted his political allies Martin Regan and Joseph Brinkley to poke fun at the bluff terrace project suggesting it looked like a medieval fortress. Councilman William Huttig added that besides looking out over the Missouri River, the terraces' primary focal point was the stockyards and factories of The West Bottoms, and why should they deliberately create a vantage point looking out on that undesirable part of the city.

As Pendergast sat back, the council absorbed his words, the room was charged with a new tension between the vision of a beautified city and the gritty realities of its most vulnerable citizens. The debate that followed no longer centered merely on parklands but on the very soul of Kansas City, laying bare the complexities and contradictions of urban progress.

Overwhelmingly, the council was divided on how to finance Meyer's project. The debate ended with the mayor agreeing that the council would take the Parks Board proposal under further consideration, but he clearly acknowledged that the complete financing of the entire plan presented by the parks commissioners would require review at the state legislature. He also made it clear to the council, this was not another parks debate, but part of a much broader improvement effort for the city.

"Gentlemen, with that, let's shift our discussion to city clean-up efforts. In our previous meetings, we decided that Chief Speers and his men were to crack down on cleaning up refuse and filth, and to begin enforcing the recently enacted ordinances we've set forth." Cowherd looked up from his podium to see Speers rise and cross the bar. He stood next to a table at the edge of the councilmen.

"Mr. Speers, can you update us on this?"

"Of course, Mr. Mayor. I have appointed one of my top men, Sergeant Ahearn, to head up this effort. He will oversee a group of officers in charge of enforcing the sanitation ordinances. We will target the worst areas of the city first, such as McClure Flats and The North End, of course, but more importantly we will engage the business owners along Main and within the core district of the inner city who continue to dump their refuse in the streets and back alleys."

"Very good. Does anyone have questions for Chief Speers?"

"What about the gandy dancers and others transients that have infiltrated our city?" asked Upper House member Oscar Dahl. "What's your plan to get rid of them?"

"And get rid of those professional beggars and unhoused persons wandering around the depot while you're at it," added alderman George Werneke.

Speers ventured a reply, but the intense gaze of Jim Pendergast cut him off.

Growing weary of the ongoing debate, Pendergast now came awake like a bear roused from his slumber. He stood at his desk and rose up. "How dare you include those less fortunate souls in the same conversation about sanitation and refuse," his voice boomed throughout the chamber. "The Chief here has been tasked with a cleanup effort, and as he mentioned, his men are going after not only the slums and less desirable areas of our city, where disease and poverty breed interchangeably I might add, but they're also looking at the business men of our city who have no regards for the cleanliness of our streets. As for these so-called transients you speak of, the Provident Association already has a hand in helping these victims of our society in getting back on the right path. And while it's true some of these sad folks may have turned begging into a profession, it is only because they have fallen on hard times in their own various professions. It's been a harsh winter for sure, and many of these people rely on farm employment during warmer seasons. Others have been maimed or debilitated in hazardous jobs and can no longer earn a proper living. You can't simply sweep them away like the refuse we're talking about."

He had a captive audience now, but few of the councilmen dared to make eye contact.

"Here we sit talking about grand designs to beautify our city, but which of our citizens benefit the most? We need a plan that accounts for *all* of our people, not just the well-off ladies who will stroll down fancy boulevards and gather for picnics in parks. We can't ignore the less fortunate men and women who need a helping hand in order to get back on their feet and contribute to our city." He slowly settled back into his chair, letting his words sink in with his fellow councilmen. Before anyone could reply further, he pounded his fist on his desk. "By God, I always say, do a man in need a favor and he will repay it ten times over in the future!"

As the session adjourned, the council members filed out with the weight of Pendergast's challenge lingering in the air. It was a poignant reminder that the path to improvement was fraught with moral and ethical decisions, shaping not just the city's skyline, but the lives of the people living in its shadows.

Chapter Seven

Two days later, in the somber confines of Chief Speers' office, Crisp sat deeply ensconced in an armchair, a fine cigar between his fingers—a tiny luxury provided by the Chief to ease the severity of their discussion. The smoke curled upwards, mingling with the weighty silence that hung between the two men.

"Thomas, I've acted on your advice and looked into one of the packing houses," Crisp began, his voice thoughtful, carrying the burden of his discoveries. "And while it's certainly fascinating to see how adept one of their workers is with a cleaver, dismembering a hog within seconds, there's one thing that doesn't quite align."

"And what's that?" Speers looked up from the assortment of paperwork that cluttered his desk, his curiosity aroused.

"These packing workers, they're toiling in the slaughterhouse for upwards of sixteen hours a day, every day. When would one of them find the time to frequent bordellos, target victims, and transport them in the dead of night?" Crisp's skepticism was not just a reflection of logistical doubts but a deeper, more troubling realization of the human condition.

Speers, ever the pragmatist, cupped his chin while he

considered this. "Yes, that would be quite the undertaking, but not entirely improbable. The slayer still has eight hours to his day by your calculations."

Crisp shook his head, the smoke swirling around him like his thoughts. "Trust me, Thomas. If you saw these men at the end of their shift, you'd understand my doubt. They are utterly spent, covered head to toe in the day's grime. They seek nothing more than to wash away the filth and collapse into whatever comfort they can find. The likelihood of them mustering the energy to then engage in such calculated brutality is... it's inconceivable."

"But the skill these workers possess—that's what's key here. Perhaps our killer is a former employee? Someone who no longer follows that grueling routine but retains the skills?" Speers suggested, trying to bridge Crisp's observations with the needs of their investigation.

"That's a possibility," he conceded, tapping ash into a tray. "But if we're to consider that our killer wields such a blade with deadly precision, then shouldn't we broaden our scope? There are butchers, hunters, even former military surgeons who possess similar capabilities."

"True, but wouldn't it make sense to start with the packing house worker? After all, we don't have a surfeit of surgeons and hunters in The Bottoms."

Crisp sighed, a deep, weary sound. "The killer may well have acquired his expertise with a blade anywhere—perhaps on the plains slaughtering bison, or in a war far from here. We must consider that his skill with a blade, while distinctive, is just one piece of this dark puzzle. We simply need more to go on."

"Agreed," Speers said, sifting through his paperwork again. "But we also need to uncover the motive behind these heinous acts. Why these women? What drives a man to not only kill, but to mutilate and display his victims so publicly?"

"The why of it..." Crisp mused aloud, his mind racing through potential motives—jealousy, revenge, a twisted pleasure in instilling fear. "The why will tell us much more about our killer than the how."

At that moment, Speers handed a folded paper, a handwritten note to Crisp, "This arrived for me this morning. Perhaps it will shed some light."

Crisp snatched the letter, his eyes widening in shock at the realization of the significance of the unnerving discovery. He devoured its short message, absorbing every nuance in a single intense sweep:

DEAR MR SPEARS,

YOU BETTER CALL OFF THOSE LADYS OF TEMPRANSS OR THERE WILL BE MORE BODIES TO COME! KEEP THEM FANCY WOMEN UPTOWN THEY HAVE NO BIZNISS IN THE AFFAIRS BELOW THE BLUFFS.

AND TELL YOUR CONSILMEN AND POLITOCOS TO FORGET THEM LAWS AGAINST OUR WAY OF LIFE! IF THEY WANT TO PRETTY UP THIS TOWN THEY CAN KEEP IT UP THERE. LEAVES US IN THE FIRST WARD ALONE!

The words crept into his mind like a slow, insidious fog. As Crisp sat in silence, their meaning gradually took shape, a dark undercurrent threading through each line. The message was a disturbing jumble, oscillating between a deranged rant and a chilling warning. It left no doubt in his mind—this killer was no opportunistic predator. "This is significant, Thomas."

Speers nodded gravely.

"It suggests our killer isn't just a random madman," Crisp continued. "He's someone entrenched in the very fabric of The Bottoms. He's not merely reacting; he's defending. These reforms threaten his world, his identity. He's driven by fear, anger, and an almost primal sense of territory." Crisp stroked his beard absently with his free hand, his mind turning over the layers of meaning within the letter. "This man is protective of his domain. To him, these changes are an invasion, an attempt to strip him of his way of life."

Speers, having read the letter multiple times, shared the same unsettling conclusions. The unease on his face was unmistakable. "Agreed. But what else does it reveal about our suspect?"

Crisp flipped the letter over, examining it closely from every angle. He held it up to the light, scrutinizing smudges of dirt on the back—marks left by the author's fingers. "It's clearly a man's handwriting, too messy and crude for a woman. And with all these spelling and grammar mistakes, I'd wager we're dealing with a man of limited education. The motive is undeniably revenge," Crisp said, rolling his cigar between his fingers. "But why target you specifically? Why not the mayor, the city council, or even the WCTU? He seems to view you—and your men—as the enforcers of the change he despises."

"Perhaps he's someone I've arrested before," Speers suggested. "A man who feels wronged for some previous punishment?"

"That's possible, but there's no direct reference to any past grievance with you. He seems to see you as a protector of these women, expecting you to act. And look here—toward the end, his tone becomes overtly political. And why mention the First Ward specifically?" Crisp mused. "That suggests a political motive, does it not?"

"Maybe, maybe not. The papers often use that name, anyone living or voting there would know that. This definitely confirms my suspicions: our killer is someone from The Bottoms," Speers stated coldly.

Crisp started to argue otherwise, but held his tongue; his instincts told him more. It was too soon to leap to any conclusions, too soon to rule out the possibility of the suspect emerging from any corner of the city.

"You say this message arrived today? Who brought it? Where did it come from?"

"One of my officers found it at the front desk. No one knows how long it had been there, or even how it got there to begin with."

"I'll need to study this letter further, examining each word and aligning them with what we know, and what we don't. May I keep this?" he asked, though more of a statement than a question.

"Of course," Speers replied. "If it aids in unraveling this mystery, it's yours."

As they delved deeper into the psychological profile of their suspect, a knock on the door interrupted their contemplation. Speers stepped away to deal with yet another crisis, leaving Crisp alone with his thoughts and the smoky remnants of his cigar.

He reread the letter, each word a clue, each misspelling a testament to the writer's raw, unfiltered emotion. This was not just a clue but a window into the soul of The Bottoms—the old world fighting against the encroachment of the new, where every change was seen as an existential threat. This was a puzzle not just of logic but of human emotion and fear, and he was determined to solve it, one piece at a time.

Speers' office door stood ajar, and through the narrow gap, Crisp caught a shadow flicker across the threshold. As he looked up, Detective Halpin stepped into the room.

"The Chief just stepped out," Crisp mentioned, rising and edging toward the door.

"Yes, I saw him heading downstairs," Halpin acknowledged, then shut the door, cutting off Crisp's exit. His presence put Crisp on edge, especially given recent tensions with Crotty.

"How is your investigation going?" Halpin asked, cutting straight to the chase.

"Looking into a few leads," Crisp replied, cautiously tucking the letter into his coat pocket. "These things take time to unravel."

Halpin's voice held a genuine note as he offered, "If there's anything I can assist you with, just say the word."

"There is one matter that's been puzzling me," Crisp replied, his thoughts shifting gears like a cable car flying down the Ninth Street incline.

"And, what's that?"

"When your men arrive at a crime scene, such as the one at the Glass residence, do they immediately move the body to shield it from public view?"

"No, we leave the body untouched until the surgeon arrives; unless he's delayed and instructs us otherwise."

"But the recent victims I've encountered were covered with tarpaulins," Crisp said, his tone puzzled as he tilted his head slightly. "They weren't just covered; the tarps were spread on the ground, the bodies placed on them, and then the edges of the tarps pulled over the top of them. It seems your men must shift the bodies in order to fully cover them."

"Those tarps aren't ours. We only adjust them to block the view from onlookers; we don't touch the bodies otherwise."

"The tarps aren't yours?" Crisp echoed in surprise. "I just assumed they were placed by your team upon arrival."

"No, the tarps and blankets were already with the bodies when we found them."

Recalling the scene at the Glass residence as the patrolmen loaded the body into the surgeon's wagon, Crisp now vividly remembered them lifting the cadaver off the tarp and wrapping it in a bundle. Once the body had been loaded, one of them roughly stuffed the tarp into the wagon. "Where are these tarps now? Surely, you must see, these are critical clues linked to the killer."

Halpin shifted uncomfortably and pulled at his collar, realizing his men's oversight in ignoring the tarps' significance. "They were sent along with the bodies to the surgeon for examination."

As Crisp paced the room, lost in thought, Halpin watched him, waiting for a response that didn't come. Finally, unable to hold back, Halpin spoke with decisive clarity. "Crisp, there's a reason I stopped by," he said, stepping into Crisp's path and grabbing his arm. "You're a smart man; I could use someone like you on my force."

Crisp hesitated, caught off-guard. "I'm flattered, Detective, but I've agreed to report directly to the Chief—no politics, no distractions, no competing priorities."

Halpin persisted, "Understood, but consider this: you can keep pursuing your current case under my watch. I've got other cases too that would benefit from your expertise."

Crisp weighed the proposition thoughtfully.

"This is a chance to clear your name, establish yourself again. I won't lie—your appointment by the Chief raised several eyebrows," Halpin admitted. His words stung like alcohol in an open wound, sharp yet sincere. "But I can see your potential. Hiring on with me would... have a certain legitimacy to it."

Crisp narrowed his eyes at Halpin, but remained silent, pondering. A stable position with Halpin's backing was enticing, a genuine chance at redemption, yet the weight of loyalty to Speers tugged at him, leaving a bitter taste of betrayal at even contemplating such an offer.

"I'll give you time to think it over," Halpin added as he opened the door to leave. "The offer stands whenever you're ready."

"Thank you, Detective. I'll take it to heart," Crisp responded heavily.

Halpin opened the door and slipped out leaving Crisp to his

own thoughts.

<hr>

Across the teeming city, life continued unabated, as ordinary citizens carried on with their daily routines. Shops opened their doors to eager customers, children played in the streets, and workers toiled away in factories and warehouses. The hum of everyday life continued undisturbed, blissfully unaware of the grave discussions and dark revelations unfolding above the bluffs. This was true for Bernie Koppelman, who fumbled through a hefty ring of keys, his eyes flickering with suspicion, as he selected one for door number ten in his tenement house on State Line.

"Rent's two dollars a month. Just you living here?" He scrutinized the younger man who stood in the dim hallway next to him.

"My brother will sleep here during the day; he works nights," the man replied, his voice even, showing no concern.

"For two of you, rent is another fifty cents." Koppelman said, taken aback. "Two fifty a month," he clarified, pushing the door open to reveal a cramped space. The room, a mere ten feet square, featured a ceiling just shy of six feet, an iron stove with a rusted pipe jutting awkwardly through one wall, and a makeshift closet cobbled together from old boards and exposed joists—a testament to transient lives past. The man stepped over the threshold, his gaze sweeping the sparse quarters. Koppelman, eager to upsell, added, "Three dollars gets you a room with a window."

The man paused, considering the dark, enclosed space before him, then shook his head resolutely. "This will do," he decided, sealing his fate to the shadowy confines of room ten.

"The privy is out back. No animals in here, and careful with that stove. It gets plenty hot with just a few sticks, don't go making a blazing fire that'll burn the place down. I'll be around the first week of the month to collect rent. No rent, no room, you understand?"

Koppelman clutched a handful of coins handed to him, his fingers nimbly counting each one to assure their full amount. Satisfied, he reluctantly parted with a key, his voice sharpening as he warned, "Lose that, and it'll cost you two bits."

With the transaction complete, he trudged down the stairs, his expression souring as he navigated through discarded rubbish. A rat, obscured beneath a heap of chicken bones, startled him, prompting a swift rebuke with his walking stick. As he reached the landing, two unkempt children darted past, their dirty faces briefly catching his glare.

"No running in here! Take that outside," he barked, authority dripping from every syllable. The children halted, their expressions blank and uncomprehending. With a dismissive wave, he shooed them, "Go on, git!" His voice carried the irritable tone of a man burdened by the carelessness around him, reinforcing his miserly dominion over the dilapidated building.

He navigated the lengthy corridor that bisected the building, his gaze fixed on the exit ahead, when a piercing squeal halted his progress. He pivoted sharply, irritation flashing across his face as he muttered, "There better not be a damned dog tied up back there." His steps quickened along the dingy hallway toward the rear of the building, where the door stood ajar, revealing the confines of an enclosed patio.

Beyond the usual clutter and disarray of the decrepit hallway, an unnerving spectacle awaited him at the rear exit. As he neared the threshold, his pace slowed, caution overtaking his initial rush. What he first assumed to be mere refuse piled against the doorstep now seemed ominously out of place. A closer inspection revealed not garbage, but something far more disturbing—a shape too deliberate to be discarded trash. The realization struck a chord of dread in Koppelman as he approached, the contours of the heap growing clearer and his heart rate quickening with apprehension.

A black and white dog, lifeless and grotesquely hanged by a rope around its neck, lay ominously at the backstep. He poked at the animal with his walking stick but it did not move. The disturbing sight was a dark prelude to the violent confrontation that was to follow. He grabbed the rope and pulled the dog off the steps muttering to himself, "Damned fool. You can't tie a dog up like that. Now he's hanged hisself." His initial confusion over the seemingly self-inflicted demise of the animal turned to horror as the truth revealed itself—the end of the rope hung loosely, ominously unattached to nothing.

"Having trouble with your dog?"

Startled by a menacing voice, he turned to find himself confronted by a man whose lavish presence starkly contrasted with the squalor of the tenement. The man was clad in an elegant black suit, his hair equally dark and neatly parted. A similarly dark mustache framed a thin, tight-lipped mouth, and deep-set eyes glowered ominously from the sculpted hollows of his face. The man's usually handsome demeanor now carried an unsettling aura that sent chills down Koppelman's spine.

"That's not my dog!" Koppelman retorted sharply, his eyes darting to size up the figure before him. In the doorway, another man loomed, his form a dark silhouette outlined against the gloomy interior. The man next to Koppelman closed the distance, and Koppelman's attitude changed from frustration to fear. "This has nothing to do with you, stay back now, you hear?" He waved his walking stick at the stranger. The encounter swiftly escalated as the man seized Koppelman's cane, pinning him against the cold, harsh brickwork of the tenement building with the wooden rod.

"Are you Koppelman?"

Koppelman's stern facade crumbled in that moment, leaving his voice weak and frail. "Please take my money, but don't hurt me."

"Do I look like I need your lousy money?" He backhanded Koppelman against the cheek. "You got a renter here named Maria Ruckaveena? A widower?"

The fear in Koppelman's eyes was evident as the stranger interrogated him, his grip tightening with every question. The man's left fist shot out clenching tight around Koppelman's throat, pushing his head back and causing his skull to crack brutally against the wall. "I understand you're trying to evict her," he growled menacingly.

Koppelman choked, gasping for breath. "She, she—" spittle formed at the edge of his lips as he sputtered, his words barely escaping. "She broke the rules, she has to go."

With a sudden release, the man spun Koppelman to face the wall, shoving his face forcefully against the coarse brick, the impact sending sparks through his mind.

"What rules?" the man demanded.

"She can't make the rent," Koppelman managed to wheeze out. "She has to get out."

"Maybe she can't make the rent because you keep squeezing her for more," the man snarled. He seized Koppelman's right arm, wrenching it upward behind his back, grinding him further into the brickwork. The jagged surface clawed at Koppelman's face, eliciting a scowl of agony.

"What's the rent?"

"Four dollars," Koppelman grunted.

The man tightened his grip on Koppelman's hair, yanking his head back violently and he spoke directly into his ear. Koppelman grimaced as the whiskey-stained breath of the man assaulted his senses, his words hissing like steam. "Her rent will now be one dollar a month, and you'll not molest this woman again," the man whispered with venomous clarity. He then stuffed a ten-dollar greenback into Koppelman's mouth, mashing his face crudely against the rough brick. "Consider her paid up for the rest of the year," he growled. He threw Koppelman into a pile of refuse lining the back wall.

The man in the doorway cut in, "Let's go Jim." They calmly stepped into the rear of the building, their presence as chilling and unfeeling as the winter air.

Trembling, Koppelman clawed the crumpled bill from his mouth, his hands shaking as he wiped slobber and blood from his face. He scrabbled on his hands and knees through the doorway into the narrow hallway where he paused on all fours, squinting into the low light of the corridor, watching the menacing silhouettes of the two men recede. At the far end, the front door stood ajar, a rectangle of daylight framing a figure in a tall derby and long trench coat—a policeman, he presumed, positioned to intercept the attackers.

A hopeful cry died in his throat as the officer stepped aside nonchalantly, allowing the menacing figures to exit unchallenged. Koppelman's heart sank further when he saw the man in black slip something into the policeman's hand, confirming his worst fears about the reach of their influence. He lay there, paralyzed by fear and disbelief, as the door swung shut, cloaking him once more in the confined shadows of the long corridor.

Crisp and Moreland entered a tunnel beneath the looming bluffs via the Eighth Street incline; the rhythmic clatter of the trolley car blended with their hushed conversation. It had been five days since they last talked and Crisp quickly caught Moreland up on his recent meeting with Speers.

They disembarked at Pennsylvania, where St. Joseph's Hospital cast a contrasted silhouette against the gray morning sky. The edifice, a blend of hope and despair, housed Dr. Charles Henwood, the police surgeon whose domain lay in the hospital's underbelly—the city morgue. They entered the hospital and were promptly directed toward a long flight of descending stairs. Here, in the subdued light of the cold basement corridors, truths were laid bare, and secrets of the deceased whispered in the otherworldly silence.

The clinical chill of the morgue seeped into their bones, as they moved deeper into the poorly lit recesses of the basement. They were greeted by Henwood's assistant who led them to an antechamber where the surgeon worked, and here, they found Dr. Henwood, surrounded by the distinct tools of his trade, hunched over a cadaver draped in white linens. An antiseptic odor clung to the fringes of death, while amber lights fluttered faintly overhead, casting queer shadows across the cold, tile floor. Henwood, a meticulous man shaped by the rigors of medical science, greeted them in expectation, his introduction brief as he paused from his work.

His expression remained somber as he relayed the details of his most recent examination, inviting the men to come closer. "Speers' men identified the victim, Marion Krause—an assignation worker from The Bottoms, early twenties," Henwood began without preamble, his voice echoing slightly in the cavernous room. He reached for the cloth covering the cadaver.

"And the cause of death?" Crisp asked, his mind jumping ahead of the surgeon.

"Asphyxiation, or strangulation to be precise," Henwood confirmed as he pulled the linen back from the prone figure. He proceeded to point out the brutal precision of the marks on her body. "You can see the cuts across her face—uneven, jagged. The work of rage, not skill. Five in total, three on the left and two on the right, all stretching from just outside the eye socket down to her lower jaw. I found lacerations on the zygomatic bone and mandibles where the blade had nicked them. The torso tells a similar story. Six incisions ranging between eight and twelve inches. Again, the blade scratched a number of bones as incisions were scene on ribs five and six on the right side, and here on six and eight on the left."

Crisp listened intently, his analytical mind cataloging each detail. Moreland looked over his shoulder apprehensively; a fly buzzed somewhere in the shadows. Crisp continued, "And these cuts—made after death?"

"Indeed," Henwood continued, his face grave. "And there's the matter of the removed breasts. Not the work of any surgeon I know—no precision there, just brutal necessity. A sharp blade, yes, but wielded with little care for finesse."

Moreland's first glimpse of the cadaver laid out on the cold, metallic table was a visceral punch to the gut. As he stood there, a deep sense of revulsion crawled up his spine. The smell of the place was clinical, yet corrupt, a blend of disinfectant and decay that clung to the back of his throat, threatening to choke him. A fly landed on his cheek, edging toward his lip. He slapped at it and fumbled in his pocket for a handkerchief. When his fingers could not find it, he covered his mouth and nose gagging into the sleeve of his coat.

The conversation shifted as Henwood pulled out his notes, revealing further horrors that the crime scene had concealed. "There's more here in my report, but as you can see, there is one even more sinister discovery that you would not have seen at first." He handed his medical report to Moreland who read the details in fascination. Crisp looked over his shoulder to see what he could interpret.

"Good God!" Moreland shoved the report toward Crisp after reading the detailed findings regarding trauma caused by a large blunt object, presumably used in the hands of a necrophile. Crisp probed deeper into the medical assessment in the report, its graphic intensity a testament to the cruelty inflicted upon Marion Krause.

"Yes, quite heinous business. Again, it seems all of the bodily damage was inflicted a few hours post-mortem, most likely," Henwood estimated, his tone objective but not without a trace of anger. "There's more," he added, pointing to a diagram of the victim's body, "I found sooty smudges on her clothing, and here on her knees." He moved across the room to a wooden crate and retrieved her personal affects. "This substance here—I included it in the report. Unknown, but possibly relevant. Tar? Pitch? Soot?"

Crisp studied the piece of attire but continued his line of questioning, "Were there signs of her defending herself?" he inquired, handing the report back to Henwood.

"Definitely. Skin found beneath the fingernails. That suggests she fought with her attacker," Henwood affirmed. He then pointed to another disturbing detail on the cadaver. Moreland looked away but listened intently. "See here—hair forcibly removed, hacked off with a sharp blade. That might indicate a struggle."

Crisp absorbed the information, with speculations swirling in his head. "You've mentioned other victims with similar circumstances?"

"Yes, there have been others. All strangled, with post-mortem mutilations. It's becoming a disturbing pattern—" Henwood's voice trailed off, tinged with frustration, the kind that came from seeing too much and solving too little.

"What about tarpaulins? Detective Halpin tells me they were brought with the victims."

"I wasn't told anything about tarpaulins. If they were with the bodies, my staff must have disposed of them."

Crisp clenched his jaw, hiding his frustrations. He spun toward Marcus, "Do you have any other questions for the Doctor?" but swiftly turned back to Henwood, Moreland's green complexion and vehement nod confirming his curiosity had been more than satisfied. "Thank you for your time, Doctor."

They prepared to leave, thanking Henwood and promising to follow up with questions funneled through his assistant, and could barely hide their desire to make a hasty retreat from the oppressive confines of Henwood's grim sanctuary.

They stepped out into the brisk air of the city, their thoughts heavy with the details Henwood had provided, with the morgue's chill still clinging to their clothes. Crisp was pensive, his instincts telling him that the key to solving the string of brutal murders lay in understanding the mind behind them.

"Algernon, the pattern is clear, but the motive remains murky," Moreland mused as they walked.

"We need to consider the broader connections—what binds these victims beyond their professions? Is it personal, a message, or merely the actions of a deranged mind?"

Moreland nodded, equally troubled. "And what about the dates when these acts were committed. Assuming the killings are linked, and the result of the same perpetrator, then why the escalating frequency? What's driving this surge in violence? It's as if the killer is becoming more desperate... or bold."

Crisp paused; his gaze distant. "I was considering the same. There were three months between the first two incidents, and according to the Chief's notes, the next three repeat themselves within a matter of only a few weeks apart. The most recent killings have all been about a week to ten days apart."

"Perhaps there is some significance to the dates, or days of the week of the killings?"

"You're right again my friend. I believe if we plot out the dates of the previous murders, we will find an underlaying pattern that ties to other events that are important in the mind of our killer. Based on the threatening letter sent to the Chief, and the flyer found on the courthouse victim, it seems our culprit is seeking retribution against the temperance movements. I would guess the dates of the past killings align closely with social events or news stories, or some other actions regarding those movements."

Crisp resumed his stride forcing Moreland to pick up his pace. He continued speculating as they walked, "We must consider the entire context—recent laws, public sentiment, anything that might trigger such extremes. This isn't just about the who, but the why. Understanding that will lead us to him. If retribution is in fact the primary motive, it would imply that our killer is affected in some way by the temperance movements. Perhaps his livelihood is at risk, or maybe his moral values are threatened in some way."

"I counted five killings that are related, do you agree?" Moreland asked.

"Five for sure, but there were two others I took note of, they might also be related." Crisp fished in his pocket and pulled out the handwritten note from Speers. "And the Chief speculates there are possibly three others. He lists out a total of eight killings he believes are linked, so seven or eight for sure."

Moreland's expression tightened as Crisp's word sunk in. The thought of so many lives cut short stirred a quiet anger within him.

The two men walked on in silence, the weight of their task as heavy as the city fog that rolled in from the river, enveloping the streets with its frigid, damp tendrils. With each step, they drew nearer to the darkness at the heart of the city—a darkness they were determined to illuminate.

Chapter Eight

Monday morning arrived with a flurry of activity in the practical confines of Pendergast's office on St. Louis Avenue. The bustling office hummed with a blend of personal errands and strategic planning, each task executed with the precision and urgency that marked the beginning of a new and busy week. Dermot Gallagher, Pendergast's attentive assistant, offered a final pot of coffee, which his boss declined with a wave of his hand.

"Thank you, Dermot. No, I'll be leaving soon for lunch."

"Very well, sir, anything else?"

"Is my suit back yet? The black one, the new one that is."

"Mr. Wyse should be back shortly with it and the other sundries you requested."

"Good, very good. And Dermot, run down to Bullene's. I'd like some new collars, and pick out a fancy bow tie while you're there. Not too fancy, but something sophisticated. I have that meeting with *The Star* and want to look sharp for their reporter."

"Of course. I'll take care of that today," Gallagher assured before exiting the room.

Pendergast then turned his attention to Banwell, who had

been quietly taking notes. "Tom, I want you to find out more about this Haff fellow, D.J. Haff, the legal assistant for Meyer I told you about. What's his background? Where does he stand on parks? And what is Meyer's angle with his employment?" Banwell jotted down the instructions, nodding along. Pendergast shared his notes from the council meeting with Banwell. "And while you're at it, look into these other parks men. It would be convenient if something turned up on one of them, bad press, or anything I can use against them," Pendergast added, his voice carrying a mix of cynicism and calculation.

The intrusive sound of boots clomping up the back staircase heralded the impending entrance of Colin Wyse. Before he could even knock, Banwell intercepted him at the door, his voice terse with anticipation. "What is it?" he demanded.

Looming heavily in the corridor, Wyse was accompanied by a figure even more imposing—Denis Skahill. Towering at almost seven feet, Skahill's presence cast an oppressive shadow, barbaric and ogre-like, in the poorly lit hallway. His features, coarsely molded as if from rough clay, coupled with the tiny, inscrutable gleam of his eyes, stirred a profound unease within Banwell. The man's thoughts were shuttered behind his brutish countenance, making him an unreadable and disquieting figure.

"Picked up the boss's laundry and took the rest of the things to Mrs. P. in the kitchen," Wyse stated in his typically flat tone.

"Very good," Banwell responded with a dismissive nod.

Wyse lingered awkwardly, waiting for further instruction, while Skahill beside him, stared vacantly with his mouth agape.

Banwell's gaze hardened as he looked at them both. "Have

you repaired that back door yet? Get on with it, and slap some fresh paint on it too. Colin, make sure he does it properly," he instructed with a sneer, doubting their competence.

At that moment, more heavy footsteps announced the arrival of Patrick Carnes coming up the stairwell. In a comical moment, the big man squeezed past the hulking figures of Wyse and Skahill as the two tried to avoid a collision. "Move it," he growled, brushing past them, "I've got matters with the Boss."

After the two men left, Carnes entered the room. As Banwell closed the door behind them, he asked in a muted voice, "Did you take care of that business with Koppelman?"

"Done," Carnes replied, looking to Pendergast who was distracted with other thoughts.

"Patrick, have you seen yesterday's paper?" Pendergast inquired, his tone indicating a shift to matters of greater import.

"Which one, sir, *The Star* or *The Times*?" Carnes took a seat across from Pendergast.

Banwell handed a folded newspaper, yesterday's *Kansas City Star*, to Carnes pointing to a short, yet significant story.

Pendergast leaned back, his voice carrying the weight of implied command as he addressed Carnes across the cluttered surface of the oak desk. "There's a gathering Thursday, Republican rally at the Schlitz beer garden. Make sure our boys are there," he said, the undertone of his words clear. "The few 'Rabbits'—as they call themselves—in The Bottoms should reconsider their affiliation after our boys mingle with them. In fact, I want our boys at every one of these rallies going forward. Let's see if we can *entice* a few of them to change party."

Carnes nodded, absorbing the directive.

Pendergast pointed to a different headline as his temper flared briefly, "If they want to see the 'Bloody First Ward', by God, we'll give it to them!"

Banwell shifted uncomfortably where he stood, a few paces behind Carnes. His features tightened, the crease between his brows deepening as he listened to Pendergast's commands. His eyes flickered with a hint of anxiety, betraying his concern for the ramifications of such strategies on Pendergast's reputation. He glanced briefly towards Carnes, searching for a reflection of his own disquiet, but finding none, he quietly resumed his watchful stance. His hands, normally steady, clasped and unclasped behind his back—a silent, rhythmic testament to his growing unease as he contemplated the potential fallout from Pendergast's aggressive tactics.

"Patrick, you've heard me say it before, this politics business is all about making friends," Pendergast's tone relaxed, his words tinged almost with humorous ease, "but I think you'd agree, some friends need a little *coaxing* from time to time."

***

When Wednesday arrived two days later, it brought with it a slow steady snowfall that muted the city's usual clamor. Chief Speers stood solemnly outside the prestigious Louis Hammerslough residence near Sixteenth and Central Streets, his expression a mix of concern and weariness. A group of his detectives, clustered nearby, were engaged in a low, urgent discussion over the day's unpleasant discovery. The afternoon chill was a harsh contrast to the dark reality laid bare beneath the covered heap before them—a reality all too common in recent weeks.

Crisp approached rapidly, his keen eyes scanning the familiar scene of despair. "H'lo Thomas, what have we found today?" he called out as he neared the cluster of law enforcement.

"Another one, I'm afraid," Speers responded, gesturing somberly towards the blanketed form on the ground.

Crisp moved closer, his presence causing the other detectives to step aside, a mix of respect and resignation in their eyes. He peeled back the blanket, revealing the tragic scene beneath. His quick, practiced gaze took in the horrid details: woman in her mid-twenties, evidence of strangulation, face and torso marred by post-mortem mutilations, clothing brutally removed, lock of blonde hair cut away. He jotted down observations in his notepad—every detail, every similarity with the previous cases, methodically recorded as he had seen in Henwood's documents.

As he worked, he overheard snippets of a conversation between two of the detectives. "Mrs. Vickers, cross the street there, mentioned a narrow horse truck here just before dawn," one of them murmured. "Woke by her dog's barking, she watched from her window. The wagon moved on quickly, and she went back to sleep."

Crisp added a note to his pad: Mrs. Vickers, horse truck, dawn. He carefully covered the body again and approached the detectives. "Did your men move this body at all, or was it found just so?"

"No, sir, untouched until the surgeon arrives," one detective replied. Crisp knelt and examined the coarse blanket haphazardly strewn around the victim.

Returning to Speers, he shared his initial thoughts. "Much the same, though this time, our perpetrator seems to have been in a rush. This victim is facedown, only a few feet from the road—unlike the others, who were carried further away. The blanket is not neatly spread, but thrown. It suggests he was interrupted, perhaps."

Speers nodded.

"Your men said the body has been here since early morning—when was it discovered?"

"We don't know for sure how long it's been lying there, but we weren't summoned until early afternoon. Seems no one had come across it yet. The snow kept it from view."

Crisp eyed the layout of the yard. "Too many footprints all about to make any conclusions," he noted. Some distance away, a wheelbarrow and two shovels sat near a hedge line. Speers caught Crisp's gaze and read his mind.

"We already confirmed those belong to a workman making repairs around the place. They've been sitting in the same place for a number of days."

Crisp jotted a note to himself. "What can you tell me about this home? Who lives here?"

"Louis Hammerslough, retired clothier. You probably recognize the name from his store at Fifth and Main, the Hammerslough building?"

Crisp considered this. "And that last victim, just a few blocks from here. Who owned that home?"

"William Glass, a prominent business man who runs a wholesale liquor distribution warehouse downtown. Do you think there is a connection?"

"Hammerslough, retired clothing merchant," Crisp mused. "And Glass, another prominent businessman. It's an uptown shift from The Bottoms; there hasn't been a body found down there in a few weeks. He's either escalating his message or diversifying his targets for greater impact."

"Could be both."

"Thomas," he began, a thoughtful tone shaping his words, "your office holds that expansive city map. By marking where each victim was found, we might uncover a pattern."

"Certainly," Spears replied, nodding. "You're free to use my office for that; there might indeed be something to your hunch."

Crisp moved away from Speers and stepped off the curb; noting hoofprints and wheel marks in the snow-covered street. He paused there, analyzing them before they disappeared from view. Catching the stares of neighbors peeping from windows and gawking from porches, he waved to Speers, who stood amidst his policemen, signaling that he was leaving.

With a determined stride, Crisp headed north for several blocks before catching an eastbound cable car. He hopped off in front of the Coates House Hotel, and found Moreland seated in the lobby. As they waited for a table in the dining hall, Crisp briefed him on the day's discovery. He pulled out a piece of twisted wire from his coat pocket. "Found this just off the curb, near where a wagon had stopped," he explained, handing it over to Moreland.

Moreland examined the wire, then handed it back. "Could this have been used in the strangulations?"

Crisp manipulated the wire between his fingers, considering. "Perhaps, if long enough. Though something more flexible, like a cord of rope, would be more effective. But the victims you'll recall, seem to be strangled by hand. The contusions and marks around the neck were not symptomatic of a line or cord." He paused, a distant look crossing his face. "This wire—it's familiar though. I can't place where I've seen this type, but it's significant."

Moreland shrugged his shoulders. "No idea. I've never seen it before."

Crisp coiled the wire into a ring and tucked it back into his pocket. From the large bay windows of the hotel, he watched the grey winter afternoon surrender to an ashen dusk, the street lights popped on one-by-one casting their deceptive amber warmth on the snow-covered sidewalks. Oblivious to the lurking dangers that nightfall could unleash, pedestrians shuffled along, their outlines meandering there on the brink of darkness.

"It will be dark soon, let's revisit the scene tomorrow," Crisp suggested after a moment. "I overheard one of Speers' men say a neighbor had spotted a wagon parked there this morning. I plan to circle back and question a few of the neighbors, would you like to join me?"

"I've got a morning appointment at ten, but after that," Moreland agreed.

"And I'd like to consult Speers' city map in his office. If we plot the locations where the victims were found, we might uncover a connection with our killer's motives and movements."

"I can't help but wonder if there's something else I may be able to assist you with. I'm happy to help; I'm just not sure where to pitch in," Moreland offered.

"I'm grappling with where these bodies have been left—" Crisp began, rubbing his chin thoughtfully without acknowledging Moreland's offer. "Both recent victims were found at the homes of well-known businessmen. There's got to be a deliberate reason for that choice."

Moreland nodded, analyzing the possible connection between them. "I assume the killer is targeting these businessmen directly."

"We must never assume," Crisp responded. "We can *presume* and follow the possible conclusions they lead to, but when you *assume*, it closes your mind to many options you may not have seen." He stared out the window for several moments. "You can help by digging into the relationships between these men and the networks they belong to, we might find something there. Perhaps you can attend some of their public gatherings, see if there are shared interests or conflicts that stand out."

"Alright, I will begin with the social clubs and charity boards they're involved with. Perhaps there's some overlap there that's not immediately obvious," Moreland suggested, his mind already ticking through potential approaches.

"Yes, exactly," Crisp agreed. "And keep an ear out for anything that seems out of place. Sometimes it's the tiniest detail that speaks volumes."

"I'll keep that in mind. It's a bit like looking for a needle in a haystack, but it's a start," Moreland concluded, his tone resolute but aware of the challenge ahead.

Their conversation deepened into the nuances of the case as they moved to dine, every word exchanged thick with the gravity of the case. With each clue examined, the looming presence of their task hung over them, yet the path forward grew clearer, drawing them nearer to the malevolent force they sought to expose.

———

Another day slipped by, and they found themselves no closer than before to uncovering a suspect. Crisp, Moreland, and Speers convened in the sullen confines of police headquarters, behind closed doors in the Chief's office, where the urgency of their mission was clear.

Speers, visibly exhausted, massaged his temples before speaking. "Gentlemen, I needn't remind you that the city's reputation is at stake here. With Chicago's Exposition drawing national attention, Kansas City must not falter, especially not now with the mayor pushing his parks and clean-up initiatives so vigorously. We must contain this string of murders swiftly." He gestured towards a copy of *The Kansas City Star* on his desk. "The press is on this, and it's only a matter of time before they start pointing fingers."

Crisp looked at the front page in shock. "Hello, what's this then?" The headline declared 'Recent Murder Committed By Ice/Coal Man'.

"Where did they get that?" Moreland asked in surprise.

"That's precisely what we need to find out, Marcus. We need to identify the source of that claim," Crisp insisted, scanning the news story, searching for clues. "Chief," he continued, his tone reflecting a mix of concern and accusation, "the details in this story suggest an inside leak. Could one of your men be feeding the press?"

Speers' expression darkened as he exhaled sharply, clearly agitated. "While I admit it's possible, I suspect the Baron might be behind this."

"The Baron?"

"William Rockhill Nelson, the founder of *The Kansas City Star*," Crisp explained for Moreland's benefit.

"He's got deep connections, possibly even deeper than we know." Speers spoke with urgency. "But let's not get sidetracked by conjectures. We need to focus on the facts and solve this matter swiftly. Do you have any suspects in mind yet?"

"Still working that, but we dug this up," Crisp interjected, pulling out his notebook. "Earlier today, Marcus and I returned to the Hammerslough neighborhood. A witness, Mrs. Vickers, reported a wagon parked near the crime scene, early yesterday morning, close to where the victim was found. She described it as a small box wagon, the type commonly used for deliveries, pulled by a single dun-colored horse. We confirmed with a member of the household staff that it was not the type of wagon used by the men working on the property there."

Speers perked up, "So, *The Star* might actually be onto something with their ice and coal man theory?"

Crisp shook his head, "Not necessarily. While the wagon fits the description of what an ice or coal man might use, Mrs. Vickers couldn't confirm any company name painted on the wagon due to the snow covering the painted letters on its sides. It could belong to any number of enterprises."

Moreland chimed in, "She did mention a red wagon with

faded white lettering that had lanterns affixed near the driver's box; those could be distinctive features. We're keeping an eye out for any wagon that matches this description." And then in a flash of inspiration, he added, "We could simply visit every coal and ice plant in town and easily find such a wagon!"

"Marcus, the Chief may have to hire you on as my assistant," he smiled toward Speers, but the humor fell flat against his desk. He took a deep breath before continuing, "The wagon may lead us to the right location, but then we need to consider the man himself. The size of the driver is also a crucial detail. Mrs. Vickers noted he was a big man, his features vague in the darkness, but he needed to hunch over to get into the driver's seat. This aligns with our theory of a physically imposing fellow capable of overpowering his victims."

"Too bad she didn't get a look at his face or give us some identifying marks," Speers said, inclining forward.

Moreland added, "Dr. Henwood told us the latest victim had fought back against her attacker. There could be visible scratches on our suspect, possibly on his face or arms."

Crisp nodded, "If we can locate someone matching this description, it might lead us right to him. But let's also consider the psychological profile. The crudeness of the handwriting in the letter to you Chief, the primitive use of language—this points to a man of very limited education, possibly someone who feels deeply threatened by the temperance movement's activities."

Speers looked thoughtful, "Perhaps a saloon owner, or someone employed in the gambling dens."

"Maybe he is an immigrant", Moreland chimed in. "That

would account for his poor use of the language."

"That is an excellent thought Marcus, and one we should keep in mind," Crisp agreed. "Now, let's shift our attention to the pattern of these crime scenes— they seem to have moved from the shadowed corners of The Bottoms, to the clear visibility of uptown neighborhoods." With a decisive stride, he approached the wall where a large city map hung. Gesturing broadly, he summoned Speers and Moreland to join him. He took a pencil and pointed out various locations on the map. "Here," he began, his voice steady and compelling as he traced the geography of violence, "are the sites where the victims were discovered. Six victims discovered below the bluffs. The first five, all found within a few blocks of the depot, that may be significant. The first discovered here on Eighth, and the next here, near the corner of St. Louis and Wyoming, the third in the rail yards near the Twelfth Street trestle, and then the other two found at the north end of the depot, here in the yards, and here beneath the Ninth Street incline," he finished by circling the identified locations.

The two men hung on Crisp's words.

"But then the pattern shifts. The next body appeared here, at Dold's. This is the first *displayed* if you will, clothing removed, laid out in the open, which marks a chilling escalation."

"Why Dold's, do you think?" Marcus asked.

"Dold is certainly a prominent business man," Speers pointed out. Crisp nodded.

"Maybe the killer worked at the plant and held a grievance against Dold," Moreland suggested.

Crisp shook his head thoughtfully. "I considered the same,

but my research has determined that Dold is esteemed by his staff, known for extending generous social benefits. Here's something interesting though. Just two days before the body was discovered, his company hosted a lecture attended by the Mothers of Kansas City."

"The killer might have been present at that gathering!" Moreland interjected, piecing together the narrative.

"Possibly," Crisp conceded. "We can't dismiss any connections. Can you look into that for me?" Without waiting for Moreland's response, he continued, "Now, moving uptown..." He shifted to the circled intersection of Fifth and Main. "The body at City Hall, found with the temperance flyer."

"Not a temperance woman herself, but another crib girl," Speers interjected.

"Correct. It suggests the killer is striking at the movement through these girls."

"But why City Hall?" Moreland asked, "there's been no parade or temperance gathering there?"

"Correct again. But this is where it gets interesting. This victim was placed the day after this this came out." He dug through a worn attaché case and pulled out a newspaper dated January 29th. On the front page, Crisp had circled two headlines: 'Mothers of KC Against Policy Shops' and 'Rev Wright Denounces Policy Shops as Evil'. "I didn't make a connection at first, but you recall Chief, the poor girl had the wad of newspaper stuffed in her mouth?"

"Of course, who can forget something like that."

"Later, when I examined the date of that page, January

29th, it matched the front page you see here. It's clear he's escalating matters, seeking broader attention, or reacting to changes happening in these areas due both to the temperance movement, and to the Parks Board's initiatives."

"Do you really believe he's targeting the Parks Board?" Speers raised an eyebrow.

"Yes, think about it," Crisp leaned in. "Both Hammerslough and Glass, their homes the locations of the most recent crime scenes; both are connected to the Parks Board, thanks for confirming that, Marcus. And remember the letter to you Chief? It directly references 'prettying up the town.' Our man is not just reacting to the temperance movement but also to the beautification efforts the mayor is pushing, which might be disrupting where he stays or conducts business."

Speers rubbed his chin, mulling over the information. "So, you're suggesting a convergence of motives? The temperance movement, the mayor's clean-up efforts, and perhaps personal grievances?"

"Precisely," Crisp confirmed. "Our killer uses the city as his stage, selecting his targets and locations to send a message. It's not just about the victims—it's about the impact on the community and those driving change."

Moreland's confusion became evident as he considered something else. "Except for the woman we aided near the depot, all the victims have been prostitutes. Why?"

Speers chipped in thoughtfully, "That would suggest our suspect isn't a brothel owner, right?"

Crisp nodded, "Good point. A brothel owner would protect his or her assets. It seems our man holds a grudge against these women, or has some morbid interest in them. Although his actions are driven by vengeance against certain movements, he's not directly targeting those members. Instead, he's making them witnesses to his brutality, aiming to instill fear."

It became clear for Moreland, "So, the women are just instruments to him; inconsequential in and of themselves."

"Correct," Crisp affirmed. "He's exploiting them to provoke fear in those who oppose him. He's trying to ruffle your feathers, Chief." Crisp paused to let this sink in, then continued, "Still, his choice of victims must mean something. He could target anyone, but he chooses these women in particular."

"Perhaps because they're accessible and seen as easy targets," Moreland speculated.

Crisp agreed, "That's likely. If our hunch is correct and the killer is a large man, he's not one to easily hide during an abduction. As a brothel patron, he'd be routinely welcomed by these women without suspicion. But there is likely something else, something about his rapport with these women. Something that triggers his aggressions."

Moreland pondered the paradox, "He's attacking the movements by using the victims of vice to make a statement about vice itself."

Crisp concluded, "We're dealing with a disturbed mind. This man, likely uneducated and from the lower echelons of society, feels powerless against the changes these movements represent. He reacts not with words, or peaceful protests, but with primal violence."

Speers, visibly shaken by the weight of their discussion,

interjected with urgency, "We need to stop him before this escalates further. We need to move faster; this is getting out of hand. Let's broaden our search—background checks on anyone linked to the parks and the temperance movements. My men will keep an eye out for anyone matching our suspect's description. I'm counting on you two to delve deeper into these connections."

They exchanged a brief glance, the same thought passing between them without the need for word. Eight victims. Eight too many.

Chapter Nine

In the hushed hours before sunrise, the flickering flame of a single oil lamp cast a faint glow in Crisp's room at the boardinghouse. Outside, the immediate vicinity was besieged by a line of thunderstorms. Flashes of lightning and claps of thunder rattled the thin glass panels in his window. Inside, the sweet, narcotic haze of opium and morphine vapors hovered above the bed where he and Cassie lay entwined after their intimacy.

He sat up, back on his pillow, feeling the warmth of her body as she snuggled against him under a heavy quilt. Her closeness, meant to be comforting, twisted his insides with guilt. The weight of borrowed money pressed on him as heavily as the opium and tobacco fumes clinging to his bedding. He had promised himself this would be the last time, yet he found himself indebted to her once again.

In his hand, he held a cheroot laced with cocaine. The drug sent his thoughts racing as he took a deep drag, letting the smoke fill his lungs and clear his mind. His eyes traced patterns in the floral motif on the peeling wallpaper while his brain worked over the details of the murder investigation. In his free hand, he toyed with the twisted wire found near the Hammerslough crime scene. Ms. Meadows had confirmed her ice man delivered canvas bags tied with similar wire, solidifying the connection in Crisp's mind between a coal and ice man, and the murderer.

Cassie sidled up next to him, and he offered her a puff from the cheroot. She blew a cloud of smoke toward the ceiling and reached to the side table, grabbed another cheroot, and lit it off the end of his. He took another large puff and instantly felt the rush from the contents within. He considered the bawdy houses he had noted earlier—the very places where the victims had once laughed and lived. He needed to understand more about that world, and Cassie was his conduit.

He sat up and moved closer, the morning light catching the earnestness in his gaze. "I could really use your insight on these murders," he murmured. He felt the tenseness in her body as she nestled beside him. She too had her demons, ones that had visited her earlier that night in her dreams. The victims were her peers, fellow spirits in the shadowy world she inhabited.

"Charlie," she whispered, her voice edged with fear, "do you think—could it be one of us next?" Her words hung between them, a specter neither could ignore.

"I won't let that happen, Cass." His mind swirled with the implications of her fears. The safety of the women, the stealth of the killer, the chaos of the brothel's workings—all these thoughts churned in his head. He turned to face her. "You've never told me how you got into the business," he said, looking at her empathetically with a reassuring smile. She drew herself up and shrugged as the covers slipped from her shoulders, exposing her nakedness to the chill of the room. Any other woman would have blushed and scrambled to cover up, but she remained indifferent. Crisp's smile lingered with a trace of yearning as he gathered his thoughts to continue. "Will you tell me?"

After a moment of reflection, she began, "When I was younger, my family fell on hard times. Papa was sickly in those days and frequently out of work. Mama struggled to keep us all fed; there were five children in the house then. She took odd jobs to make ends meet—sewin' and laundry for the wealthy families in St. Joseph—while I cared for the young'uns. Then, in the winter of eighty-four, consumption took Papa. I went to stay with my aunt Sophie and cousin Emma in Kansas City. Sophie was a successful dressmaker, with her own downtown shop, or so the family thought."

He put his arm around her, drawing her close. Her hand rested on his chest as she thought back on those dark years.

"Once I got to the city, I quickly learnt Sophie's nice house and luxuries were paid for by the brothel she ran. It wasn't Madame Chambers' place, but decent enough." She sighed, "I guess I was desperate; I saw Sophie's and Emma's glamorous lifestyle compared to where I'd come from. They swayed me with promises of quick money and an early retirement, and luxuries far beyond reach in my former life." She rolled away from Crisp, still nestled in his arms.

"At first, I felt betrayed, like I'd been lied to." Her voice broke; though he couldn't see the tear running down her cheek, he sensed it, and his heart ached with a tenderness that made him hold her tight. "I turned sixteen that year, but I was still just a child. I mean coming from the country and all, I didn't know much about the ways of the world. My aunt convinced me my beauty and charm were an asset." She sniffed and regained her composure. "Like I said, I was in dire need. My cousin Emma taught me everything."

She hesitated in trepidation, pondering on how much to share. "I sent the money I earned back home to Mama. Sophie provided for me, and I knew Mama could use the money for food and send the young'uns to school." Then she laughed bitterly through sniffles and wiped at her cheek. "Sophie promised I could retire at twenty-two, with enough money to do whatever I wanted. I dreamt of owning a flower shop or my very own boardinghouse. But twenty-two came and went. I decided to help the new girls instead of leaving the business. I saved some money, but not enough to start my own business. But now, I have enough, and I have you, Charlie. Everything is good now. I want things to be different for us."

He tilted in and kissed her cheek softly. "Yes, everything will be different." He rocked her gently to ease her sorrow, his touch tender and reassuring, but the mystery of the killer still weighed heavily on his mind, casting a shadow over their fragile moment of solace. "Cass," he continued, his tone more serious, "I want to know more about the girls you work with. Do any of the men ever get violent with them?"

"It's part of the job," she sighed. "Most of the men are drunk to begin with. If he wants to play mean, or maybe the girl ain't doing everything he wants, sure they sometimes get rough you know. Most of these men start their nights with a bottle and end them with their fists."

His expression hardened at the casual acceptance of such harsh realities. "And how often do you see that sort of thing? Is it just the occasional outburst, or is it more commonplace?"

"More frequent than any of us would like to admit," she said, her voice dropping a notch. "Especially with new customers who think a few dollars buys them the right to leave marks."

He continued, his tone edged with urgency, "I'm digging deeper here, Cass. Has there ever been talk of someone not just mouthing off, but really meaning harm? Serious threats?"

"I've heard stories, never happened to me that way," she paused, considering his question as she drew the sheets closer. "It's rare, but yeah, some fellas lose their heads completely, especially after a few drinks too many. If one of 'em thinks he's been conned or laughed at, then the threats start flying."

"That's it," he nodded, his voice tightening with the weight of his thoughts. "It's the serious threats I'm interested in. Have you ever been frightened by someone's words?"

She exhaled slowly, her eyes closing as she sifted through her memories. "There was one fella," she began, her voice dropping, "talked like he'd kill someone one day. But it's all talk until it isn't, isn't it?"

Crisp's eyes met hers, searching for any flicker of evasion. "It's those kinds of men I need to find out about, Love. Anyone who's crossed the line from just talking to doing something about it."

Cassie nodded slowly, understanding the gravity of his quest. "I'll think on it, these are not light matters, Charlie." Her voice held a wary edge. "What are you driving at with all these questions?"

His tone softened; his concern evident. "Cass, have you known any of the women who've been found dead recently? Even just by reputation?"

She shifted uncomfortably, wrapping the sheet a bit tighter around herself. "Only what's been whispered around. I heard one girl used to work under Madame Lovejoy. I never did myself, but Susie, from our place, she did. She knew the poor girl."

"Did Susie ever mention anything about her, or any threats, anything like that?" Crisp probed, his gaze intense.

She frowned, a flicker of anxiety passing over her face. "Should I be worried? Is there something you're not telling me Charlie?"

"No, Love. I'm just trying to understand the type of bloke that's behind all of this." He sensed her hesitation, aware of the weight of his questions. Though reluctant to push further, he understood the necessity; she could be a pivotal piece in unraveling the mystery. He felt the urgency to delve deeper, knowing her insights could be crucial to the investigation's success. "The house where you work... I've been wondering how things operate there. Will you tell me?" His mind, fueled by the stimulants coursing through his system, sped through the logistics of his investigation. "I need to understand how it all happens—the girls, the customers, the money, everything." It was a delicate request, one that bridged their personal intimacy and his professional conviction. But for him, understanding the predator's perspective was crucial, and he trusted no one more than her to guide him into this dark world.

She shifted; her interest piqued despite the morphine's heavy veil. "Where do you want me to start?"

"How many other houses have you worked in? How does it work?"

"I've been in three others, including Aunt Sophie's. Men come, choose a girl, go to a room. What makes you ask?"

He chewed at his bottom lip, his detective's mind piecing together a haunting puzzle. "I'm trying to figure out how a killer could get to a girl without drawing attention; how he could abduct her and move her without being seen. It's a busy place, surely."

"Some men request the last appointment of the night, or pay extra for privacy. Many girls have regulars that ask for them each time. Not all the girls are careful about who they trust."

The implications hung heavy in the air. "You need to be careful," he said softly, the protective edge in his voice sharp. "Promise me you'll be careful."

"I always am," she reassured him, though her voice was distant, drifting under the influence. After a moment of further contemplation, her eyes cleared. "Now you got me scared," she said, clutching at his arm.

Crisp reached out, his hand gently squeezing hers. "I'm sorry Love," he said, his voice steady with reassurance. His eyes, full of a soft intensity, held hers. "I didn't mean to frighten you. I appreciate you more than you will ever know." He rolled over to kiss her on the forehead and looked into her eyes; his face set with determination. "Will you show me?" he said, his voice low and urgent. "Take me to where you work. I need to see it through the eyes of this fiend."

"Okay."

He resisted the urge to press her further, knowing that patience would yield more insights into her world. For now, he chose to tread carefully, aware that pushing too hard might close the doors she was only just beginning to open. "Later, Love. Let's not talk about it anymore, just relax." He lay back, pulling her close as she succumbed to the opium's lull. His mind, however, could not rest; too many unsolved puzzles kept his eyes wide open. As her breathing deepened into sleep, his gaze drifted to the faint light seeping through the curtains. The dawn neared, and with it, another day of danger in the tangled streets of Kansas City.

In the silence of the room, with her soft sighs as the only sound, he made a silent vow to unravel the mystery of the murders—to protect her and the others entangled in this sinister web.

By evening, the storms had cleared out, leaving The Bottoms draped in an inescapable dampness. The back alley to Cassie's assignation house was narrow and poorly lit, and littered with the debris of the city's less savory transactions. Crisp had not been there in some time, but knew the boardinghouse where she rented a room by the day, sat on State Line just one block away from his own. As they slipped through the shadows with his faithful companion Percy, they avoided stagnant puddles of filth, making their way to the rear of her building. She stopped them sooner than Crisp expected. Here, the buildings loomed like shadowy monoliths, their identities indistinguishable in the murky gloom, each offering a non-descript rear entrance. He looked upon boarded-up windows on the second floor of her building, barriers that told tales of vulnerability and fear. She pointed out a discreet back entrance, and opened a sliding door where he inspected the ingress in earnest.

"Is there a way to secure this from inside?"

"No one knows about this door," she said, leading him into the portal.

"Wait for me around front," Crisp instructed the boy, his tone firm and impatient. "This won't take long."

They stepped into a poorly lit hallway, separated from the front of the house by a set of heavy drapes, and her hand trembled slightly in his as it struck her for the first time that someone could easily gain access to the boardinghouse and conceal themselves here unnoticed. She pointed to her room and the one opposite which were concealed behind the curtained partition. "If someone wanted to stay hidden, coming and going, this would be the spot," she murmured.

She unlocked the door and moved to the center of the room where she tugged on a short brass chain hanging from a suspended light fixture. The scent of her perfume hung heavily in the pink glow cast by the shaded light. Crisp was accustomed to the scent, yet its intensity in this particular setting felt strangely overwhelming to him. The familiar yet foreign room, cramped and sparsely furnished, sat as a poignant reminder of their first encounter before life had woven their paths so tightly together. This was the place where she worked; the thought of it stirred a quiet revulsion in him, an instinctive unease he couldn't suppress, yet he forced down the discomfort rising in his chest, willing himself to stay focused.

He moved to the window facing the rear alley, his fingers brushing the frame as he inspected the bolts. Secure, but not beyond tampering—anyone could unlatch it with ease and slip back in undetected. Something deeper stirred within him; beneath the surface his mind wrestled with more than the mechanics of the window. It was a mix of concern for her safety and the feelings he associated with this room. It was more than just her place of work; it was where their paths had first crossed, a moment bound by a significance she seemed to overlook.

"Is there not another room you could choose?"

"I like this one, it's quieter than most," she said, oblivious to the turmoil hidden behind his words.

As if on cue, he heard a rhythmic, muted thumping on the floorboards above his head, and forced himself to ignore its implications. Absorbed in every detail, the layout of her room embedded itself in his mind alongside the throbbing realization that his encroachment had changed the stakes of their relationship. Despite the dire context, his heart ached with a complex emotion that was neither jealousy nor simple sadness. It was a deeper, more consuming sorrow mingled with a fierce commitment to protect her, a conviction that tightened his chest as they exited the room.

"You should always make sure that window is secured."

She locked the door to her room. "The window is jammed; it doesn't open anyway."

She showed him around the rest of the house. An undersized parlor at the front served as a waiting area for the clientele who frequented the brothel. Three or four other women, rouged and powdered, and dressed provocatively in tight-fitting bodices adorned with feathered boas, hung there awaiting the arrival of new customers. Two additional floors upstairs held a total of twelve modest rooms; and for those unoccupied that he was able to view, each was sparsely furnished like Cassie's, and each harbored its own secrets and indiscretions of the illicit activities that transpired within.

Exits from each floor leading to a rear fire escape had long since been boarded up and showed no signs of providing entrance. At least in her assignation house, the only way in and out seemed to be through the front of the building, or the secret entrance she had shown him. He decided his next steps must include visits to other brothels in the area. Each would offer new clues; each could reveal something different from this place.

They stepped out the front entrance into the cool night air where the city's sounds were muffled by fog. Percy waited obediently under a street lamp, smoking a cigarette and twirling a piece of chain. Crisp felt the weight of the task ahead but relied on the wiry, gutter child who knew every shadow and corner of the neighborhood, to aid him in his investigations.

Cassie remained behind while Crisp and Percy traversed the grimy backstreets of The Bottoms. Their goal was narrow and precise: they searched for brothels with discreet back exits—rooms and windows that faced the anonymity of alleyways, the sort where secrets were kept with ease.

As they prowled through the labyrinth of alleys, Crisp pointed out fire escapes and rickety stairs clinging to the backs of buildings like skeletal hands. "These make quick exits for anyone looking to avoid the main streets," he muttered, making mental notes of each configuration. The pair also scrutinized the narrowness of each corridor they inspected, assessing whether a cart or wagon would be able to fit through the alleys without catching on the clutter and refuse that lined the ground, and determining if there were enough room for a horse to maneuver and turn a cart around.

Their inquiries extended to the locals as well. Crisp, with his authoritative demeanor, questioned a few loitering neighbors. "Seen any carts or wagons around these parts often?" he asked. The responses were mixed, but no one recalled anything unusual—just the typical deliveries and pickups, coal and ice men making their rounds, other occasional visitors, nothing that stood out. Yet, the mention of the ice and coal deliveries struck a chord in Crisp's analytical mind.

Exiting an alleyway, Crisp looked up and down St. Louis Avenue. "You're sure you got straight answers, from the ice dealers; they didn't give you the run around?"

"I swear Colonel, I checked every coal and ice plant in The Bottoms; our red wagon weren't from any of them."

Seeking a broader perspective, Crisp clapped a hand on the boy's shoulder. "Let's get a better view," he suggested. They found a nearby fire escape, its metal cold and unwelcoming under their hands, as they began their ascent. From the fire escape, they climbed a rusty ladder leading to a rooftop, where they surveyed the sprawling district below. The West Bottoms stretched out like a patchwork of desperation and decay, a perfect backdrop for the dark deeds they aimed to unravel.

The fog hung in pockets along Ninth Street, obscuring details in the ethereal glow from amber gaslit street lights. Yet, from their elevated vantage point, Percy's keen eyes caught movement in the street below. "Look Colonel, that horse truck; it's red or I'm an honest injun!" he shouted, pointing towards a cross street where a dun horse pulled a boxed freight wagon. The wagon turned a corner and disappeared into an alley off St. Louis Avenue, its movements seemingly purposeful.

Wasting no time, they descended from their perch, their steps quick and sure as they carefully descended the fire escape. When their feet hit the ground, they raced toward St. Louis Avenue, searching every side street and corridor in the vicinity. Their first turn led them astray, a turn into the wrong lot filled with the clatter and clang of a metal works shop. Doubling back, they corrected their course and soon found the location they sought. A few frantic minutes had elapsed since they had first caught sight of their target, but now, they were sure they had found the right spot. Here, parked at the far end of the enclosure, hidden from casual view, sat an ice and coal wagon—precisely the kind they had been searching for.

Crisp chewed his lower lip as he surveyed the scene, rearranging the pieces of the puzzle in his mind, and forming a picture he had only glimpsed in fragments before. He felt a surge of anticipation—here was the tangible link to the murders that had eluded them until now. He cursed the incoming fog and the darkness descending upon the lot. "Perhaps we should come back in the morning," he said aloud to himself.

"What if the wagon is gone by then?"

"At least we know where it is kept. We can watch this place from a safe distance in the daylight; see who comes and goes." His instincts warned him of unseen peril lurking within. Was it real danger, or merely his own fear playing tricks on him? He couldn't be sure, but the uncertainty gnawed at him. His concern for the boy's safety was paramount, he reassured himself, though deep down he wondered whether it was his own trepidation holding him back. The shadows seemed to whisper with possibilities—none of them good.

"Let's look now. I ain't afraid, Colonel."

"I am. I am, my boy."

In the muted light of the cloudless, grey morning the next day, the lot revealed itself to be a scrapyard of twisted metal and mystery stretched out before Crisp and his young companion. They stood with renewed courage at the threshold of a discovery that promised to turn the tide of their investigation. The lot they'd chanced upon the night before, was cluttered with the skeletal remains of discarded machinery and rusting carriages; it seemed almost to whisper secrets as the wind howled softly through its confines.

As they ventured into the scrapyard, Crisp's eyes fixed on a cluster of wagons tucked away behind piles of debris at the rear of the lot. Moving deeper into the lot, he realized a narrow alley fed the lot from the backside along with other businesses between Ninth and St. Louis Avenue, and offered the only potential egress. As they neared the wagons, Crisp clearly saw the first was a flatbed, farm-style wagon that he discounted immediately, the other a box-frame commonly referred to as a horse truck. Its boxed sides bore the scars of frequent use and neglect.

With deliberate care, Crisp and Percy approached the wagon. Even in the soft morning light, they could make out its worn, red paint and faded, white lettering. Lanterns were affixed on either side of the box near the driver's seat. They began a thorough examination; Percy measured the wheels while Crisp inspected the ground nearby. There, imprinted in the soft earth beneath the wagon, were small horse prints, eerily similar to those he had examined at the murder scenes.

The discovery sent a shiver down his spine. There was no door on the boxed frame, and Crisp saw laying just inches inside its dark enclosure a discarded tarpaulin. He carefully lifted the tarp's edge, his eyes narrowing as he peered into the faint twilight underneath. A dark stain marred the floorboards of the wagon. Blood? His mind flickered with uncertainty. It was too thin for paint, possibly oil, or some other substance. His fingers hovered over the stain, his thoughts racing through the possibilities, none of them sitting comfortably. Beside it, a piece of wire lay discarded, bent and unremarkable at first glance. He reached for it, feeling the familiar texture as he tucked it into his coat. It was similar, almost identical, to the wire he'd found earlier.

As he pondered his findings, his gaze inadvertently drifted to the towering building beyond the scrapyard's chaotic borders. The backside of the Pendergast Hotel loomed overhead, its windows staring blankly back at him. A thought struck him with the force of a thunderclap: could there be a link between this wagon, the murders, and the man known as Boss Jim Pendergast, whose notorious influence ran through the veins of The West Bottoms like poison?

Before he could sink deeper into his hypothesis, Percy tugged at his sleeve. "Look there, Colonel!" he whispered, pointing to a neatly kept buggy parked not far from their current fixation. "That's Boss Jim's ride. Seen it myself, takin' him uptown more times than I can count."

The proximity of Pendergast's personal carriage to the red wagon stood out as a clue too pointed to be mere coincidence. The threads of the web began to connect, leading them ever closer to the heart of the conspiracy.

Their investigation was short, interrupted by a gruff voice. "You! Get away from there!" A shabby man, bearing the stains and stench of the scrapyard, strode towards them, his face set in a forbidding scowl as he waved a dirty rag in their direction. "That's Pendergast's property, and he don't like no one sniffin' around. Clear off, or it'll be the worse for ya!"

Crisp sized up the short man, his grimy clothes bespoke of the labors he had seen, similar to any other worker in The Bottoms, yet he instantly decided the man likely was not the wagon driver they pursued due to his short stature. "Apologies my good man; me and the boy were simply cutting through the lot. You say this is Boss Jim's rig? Does he own this lot?"

"Rex Jackson, my boss, owns the lot, Pendergast just parks his wagons here, keeps his horses round the corner, if it's any bizniss to you'uns, but it ain't, so beat it!" he said threateningly.

"Of course, sorry for the imposition."

Reluctantly, Crisp and Percy began to retreat, their thoughts spinning like the wheels of a speeding carriage as they grasped the significance of their discoveries. However, as they turned to leave, Crisp's eye caught a peculiar sight—a large boot print in the mud, markedly similar to one he had seen near the crime scenes. With a sense of renewed purpose, he motioned to Percy to follow the trail. The footprints led them around the back edge of the lot to a narrow alley behind The Pendergast Hotel.

The alley sat quiet, save for the distant clatter of the city beyond. The footprints continued to a back door at the rear of the neighboring hotel, standing slightly ajar as if inviting them to uncover its secrets within. They followed the prints and with a cautious glance, Crisp pushed the door open wider, the creak of its hinges echoing like a warning. He held a finger to his lips and motioned the boy to follow him.

What lay beyond this threshold could very well change everything. They stepped into a darkened hallway, their hearts pounding with the thrill of the chase and the fear of what they might find.

Chapter Ten

I nside Police Headquarters, Crisp sat across from Chief Speers, whose robust demeanor was softened by a hint of skepticism in his eyes. Crisp, with the weight of his recent discoveries pressing upon him, wasted no time in delving into the heart of the matter: the unsettling ties between the grisly murders and the notorious Pendergast machine. He carefully recounted the events of the past few days, detailing every moment that had led to his grim discoveries at the vacant lot, and then paused, giving Speers time to mull it over.

"Surely you don't think Pendergast is behind these frightful murders," Speers exclaimed, his voice a mix of disbelief and concern. The name Pendergast alone was enough to stir a palpable tension in the room, a testament to the man's dark repute in the city's underbelly.

Crisp leaned forward, his expression earnest as he outlined his suspicions. "No, I don't suspect Pendergast himself," he clarified, "but consider this—it must be one of his men. Everything aligns; our suspect likely works in The Bottoms, and fears losing his job. If movements to reform The Bottoms succeed, Pendergast's operations could suffer significantly. It's likely someone within his ranks is trying to maintain their grip by instilling fear or removing certain... obstacles. Maybe they've even been directed to take these actions. It's not the first time you've seen violence from his men."

"I just don't see it," Speers argued, "Pendergast wouldn't take the risk of stirring up negative publicity in his ward. He has enough of that with the movements and religious groups aimed at eradicating the tenderloin district and shutting down the gambling and saloons. No, the way I see it, Pendergast would like nothing more than to shift the focus elsewhere." He rubbed a hand through his thinning hair. "And how do you know this red wagon you found is the one connected to our murders? Are you sure it belongs to Pendergast? Maybe someone else parks it in the lot."

Crisp chewed on his bottom lip as he contemplated Speers' words. "I've got eyes on it as we speak. I'll soon know for sure who uses it, but everything points to Pendergast. It's parked directly behind his hotel, alongside his own private carriage, and just around the corner, at a stable, one of the six horses housed there is a small dun that belongs to Pendergast. That also aligns with our suspicions, and links to the wagon."

Speers deliberated on this for a moment before shifting his thoughts to the rest of Crisp's details. "You said you entered his hotel; did you find anything there?"

"I didn't get very far, just a hallway at the rear where the staff comes and goes. Hotel employees were there, kitchen staff, and I wasn't prepared to justify my presence. I got in and out but I came across something interesting, a possible clue: a set of large boot prints. Someone had spilled paint just outside in the alley, and tracks led from the alley, through the paint, and into the corridor. If you recall, at every crime scene we've seen large boot prints."

"Horsestuff!" Speers cleared his throat expressing his concern, "We need concrete proof. We can't move on Pendergast until we have something solid." The room grew tense as Crisp's theory hung in the air. Speers knew the dangers of meddling with Pendergast's empire, yet the potential breakthrough in the murder investigation, too significant to ignore, required action. Speers frowned, shaking his head. "Crisp, you're seeing shadows where there aren't any. Pendergast's men are crooks, yes, but they're not killers. You're wasting your time chasing phantoms."

Crisp leaned forward, his voice steady and persuasive. "Chief, the evidence points to someone meticulous. The precision, the method—it's not random. These aren't just street thugs we're dealing with. Pendergast's men fit the bill. His influence reaches farther than you think."

Speers glared at Crisp; his voice edged with frustration. "Don't patronize me. I know all too well how far Pendergast's influence reaches. I've been dealing with his tentacles in this city longer than you've been advertising Inquiry Agent for Hire." Speers took a deep breath, letting the air fill his lungs, and slowly exhaled, regaining his composure. "But again, we need solid proof, Crisp, not just theories and hunches."

Crisp began to craft a daring strategy. His next move would be audacious: he would infiltrate Pendergast's organization to unearth the identity of the murderer. "I need to get inside Pendergast's circle," he stated resolutely, his mind already racing through potential approaches to breach the ironclad inner sanctum of the city's most elusive figure. "From the inside I can learn which of his men are at the heart of this."

Speers, clearly concerned, frowned. "I don't know. That's a big gamble. Have you ever met Pendergast? Are any of his men familiar with you?" His questions were pointed, seeking to gauge just how familiar the Crisp name had become in The Bottoms.

"Everyone in The Bottoms knows Boss Jim of course, but no, I've never met him directly or worked with his men. I've seen a few of them around, particularly at his saloon during paydays, or at Christmas when Boss Jim plays the benefactor, doling out coal and holiday turkeys to the needy. But I don't know them well—just faces in the crowd."

"What do you have in mind?"

"I can begin by tailing his men. See who comes and goes, learn how many men there are, figure out who's who. But that will take time. Unless you already have that information."

"I keep tabs on a few of his boys, but I don't interfere in his day-to-day business." He jotted down a few names on a piece of paper and handed it to Crisp. "You'll find their photos in with the others," he said pointing to the room across the hall. "That will save you some time. I'll see what else I can dig up for you, but it won't be much." He offered Crisp a cigar, his mind still tossing ideas back and forth as he lit one for himself. "I'd start by figuring out who uses that wagon."

Crisp nodded in agreement. "I still think my best hope is to get inside his organization. I need to be in his office on a regular basis. I should pose as a person who has a reason to be there. Maybe someone from the hotel staff?" he inquired more to himself than to Speers. "Do you have any ideas?

"Pendergast has two offices, you know—one in The Bottoms and one here, uptown. You'll need to get inside both if you want a real view of how his operations work."

Crisp's eyes widened noticeably at the revelation. "Two offices? That complicates things more than I anticipated, but it also means there are more places where we can find the proof we need."

Speers stepped to his window and pointed across the street to an otherwise non-descript establishment. "That's Pendergast's Saloon there," he said, his voice low and measured. "What most people don't realize is that he has an office right above it, keeps close to the courthouse for his legitimate council errands. But don't let the facade fool you. Pendergast may have different men working from the office in The Bottoms, the ones who handle the seedier side of his businesses. Still, you'll need to infiltrate both locations to get the full picture. It's a dicey endeavor, Crisp."

With a glint of excitement in his eye, Crisp began voicing his thoughts aloud, almost as if he were speaking to himself rather than directly to Speers. "Posing as a hotel employee would get me through the door, but he'd likely smoke me out if I show up too often or poke around his office too much. No, it should be someone who can move freely through his private quarters without raising suspicion." Suddenly, he shot out of his chair and began pacing the room, his thoughts spilling out in rapid succession. "As for the office here in town though—that's a whole different beast. I could blend in as a patron or an employee, but again, that won't grant me unfettered access to his inner sanctum. This is not a quick-in-and-out job. I need time to observe, to gather details, to figure out who is who. I'm afraid you're right, this will be no easy task."

Speers tapped his fingers on the desk. "A legal assistant might work. Pendergast is always looking for legal advice, ways to cover his tracks. Or maybe a liaison from my office."

"Legal assistant," Crisp reflected. "I like that angle. Can you help me get my foot in the door?"

"This is risky business. If they suspect anything, you're as good as dead. And if things go south?"

Crisp smiled confidently. "Then I'll rely on my wits. It's our best shot; I can do this."

"What if you're wrong? What if his men aren't at the heart of this?" Speers sighed, exasperation creeping into his tone. "I'm worried you'll spend all your time infiltrating Pendergast's operation, while the real killer slips through our fingers."

Crisp met his gaze, unflinching. "Give me a couple weeks, Chief. Let me dig a little deeper. If I'm wrong, I'll drop it. But if I'm right, we could bring down not just a killer, but the whole corrupt network."

Speers hesitated, then nodded reluctantly. "Alright, Crisp. Two weeks. But don't make me regret it. And remember, we're just after the killer. I'm not concerned with Pendergast's other business."

Crisp's thoughts tumbled over each other, knowing that finding the killer could unravel more of Pendergast's empire than Speers was willing to acknowledge; it wasn't just about seeking justice for the murders, but the possibility of exposing a much larger web of corruption. He sensed there was something else, Speers was tied closer to Pendergast than he was willing to admit. "I don't want to put you in a bad spot."

Speers nodded slowly. "I can't make any promises, but let me see what I can arrange. Pendergast owes me a favor or two; I think it's time I cashed them in." The weight of his words hung in the air, a reminder of the peril ahead. "With Pendergast, it's always a matter of what you owe him at the end of the day. He has a way of turning the tables in his favor. Don't worry, you're not putting me in a bad spot; it's an ongoing game we play."

Crisp's determination was unshaken, knowing his employment by Pendergast might very well be the key to solving the mystery in The Bottoms.

It was no coincidence that Speers found himself in Pendergast's downtown office later that afternoon—the two men routinely met multiple times throughout the week. The office at 520 Main Street exuded the distinct contrast between legitimacy and the illicit undercurrents that ran through the city's veins. Here, perched above Pendergast's bustling saloon in the heart of the city, Boss Jim orchestrated his empire in downtown Kansas City. The opulent decor served as a facade that masked the less savory aspects of his control over Kansas City's gambling, prostitution, and political dealings.

Pendergast pushed back into his leather chair, holding a glass of whiskey, and swirling the amber liquid thoughtfully before taking a sip. Speers sat across from him, his posture stiff, eyes wary. "Thomas," he began, his tone casual but with an undercurrent of authority, "I want to talk about this new city clean-up effort. Sounds like quite the undertaking."

Speers nodded, his fingers tapping nervously on the armrest of his chair. "It's a comprehensive plan, Jim. We're targeting all the unsavory elements—starting with the slums and back alleys of the city."

Pendergast smiled, a slow, knowing smile. "That's commendable, Thomas. Truly. But you know, I have certain… interests in this city. Businesses that keep a lot of people employed, keep the money flowing." He bent forward, his eyes locking with Speers'. "I'd hate to see those businesses disrupted." Speers fidgeted nervously, recognizing Pendergast's implications.

"Jim, I understand your position. But the mayor's office is pushing hard on this. They want to see results."

Pendergast's smile widened, but his eyes remained cold. "And I want to see you continue as Chief. You've done good work. Work that's been beneficial to both of us." He paused, letting the inference settle. "All I'm asking is that my businesses remain untouched. Just go after the real troublemakers."

Speers took a deep breath, the weight of Pendergast's words pressing down on him. "Jim, I… I'll do what I can. But there are limits to what I can control. But honestly, I don't think you have anything to worry about. Give me a list of places to avoid. I'll have my men start elsewhere. I'll keep your name out of things of course."

Pendergast raised his glass in a mock toast. "Good, that's all I ask, do what you can. Remember, we're in this together. Your support ensures my support." He took another sip, his gaze never leaving Speers. "And what's all this ruckus about policy shops lately?"

"That spark was ignited when the shop near the high school was caught selling to minors. I know this wasn't one of your operations, but it caused quite the stir with the mother's and women's groups. You heard their complaints at City Hall. I'm afraid they won't go away anytime soon."

"I'd like to keep their attention here downtown, not below the bluffs," Pendergast said, offering Speers a cigar. "Would it help if we gave them more situations like that policy shop?"

"What do you mean?"

"Something to stir them up. We can stand up a phony operation, let your men shut it down, give them a few small victories. Lots of press; I'm sure the Baron and his rivals would jump all over that kind of thing."

Speers nodded, a reluctant agreement forming. His career, as much about policing as politics, forced him to carefully navigate the treacherous waters of their conversation. Most of his men, including himself, were on the Pendergast payroll, not just for protection, but also for complicity. The arrangement required Speers to occasionally turn a blind eye to the vice districts under Pendergast's control, a task that weighed on him differently on different days.

But today, Speers had come with a different agenda. He needed to broach the delicate subject—the employment of Algernon Crisp. Crisp an outsider, represented a variable that might upset the careful balance of power and secrecy Pendergast maintained. He had rehearsed his words mentally earlier in the day, and waited for the right angle to introduce the idea without arousing suspicion. Too soon. He decided to play their conversation a little further. "Who can help me on that effort?"

As if on cue, Pendergast leaned back in his chair, steepling his fingers. He smiled at Speers. "Tom," he barked into the adjacent room, summoning his attorney. Moments later, Banwell appeared, his face drawn, the lines deeper than usual from the weight of managing both the legitimate and underworld facets of Pendergast's operations. "I have a little project for you."

Banwell didn't waste time on pleasantries. "Between City Hall and The Bottoms, I'm stretched thin," he complained, his frustration evident as he continued, "What is it?"

"I'll let you coordinate the details with the Chief here, but let's create some sort of rabble that will keep the temperance ladies off Ninth Street; shift their attention here, up town. Have Findlay set up some of his street games here in town, somewhere visible. Let's stir up a ruckus of some kind; Carnes' boys can probably help."

"I can't keep dragging his thugs—excuse me, *our men*—up from The Bottoms to handle things here; they're not cut out for it, and it's starting to show. I could really use some help, someone more capable; someone more genteel."

Pendergast listened; his expression unreadable. The mention of 'thugs' was a sore point; they were necessary for his control, yet he knew their rough edges were unfit for the polished halls of political power.

Banwell's concern was more a testament to the balancing act required to keep their operations afloat. He considered informing Pendergast about how 'the boys' were degrading the clientele in the Main Street saloon by hanging around all day drinking, cussing, and whoring, but he checked himself. Another time, no audience. Instead, he turned to Speers and in a resigned voice said, "Perhaps we can meet in the morning and work out a plan? I have business at the courthouse then."

Speers nodded.

Reading nothing else in Pendergast's eyes, Banwell returned to his office, somewhat mollified that he had at least made his point about being stretched thin.

Satisfied, Pendergast said, "Now, let's enjoy this whiskey." He filled his glass and offered another to Speers. "Do we have anything to discuss?"

Speers saw his opportunity. He spoke slowly at first, his voice low. "Jim, I might have a solution for Tom's problems," he ventured cautiously. "There's a man I know, a trusted friend, sharp and discreet. Algernon Crisp is his name. He could be just the clerk to keep Banwell's affairs in order, both kinds. It's obvious he needs help." Speers held his breath, watching for any flicker of recognition in Pendergast's eyes, but the man's expression remained unreadable, giving nothing away.

Pendergast eyed Speers, a flicker of interest crossing his features. Speers' intriguing proposal played over in his mind—a new player could indeed smooth over the rougher edges of their operations, or could just as easily become a problem. "Tell me more. How do you know this man? What talents does he possess?"

"You may remember the name Crisp, Jonathan Crisp?" Pendergast's face was a stone mask. Speers continued, "The real estate man caught up when things collapsed in '88. His nephew, the man I suggest, was in his employ at that time. I don't believe he was directly involved in his uncle's schemes, but he is a discreet fellow; certainly, anything he may have known at that time hasn't been revealed. He's got a good business sense and some legal background to boot. Honestly, I think he's the perfect man to help out Banwell, and he could start right away."

"Speers, you know I don't trust easily. Why do you think we need another man now? What's driving this urgency?" Pendergast's eyes sharpened as he studied his companion.

Speers took a deep breath. "Jim, your influence is vast, but it's stretched thin. Banwell's operations are becoming more complex, and your enemies are getting bolder. Having a legal advisor like Crisp could safeguard our interests, cover the loopholes, and keep our hands clean. Besides, with the political climate shifting, we need someone who can navigate the legalities with finesse."

Pendergast leaned back in his chair, swirling the whiskey in his glass. "And why Crisp? Why not someone already within our circle?"

"Because Crisp is an outsider, but one who understands our world. He's not tainted by our past, which gives him a level of plausible deniability. Moreover, his discreet nature means he can operate without drawing attention. We need someone who can handle both the legitimate and the not-so-legitimate aspects of your business. Crisp fits that bill."

Pendergast's expression remained unreadable, but behind that stone façade, his mind was tossing over the implications. The thought of having a man who could legally shield them was appealing. "Alright, Speers. I'll give him a chance. But mark my words, if he falters, it'll be on your head." A gambler at heart, Pendergast knew that Speers had never steered him wrong. "Bring him in," he decided, his voice carrying a finality that left no room for doubt.

Speers nodded; his relief mingled with the anxiety of what he had just set in motion. "Understood, Jim. I'll make the arrangements."

Pendergast raised his glass, signaling the end of the discussion. "To new alliances, then. Let's hope this man Crisp is as sharp as you say."

They clinked glasses, each man lost in his thoughts about the uncertain future that lay ahead.

Crisp's initial steps into the Pendergast organization at 520 Main Street two days later, felt more mundane than he had anticipated. As the newly appointed assistant to Thomas Banwell, his schedule was filled with typing, delivering messages to the courthouse, and attending to paperwork, lots of paperwork—far from the intrigue and danger he had braced himself for. Beneath the veneer of administrative monotony, the undercurrents of a much darker world pulsed, and Crisp was keen to learn.

It quickly became apparent that his appointment also worked against him. Just a few days into his assignment, he was no longer able to supplement his income with card games, nor able to continue his investigations in The Bottoms. He now had to rely on both Cassie and Percy to keep their eyes and ears open for telltale signs of the killer he pursued. By day, he worked from the office seeking to unravel the mysteries within, and by night, he orchestrated a street-level investigation. Percy, with his network of street urchins, monitored the vacant lot, tracking the comings and goings of the wagons and the men who drove them. Cassie, meanwhile, leveraged her 'sisters' in the trade to keep a close eye on The Bottoms, gathering whispers and rumors from clients about the girls who had fallen victim.

Yet, from his modest desk strategically positioned just outside of Pendergast's private office, Crisp meticulously monitored the activities of the organization's key players and began to understand the inner workings of the organization. Each day, he observed their movements, piecing together the intricate web of the Pendergast machine from within. He quickly became familiar with the men on a first-name basis, learning their responsibilities and schedules. Some were familiar faces, while others he rapidly assessed, building a detailed profile in his mind on each of them.

He immediately recognized Ed Findlay from the gaming halls on Ninth Street. His meticulous dress and confident swagger marked him as the overseer of the gambling rackets. The papers had labeled him 'Policy Boss', furthering his notoriety in the city. Findlay, with his rakish appearance, and stylish clothing, carried himself with an air of superiority, often accompanied by admiring glances from the ladies who frequented the saloon beneath the office.

Next, there was Felix Wexler, the accountant, a man of precise habits and conservative dress, who managed the financial lifeline of the operation. His turned-up collars and oiled hair parted down the middle were as orderly as the precise books he kept. Wexler moved quietly through the halls, often carrying stacks of bills and ledger books that detailed the flow of money throughout the enterprise—details that never left his person.

In contrast to both, Thomas Banwell commanded a different kind of respect. Approaching sixty, his demeanor was calm yet authoritative. He had dark hair speckled with grey, and a white beard framing his face, and he dressed for daily appearances at the courthouse. As Pendergast's attorney and fixer, he acted as linchpin in the operation, his advice crucial, his actions deliberate. Banwell made things happen, ensuring that all parts of the Pendergast empire worked in seamless harmony.

Patrick Carnes, the bodyguard, was hard to miss. Towering over most, his broad frame and pugilistic face spoke of his primary role—protection. Carnes was a stark figure, his presence a clear message to any who thought to challenge Pendergast. His interactions were brief, often laced with a sternness that left no room for argument. He and his men held the press at arm's length, shielded Pendergast during public appearances, and when directed, they delivered a clinched fist to sway public opinion in the desired direction.

Crisp's daily work load doled out by Banwell kept him from interacting with most of the men directly. He shared a tiny space with Banwell adjacent to Pendergast's office, but Crisp's interactions were limited primarily to Banwell, and Pendergast's personal valet and butler, Dermot Gallagher. Gallagher was a proper man, with waxed mustache and impeccable attire, he managed all of Pendergast's personal and domestic affairs with a precision that bordered on the obsessive. To Gallagher, everyone besides his employer merited a certain disdain, which he barely bothered to hide.

Crisp spent his first days getting situated, trying to discern the intricate web of who was who. Despite spending nearly twelve hours a day at the office, the hierarchy within the organization remained an enigma. He had yet to find the opportunity to get to know his colleagues within the organization beyond casual chats, as Banwell had kept him tightly by his side throughout the first week. Their time had been split between long days at the courthouse and afternoons that drug wearily into the evening at the Main Street office.

Spending so much time on Main Street had kept Crisp away from the men whom Speers had identified as targets of interest: Wyse, Taffe, Haggan, and Dowling. He'd found a photo in Speers' rogue's gallery of each of them and had been on the watch all week. The men were notably absent from the downtown office for most of that initial week, and Crisp was only briefly introduced during their passing. Crisp speculated there likely were others on the payroll working exclusively from The Bottoms whom he had yet to encounter.

It was the end of the first full week in the office before he got his first opportunity to delve deeper. With a batch of correspondence to deliver to Pendergast himself, Crisp noticed four men had entered the boss's office and had not yet emerged. Seizing the moment, he paused by the ajar door. Inside, a heated discussion unfolded among the men. Findlay debated the logistics of an upcoming dice game, while Wexler expressed concerns about cash flow disruptions. Carnes grumbled about new security measures, and Banwell, orchestrating the conversation with a firm yet conciliatory tone, steered the men back to focus.

Crisp's ears pricked up as he caught fragments of Pendergast's voice, giving direction to his men. From what he could make out, Pendergast schemed with instructions to relocate a dice game from The Bottoms to the downtown area. It was clear Pendergast intended to shift attention away from The Bottoms, to draw eyes away from his more nefarious activities still operating there. Crisp sensed a calculated move, one that hinted at deeper layers of Pendergast's strategy.

He lingered a moment longer, absorbing every word. Though the brief eavesdropping session revealed nothing incriminating, it offered invaluable insight into the tangled web of duties and loyalties. He knew this was the first step to unraveling the mysteries at the heart of the Pendergast empire. He pressed his ear closer to the sliver made by the ajar door, straining to catch every word of Pendergast's conversation. His concentration was abruptly broken by the sound of footsteps approaching. He straightened up just as Gallagher entered the room, eyes narrowing with immediate suspicion.

"Mr. Crisp," he acknowledged after they made brief eye contact, his voice edged with apprehension, "something I can assist with?"

Crisp forced a smile, trying to appear nonchalant. "Ah Dermot, good timing. I have some papers to deliver to the Boss. Not wanting to interrupt, I was waiting for the right moment. But now that you're here, perhaps you could leave these on his desk for me? I'll pick them up later."

Gallagher's eyes darted from Crisp to the door behind him,

his manner still guarded. "I'll take care of it," he replied in a haughty tone, clearly put off by Crisp's request.

"Thank you," Crisp said, handing over the documents. Gallagher entered the meeting, closing the door behind him. Crisp returned to his desk, retreating into the quiet corner of his office, immersing himself once again in the mundane flow of administrative tasks.

Beneath the surface, his mind buzzed, turning over the fragments of conversation he had overheard, each detail a potential key to the puzzle he was determined to unlock.

Chapter Eleven

The rain had ceased, and as Crisp finished a quick meal at a diner on Main Street—ham and beans, and coffee for two bits—he watched a streetcar trundle by, slowing at the intersection of Fifth and Main. His Monday morning had been a blur of tedium and fatigue as he plowed through a stack of letters and correspondence, each prepared by Banwell over the weekend. The monotony wore on Crisp until he finally seized a moment of reprieve, delivering the paperwork to the courthouse and pausing just long enough to grab a quick bite to eat. The thought of returning to the office was unappealing, and he considered his next move in his investigation.

Crisp toyed with the idea of heading directly to Pendergast's office in The Bottoms, crafting a simple enough excuse—Banwell needed some documents fetched. Once there, he could quietly observe which of Pendergast's men were active in that corner of the city and identify any faces he'd yet to place. Percy and his gang had been keeping a diligent watch on the back lot behind the hotel, but the wagons, their drivers, and their movements had remained frustratingly elusive. It left Crisp no closer to unraveling the activities at the hotel office than a week ago. Still, he knew better than to rush in. He'd hold off visiting until he'd had a chance to review Banwell's schedule, waiting for the opening he needed to slip away from Main Street.

Similarly, Cassie's inquiries had turned up little of value. The most intriguing—and absurd—rumor she'd uncovered was that an escaped circus animal had been responsible for mauling some of the recent victims.

He laughed to himself as he finished a cup of coffee while staring through a large plate glass window looking out onto Main Street. By a stroke of good fortune, his gaze caught Jim Dowling, Rory Taffe, and Bill Haggan boarding a streetcar just as it jolted back into motion. He hadn't realized the trio had been in the Main Street office, likely missing them while they loitered in the saloon downstairs. He'd left through the rear of the building, oblivious to their presence, and now cursed himself for the oversight.

Quickly paying his bill, he dashed into the streets, eyes fixed on their trolley car as it trundled toward The Junction, the aptly named corner at the convergence of Delaware and Main. He hurried uphill, weaving through pedestrians, and in the distance, spotted the three men disembarking from the trolley further down the street. They crossed Main and headed east along Seventh Street, slipping out of Crisp's view.

He raced headlong up the block and crossed the busy intersection, continuing down Seventh. The three men were nowhere in sight, as he cautiously maneuvered along the sidewalk, inspecting every shop window he passed. When he reached the corner of Seventh and Walnut, he couldn't help notice a crowd gathering on the south side of the block outside the Grand Opera House. On the opposite southeast corner stood the magnificent Midland Hotel, bustling with a throng of visitors. Both venues seemed far too grand for Pendergast's men.

Looking north up Walnut, his attention was drawn to a round sign glowing with white light: a pool hall—an obvious destination for the three ruffians. He moved down the block and, as he passed the hall's large window, he spotted the three men inside, huddled around a billiard table. The room was populated with several other patrons, both men and women, all drinking, and all engaged in animated conversations and competitive billiards. He continued several paces past the pool hall as he deliberated his course of action. From a hotel lobby across the street, he could survey their movements, but that offered no insight into their conversations; he wanted to be within earshot.

He decided to venture inside, moving stealthily to avoid being noticed by the three men, and found a spot at the end of the bar, keeping a watchful eye on the billiard table where they huddled. For several minutes, he sipped a beer, watching as Taffe and Haggan played pool and steadily grew more inebriated, meanwhile, Dowling lounged off to the side with a dolly mop he had picked up. The faint glow from the gas lamps and the lingering fog of tobacco smoke painted these men in their natural habitat, their rough edges softened by the shadows. After nearly an hour, Crisp concluded there wasn't much to learn from his targets. He decided to move across the street and wait until the three men left so he could follow them from there. But his plans were abruptly cut short when Taffe approached the bar and asked for a bottle of whiskey. Crisp turned his back and tried to hide his face, but Taffe spotted him immediately.

"Mr. Crisp, what are you doing here?"

He feigned a surprised look. "Just stopped off for a pint after a day at the courthouse."

"Why don't you join the boys," Taffe insisted, putting his arm around Crisp's shoulder and urging him toward the billiard table.

As they approached the table, Taffe announced, "Look who I found at the bar."

"Didn't know you were an admirer of billiards, Mr. Crisp," Dowling said with a derisive tone, his eyes declaring his unmistakable suspicion.

Crisp attempted to deflect with a casual tone. "I've knocked a few balls around in my time," he said, forcing a lighthearted smile.

Taffe and Haggan couldn't resist the opportunity and tempted Crisp with a sizable bet, eager to relieve him of his newly earned pay. They played several rounds, and Crisp, to his own surprise, managed to hold his own, and broke even after two hours. As he played with Taffe and Haggan, Dowling sat the entire time, perched on a stool, swigging from a whiskey bottle, and entertaining his girl with watchful eyes never straying far from Crisp.

His camaraderie with Taffe and Haggan finally gave him the chance he had been waiting for; a chance to carouse with the Pendergast boys and learn more about their business out of the office. He broached the topic with a calculated nonchalance. "Thought you usually hung around The Climax? What brings you boys downtown?"

Taffe, always eager to talk, grinned. "This is our favorite spot when we're working on Main."

Dowling hung back, his eyes watching with suspicion, clearly reluctant to share much. Crisp pressed on. "Do you all stay close by when you're downtown? Seems like a long jaunt back to the hotel after a long night."

Haggan shrugged. The sharp crack of the cue in his hands echoed through the hall as the cue-ball collided forcefully with the six-ball, sending it spinning across the green felt and into the corner pocket with a satisfying thunk. "We just stay at the hotel."

Taffe, unable to help himself, added, "We ring up Wyse to give us a lift. He brings the boss's carriage around so we can travel in style." He chuckled, "We come here to let off a little steam, if you know what I mean."

Dowling's glare silenced Taffe, and he sneered at Crisp, "What about you, Crisp? You can't afford to stay downtown. Must be quite an inconvenience having to work on Main when your gambling and whoring is centered down in The Bottoms." Crisp took the jibe in stride, his face impassive. Although the taunt suggested Dowling was more familiar with his own private choices than he was with Dowling's. He lined up a shot, but then had second thoughts, and moved to the other side of the table. "True, downtown hotels are too rich for my blood." He chose to let it lie. Still, Dowling's comment resonated sharply as he considered its implied meaning. He'd seen Pendergast's men in The Climax Saloon and others in The Bottoms on too many occasions to count, but never realized he'd been under watchful eyes too.

He decided to steer the conversation back to his line of questioning; it was apparent, Taffe was the talker. "What about the others? Does Wyse ever join you away from the office?" Crisp hunched over the billiard table with refined skill, his movements smooth and calculating. With a precise stroke, he sent the cue ball gliding effortlessly, sinking both the two-ball and the five-ball into their respective pockets in a single, elegant shot.

Haggan scowled in frustration and Taffe laughed aloud. "Boss has him and that new fella Skahill working all the time, moving goods, picking up deliveries, running him and his family around town. Besides, they ain't got the brains for gamblin' and lord help us if they ever get liquored up – they'd be no match for anyone trying to contain them." Haggan nodded in agreement.

Crisp was about to delve deeper when a commotion erupted at the other end of the table. The sudden noise drew everyone's attention, effectively ending his line of questioning. He watched as the boys turned to see what was happening, his thoughts already piecing together the fragments of information he'd gathered. At some point during his queries, his attention had wavered away from Dowling, and now Dowling's voice sliced through the air, halting their game. Taffe and Haggan looked up, concern etched on their faces, prompting Crisp to follow their gaze.

Dowling stood face to face with a man of equal stature. "I said apologize to the lady," Dowling demanded, his tone cold and unwavering.

The other man stood his ground, casting a sideways glance and a sly smile at his friends. He began to reply with a clever smirk, but before the words could form, Dowling's fist crashed into his jaw with brutal precision.

Taffe and Haggan leaped into action, holding the surrounding men at bay with their pool cues while Dowling continued his assault. Dowling, the more skilled fighter, swiftly gained the upper hand. After delivering several punishing blows, he seized the man by the arm, twisting him around and slamming him face down on a pool table, shoving Crisp aside in the heat of the scuffle. Blood and spittle oozed from the corner of the man's mouth, staining the felt.

Dowling pressed the man's head against the table. "I said apologize to the lady."

"Fuck you," the man grunted, struggling to break free, but Dowling held him firmly pinned. With a sadistic grin, Dowling motioned to Taffe, snatching a cigar from his hand. Slowly, he brought the glowing tip close to the man's cheek. The man thrashed harder, but Dowling's iron grip, concealed beneath his cultured attire, was unyielding. Dowling pressed the burning end of the cigar against the man's face, the sickening sizzle mingling with the man's shouts and curses. Finally, the man succumbed to the agony. "I'm sorry, I'm sorry, Jeezis!"

Dowling pulled the man up and turned him to face his girl, who watched in shocked fascination. "Now say it to the lady."

"I'm sorry, miss. I didn't mean anything by it," the man stammered.

Dowling shoved the man into the waiting arms of his friends, who stood by in apprehension under the watchful glare of

Taffe and Haggan. "Does anyone else have something to say to my lady friend?" Dowling challenged, his voice dripping with menace. When all eyes averted his, he returned to the woman, who began to massage his tender knuckles while he took a long swig from the whiskey bottle. He scanned the room with a cold, triumphant glare, but everyone had moved on.

With a fierce brutality, Dowling closed the gap with his woman and slapped her with the back of his hand threateningly, "Next time I catch you making eyes, you'll get it even worse." He motioned again with his hand, causing his girl to cower in fear. He then took another swig of whiskey and pulled her close to his side.

Taffe put his arm around Crisp's shoulder. "You should hang with us more often, Mr. Crisp. Never a dull moment!"

———

The next morning, Crisp sat across from Banwell, who was hunched over his cluttered desk littered with papers and ink bottles. A chill seeped through the tall, narrow windows across from them, but neither man seemed to notice, absorbed as they were in their work. Banwell had remained silent most of the morning and Crisp couldn't decide if he was still upset with Crisp's weak explanation for having not returned to the office yesterday, or whether he was just overwhelmed with the workload in front of him. Crisp had been walking on eggshells with Banwell, but finally chose to test the waters.

"Thomas, for this next letter to the city council, how do you suggest we phrase our concerns about the sanitation issues in

The North End?" Crisp asked, his pen poised above the paper.

Banwell rubbed his chin thoughtfully. "Start with acknowledging the ongoing efforts, then transition into the more specific issues. It's always good to begin on a positive note."

Crisp nodded, making notes. "Good point. It's about gaining their trust, isn't it? Speaking of which, Thomas, I've been wondering about something else... How do you think I might get better acquainted with the others here? They view me as an outsider?"

Banwell looked up, surprised by the shift in topic. "Trust takes time, Crisp. Why? Is there someone you're having trouble with?"

"Just a thought," Crisp murmured, his mind ticking through possibilities of how to deepen his strategic alliances within the complex political landscape. "Perhaps if I had a chance to work from the hotel office occasionally, I would have a chance to engage with the others?"

With a perturbed look, Banwell added, "You'll get your chance soon enough." Without another word, he buried himself back into his work.

In the preceding days, Crisp had only had a chance to bump into a few of Pendergast's men. Colin Wyse and Denis Skahill, both known for their routine work in The Bottoms, had been spotted making deliveries to the Main Street office where Crisp worked, but he'd had no opportunity to socialize with either of them. Their mere presence in the Main Street office revealed that there were more men behind the scenes, working seamlessly between both locations. It was a clear sign that Crisp still had much to learn about the full extent of Pendergast's operations.

He weighed the likely suspects among Pendergast's men that he had seen thus far, focusing on those of formidable stature. If he followed his instinct and looked for a towering figure, it narrowed the field to Wyse, Skahill, and Carnes. Carnes, noted for his temper, and Skahill, for his sheer physicality, were obvious suspects. Yet, Wyse, with his quiet demeanor and routine access to the boss's resources—horses, wagons, and the like—seemed oddly suitable. However, Wyse's reserved nature made him an enigma, elusive in both personal detail and character.

Seeking more, Crisp broached the topic with Banwell. "How long have the others been in Mr. Pendergast's employ?" he inquired cautiously.

Banwell looked up, the irritation apparent in his expression. "Most have been here from the start," he answered briskly, returning to his paperwork. Pausing, perhaps to forestall further inquiry, he added, "You're the newest, aside from that Skahill fellow."

Crisp held back, acutely aware of the delicate nature of his inquiry.

Banwell, sensing an undercurrent, remarked with a dismissive tone, "Seems like you and Denis have both benefited from Mr. Pendergast's patronage," making it clear he had no interest in delving deeper.

Crisp realized that with the burden of tasks Banwell had piled on throughout the week, his sole chance to conduct any personal investigations would arise only after Banwell had called it a night. Then, he could stealthily follow one of his colleagues to ascertain their residences and activities during the evening hours. He had stationed Percy in the vicinity of St. Louis Avenue in order to keep an eye on the hotel throughout the week, but hadn't yet found a moment to rendezvous with his young accomplice to catch up on his observations. He decided to test the waters. "Thomas, I've finished up with this correspondence. Would it be alright if I pop off a tad bit early today... to handle some personal matters?"

Before Banwell could reply, the door creaked open and Colin Wyse stepped in, his presence filling the room with an air of expectancy as he answered Banwell's summons from Gallagher. Banwell was prompt with his orders, "Mr. Pendergast has changed his plans; he's decided to walk today. No need for a carriage. But if you can take care of that list, the one I gave you yesterday, get it done by end of day, if you please."

Wyse lingered by the door, clearly waiting but seemingly aimless. An idea sparked in Crisp's mind, a way to utilize this change of plans to his advantage. It seemed that Banwell read his mind.

"Colin, since you're here, and it seems Mr. Pendergast won't be needing you right away, would you mind if Crisp tags along on your other errands? He has to drop off some correspondence at the courthouse and could use a lift." Banwell winked imperceptibly toward Crisp.

Wyse, caught off guard, nodded. "Okay. C'mon, I'm headed to the market district now."

As they stepped into a fine mist of rain, a steady drizzle too subtle to notice but impossible to ignore, Crisp pulled his coat tight around him to fend off the pervasive dampness he felt more than saw. Within seconds, unseen droplets of water moistened his face and a breeze chilled his wet skin causing him to hunch his shoulders in an attempt to cover the back of his neck with his collar.

The walk was brief and quiet at first, but Crisp's mind was far from still. They moved out the front of the building, idling to the side alley adjacent to Pendergast's uptown saloon, and he was already formulating questions, ways to casually extract information from Wyse without seeming too pointed.

"So, Colin, how long have you been driving for Mr. Pendergast?" Crisp ventured as they approached Pendergast's carriage.

"Dunno, maybe two years," Wyse replied flatly, untethering his horse. "We have to go change out wagons. I can't be carrying boxes in this fancy chaise."

"Understood," Crisp replied, easing into the seat beside Wyse. He settled in, admiring the carriage's plush velvet upholstery and thankful for the canopy taut above them. Hoping to coax more information from Wyse, he probed further, "I'd imagine driving Mr. Pendergast around provides you with quite a unique view of the city's affairs, does it not?"

Wyse shrugged his shoulders noncommittally, "Mebbe." He tugged at the reins and the black gelding attached to the carriage responded, pulling them out into the bustling traffic on Main Street. Crisp scrutinized Wyse with a discreet, yet sharp eye as they traveled. Wyse was a broad-shouldered, gruff-looking man, his face hardened from years of toiling under the sun. His hands, large and calloused, spoke of physical labor, and his clothes, though well-worn, were clean and functional. The brim of his hat cast a shadow over his deep-set eyes, adding an air of mystery that Crisp found simultaneously intriguing and alarming.

Turning the carriage away from Main, Wyse steered them down Fifth Street, eventually pulling into an empty lot on Grand Street, nestled between Fifth and Missouri Avenue. Here, they switched to a flatbed farm wagon, its sideboards slick and reflecting the morning light. It wasn't the enclosed wagon Crisp had anticipated, which he guessed remained in The Bottoms for other uses, but this change reinforced his notion of Wyse maintaining a separate set of vehicles for different tasks uptown.

While Wyse busied himself transferring the horse between wagons, Crisp decided to probe for information. "How many horses do you have?"

"Four," Wyse said flatly. "Why?"

"Just wondering. I suppose you have different ones for different purposes—" it was intended to be a question, but he sensed Wyse's growing irritation.

Wyse ignored the comment with a roll of his eyes, making it clear he had nothing more to say. He hopped into the elevated driver's seat mounted on robust springs, and Crisp squeezed in beside him to avoid the discomfort of riding in the back, which offered no accommodation, even for a short trip. Crisp fished an umbrella from under the seat and huddled beneath its flimsy covering, finding scant refuge from the encroaching mist. The trip over to the courthouse was quick, and he tried eagerly to pry more out of Wyse while he had the chance. "I see you routinely move between the hotel office and the one on Main? Are there certain days when you work at one location or the other?"

Wyse's tone was tinged with annoyance as he gave a heavy sigh, "Depends on what the Boss wants." Approaching the courthouse, Crisp tried to get one last query in, "You seem to have access to a variety of wagons and carriages. Are they split between uptown and The Bottoms, or do you maintain a single fleet stored elsewhere in the city?" Just as he was about to push farther, Wyse interjected sharply, halting the inquiry and the wagon in the same motion, "Look cove, I ain't lookin' for a new friend… I got stuff to do for the Boss. This is where you get off."

Crisp stepped down from his perch and reached out to hand Wyse the umbrella, but Wyse snapped the reins and moved on, ignoring Crisp entirely.

Despite the rain, downtown Kansas City pulsed with the vibrant thrum of progress. The streets were alive with the clip-clop of horse-drawn wagons and the incessant clanging of streetcars. Outside the courthouse, men in tailored suits and women in long skirts moved purposefully along the sidewalks beneath parasols and umbrellas, while newsboys shouted the latest headlines at passersby. Amidst this bustling scene, Crisp stood, his eyes tracking the movements of Wyse—a man he still suspected could be the murderer he sought. Wyse's emotions were clear, he had no interest in conversing with Crisp.

Undeterred, Crisp followed Wyse on foot at a discreet distance. As he navigated through the crowded streets, he saw Wyse make his way back to the Junction, a well-known hub where local businessmen and workers converged for quick transactions and casual chatter. Wyse parked the wagon, but didn't linger; he made brief visits to retail stores along the block, each stop seemingly pre-planned and efficient. From there, he traveled by wagon to a cigar shop on the corner of Seventh and Delaware, barely pausing as he exchanged a few words with the shopkeeper from his seat in the wagon. A swift handshake sealed the encounter, something discreetly changing hands. Crisp's curiosity intensified—what kind of dealings was Wyse involved in that demanded such secrecy?

Next, Wyse headed to a liquor wholesale warehouse several blocks south on Main, where he spent some time inside before a group of men emerged with another set of packages, loading them into the back of his wagon with practiced ease while Wyse watched nervously, casting furtive glances along the street.

Finally, Wyse drove his wagon into a narrow alley off Fourth Street and Main Street. He parked and glanced around cautiously before stepping down and securing the horse and wagon. With a swift look over his shoulder, Wyse slipped through a nondescript door—a door that Crisp knew led to one of the city's quieter brothels.

Crisp lingered at the mouth of a nearby alley across the street, exhausted from his foot chase. His mind worked overtime with all the day's observations which had provided more questions than answers; but he was now certain that Colin Wyse was deeply embedded in the underbelly of Kansas City. As Wyse disappeared into the shadows of the brothel, Crisp made a mental note to dig deeper into the man's connections at another time. He hunkered under his umbrella, just inside the alleyway, the shadows wrapping around him as he contemplated his next move. If Wyse's afternoon respite didn't last long, he would continue tailing the man for the remainder of the day; otherwise, he felt he was wasting time. Wyse had become his prime suspect, yet he pondered whether to spend all of his time in this single pursuit and wondered instead if Percy had noted any unusual behavior of the various men working at the hotel below the bluffs.

By coincidence, or perhaps serendipitous fortune, Crisp looked up to see young Percy on the opposite side of the street, heading south towards Pendergast's saloon. A sharp whistle from Crisp caught the boy's attention. The boy swiftly dodged a streetcar and meandered around busy horse traffic on Main to arrive at Crisp's location.

"H'lo, Colonel. I was just coming to find you."

"Have you got anything for me?"

"I watched the hotel like you said and kept my eye out for those big men. The one named Carnes, he stays in Toad-a-Loop, a little shack where he keeps his girlfriend. She has three kids running around, but I don't think they're his."

"I see," Crisp pondered, recalling the slum district perched on a bluff on the extreme south side of The Bottoms. "What else?"

"Them other two big fellas, Wyse and Skill, they keep rooms at Pendergast's and only leave when they're doing jobs for Boss Jim."

Crisp nodded, taking in the information.

"And then you got the rough boys, I call them. Taffy and Haggan must keep rooms at the hotel too cause they're always hanging 'round The Climax and never seem to leave the hotel. Dowling, he visits lots of soiled doves and must sleep in their rooms, otherwise he's at Pendergast's playing cards and drinkin'. I ain't seen most of them around at all today, so that's why I headed down here."

"That is all very good, my boy," Crisp said, fishing a handful of coins from his pocket for the boy. He considered all that Percy had shared. He could see Percy awaited his next assignment. "Let's keep an eye on Wyse and Skahill. I've been tracking Wyse today. You head back to the hotel and watch the movements of Skahill. Specifically, watch that backlot and see if he goes there. You remember we saw Pendergast's carriage there? Wyse is the boss's personal driver, but we need to know if Skahill, or any of the other men use that red wagon."

The boy nodded eagerly and rushed off, ready to grab something to eat before returning to his duties in The Bottoms. As Crisp waited out Wyse's afternoon repose, he knew it would take all his efforts, plus the aid of his companions Percy, Cassie, and Moreland, to keep track of all of Pendergast's men, but he also knew he only a had a few more days to meet the deadline Speers had given him.

By the end of the next week, Crisp finally got his chance to visit the Pendergast office in The Bottoms, located at the rear of the building above his notorious hotel. He'd been instructed to enter through the lobby, where he'd find a flight of stairs tucked behind the front desk, ascending to Pendergast's suite.

While Crisp had visited the adjoined Climax Saloon on numerous occasions, he had never set foot into the hotel proper, and on this first visit he was impressed with the lavish décor. Crystal chandeliers cast a soft, golden glow over the entire space.

Richly patterned carpets, woven with intricate designs, hushed each step, while plush velvet armchairs invited guests to bask in the luxurious surroundings. Gilt-framed paintings adorned the walls, depicting serene landscapes and classical scenes, adding an artistic touch to the ambiance. Elegant marble statues, polished to a high sheen, stood proudly, reflecting the soft light and enhancing the sense of grandeur. The atmosphere was a perfect blend of sophistication and warmth.

The steps behind the front desk took him into another world, stark and utilitarian, and stripped of any unnecessary ornamentation. Its bare wooden floors and plain furniture spoke of a no-nonsense approach to business.

He stepped into the bustling office of Pendergast in the midst of a murmur of scheming voices, and was greeted with cold derision and furtive glances laced with icy contempt from some of his peers. He handed a packet of letters to Banwell and took a position on the far side of the room near the wood-fired stove for warmth.

From his vantage point, he surveyed the Spartan surroundings, suspecting that only Pendergast's inner circle ever met here, conducting their affairs with an emphasis on efficiency and discretion. In contrast to the Main Street office's close proximity to the courthouse, where Pendergast entertained guests and conducted more formal business, the juxtaposition of the two locations underscored the dual nature of Pendergast's operations—one side polished and public, the other shadowy and secretive.

Pendergast, with a portly figure and commanding presence, sat behind his massive oak desk covered in papers and ledgers.

Today he orchestrated the distribution of coal to needy families—a usual winter benevolence that doubled as a political maneuver to secure the loyalty of his constituents. Around him, his staff moved with a well-practiced efficiency that spoke of numerous operations conducted from this very room. Crisp had nothing to do with the effort, but remained near the side of the room when he had not been asked to leave.

Carnes discussed security arrangements with his enforcers. Among them, Jim Dowling stood out to Crisp with his neat mustache and handsome features that contrasted his readiness to inflict pain at Carnes' command. Beside him, Rory Taffe adjusted his wide-brimmed fedora and scanned the room through beady eyes. His thin mustache twitched as he cracked a sly joke under his breath to Bill Haggan, who responded with a youthful, reckless laugh. Haggan's slicked hair and juvenile demeanor contrasted sharply with the hardened lines of violence etched into his face. Carnes' frigid look warned the men to listen seriously to Pendergast's plans.

"Patrick, your men will keep things orderly today, no rough stuff," Pendergast interjected as the banter among the men grew louder. "Just make sure everyone gets their fair share without any commotion; nice and orderly."

On the periphery, Denis Skahill loomed silently in the back of the room opposite Crisp. His large hands, misshapen face, and over-sized chin made him an imposing figure, yet his movements were gentle—in stark contrast to the brusqueness of Wyse who stood next to him. They talked in hushed tones; Wyse shirking a menial task and delegating it to Skahill.

Pendergast's voice, authoritative and impatient, sliced

through the babel of the room, reaching the two men with the same veracity as those huddled around his desk, ensuring no detail was overlooked. "Colin, you two bag the coal into bundles; it's easier to hand out than shoveling into random containers."

Pendergast briefed Banwell on leveraging the event for maximum exposure. "I'll deliver a brief speech and meet with the public. Ensure the press captures the goodwill we're spreading. As the winter chill deepens, our generosity must shine even warmer," he directed. Banwell acknowledged, his thoughts swiftly crafting potential headlines around those words that would cast his boss in a benevolent light. He had arranged for one of the Baron's men to spotlight the distribution, aiming to generate some positive news from The Bottoms in *The Star* for once.

"When the wagon is empty, let's parade back to The Climax and dole out pay as usual. Felix, you should head there first thing and line that up, Carnes will follow to secure the area before I arrive."

With the plans set and everyone briefed, the group began to disperse. Crisp, who had been a silent observer until now, lingered at a desk just outside Pendergast's office, his involvement in the coal scheme conspicuously absent. Banwell had assigned him to a stack of paperwork piled high to keep him occupied while the others took part in the elaborate publicity stunt. As his colleagues filed out, their chatter fading into the distance, Crisp methodically shuffled through the papers, biding his time.

This was the first opportunity he'd had to be alone in one

of the offices. He'd considered a nighttime break-in to either location, but the logistics were too complex, the risks too high; instead, he chose to wait for the right opportunity which now appeared at hand. As the office settled into a hushed stillness, Crisp took a chance. His heart quickened with anticipation and doubt. Was everyone truly accounted for? Could there be anyone else who might appear unexpectedly? Despite his second thoughts, the opportunity was too good to overlook.

With careful, measured steps, he rose from his seat and approached Pendergast's office door. He took a deep breath, steadied his nerves, and slipped inside, ready to uncover the secrets hidden within. The room was now quiet, the air cool, yet the scent of tobacco and whiskey lingered heavily. He began by examining the papers on Pendergast's desk, searching for any clue that might link the political boss to the ongoing murders. It was a long shot at best as Crisp really didn't suspect Pendergast's involvement, but still, he hoped to find something—a missive or other directive suggesting Boss Jim had given instruction on the retributions. Crisp's heart pounded. He knew the risk involved in snooping around Pendergast's inner sanctum, yet he pressed on.

All of the paperwork on Pendergast's desk seemed legit; he found nothing in writing that could be used against the man. Everything was on the up and up. Then Crisp reflected on his recent attendance in other meetings. It was Banwell who normally took notes, Pendergast never put anything in writing regarding his schemes. If there was anything to be found, it must be in Banwell's personal notebook, which he carried with him everywhere he went.

Crisp's focus shifted as he stumbled upon a partially finished letter from Pendergast to a fellow councilman, written in Pendergast's own hand. The incomplete message revealed Pendergast's irritation with the Parks Board. While the letter didn't provide any evidence to speculate on Pendergast's planning to retaliate against the parks movement, the terse phrasing made Pendergast's dissatisfaction with the recent proposals of the board palpably clear. Yet it wasn't the letter's content that held Crisp's interest. There was something else—had he seen this before? Lost in thought over the meaning of the message, he was startled when he heard the sudden creak of the office door behind him. His breath hitched as he turned, finding himself frozen with his hand still on the letter—an incriminating pose that left no room for excuses.

Banwell stood framed in the doorway, his expression a mixture of surprise and suspicion. He entered the room, as Crisp snapped shut a drawer at Pendergast's desk. His fingers had barely left the handle when he turned to face Banwell, his expression a careful blend of innocence and surprise. "Ah, hello, Tom, just looking for a blank envelope. Need to send some correspondence over to the courthouse," he explained, his voice steady despite the rush of adrenaline.

Banwell raised an eyebrow, his gaze lingering on the desk before meeting Crisp's eyes. "You'll find supplies in the other room, Crisp," he said, his tone light but with a firmness that hinted at unspoken boundaries. "Pendergast's desk isn't the place for everyone to rummage through."

Crisp straightened up, feeling a flush of embarrassment rise to his cheeks. "I'm sorry, Mr. Banwell," he began, his voice earnest. "I didn't mean to overstep. Still learning the ropes," he added with a mock grin.

Banwell's expression softened, but his voice remained stern. "I understand, but there are protocols to follow. You should not be in the boss's office again without express orders, or going forward, without my accompaniment for that matter."

"Understood," Crisp nodded, his mind racing for a way to redirect Banwell's attention. He straightened, adjusted his jacket as though setting his thoughts in order, and moved toward the door where Banwell waited. "Speaking of the courthouse, do you still need me to confirm the schedule for next Friday? I haven't heard back yet but can reach out first thing tomorrow."

Banwell paused, his initial suspicion momentarily redirected by the shift in conversation. "Yes, make sure you do that." Once Crisp had crossed the threshold into the adjoining room, Banwell promptly closed the office door behind him. Crisp exhaled slowly, relieved at the change of topic and Banwell's acceptance of his explanation, at least for the moment.

As he returned to his desk, his sorted the pieces of the puzzle he had begun to uncover, and the realization of just how dangerous his investigation had become. Banwell made a deliberate show of locking Pendergast's door. He turned to Crisp, glancing at his pocket watch before speaking. "I think it would be best if you head to the courthouse now. There's still time to make the arrangements with the clerk."

Crisp nodded, noting the firmness in Banwell's tone.

"And once you've finished, return to the Main Street office; I'll meet you there in about an hour. Make sure everything is in order before I arrive." Banwell stood firm, watching Crisp intently, waiting for him to exit before he, too, descended the stairs.

Crisp left immediately for the Main Street office, but not before diverting for a brief rendezvous with the street boy Percy. His instructions were clear: find Cassie and Marcus, and all three of them were to meet Crisp at 6:00 around the corner from the Pendergast Hotel.

He hung around the downtown office for the remainder of the afternoon, thankful that Banwell did not keep him late, and once his work was complete and Banwell agreed to call it a night, he finally took the Ninth Street cable car down to The Bottoms and looked for his friends. As expected, he found them at the designated location and wasted no time with his instructions for the plan he'd been formulating all afternoon.

As dusk settled over the city, Crisp entered the hotel anticipating an empty office suite waiting for him upstairs. Percy was stationed at the rear of the building while Moreland sauntered in the lobby; both were prepared to signal the arrival of any of Pendergast's men. Cassie, whose charm was unmatched, accompanied Crisp to the office upstairs and waited near the top of the stairs. Her task was clear: if any of Pendergast's boys appeared, she would divert them back downstairs to The Climax, ensuring Crisp's operation proceeded without disruption.

Coming out from the dimly lit stairwell into the lighted office loft, he expected silence but instead found Felix Wexler still at his desk, deeply immersed in recalculating figures. Maintaining an air of nonchalance, Crisp approached his own desk, shuffling through a stack of papers he'd left there earlier.

"Burning the midnight oil?"

Wexler, marking his place in a ledger, looked up reluctantly. "Good evening, Mr. Crisp. Just revisiting some numbers for Mr. Pendergast."

"I'm just dropping off some paperwork for the boss," Crisp replied, noting Wexler's apparent indifference. The man was obsessed with his figures, and if Crisp's unexpected appearance should have raised some concern, Wexler didn't show it. However, the accountant's demeanor swiftly changed when Cassie entered a few steps behind Crisp, her alluring presence eliciting a double-take.

"Felix, let me introduce you to my friend, Miss Cassie."

Felix nodded, Cassie's curtsy caused him to bury his head back into his work, flustered.

The door to Pendergast's private office was predictably locked, but he knew a spare key resided in Banwell's desk. Sharing a knowing glance with Cassie, she moved between him and Wexler.

"What exactly do you do here, Mr. Wexler?" Cassie inquired, sidling up to him.

"I handle all the accounts for Mr. Pendergast's business. All the money that is."

"That sounds very important. Must have required a lot of schoolin' to work with all those numbers."

Wexler blushed noticeably.

Crisp, clutching letters in his left hand, moved to Banwell's desk and found the keys in the upper right-hand drawer. "Cass, Dear, I'll just be a moment, need to leave these letters for Mr.

Pendergast to sign first thing in the morning." He moved to Pendergast's door with routine precision.

Cassie edged closer to Wexler, her ample bosom capturing his furtive glances. She tried to hold his interest, but his eyes betrayed him as he glanced past her toward Crisp entering Pendergast's office.

"Is that all dollars? That's a lot of money you manage, Mr. Wexler." She nudged closer and laid a hand on top of his.

Wexler quickly turned a page in his ledger and withdrew his hand. "Yes, ma'am. But those are confidential numbers. Please don't pry."

Cassie gently touched Wexler's cheek, drawing his gaze back. "Understood. Once Algernon drops off those letters, we'll leave directly."

Inside Pendergast's office, Crisp worked with purpose. With his eyes knitted together in deep concentration, he moved to Pendergast's desk and rifled quietly through the drawers. He searched Pendergast's desk with hyper-focused intensity, his eyes scanning every detail for clues. He frantically sifted through the desk, hoping to find information on Pendergast's employees or any link to the recent murders, but found nothing of substance. A desk calendar caught his eye, but the few meetings penciled there seemed routine, nothing out of the ordinary. He cursed himself for risking this search—his earlier visit to Pendergast's office had revealed nothing noteworthy, and yet here he stood just a few hours later, desperate for any lead, desperate for something that lay hidden in plain sight.

Downstairs, Percy hid in the long corridor leading out the rear of the hotel. He hid behind a stack of chairs near the kitchen where he eyed a fresh loaf of bread cooling on a counter top. Ever the keen observer, he had carefully timed the routine of the bustling kitchen staff and watched intently, noting the patterns of their movements. In a matter of seconds, he seized his opportunity and darted forward to snatch the warm loaf, then hastily retreated to the shadows to savor his prize. His primary duty of watching for Pendergast's men temporarily forgotten, he munched contentedly, concealed from view.

Back upstairs, Crisp moved to the corner of the office where an old file cabinet stood. Following Percy's earlier tip, he assumed most of Pendergast's men kept a room on the premises, but a quick view of the register at the front desk earlier that day revealed nothing. Nor did an attempt to garner the information from the desk clerk, bellhop, or hotel staff. Everyone was tight lipped on the lodgings of Pendergast's men. He hoped there were something in the files to shed light on the mystery, but browsing through the drawers, he found much the same: business letters, invoices, all apparently normal correspondence, nothing that hinted at where Pendergast's men stayed.

He closed the last drawer and took another glance around the room. Something called out to him, but he couldn't place its whereabouts. There had to be something here, some clue, something he had missed. Then it came to him in a flash. The letter to the councilmen he'd set eyes upon earlier in the day. He rushed to Pendergast's desk and to his relief it was still there. He picked it up, examining it from different angles in the diffused light coming in from the window. He was certain, this was the same type of paper used for the cryptic note sent to Speers by their suspect.

He placed the letter back where he'd found it and searched through a few drawers before he found a folder of stationary containing a sheathe of the same type of paper. He retrieved a blank sheet and folded it into his pocket as a subtle thump on the wall—the planned signal from Cassie—alerted him that it was time to go.

He made one last sweep of the room to ensure that he'd left no trace, and started for the door. Prying it barely ajar before exiting, he heard heavy footsteps echoing in the stairwell signaling that Pendergast's men had arrived. He knew if he were discovered this second time in Pendergast's office, it would mean dire consequences.

"Well, if it ain't Cassie Diamond, Crisp's whore. What are you doing here?" The unmistakable voice of Jim Dowling cut through the tension.

Before she could reply, Crisp recognized a second voice that chimed in. "Maybe she's here for him." It was Rory Taffe; like two sides of a coin, he seemed inseparable from Dowling.

"Can't be, we know ole Felix ain't interested in anything but his numbers." Both men laughed mockingly.

"I came to meet Algernon. Said he'd be working late, but Mr. Wexler assures me I just missed him." Cassie smiled at Wexler, who nodded nervously.

A third set of boots thudded up the stairs. Crisp couldn't see the newcomer but guessed it was one of Pendergast's other toughs, Wyse, Skahill, or Carnes.

"We were just looking for the man ourselves," Dowling said. "No one 'cept Felix here is supposed to be working late."

"Yet, the three of you are here," she jabbed at Dowling.

"He's probably out getting drunk and losing money at cards again," Taffe snorted.

"It appears he must've stood you up Cass." Dowling glided through the room, lighting a cigar as he passed Crisp's vantage point, his presence exuding an intimidating aura that made it clear to Cassie she could not leave on her own. "What do you see in him anyway?" He continued; his tone dripping with derision.

"I see a good man, one winning hand away from leaving this place," she said, strolling closer to Dowling. "But you're right, he's obviously forgotten about me tonight." Crisp peeked out to get a better view, but could only account for Wexler and Taffe. A chair scraped on the far side of the room—must be Wyse or Skahill, Crisp assumed; if it were Carnes, he would surely have spoken up by now.

Turning her charms towards Dowling and Taffe, Cassie suggested, "Since he's not here, what do you say we all go downstairs? First round's on me. You too, Mr. Wexler?"

Wexler looked up, surprised. "Thank you kindly, ma'am, but I have work to do."

"See, he ain't interested in pretty women and smooth whiskey," Dowling interjected.

"But we are," Taffe added.

"What are we waiting for then?" Cassie hooked her arm through Dowling's, leading him toward the stairs.

"Stay here. If Crisp shows up, let us know. Don't let him out of your sight," Dowling ordered toward the quiet man in the chair. Accompanied by Taffe and Cassie, the three descended the stairs. Crisp pried the door open an inch further and spied another look into the outer room: Wyse sat idly picking at his fingernails with a pocket knife, and Wexler, still absorbed in his ledgers, had seemingly forgotten about Crisp.

He was trapped. The only other door from Pendergast's office led to an adjacent room, a cramped windowless library that offered nowhere to hide. The long and narrow pane glass window behind Pendergast's desk was a transom type, likewise offering no way out. Each second stretched into an eternity as Crisp waited, but Wyse remained unmoving, and Wexler appeared oblivious to Crisp's presence. Each minute slipped away with alarming speed. If Pendergast were to return and find him, it would spell the end of his employment and his ongoing investigation into Pendergast's operations. Even worse, he knew it would likely culminate in a violent confrontation.

Desperation drove him to search the office for any disguise. All he could find were Pendergast's oversized coat and a bowler hat. It was far from ideal. The hat hung awkwardly over his ears, but it covered his brow, and with his head tucked down, it might obscure his face. The overcoat, tailored for Pendergast's bulky frame, draped loosely over Crisp's lean body, but it was all he had to work with.

He peeked through the door crack again watching Wyse and Wexler.

Suddenly, Percy's voice startled them all. The boy appeared from nowhere, his voice strong and confident, "Boss wants to see you. Now."

Wyse jumped up. "Who the hell are you?"

"You gonna make me repeat the boss's orders?" Percy said, striving to inject authority into his voice. Before he could react, the dimwitted Wyse lunged, grabbing Percy in a bear hug.

"Got you, runt! I never seen you around here before." Percy fought in desperation to free himself but the massive hands and arms of Wyse were too much. Wyse grinned as the boy struggled.

"Let me go! Let me go!"

Crisp bolted into action. He kicked the door open causing it to bang loudly as it hit the wall on its backswing. With his cloaked silhouette framed in the doorway, and mimicking Pendergast's gruff voice, he barked, "What's all this hullabaloo about?"

Wyse, momentarily confused, released Percy, who bolted down the stairs. "After him!" Crisp commanded. Wyse clumsily followed, his heavy boots clopping down the stairs, but Percy had already vanished into the rear corridor before Wyse had seen which way he'd gone.

Crisp discarded the coat and hat into an empty chair, and retreated from the office, leaving Wexler bewildered by the bizarre engagement.

From The Climax Saloon, Cassie had managed to keep her eyes glued to the stairs without raising Dowling's suspicion. Once Percy had darted into the rear hallway and Wyse came fumbling into the front lobby in search of his prey, she wrapped up her act with Dowling and Taffe. Crisp was able to squeeze by unnoticed and met Percy in the back alley, and moments later, Cassie joined them both. Moreland arrived shortly, assuring them it was clear, and all three dodged through the backstreets and alleyways of The Bottoms in an effort to reconvene at Crisp's boardinghouse.

The gamble had been risky, and much like his luck at the saloon table, the payout had fallen short. Still, his plan had merits; utilizing his team of resources had been the only thing that kept him from being caught in the act. Moving forward, he knew that his only chance of cracking the case lay in leveraging all three of them to their fullest potential.

Chapter Twelve

The night lay thick over the back lot, a secluded patch of land shadowed by the sprawling bulk of industrial buildings. Here, the silence in the dead of night was dense, broken only by the distant hum of the city and the occasional rattle of a passing train. In this hidden expanse, under the scant light of a half-moon, the true terror that stalked Kansas City was about to manifest itself again.

Under a veil of darkness, a towering figure, colossal and obscured, lumbered from the rear of a covered, box wagon. His heavy boots left deep impressions in the soft earth muddied by recent rains as he moved. His overalls, grimy and worn, clung to his vast frame, each stain chronicling countless similar nights. The shadows twisted around him, cloaking his features in a spectral distortion that seemed almost otherworldly.

Tucked in the wagon's shadowed depths, a figure lay motionless, faintly visible under the sparse moonlight. With hands that seemed more like tools of iron than flesh, the man reached in, his grip encircling a lifeless body of a young woman. Her limbs dangled, devoid of will, a reminder of the struggle subdued hours before. He lifted her with a chilling ease, her form draped over his shoulder like a rag doll, as he moved with purpose towards a darker corner of the abandoned lot. The night air seemed to thicken with dread as he vanished into the darkness, leaving behind only the heavy imprint of his passage.

In a shadowed enclave shielded from prying eyes, he ignited an oil lamp. The weak flame illuminated his makeshift lair with a pallid glow. Here, away from the world's gaze, the sickly light cast haunting shadows that danced across the walls, each movement a ghostly whisper in the stillness of his hidden sanctum. Setting the body down, the man crouched beside the woman. He observed her for a moment, her chest rising and falling shallowly. The thrill of control, of power over life and death, surged through him. He relished the feeling; it drove him to these dreadful acts. With a grunt, he tightened his grip around her neck, his fingers pressing deeply. The struggle was brief; her weakened state allowed for no real fight. The life faded from her body, extinguishing the last bit of her spirit under his crushing force.

Breathing heavily, he stood and looked down at the now still figure, her taunts and mockery silenced forever. The act of strangulation hadn't satiated the dark hunger within him, it was only a prelude to what he truly savored. He slowly undressed her, his eyes feasting on the now lifeless body. He stood there for countless minutes, perversely looking upon his victim, capturing every detail of her nakedness.

Reaching into the rafters of his den, he retrieved a package wrapped in brown paper and coarse twine. His hands, almost gentle, unwrapped it to reveal a new butcher knife, its blade glinting malevolently in the lamplight. A sinister smile twisted across his face, shadowed and obscured, lending his features an eerie, distorted appearance that seemed to meld with the surrounding darkness. He admired the new blade; this was his instrument, a tool to express the darkness that clung to his soul.

He tore a strip from her soft blouse, a long swath of fabric, and grabbed a handful of her hair. Tying it off with the torn cloth, he then tested the sharpness of his knife. Satisfied, he sliced the lock close to the scalp with a clean, decisive stroke. In his hand lay a new trophy, a gruesome memento to join the others collected from his macabre pursuits.

In the murky light from the lamp, he hunched over the body. His fingers traced the soft skin, still warm to the touch, with a perverse delicacy, savoring the stillness of what he now claimed as his own. The night stretched on, and on, and he, enveloped in his ghastly ritual, lost himself to the dark whims that commanded him. Finally, he knelt beside the body, and placed the tip of the knife against the now clammy torso. With a practiced hand, he began to carve, each gash a grotesque violation of the human form he had already robbed of life. The sound of the blade slicing through flesh was a melody to him, and with each cut, his excitement grew.

As the night wore on, he worked with a joy that belied the horror of his actions. Each incision deeper, more assured than the last, his movements were both brutal and precise. When he finally paused, stepping back to admire his work, the body before him bore little resemblance to the woman it had once been. As he finished, a fleeting shadow of remorse flickered through him; his mood darkened abruptly, as the macabre acts he'd committed began to weigh against his conscience. He quickly wrapped the body in an old blanket and moved it back to his wagon.

Under the waning moonlight, the worn box wagon creaked over the Fourth Street Viaduct, its faded paint merging with the shadows of the night. Emerging atop the bluffs onto Washington Street, it navigated the still-slumbering city with a quiet persistence.

As dawn lingered somewhere beyond the eastern horizon, the wagon continued its discreet journey, its wooden wheels clattering against the cobblestones in the Quality Hill neighborhood. Eventually, it came to rest at the curb on Bank Street, nestled in the serene pre-dawn between Seventh and Eighth Streets, where it stood silent.

He didn't have much time.

As a pale, ash-grey light began to seep across the edge of the sky, it hesitated, the winter night keeping dawn from breaking too soon. He jumped into action, depositing his sinister token of evil. The placement was always important—just hidden enough to delay discovery but sure to be found, a nightmare made inevitable. His chosen spot tonight was beneath an old oak, its gnarled branches a silent witness to his brutality. The tree cast a shadow over the sidewalk leading to the front porch of the grand Quality Hill mansion looming in the enveloping darkness.

As he moved, his mind worked methodically. This wasn't just about hiding a body; it was about sending a message; one he took perverse pleasure in crafting. The elegant lawn was now merely a canvas for his macabre artistry, a silent testament to the raw, unyielding force of the antagonist that haunted the streets of Kansas City.

Amongst the somber, low light that cast deep shadows across his stern face, Speers sat behind his cluttered desk. The normally austere walls, lined with maps and crime photos, created an atmosphere of ceaseless vigilance. It was just before noon on Sunday, but his morning's ghastly work required a stiff drink. He pulled a bottle of whiskey from his desk and poured two fingers into a glass. Another victim, another savage mutilation.

He sat back with an audible gasp, and looked up as Crisp entered the room, his face set in grim determination. Speers swigged his drink and gestured to the seat across from him, his expression weary yet expectant. He motioned to the bottle, but Crisp declined his offer. "Hadn't heard from you all week; I was getting worried," Speers poured himself another glass as Crisp settled in.

"I think we're close to a breakthrough," Crisp said, his voice low but carrying an undercurrent of excitement. "Colin Wyse, one of Pendergast's men."

Speers sat forward, clearly intrigued. "Wyse? Pendergast's driver?" He raised an eyebrow, skepticism mingling with interest, "What makes you suspect him?"

"A number of things. First of all, he has access to wagons and horses. We know our suspect needs transport for his activities. Wyse not only has access but spends a lot of time supposedly on his own schedule. Second, he works in both The Bottoms and here downtown, so he has reason to be in both places without suspicion. Third, well, you've seen the man, strong as an ox.

And lastly, I've tracked him—on one occasion this past week, he entered a brothel we know some of the victims came from."

"Which brothel?"

"Eva's on Fourth."

Speers mused, rubbing his chin. "And the evidence? What have you got tying him to the killings?"

Crisp paused intentionally; his eyes intent. "Paint, Thomas, paint splatters on his boots, the same type found on a tarp wrapping one of our victims, the same as I saw at the rear of the hotel. And his boots are the size of the footprints I've seen at the crime scenes. And here's the big one; I told you, I tracked the large boot prints from the lot to the back door of the hotel, where the door and the fence lining the alley had just received a fresh coat of paint. We found paint cans in the lot near the wagon, and upon closer inspection, I found where he had stepped in paint and left a footprint on the floorboard of the wagon. It's got to be Wyse's boot. It's too much of a coincidence."

Speers nodded hesitantly. "What about motive, what have you got there?"

"Well," Crisp began counting on his fingers, pointing at his thumb, "First, he's one of Pendergast's men, so his employment is tied to The Bottoms and the vice that Pendergast controls; that's the at-risk element we've discussed." He withdrew his index finger, "Next, I snooped around Pendergast's desk, and there within easy access, in plain sight, I found lists of the parks men and correspondence to them complaining about the impacts to Pendergast's business. It would be simple to target those men." He pointed to his middle finger, "Wyse has been in the Pendergast office, along with most of us, a number of times when Pendergast himself goes on a tirade about the movement. Wyse usually stands at the back of the room, listening, absorbing everything."

Before Speers could get a word in, Crisp triumphantly announced, "and there's this. Matches the type of paper from the letter you received." Crisp handed both to Speers for his inspection. "Found that in Pendergast's desk."

Speers compared the pieces of paper, noting their similarities before handing them back to Crisp. "You say 'us'; so, are not there other Pendergast men who have access to the same information—they share the same risks—could one of them be suspect as well?"

Crisp nodded. "I'm not ruling them out. You've got Patrick Carnes, he's the muscle, keeps the others in line, coordinates Pendergast's strongarm tactics. Under him, you have Bill Haggan and Rory Taffe, a couple of thugs, real delinquents. And there's Jim Dowling too. He's a piece of work, enjoys the rough stuff too much. Certainly, all of them are prone to violence, but none of them meets the stature of our man, well except Carnes, he is a big fellow. Let's hold that thought for a moment," Crisp paused pulling a cheroot from his pocket. "May I?" With Speers approval, he struck a match before continuing, "Thomas Banwell is the brains. As Pendergast's attorney, he keeps them all out of legal heat. He's also the adviser to Pendergast, and acts as his right-hand man. Whatever Pendergast wishes, its generally coordinated through Banwell. Then there's Wexler, manages the books, smart but a meek man, hasn't got a backbone. Dermot Gallagher, Pendergast's valet and man-servant, knows all the secrets but sticks to his own business. A very proper gentleman." Crisp paused thinking of his other interactions within the Pendergast ring.

Speers recognized every name that Crisp mentioned, each one a cog in Pendergast's intricate machine, but he kept a poker face, neither confirming nor denying any recognition, his expression betraying nothing. Then he recalled one man Crisp had not mentioned; a shadowy figure who he'd seen coming and going from Pendergast's on a few occasions. "What about that other big fellow, I believe Skahill is his name?" Speers interjected.

"He's a brute for sure," Crisp shrugged, "I actually thought maybe he was mute when I first met him. Does what he's told, no questions asked, hardly any brains it seems. He just recently joined Pendergast, so he's got the least at risk."

"Have you been able to rule out any of these men?"

"Assuming that the same man is committing these murders, we can cross off Taffe and Haggan from our list. I found train tickets for both, that place them in Hannibal, Missouri during the weekend of one of the murders. And although a train ticket might easily be used as a ruse, other correspondence points to their whereabouts at the time. If we just focus on the big men, that leaves Carnes and Wyse, but Carnes has too many alibis. My source has tracked him routinely to Toad-a-Loop; he spends most of his time away from Pendergast there."

"If you're gut says Wyse, we should follow that through," Speers instructed firmly. "What's his educational background?" he asked, thinking back to the threatening letter. "Is he literate? Dumb-spoken?"

"I haven't uncovered that yet. He's a quiet man for sure, not interested in idle chat. I'll have to see if I can dig something up on him from one of the others."

Speers reached into his drawer and pulled out a large piece of cloth, concealing something. He placed it on the desk before Crisp. "Do you suppose he has a professional background with this?"

Slowly unfolding the cloth, Crisp could not hide his disbelief as his eyes settled on a pristine butcher's knife.

"That came from the latest scene, another victim this weekend," Speers added solemnly. "She was found on Banks Street on The Hill; that was laying several feet from the body; we guess dropped in haste."

Crisp's eyes widened and he felt his stomach clench. The room fell silent, save for the distant sounds of the busy police headquarters beyond Speers' door. Finally, almost reluctantly, he carefully picked up the knife. "This may be the break we need, if I can link it to Wyse that is." He turned the blade over in his hands, inspecting it from every angle.

"I need you to make that link, Crisp," Speers said gravely. "We need more than paint and coincidences. We need conclusive evidence."

"I understand," Crisp replied, the weight of the task settling on his shoulders. "If Wyse is our man, I'll find the proof."

Speers nodded, his expression hard as stone. "Do it fast, Crisp. Every day we linger, puts another helpless victim at risk."

Crisp wrapped the blade in the cloth. "You'll have your proof, or I'll find out if we're barking up the wrong tree. Allow me to take this and I'll tie it back to Wyse."

As he stood to leave, Speers said, "Be careful, Crisp. This isn't just about catching a killer anymore. It's about cutting the head off a snake." With a knowing bob of his head, Crisp walked to the door, the weight of the butcher's knife as heavy as the fate of the investigation.

Speers called behind him as he paused there, "I'll get you the details of this latest victim once I hear back from Henwood," but he could not be certain his words reached Crisp who shuffled into the hallway in deep contemplation.

———

In the opulent parlor of Annie Chambers' brothel, the pervasive scent of perfume hung in the air eclipsing the murmur of clandestine conversations. Velvet drapes and gilded mirrors adorned the walls, projecting an aura of exclusivity and sin. The 25-room mansion was nestled in the red-light district just south of the Missouri River, near the bustling City Market. Operating within vicinity of City Hall and Police Headquarters, Madam Chambers catered to a clientele of prominent businessmen and high-ranking city officials.

While most men relaxed on porch fronts on Sundays after church, sipping lemonade and enjoying the spring-like weather, Jim Pendergast sat with Thomas Speers at a secluded corner table in the foyer of the brothel, the mood tense, and underscored by the importance of their discussion.

Annie Chambers, renowned across The West for her shrewd business acumen and the first-class status of her establishment, approached their table with the poise of a queen ruling her court. Her gown rustled softly as she moved, the sound mingling with the hum of voices that filled the room.

"Gentlemen," Annie greeted, her voice smooth as silk. "I trust everything is to your liking? Can I offer either of you a special companion for the afternoon?" Her eyes twinkled with a mix of business savvy and mischief, knowing well the influence these men wielded in her city.

Speers waved off the offer with a polite smile, his mind clearly preoccupied. "Thank you, Annie, but we have pressing matters to discuss. Perhaps another time."

Annie nodded; her gaze sharp. "Speaking of pressing matters, there's been talk among the girls—fears about these dreadful murders. It's bad for business, and frankly, it's bad for the girls' spirits. What are you doing about it?" This was aimed at Speers.

He sipped a glass of sweet wine—Chambers never served whiskey in her place—choosing his words carefully. "We're doing everything we can, Annie. I've even appointed a special detective to oversee the investigation. I've got my best men on it; more patrols, more eyes on the street."

"I pay for those eyes here in the heart of town, not down in The Bottoms," Annie said pointedly, her voice laced with concern. A steady stream of bribes and fines shielded her establishment from police interference, ensuring not only official immunity but also an unseen layer of protection.

Speers started to reassure her when Pendergast interjected, his voice smooth but carrying an edge. "Annie, you know I take care of my constituents. I can offer you protection, real protection—not just the badge boys walking the beat."

Speers bristled at the interruption. "Jim, my men are already covering the Ninth Ward. We don't need civilians stepping in where they don't belong."

Pendergast chuckled, a low sound that filled the tense space between them. "Yes, but I can get my men inside. They can mingle, blend in with the crowd. Who better to catch a murderer than someone who doesn't look like a cop?"

Annie considered this, her eyes flitting between the two men. She was no stranger to playing one against the other if it meant the safety of her girls. "Chief, I appreciate your efforts, really, I do. But Jim has a point. His men can blend in, watch without being obvious."

Speers' jaw tightened. "That may be, but it's my job to ensure law and order. Pendergast, your men are hardly the type we want patrolling an area already on edge."

"But think of it, Tom," he said, his voice persuasive. "My boys could watch from the inside. They can provide security discreetly while your men handle the streets. It's about keeping the peace, isn't it?"

Annie watched the exchange, toying with the implications bouncing in her head. Speers was a good man, but Pendergast's offer was tempting. More protection without the overt presence of law enforcement would indeed be less disruptive. "Chief, perhaps a compromise can be reached," she suggested smoothly. "Maybe a trial period to see how it goes with Jim's men?"

Speers sighed with the weight of the city's safety heavy on his shoulders. "Alright, Jim. We'll try it your way. But remember, any slip-up, and it's back to my men alone."

Pendergast grinned, satisfied. "Understood, Chief. You won't regret this."

As the men settled their strategy, Annie excused herself, her mind somewhat at ease but wary of the tenuous peace they'd brokered. She knew all too well the delicate balance of power in Kansas City, and with a murderer on the loose, everything felt like a house of cards, waiting for just a breath of wind to tumble it down.

Pendergast leaned back in his chair; his eyes wide with interest. "Tell me more about these murders. I'd seen a few headlines, but didn't realize the gravity of the situation."

Speers sighed, rubbing his temples. "As I told Annie, I've got my best men on it."

Pendergast nodded, a hint of concern showing in his eyes. "Why is she so riled up?"

"Many of the victims have been prostitutes," Speers explained, watching Pendergast's reaction closely. "None working for Annie that I know of, but it's still a blow to her business and reputation." Pendergast's face remained unreadable; his expression carefully neutral. Speers continued, "Most of the women were from The Bottoms. I thought you would've known that?"

Pendergast shrugged nonchalantly. Reconsidering his offer to Annie, he continued, "I don't have any men to spare right now on a full-time basis, but a few of my boys have been spending too much time in my saloon. I'm sure they'll be more than happy to hang around here and sample the pleasures Ms. Chambers has to offer, but I can't let them stay here permanently."

Speers nodded, still trying to gauge Pendergast's true feelings. "That will give her peace of mind I suppose, might just help keep things under control."

Pendergast's lips curled into a faint smile. "Let's hope it does, for everyone's sake."

Chapter Thirteen

Within the walls of 520 Main Street, the game was changing, and allegiances, however hidden, were being tested under the watchful eyes of those who played for the highest stakes.

Banwell, his sharp features tightened in concern, approached Pendergast with a subtle caution that belied his usual confidence. "Jim, there's something about this Crisp fellow that's nagging at me," he started, his voice low. "Do we know where he comes from? His name strikes a familiar chord, but I can't quite place him."

Pendergast looked up from his correspondence, his gaze sharp and assessing. He took a puff from a cigar, and sat back in his chair. "He came highly recommended by Speers," his tone dismissive yet not without a hint of caution. "You know Speers has been a solid ally. Why the sudden distrust?"

Banwell shifted uncomfortably, his instincts honed by years in the murky waters of city politics warned him of unseen currents. "It's not distrust, exactly. But what if he's been planted here? We can't ignore the possibility."

Pendergast's eyes hid his inward contemplations. The implications of Banwell's words were not lost on him, however, his expression remained composed as he responded, "Speers wouldn't play us like that. He knows better than to bite the hand that feeds, especially with the city cleanup movement gaining momentum. He needs us on his side, and he knows it."

"Still, there's something suspicious about this man. I asked him a few legal questions the other day, and I'm convinced his answers were quite made up," Banwell said. "And he's always asking about the other men, their whereabouts, how to get in good with them, that kind of thing."

Pendergast leaned back, considering. "If you've got concerns, you know how to handle it. I certainly can't get rid of him, not just yet. But let's keep him where we can watch him. Maybe post him here on Main exclusively."

Banwell shook his head. "No good, I am here less than any place. If I'm not at the courthouse, I'm at the hotel."

Pendergast's eyes narrowed thoughtfully. "Then make him accompany you everywhere you go, keep him in your vest."

"He's too smart for that. He'll know I'm on to him," Banwell sighed, frustration evident.

"Bury him in work then, keep his mind occupied until we can get a better read on him," Pendergast decided, his voice firm and unrelenting. "And get someone to keep an eye on him, follow him around, see what he's up to. Not one of our regulars that he knows." Banwell nodded, though his doubt lingered like a persistent shadow. As Pendergast stood, adjusting the cuffs of his impeccably tailored suit, he added, "I have a meeting at City Hall. We'll discuss this later."

Once Pendergast had left, the weight of the office seemed to grow heavier, the luxurious decor doing little to dispel the growing tension. Banwell went to the saloon on the first floor where Dowling and Haggan hung at the end of the bar accompanied by two trollops, their presence unobtrusive yet unmistakable.

With a whistle, Banwell summoned the men into the stairwell, his voice carrying a new edge of authority. "Where's Crisp?"

Dowling shrugged his shoulders, but Haggan chimed up, "Think he's over to the courthouse."

"I want eyes on him. When he gets back, don't let him out of your sight. He's up to something, I can feel it. He's too smooth, too composed. No one is that clean, not in this city."

Dowling, his dark hair slicked back and his mustache neatly trimmed, gave a slow, menacing smile. "Consider it done," he replied, his voice silky with the promise of trouble. "If he's hiding something, we'll find out."

Haggan, his youthful face belying the cold hardness in his eyes, nodded in agreement. "No one fools us," he added, his tone light but chilling.

As Banwell watched them leave, his mind churned with possibilities and plans. If Crisp were indeed a plant, the ramifications would be disastrous not just for their operations but for Pendergast's hold over the city's shadowy corridors of power. The thought left him restless, his unease growing as he grabbed a bottle from the bar and turned back to the steps leading to the stacks of paperwork on his desk.

***

Late in the day, under a sky heavy with thick, brooding clouds that cast queer twilight over Ninth Street, Crisp made his way to the local druggist. The sun lay hidden behind the oppressive gray, offering no warmth or light, and leaving the world in a cold, shadowed gloom. Flurries began to swirl in the biting wind, a prelude to the impending snowfall. The streets were eerily quiet, the usual bustle muted as people hurried to seek shelter from the advancing wintry onslaught. With any luck, Mr. Byers' shop would still be open. Crisp's purpose was twofold: procure some relief for Cassie's unending needs and fortify himself against the cold that seeped into his very bones.

The bell jingled as he entered the quaint shop, where rows upon rows of bottles, jars, and other vessels crowded the wooden counters, each teeming with a seemingly endless array of drugs, herbs, and patent medicines.

"Evening, Mr. Crisp," Byers called out. A portly man with a face as pallid as the opiate concoctions he dispensed, asked, "The usual for Miss Cassie?"

"Yes, and something for the cold night." Crisp replied, his voice steady despite the tremor he felt within. Byers nodded, turning to mix a draught of opiates and cocaine, a potent blend that promised oblivion. Crisp watched, his mind torn between the necessity of the act and the knowledge of its danger.

"Looks like snow."

Crisp, his gaze distant, responded vacantly, "Yes."

"Well, that's March for you. Calendar says spring."

Crisp, still lost in his thoughts, nodded, barely acknowledging the conversation. "Mm-hmm."

Armed with the illicit goods tucked securely in his coat, Crisp left the warmth of the druggist's shop for the cold streets, feeling a tug toward the lot behind Pendergast's Hotel as he reached that stretch. The area lay under the shadow of the hotel like a dark secret. As he approached, the gas streetlights flickered on, announcing evening's onset and casting eerie patterns on the ground. With each step deeper into the gloom, a profound chill seemed to seep from the very ground, as if the earth itself whispered secrets of forgotten misdeeds.

The evening air bit at Crisp's ears and lashed his face with an icy sting as he ducked through the broken fence at the lot's edge, grateful for the respite from the wind. He paused there, scanning the jumble of discarded metal and broken machinery; with fingers numbed by the cold, he fumbled for the little pipe and bowl tucked in his pocket. Lighting a pinch of Cassie's concoction, he drew in deeply, the smoke's bitter warmth seeping through his veins, a temporary bulwark against the encroaching cold.

The lot reeked with the tang of rust and oil which hung in the air—a sharp contrast to the breezes blowing outside the fenced enclosure. Just then, a soft light emerged out of the inky blackness, held aloft in the hand of the scrapyard worker, the man he'd spoken to before. His presence was an unexpected barrier. "Thought I made it clear last time, you ain't welcomed here."

"Just a quick look around, not taking anything," Crisp clarified, his pulse quickening. Undeterred, he waved a new greenback at the man.

The man eyed the money and snatched it from Crisp's hand in a blink of an eye, "Five minutes."

"Another five if I can borrow your lantern for that time…"

Ten dollars well spent.

The man disappeared into the stygian gloom of the empty lot. It was a graveyard of cast-offs, the detritus forming grotesque silhouettes under the lantern's pale scrutiny. Crisp's hands shook, not just from the cold but from the fear of what lay hidden in this forsaken place. He moved toward the rear corner of the lot with heart pounding and lantern sputtering. The lantern revealed what he searched for; its flames threw dancing shadows across the decrepit red wagon parked alongside Pendergast's stately carriage.

An unsettling silence hung about the lot like a wet blanket, punctuated only by the distant, haunting nicker of horses from the nearby stable where Pendergast's beasts were boarded. The light wavered, transforming the ordinary into specters of twisted metal and wood, as if revealing the very essence of decay and neglect that pervaded the lot. He moved closer to the red wagon, his shadow elongated and distorted, merging with the oncoming darkness. Each step seemed heavier, weighed down by the palpable presence of something unseen, yet overwhelmingly oppressive. The rustling of the wind through the debris sounded like hushed voices, as if the night itself conspired to keep its secrets, guarding them with a blanket of darkness and a cloak of silence.

Crisp, solitary and watchful, examined the still wagon. It revealed nothing but emptiness within its confines. His eyes caught the impression of booted footprints in the dirt, not meandering towards the expected safety of Pendergast's hotel, but veering toward an adjacent building hugged by shadows.

He followed the trail, his steps measured and silent, the ground beneath his feet whispering tales of trespass.

Nearing the old brick building that framed the western side of the abandoned lot, Crisp discerned an old section of fence haphazardly propped against the weathered brick, concealing more than just the building's flank—it masked a secret passage, a hidden doorway shrouded beneath the piled timbers. His hands, guided by a blend of curiosity and dread, pushed against the course, weathered wood. The fence gave way with a groan, as if protesting the intrusion into its guarded secrets.

The barrier moved aside, revealing not just a gap but a gateway to deeper shadows—a hole that served as a silent invitation to a dark threat. Crisp paused, the lantern light trembling in his grasp, and casting an eerie glow that seemed to breathe life into the darkness ahead. He steeled himself and stepped closer, peering into the void beyond, where the boundaries between the known and the unseen blurred.

His head swam now; Byers' medicinal concoction began to course warmly throughout his bloodstream, sharpening his senses before clouding them with wraiths that danced in the shadows on the periphery of his vision. The whispers of the night, echoed inside his head, growing louder, like voices of victims murmuring through the veil between worlds. His skin crawled as the boundary between the living and the dead thinned, haunted by the echoes of those lost souls.

The crunch of gravel somewhere close snapped Crisp back to the present. His breath caught in his throat at the realization that he might not be alone. Whether the workman had returned at the allotted time limit, or another ominous soul crept within the lot's confines, he didn't care, and swiftly doused the lamp. Pressing himself against the brick wall, he tried to blend into the shadows. His heartbeat thumped heavily in his ears as he crouched there, too terrified to move, enveloped by the thick, oppressive blackness. His eyes, useless now, strained against the dark. His breath turned to mist in front of him, hanging in the still, cold air like a spectral presence.

He waited, each second stretching interminably. He slowly turned back to the hole; had the sounds come from within? With his mind clouded by the pharmacist's compound, he groped frantically for any semblance of protection until his fingers found and clung to a piece of wood that lay abandoned next to the extinguished lamp.

Other than the constant murmur of the city's hum in the distance, the lot was now silent. He finally stood, while shadows swirled and danced around the jagged portal that beckoned to him. He couldn't do it, not yet. He had to get away. Filled with the oppressive weight of unseen watchers, he propelled himself forward. That initial step was the most torturous, his heart hammering as he hurled himself away from the wall.

The chill of the night air seared his lungs as he bolted to the front of the lot, tripping and stumbling with each footfall. He set the lamp down without thanking the owner, and squeezed through the ruined fence, emerging onto Ninth Avenue. He ran as before, in his nightmare, and did not stop until he secured the locks on the back of his bedroom door. Several blocks away, the backlot lay shrouded in stillness once more. It had become a guardian of sinister secrets cloaked in shadow, biding its time until the dawn—or until the next daring soul ventured too close to its dark heart.

———

The morning light seeped weakly through the tattered curtains of the boardinghouse where Crisp had spent another restless night. Beside him, Cassie lay in a haze, the glass pipe still warm in her hand as delicate swirls of opiate smoke rose and vanished into the stale air. He watched her for a moment, her features softened by the drug's embrace, sharply opposed to the torment brewing within him.

He'd made a vow to himself earlier in the dark hours of the night—a vow going forward, to stay clean, to keep his mind sharp; the urgency of the investigation demanded it. With a silent sigh, he slipped from the bed, careful not to disturb her.

He dressed quickly and quietly, pulling on his coat with a kind of desperate haste. He needed to put distance between himself and the temptations that filled his room—the substances, the escape they offered, and the comforting presence of Cassie, lost in her chemically induced peace.

The streets of the city were bustling as he made his way to the corner of Ninth and Genessee. From there, he rushed toward his office, and knew Banwell would give him hell for being late, but nonetheless, he needed to make one quick stop. The morning air nipped at his nose as he walked, helping to clear the last cobwebs of temptation from his mind. His destination was a nondescript butcher supply shop known for its quality cutlery—a place where professionals came to procure tools of the trade.

Inside the store, the sharp scent of metal and oil greeted him, mingling with the underlying aroma of fresh sawdust. Rows of knives glinted under the shop's bare bulbs, each blade promising precision and cleanliness unlike the grotesque scenes Crisp had witnessed in recent days. He approached the counter, where an elderly man with spectacles perched on the end of his nose peered up at him.

"Can I help you, sir?" The owner's voice echoed in the confines and quietness of the shop.

Crisp shifted, adopting a conspiratorial tone. "I work for Mr. Pendergast, and I've been sent to procure cutlery for the kitchen staff."

The shop owner eyed Crisp with a hint of uncertainty, perhaps searching his memory for a flicker of recognition. "What kind of cutlery do you need, sir?"

Crisp responded smoothly, "I was told they'd already sent a list of utensils to be picked up. Did you not receive it?"

"No one's brought a list round that I know of," the owner replied, his tone laced with suspicion.

"Perhaps you remember Jim Dowling or Bill Haggan? They mentioned having purchased here before."

The shop owner squinted, assessing Crisp through his eyes. "Can't say I recall those names," he replied cautiously, his gaze flickering to the door as if expecting someone else.

"Did anyone from Pendergast's Hotel make a purchase recently? Perhaps Colin Wyse? Specifically, a butcher knife or other such cutlery?"

Just then, a young apprentice stepped forward from across the room, wiping his hands on a cloth. "I knows Dowling. Him and another big fellow who works for Pendergast, they comes around sometimes to get blades sharpened," he cut in, his eyes bright with the eagerness of youth. "I've seen Dowling plenty of times, the big one doesn't talk much. Just stands there watchin' me work the grinding stone. Dowling puts everything on Boss Jim's account. I think the big fella just drives Dowling around."

With his interest sparked, Crisp tilted in a bit closer. "This big man, can you describe him? It's important." The shop keeper listened to the young man; his gaze held a mix of deep doubt laced with an underlying fear. To his dismay, the apprentice nodded, eager to be helpful. "Tall, much taller than most. Has a way of filling the room, you know? Quiet, like I said, but you remember him. Always wears these big, heavy boots and his overalls are always a bit dirty. Sometimes he just sits outside in a carriage waiting for Dowling."

The description matched the mental image Crisp had begun to form of the murderer—a giant of a man, capable of overpowering anyone with ease, silently carrying out the darkest deeds. It was the image of Colin Wyse sitting atop the driver's box of the red wagon.

"Is this one of the blades they acquired here?" Crisp asked, unwrapping the butcher knife he'd taken from Speers.

The youth examined it with the keen eye of the shop keeper looking on. He turned to the owner, "I think this is one of ours." The owner glanced at the knife unwillingly and then agreed, urging the apprentice to hand the knife back as if he didn't want to touch it himself.

"Have they been here recently?"

"Maybe a week back."

Crisp realized he wasn't getting anywhere, and the recognition of Dowling and Wyse was enough to satisfy him for the moment. He looked at them both. The shopkeeper's trust was clearly failing. Too many questions.

"You say you work for Mr. Pendergast?" he asked, his tone edged with doubt.

"Yes, that's right."

"Did you say you were sent to get something? Is there anything I can help you with?"

"My apologies, seems there's been a mix up. Let me follow back with my staff and make sure I understand their request."

He thanked them both, and stepped back into the street with a new thread to follow. His heart raced as the pieces of the puzzle started to click together.

He paused on the sidewalk outside the shop pondering the possibilities. Could Wyse and Dowling be acting together on the killings? Dowling certainly had the cold, calculated demeanor, and perhaps he used Wyse to drive him around during the abductions and placement of the bodies. Maybe Wyse was none the wiser to Dowling's schemes, or perhaps he was simply too ignorant, or too afraid, to ask questions or challenge Dowling. Crisp had observed Dowling's gruffness with the other boys, a subtle intimidation that permeated their interactions.

But then again, maybe Dowling wasn't involved at all. Maybe Wyse was the opportunist, laying low, chauffeuring Dowling around, and all the while plotting his next move.

Crisp was no closer to nailing this down. He had to dig deeper, needed to follow each of these men, needed to catch one of them in the act. To monitor them all, he'd need help—Percy and Moreland. Between the three of them, they could set up a watch, shadowing Pendergast's men one by one, until one of them slipped up and revealed the missing clues.

Chapter Fourteen

C risp returned to his desk outside Pendergast's private office at 520 Main. It had been a long week, and Banwell had kept Crisp overwhelmed with loads of work, and also kept him at the Main Street office, despite ongoing meetings he'd heard taking place in The Bottoms. He was concerned that something was up, but with no one to tip him off, it was only a hunch. Regardless, he had to move quick.

Throughout the week, he'd kept busy with menial tasks and light correspondence waiting for the moment when Banwell would leave him alone. He finally got that chance late that afternoon; Banwell announced a meeting with the boss at the courthouse which would keep him away for a few hours, but he expected Crisp to join once his paperwork was complete.

Crisp watched from a second story window as Banwell left the office and once he had crossed Main and neared the courthouse, Crisp went into action. With eyes knitted together in deep concentration, he flitted across the room and rifled quietly through the drawers of a heavy wooden desk that wasn't his. Each drawer of Banwell's desk offered a glimpse into the minutiae of Pendergast's enterprise—ledgers, rough notes, and miscellaneous correspondence. He looked for anything that might tell him where Wyse or Dowling resided when not lurking in the shadows of Pendergast's operations, but like Pendergast, Banwell kept little evidence of his transgressions. Crisp assumed any incriminating details were kept on Banwell's person, but he pressed on searching for clues.

As he pulled open another drawer, the faint noise of the old wood seemed to echo too loudly in the silent room. He paused—sounds from the tavern below drifted up the stair case—but something else had alerted his keen senses. He waited, listening more intently and sorted out the various sounds as they came: laughter from somewhere in the barroom, the slam of a door at the rear of the building, the clanging of a passing trolley below his window, and the harsh peep-peep of a police whistle outside in the distance.

He continued cautiously, his search meticulous; he knew what needed to be done, he needed to find where Wyse could be confronted away from the eyes of the posse he ran with. His fingers brushed against a tiny, leather-bound book. Pulling it out, Crisp flipped through the pages quickly, revealing names and addresses—a treasure trove of information that might provide useful in connecting Pendergast's operations in the city, but it did not have any details on those that he employed. As he flipped through its pages making notes of various names that were familiar, a shadow moved across the room.

"Lose something, Crisp?" The voice was cold and sharp.

Crisp turned slowly to see Bill Haggan and Jim Dowling standing in the doorway. Denis Skahill loomed menacingly behind them. Dowling's lips curled into a cruel smile as he stepped forward, cracking his knuckles ominously.

"Just routine business if it's anything to you," Crisp said, trying to maintain a calm he did not feel. His heart pounded in his chest; his hand tightened around the book, but in that moment, he decided to let it lay where it belonged in the desk. He pushed the drawer closed, and shifted as if organizing other paperwork on Banwell's desk.

"Not so fast," Haggan growled, moving closer. "Tom don't like you snooping around."

"What are you suggesting?" Crisp shrugged his shoulders casually as if ignoring the accusation.

Before Crisp could even brace himself, Haggan closed the distance between them and struck him hard in the midsection, driving the air from his lungs. He staggered, attempting to maneuver Banwell's heavy chair between them as a shield, but Haggan, reading the move, seized him by the shoulders and hurled him across the room. Skahill caught Crisp deftly, holding his arms in a vice-like grip, while Dowling rushed in, delivering cruel, calculated blows to his midsection.

The intensity of the assault escalated as Dowling forcefully grabbed Crisp, spun him around, and slammed him against the solid wood of Banwell's desk, scattering papers across the room. Skahill joined in, helping to pin Crisp down. Sharp pain radiated through Crisp's back as he feared the onslaught of some tortuous act as he'd witnessed in the pool hall. He couldn't move under the oppressive weight pressing him down and he knew the worst was yet to come. Dowling seized Crisp's left hand, flattening it on the desk. Crisp clenched his teeth, gripping the edge in a futile attempt to resist Skahill's massive hands which held him in place.

"Time you learned your place, Crisp," Dowling hissed, as he forcefully slammed the desk drawer on Crisp's fingers curled over the edge of the desktop. His cries of agony filled the room as Dowling pressed his weight onto the drawer, ensuring maximum pain. Crisp's eyes teared up from the intense pain and the stark realization of his vulnerability. Dowling leaned in close, his foul breath washing over him. "Remember this pain, Mr. Crisp. It will be worse next time," he sneered.

Laughter broke from Haggan, a cruel echo in the confines of the room. Just as they moved to restrain him again, footsteps resounded along the corridor in the adjoining hallway. "Mr. Pendergast? Are you in?" It was Speers' voice, timely and unaware of the brutality unfolding inside. With a surge of adrenaline, Crisp wrenched free from Skahill's grasp and staggered toward the doorway. Haggan lunged for him but missed, and Crisp, driven by desperation and pain, burst into the hallway. Speers looked up, startled, as a battered Crisp emerged, clutching his mangled hand to his chest, his face etched with pain and shock. "Algernon! What in God's name happened?"

Crisp, gasping for breath, managed a weak smile through his pain. "Nothing I can't survive." He shrugged his head over his shoulder, motioning toward the doorway where Haggan and Dowling stood, their faces twisted in frustration. Skahill's hulking form hovered just beyond the door frame, all three realizing their chance to permanently silence Crisp had just evaded them. As Speers moved to support him, Crisp knew this was only the beginning. Now more than ever, he was committed to bringing down the men who ruled the underbelly of Kansas

City, no matter the cost.

The next day was Saturday, offering Crisp a rare respite from his office tasks. Although Pendergast toiled seven days a week, there was little for his men to do during the weekends. The only exception was Banwell, whom Pendergast kept perpetually busy with planning and scheming, ensuring the wheels of their operation never stopped turning.

Beneath the subdued lighting in Shure's Hall on Ninth Street, the click of poker chips and the murmur of conversations created a familiar backdrop, but today, Crisp's heart wasn't in the game. He sat across from Moreland at a secluded table, his mind miles away from the high stakes that usually thrilled him. The smoke-filled room, once a sanctuary where he could lose himself in the thrill of gambling, now felt suffocating.

He raised a glass of whiskey to his lips with his good hand while his bandaged hand fumbled aimlessly with a deck of cards he had no intention of dealing.

"Marcus," he began, his voice low, his eyes not meeting those of his friend. "We know where he does it—the back lot behind The Pendergast Hotel. That's his stage for these atrocities." His hand gestured vaguely, the motion encompassing the magnitude of their hunt. "I found a room in the basement of a building, near where the wagons are parked." He gave an involuntary shudder, the memory of that grim, shadowed place crawling back over him like a cold wind. "I've got to get back there. I'm convinced it's the lair where he dwells."

Moreland shifted forward; his face serious in the flickering light of the oil lamps. "Yes, but knowing the devil's lair and catching him are two different matters. How do you intend to draw him out? Can you stop him before another life is lost? And are you entirely certain Wyse is the man?"

The torrent of questions silenced Crisp. His brow furrowed as he ran through the list of suspects, his voice a whisper lost amidst the saloon's clamor. "Wyse is the prime suspect—large and silent, always lurking. Taffe and Haggan aren't any less dangerous, slick and cruel. But then there's Dowling, impulsive and violent. He's responsible for this," he said holding up his bandaged hand which throbbed incessantly. We're dealing with Pendergast's worst, Marcus. Any one of them may be our man. Wyse is who I've been focused on, but I'm now second guessing that. Speers' men found a knife at one of the crime scenes. I took it to a cutlery merchant and they confirmed Dowling had been there on multiple occasions, but they also mentioned Wyse as waiting in the wings or parked outside in a wagon. It could be either of them individually, but now I have to wonder if they may be working together."

"From what I've seen, and the details you and Dr. Henwood have shared, I just don't see how this could be the work of multiple men. Something so cruel, so gruesome, isn't committed with an audience," Moreland suggested, his voice hushed as if the darkness of their conversation could summon the horrors they spoke of. Crisp listened intently, knowing Moreland's legal expertise and familiarity with criminals was invaluable. "Assault and rape, yes, those often times can be the work of a gang of perpetrators, but the carvings, the dismembering, the brutality, that is not something lightly witnessed," Moreland continued, his eyes darkening with the weight of his suggestion.

"But what if they are following directions?" Crisp countered, his mind working through the possibilities. "Any of these men would do whatever Pendergast told them to, alone or in concert."

Moreland shook his head, a shudder running down his spine. "No, I'd wager this is something far more sinister. This level of savagery—it's personal. Your only hope is to identify the specific man behind these crimes and catch him in the act."

Crisp nodded in agreement, the bleak reality of their task settling heavily between them. "I don't know if I would use the word savage, but sadistic could certainly be used to describe Dowling. I looked through the Chief's records and he's been in trouble before. Violent brawls, beatings, aggressions." The shadows around them seemed to grow darker as they contemplated the evil they were hunting, their resolve steeling against the fear that threatened to creep in. "So, if our man is Wyse, or Dowling, or any of the others, our only hope is to catch him in the act. We will have to lurk there, near that vile place I discovered, and wait to see which of them comes prowling." Crisp shuddered with the thought.

"Why don't you have Speers send some of his men around?"

"It's no use. He won't move until I give him proof positive. Any chance I could convince you to accompany me?"

"You know I've got your back. How shall we go about this?"

"From what we know thus far, it seems the killer operates at night. I can have Percy and his boys watch during the day for any signs of movement there, but I'd rather keep them out of danger after nightfall."

Moreland nodded; his face etched with concern. "What if he's there? How will we take him?"

Crisp waited for a waitress to pass. "Do you own a gun?"

"Yes."

"This will be dangerous."

As they plotted, the saloon doors swung open, admitting a gust of cold night air and Percy rushed in from the street. The boy's eyes, wide with urgency, scanned the room, finally landing on Crisp. He rushed over, breathless.

"Colonel, it's Miss Cassie! She's hurt bad—real bad."

———

The next morning, in the unadorned, clinically, white corridors of the City Hospital, Crisp stood vigil in a waiting room, his eyes fixed on the doorway to Cassie's room where she lay under constant medical attention. The cold reminder of the morgue in the building's basement sent shivers down his spine, as he thanked whatever fortune had spared her from that grim fate. Somewhere in the distance outside, church bells rang, but their tones provided no comfort. Moreland stood by his side, occasionally offering words of consolation.

The bustling of doctors and nurses created a backdrop of urgency that heightened his own anxiety. Each time one of them emerged from her room, his reaction was the same. He bombarded them with questions, but the answers never changed: "Rest is what she needs." Each time, a pang of dread twisted in his stomach, chipping away at his fortitude.

Speers burst through a set of doors in the corridor where Crisp and Moreland sat. "I came as soon as I heard," he declared, his voice laden with both sympathy and apprehension.

Crisp looked up, his features etched with worry and barely contained fury, before sinking deeper into the chair opposite his friend. "She was found half-dead near Ninth, strangled, Thomas—like the others. They say she's stable for now," he murmured, his voice a low blend of anger and despair, his hand wearily rubbing his forehead.

Speers leaned in, his face a mask of solemnity, and placed a hand on Crisp's shoulder. "I'm truly sorry, Algernon. I had no idea she was at risk," he said, pausing as his voice thickened with emotion. He turned to Moreland for more insight.

"Much like the others, though she fought back hard. Still, she received quite the beating," he offered gravely.

Speers angled to Moreland and whispered. "Were there any cuts or slashes?" When Moreland shook his head no, Speers turned back to Crisp, "We have to catch this man quickly. Have you got anything to act on?"

Moreland, feeling the gravity of their exchange, quietly excused himself. Crisp and Speers lowered their voices, discussing the ongoing investigation with intensity. "I've given this a lot of thought this morning, and now I suspect Jim Dowling may be our man," Crisp shared, his eyes brightening as he laid out his findings.

"Dowling? I thought your suspect is Wyse," Speers countered, his expression tightening into a thoughtful frown. He took the seat vacated by Moreland.

Crisp shook his head. "I connected Dowling to the butcher knife. He's often near the crime scenes, and something about him doesn't sit right." He cradled his wounded hand, but lifted it for emphasis. "And there's this. He didn't finish the job on me and now he's taken it out on her. It fits his violent profile, now I'm more convinced than ever."

Speers nodded thoughtfully, tapping his fingers on the armrest. "Dowling has a dark history for sure... He's been trouble before he ever got under Pendergast's wing. If you're positive, I'll get some men to pick him up discreetly. But—"

Crisp stood abruptly, fueled by a surge of determination and with anger flaring said, "I knew I could count on you. Let's head to Main Street, he's likely at Pendergast's now."

But, as he turned to leave, Speers grabbed his arm. "Algernon, wait. There's more you should know." His tone revealed a vulnerability previously unseen in the police chief. "Let's step outside, get some air," Speers suggested gently. Crisp nodded, the weight of his mission pressing down on him, yet his thoughts, for the first time, seemed sharpened with an unusual clarity.

Before they could leave, a nurse approached them, her expression serious, yet gentle. "Mr. Crisp, she is awake now and asking for you. You can see her, but please keep the visit short. She needs her rest."

Speers nodded and placed a firm but gentle hand on Crisp's shoulder. "Go to her."

The dull light in Cassie's room painted shadows across her pale face, accentuating the frailty brought on by her injuries. Crisp lingered at the door, his heart heavy with grief for what she had endured. Yet even in her weakened state, he couldn't help but marvel at the quiet strength that still radiated from her. He thought she was asleep, and tiptoed into the room, but her eyes flickered open as he entered, revealing that same unyielding spirit that had captivated him from the start.

"How are you feeling?" he took her hand gently.

She managed a weak smile. "Better, now that you're here," she whispered. "They say I'm lucky to be alive."

A flood of emotion washed over him as he gently squeezed her hand for reassurance. "You're stronger than any of us," he said softly, though the weight of her ordeal hung heavily between them.

He hadn't spoken to her since Friday afternoon, when she had tenderly cared for his wounds, her touch soft and reassuring despite the chaos surrounding them both. Now, standing at her bedside, the words caught in his throat. He stammered for a moment, unsure of how to proceed, before deciding there was no time for delicate pleasantries. He cleared his throat. "Cass, I need to know what happened. Can you tell me, who attacked you?"

A shadow of horror crept over her face, and her voice quivered as she forced herself to remember. "He was a behemoth... with hands so large," she shivered, "they encircled my entire neck." She shut her eyes tightly, and pulled her covers up tight around her neck, trying to banish the vision. "I can't shake the feeling of those filthy hands, scarred and grotesque."

"Did you see his face, Cass? We need to know who he is."

Her voice broke as she spoke, "Yes, it was horrifying. He had the face of a hideous beast—beady eyes and an oversized chin and mouth like some wild animal." Tears overwhelmed her again. "Oh Charlie, that monstrous face will be etched into my mind forever!"

In that moment, as he held her close, a revelation struck him. He remembered Denis Skahill's oddly proportioned and disfigured hands and face with an overall physical appearance pitilessly altered by some abnormal condition. He flashed back to enormous hands forcing him against Banwell's desk, a vivid image permanently imprinted in his mind. Skahill's hands bore deep scratches, with grime and dirt beneath his nails, a vivid contrast to Dowling's pristine, unblemished hands. But another detail from that brutal encounter now surfaced: as he lay pinned on the desk, his eyes had caught a glimpse of boots on the floor. It was Skahill's boot, side by side with Dowling's and his own, exceptionally large and outsizing both of them, and unmistakably marked with white paint along the sole.

Cassie's sobs broke the silence, sharp and sudden, drawing the attention of a vigilant nurse who came rushing in to comfort her. "Mr. Crisp, I must ask you to leave, she needs her rest!"

He gently released her hand, stepping back as she looked up at him with weary eyes. "You're safe now, Cass. Get some rest. I'll be right outside." His voice was soft, carrying a reassuring tenderness that belied the intensity of his concern.

In that fleeting moment, the scattered threads of his investigation wove together with absolute clarity. As he stepped out from her room, Moreland stood waiting outside, concern etching his features.

"What's the matter? You look as though you've seen a ghost."

Crisp turned to him, his face pale but his eyes burning with a fierce lucidity. "Marcus," he said, his voice barely above a whisper but laden with a chilling certainty, "I know who the killer is."

Chapter Fifteen

Crisp stepped outside to find Speers waiting on the steps of the hospital. One look at his face, and Speers immediately recognized the stunned expression—the shock of an unexpected revelation written all over him.

Everything was perfectly clear in Crisp's mind. The description of the towering figure of Skahill aligned unmistakably with the puzzle pieces he had been gathering, a truth so evident yet obscured in the tumult of the past few weeks, now stood out with piercing acuity. Skahill, scarcely around during Crisp's tenure at the Pendergast offices, had often been dispatched on errands that kept him from Crisp's scrutinizing gaze. Dismissed by all of his peers, including Pendergast, as nothing more than an imbecile, Skahill had strayed just far enough from view, never to be considered a figure of consequence.

And now, his physical form could not be overlooked. His enormous, scarred hands, bearing the marks left by the desperate struggles of his victims, his grotesquely twisted face, often the target of ridicule among Pendergast's men, and his oversized boots, far larger than those of an ordinary man, all marked him as a figure both fearsome and pitiable.

Crisp chastised himself for having jumped to conclusions about Wyse, and for overlooking the man who he now considered to be the killer. He stared past Speers as he approached. "What was it you wanted to tell me?" he said vacantly.

Speers sighed; the sound deeply heavy with burden. "My ties with Pendergast... they're more complicated than you know." He rose from the steps and motioned to Crisp to walk with him. "He's not just a man I keep tabs on for the city's sake. He's a sort of silent benefactor to the force, and to me, personally. He's a powerful man."

A cold realization washed over Crisp as the implications dawned on him. "What are you saying, Thomas? Is our investigation for nothing?"

Speers met his gaze squarely, the conflict evident in his eyes. "It's not black and white, Algernon. I've had to make hard choices, difficult ones, for the greater good of this city. Yes, he is involved in shady dealings, but he also supports the city in many ways. It's a delicate balance."

As Crisp absorbed the revelation, a nagging unease twisted inside him. He had long suspected a connection between Pendergast and Speers but had always dismissed it as inconsequential, a necessary alliance to navigate Kansas City's political landscape. Now faced with the undeniable truth, the weight of it pressed down on him. His chest tightened, and a thousand thoughts clashed in his mind—loyalty, justice, and the blurred lines between them. He finally spoke, his voice edged with a tension he could no longer hide. "So where do we stand, Chief? With the law, or with those who bend it?"

"That's a good question," Speers murmured, one he seemed reluctant to answer. "For now, let's focus on stopping the killer. We'll deal with the rest as it comes." They walked a few steps further and found a cramped, little courtyard where a marble statue of a guardian angel loomed above them, wings outstretched in a gesture meant to comfort. Three cherubs clustered at her feet; their innocent faces carved in delicate detail. Yet despite the angel's watchful gaze, the cold stone offered no solace, and the air in the courtyard remained heavy with an unshakable chill. "Are you sure about Dowling? There can be no doubt."

"I was wrong; it's not Dowling. It's Skahill. Cassie just told me everything." Crisp spoke softly, the weight of his discoveries etching deep lines into his weary face. "Thomas, I believe I've unearthed his lair—the very heart of his atrocities. If we wait there for him, we can catch him alone for sure."

Speers gestured toward a pair of weathered park benches, prompting Crisp to sit. They positioned themselves across from one another, the space between them charged with the severity of their conversation. Speers pitched forward; his features taut with concern as he drew a sharp breath. "Tell me everything."

The sun vanished behind the clouds just then as the distant church bells fell silent. Crisp glanced around, taking in the sudden, eerie silence that blanketed the courtyard. He tried to assemble the chaotic fragments of information into a clear narrative, as he recounted the macabre details he'd uncovered behind Pendergast's Hotel.

Speers listened intently, to every detail, every clue, every thread that Crisp provided. He absorbed the information with a heavy brow. After a moment of reflection, he spoke decisively. "Did you enter this place you describe?"

"I didn't have time, but I'm sure if we return, all will be revealed. It lies hidden just behind the wagons that are used to move the bodies."

"Waiting to trap Skahill at his den might prove disastrous. Your theory hinges on him snatching his victims elsewhere, only to bring them there—either dead or barely clinging to life—for his dark ritual. If you're wrong—" His words hung there while he paused considering the consequences. Eventually he continued, "We need to be sure. We cannot risk another innocent suffering as Cassie did under this man's hands. Chances are, whether it's Skahill or another man, he is on to you." Speers, suddenly looking older and more worn than his years, leaned back on the bench, the lines of his face drawn tight with weariness that went beyond physical exhaustion. He began, his voice low, "There's more. You need to understand the position I'm in. I can't openly act against Pendergast. Not directly. His reach extends not just into the streets of The Bottoms, but into the very fabric of this city."

Crisp listened intently, his jaw set, as Speers continued.

"I'm on his payroll, for protection, but there's more to it than that. He ensures that his part of the city operates under his rules, which means turning a blind eye to the vice rampant there. It's politics—ugly, but necessary. He controls the First Ward, and he's angling to tighten his grip on the city."

Crisp, absorbed the full weight of Speers' words, as he ran his unbandaged hand through his hair. "Just stop," he interrupted. He knew the complexities of law and order in this city were intertwined with corruption and survival, but it had gone too far. "What you're telling me," he said slowly, "is that we're hackled when it comes to moving against him directly."

"Exactly," Speers replied gravely. "If Pendergast even suspects you're working against him, he won't hesitate to cut you loose—and I don't have to tell you, he won't do so gently. My hands are tied, Crisp. Even I can't protect you from what he might do."

Crisp nodded, his mind whirred with possibilities as he considered his next steps. "So, even Cassie's testimony identifying Skahill counts for nothing?" he asked, though he already knew the answer, the bitter truth that her reputation would be used against her.

Speers shook his head. He needed undeniable proof, something irrefutable.

"We need specific evidence," Crisp said, more to himself than to Speers. "So, if I catch Skahill in the act, or somehow coerce a confession out of him, that's the only way you'll be able to act?"

Speers sighed; the sound heavy with resignation. "Yes, and even then, it will need to be handled delicately. Even if I send my men to this lair you've discovered, it may tip him off. He may go into hiding, or he may just take a respite from his crimes. We won't have anything on him. If we move against any of Pendergast's men without ironclad proof, it could blow up in our faces."

Crisp's eyes hardened with determination. "Then that's what I'll do. I'll get the evidence we need to move forward. I'll set a trap and lure him in."

Speers looked at Crisp with a mixture of admiration and

concern. "Be careful, Algernon. You're playing a dangerous game. Make sure you're not the one who gets caught."

Crisp hesitated as he turned to go back into the hospital, torn between moving against Skahill or staying by Cassie's side. His heart pulled him in both directions.

Speers read his concern, "She's safe now. There's nothing for you to do here. Go get the evidence we need," he said reassuringly.

Crisp extended his good hand to Speers, who took it with a firm grip and clasped his left hand over top reassuringly. "I'll do what must be done," he affirmed, his voice steady despite the storm of emotions inside him. "But not yet. I need time to think." He moved up the steps to the hospital and glanced back at Speers.

In a pensive tone, Speers called from the park bench, "I'm afraid you will have to do this on your own, Algernon. I cannot help you." He waited, letting his words sink in. "You're a good man caught in an impossible situation. Just... make sure you come out of it alive."

In the shadowed sanctuary of the old stone church located in the West Bottoms, the confessional booth stood as a silent witness to the sins of its congregation. The last of the penitents had departed, leaving their burdens with the priest and accepting their penance for absolution. However, one figure lingered in the shaded recesses, shrouded in shadows, hesitant yet waiting for the right moment to step forward.

The heavy velvet curtain whispered shut behind the hulking figure of a man whose large hands trembled as he sat down. It was well past vespers, and the church was draped in the kind of oppressive silence that weighed heavily on the soul. The man sat in the confessional booth, feeling the hard wood of the bench beneath him and the coolness of the enclosed space. The blood rushed in his ears in the stillness, throbbing dully as he grappled with the weight of his sins and the depth of his desire for absolution. Through the tiny grille separating him from the priest, he could barely make out a flickering candle; its light cast ghostly images on the wooden walls, mirroring the turmoil within him. The simple, dark interior of the booth seemed to close in around him, heightening his sense of isolation and reflection as he prepared to unburden his soul.

"Bless me, Father, for I have sinned," the man's choked voice was nothing more than a deep whisper, breaking the solemn hush that filled the confessional.

Father McClary, separated from the man by only the thin lattice of the confessional screen, stiffened. A familiar voice—a voice that had haunted his nights, a voice that brought with it not only the sins of the man confessing, but his own. His heart sank as he immediately recognized the deep-set tone. The man on the other side was no stranger. It was his son—the product of McClary's own sin—born out of a moment of weakness that had damned them both.

"What troubles you, my son?" His words were hollow, trembling slightly as he forced calm into his voice, yet the dread already burrowed into his core.

A ragged breath, then a sob. "Father, I... I've done things. Bad things. The demons… they've come back. I couldn't stop them. They control me."

McClary's hand gripped the rosary he always held during confessions, but this time, it wasn't in prayer for the penitent. He squeezed the beads so tightly they bit into his palm, the pain keeping him grounded in the storm of emotions that raged beneath his cassock. A flash of a memory—the heat of summer years ago, the soft whisper of temptation, the fall into sin. He had sought his own absolution after it happened, kneeling in a similar confessional booth, muttering his sins of fornication and guilt for the child conceived out of wedlock. But the penance had never been enough. He had sinned again by hiding his son, cloaking the boy's identity under a false name. And now this—this abomination—had returned to claim him.

His voice cracked, betraying his inner turmoil. "What have you done, son?" But in his heart, McClary knew. He had always known. The darkness that Skahill carried, the evil that had taken root, had been festering since birth. This was his sin to bear. His punishment for breaking his vow of celibacy.

"I tried, Father. I tried to be good, but the urges, the needs—they're too strong," Skahill wept. His sobs were broken, childlike, but there was no innocence in them—only desperation.

McClary closed his eyes, fighting the swell of emotions—anger, guilt, fear. He had failed as a priest, as a man of God, and most damning of all, as a father. His betrayal to his holy vow had given birth to a monster. And yet, there was still a flicker of love, buried beneath the weight of his shame. A father's love, but one twisted by the need for redemption.

How many times had he begged God for forgiveness for the sin of fathering Skahill? How many sleepless nights had he spent praying to atone for his fleshly weakness?

He recalled the day he had whispered his own confession to the priest behind the grille. "Bless me, Father, for I have sinned. I have broken my vows. There is a woman, and a child…" The absolution given then felt hollow. How could any prayer erase the living, breathing reminder of his fall from grace? Now, that same child, a grown man lost to madness, sat on the other side of the grille, begging for forgiveness.

"I can't help you anymore," McClary's voice hardened. His hands shook, his heart heavy with the burden of knowing his son had become a murderer, a demon birthed by his own sin. "I gave you a chance. I helped you change your name, gave you a path forward, and still, you have fallen. Do you expect me to save you now?"

Skahill's sobbing stopped, and for a moment, there was only silence between them. "Do you still love me?" Skahill's voice was small, fragile, as though he were still a boy asking his father for comfort after a nightmare.

McClary's chest tightened. Love. That word felt like a curse now. "No," he said finally, his tone low, bitter. "I cannot love what you have become. You are my punishment. And I cannot shield you any longer. Your path leads to ruin, and I will not be there with you."

"I'm sorry, Father. I wanted to be good," Skahill whimpered, the child in him surfacing once more, but McClary's heart had hardened.

"Go to Hugh McLaughlin in The Patch. He will keep you

hidden. I will not help you anymore." His voice broke, but he recovered quickly, his tone resolute. "Leave now. And do not return to this church. Ever."

Skahill rose, the weight of his father's rejection pressing down on him, and for a moment, he hesitated. McClary watched the shadow of his son pause, but his own guilt, his own fear of damnation, held him back from speaking more.

"I have no more words for you," McClary whispered, his hands clutching the rosary tighter. "Do not bring your shame back here."

With a strangled cry, Skahill ran—like a child fleeing from punishment. His heavy footsteps echoed through the sanctuary, and McClary remained seated in the confessional, the tears he had held back now spilling down his cheeks. His sin had returned, not just in the form of Skahill's crimes, but in the undeniable truth of his own guilt. McClary wept.

As soon as his conversation with Speers had ended, Crisp wasted no time in hurrying to check on Cassie once more. The doctor's reassurances had done little to ease his growing sense of helplessness. Marcus had remained by Crisp's side at the hospital well into the afternoon, offering what comfort he could as he watched his friend burdened by the bleak circumstances thrust upon him. Eventually, he had said, "I must go now, Algernon. I've an early start tomorrow and some matters to attend to. If you need anything, send your boy around, and I'll do my best to rearrange my schedule. Be careful my friend."

Now, Crisp lingered by himself, the weight of guilt tugging at him as he watched Cassie resting inside the modest comfort of her room. He felt obliged to stay as long as he could. He'd promised to protect her, yet the urgency to act against Skahill prodded him relentlessly. He knew time was slipping away, and despite the ache of leaving her, he had no choice but to move swiftly.

As the setting sun raced toward the horizon, Crisp ventured back to the desolate lot behind the Pendergast Hotel, this time with Percy stationed on Ninth Street to keep watch. The lot attendant was conspicuously absent, likely taking advantage of the single day of leisure afforded to him on a Sunday. Since his last visit, Crisp's determination had solidified into an unyielding conviction. With nerves of steel, he moved through the lot with a newfound confidence, ready to face whatever discoveries lay ahead.

He grappled with his thoughts, the weight of what lay ahead pressing down on him like a vice. He wasn't entirely sure what he would do when he arrived, only that the inevitable confrontation loomed before him like a dark, jagged cliff. If Skahill was there, he knew with chilling certainty that he would have to kill him—there was no other way. But if the man wasn't there? The notion lingered, unsettling him. He tried to reassure himself, telling himself that Skahill likely wasn't there now, that he should turn back, that it wasn't time yet. Yet, despite the inner turmoil, something deeper pulled him forward, a need to see for himself, to confront whatever fate awaited him.

He made his way to the shadowed corner of the lot where the wagons hunkered in silence. Nearing the broken fence, he'd discovered previously, Crisp uncovered the dark void of what turned out to be an empty window frame—a portal into a makeshift underworld. He exhaled a sigh of relief, the tension in his shoulders easing as he took in the empty space. Yet beneath that relief simmered a darker wish—he almost wanted Skahill to be there, to have him in his sights so he could end it all with a single shot from his Derringer. The absence of the brute brought a fleeting sense of peace, but the unfulfilled urge to deliver justice ate away at him, leaving him torn between relief and a thirst for finality.

Clutching a lantern tightly in his good hand, he forced himself to descend into the obscurity. The cramped space was only accessible via a haphazard staircase crudely fashioned from stacked boxes of various sizes that formed primitive steps leading into the basement of a building lining the western side of the lot. Each careful footstep took Crisp deeper into the gloom, his heart pounding a frantic rhythm against his ribs as he climbed in.

The metallic tang of blood clung to the damp walls of the space and seemed to seep into the earth itself. As his eyes adjusted and the lamp sputtered to life, its feeble ochre light cast flickering shadows across the chamber. Every corner whispered secrets; every shadow shifted with the weight of dark deeds. This was a sanctum of horror, a shrine where unspeakable acts were sacraments. A chilling realization washed over Crisp like ice water: this was the very heart of darkness, a place where Skahill's perverse rituals gave birth to nightmares.

On top of a barrel used as a table, lay an old butcher's knife, its blade stained with the evidence of countless horrors, the handle worn smooth by malevolent hands. Above it, a lock of hair tied with a pink ribbon hung grotesquely from the rafters, swaying in an unseen breeze that whispered through the darkness. On the ground below his feet, a scattering of women's garments—a torn garter belt among them—painted a tale of terror. Each piece, soiled and ripped, served as a macabre trophy from the killer's gruesome conquests.

He carefully stepped around the pieces of fabric with heart racing, and knelt to examine the dirt floor of the dimly lit chamber, tracing the faint impressions of heavy boots. The evidence was damning, a silent testament to the horrors enacted in this secluded chamber of hell. But as he pieced together the fragments of Skahill's macabre rituals, the tiny room seemed to pulse with a sinister life of its own, as if the walls themselves were complicit in the deeds performed here. He contemplated on which pieces of evidence to take, which could he tie directly to Skahill? Yet, if he took something now, and Skahill returned later to find it missing, as Speers had suggested, he would likely move his den of horror elsewhere, or simply go into hiding. He decided he must wait.

Suddenly, a noise echoed from the lot above, piercing the heavy silence of the lair. Could it be the salvage worker, or someone else nosing around? With his heart in his throat, Crisp cautiously peered through the ragged window frame. His blood ran cold as he spotted Skahill, the giant of a man, solemnly hooking up a horse to the ominous red wagon. The very sight of Skahill, moving with a purposeful grace, sent a wave of panic through Crisp. Just then, Skahill unexpectedly began to move toward the lair. Crisp frantically searched for an escape. The room felt smaller, the air thicker. Seemingly trapped, he spotted, at the last possible second, an old battered door cut into one wall, hidden behind a pile of boxes. With no time to spare, Crisp scrambled behind the door into a darker, adjoining enclosure and hastily extinguished his lantern.

Silently, he pulled the door closed toward him; it latched tight with a soft, ominous click. From his precarious hideout, he watched through a crack in the broken door as Skahill descended into the chamber, his presence, like a shadow falling over the world. Through the narrow slit, Crisp observed Skahill pacing about, his movements restless, as if hunting for something elusive. Finally, abandoning the search, Skahill drew a piece of fancy red fabric from his pocket, holding it close as he carefully studied its intricate pattern and texture. He brought it to his nose, inhaling its scent, before casually draping it over a rusted nail sticking out from the rafters. With deliberate care, he then picked up the stained butcher's knife and raised it close to his face.

With an unsteady hand Crisp silently retrieved the Derringer from his pocket and reached for the edge of the door. He had two shots, one to wound, the second to kill. He was frozen in hesitation. Could he do it? Could he stop this monster? He tugged gently at the door, but it was stuck and would not budge. His bandaged hand only hampered his efforts further. He peered through the cracked door watching Skahill. There was no chance for a clean shot through the gap where he spied his prey.

Skahill inspected his blade with a practiced eye, oblivious to Crisp's presence. He looked around the room again, his beady eyes searching.

Crisp felt for the edge of the door once again. If he tugged harder it might jar open. As he applied pressure, he considered using his boot for leverage, but it was no use—the door would not budge. He peeked through the gap again, but Skahill was gone. Now he realized he was trapped; the door had latched from the outside. He struggled with relighting his lantern, but after expending three matches he gave up. There was no visible way back to the lot, no other egress from this dark tomb. Desperation clawed at him as he groped his way through the pitch blackness, guided only by a faint glimmer of daylight peeking through a crack somewhere in the inky blackness. Striking his last match, he stumbled toward the source of light, revealing an old, grimy window. After battling to slide it open and failing to do so, he held his handkerchief up to one of its panes and punched through the old glass. His voice, hoarse with fear, called out into the chilling air, "Percy! Down here."

The boy, who had seen the red wagon pulling away from the back of the lot, and had already begun searching for Crisp, now rushed to his aid. Together, they pried the window open just wide enough for Crisp to squeeze through, but it was no use—he became stuck. Panic clawed at him as he struggled, knowing every second lost was another step Skahill took toward escape. Percy's sharp eyes spotted a hole further down the outside of the wall, and without wasting time, Crisp wriggled free and plunged back into the darkness. His hands searched frantically through the pitch-black, finally finding another door that led to the room with the hole. With Percy's help, Crisp clambered out of the gap, emerging into the harsh light of reality. They realized that Skahill was on the move and that he must be stopped before he vanished into the city's shadowy depths.

They tore through the back alley where Skahill had vanished, their footsteps slapping against the moist ground and echoing off the alley walls. It led them to Hickory Street, but Skahill was nowhere in sight. Crisp sent Percy running north toward Ninth while he sprinted the opposite direction to St. Louis Avenue. From the corner of each street, they exchanged desperate signals—nothing. Skahill had seemingly vanished into the labyrinth of streets. Crisp pointed to the east and raced down St. Louis Avenue, Percy following parallel along Ninth. As they ran, their eyes scanned every nook and outlet along their paths for the telltale red wagon, but as daylight faded, Skahill could not be found. After combing every narrow pathway and side street within a four-block stretch, Crisp finally gave in and enlisted Percy's crew of street boys to widen the search. By nightfall, it was clear—Skahill had slipped through their fingers.

Returning to the lonely confines of Meadows' Boardinghouse, Crisp spent a sleepless night, his mind tossing and turning over every misstep, every lost moment that had allowed The West Bottoms killer to escape.

Chapter Sixteen

It had been a long and tumultuous weekend starting with Crisp's capture by Dowling and his crew, followed by the brutal attack on Cassie, and ending with the fruitless search for Skahill, and now Crisp felt weary and dragged out. Although it was Monday, he was hesitant to return to Pendergast's office. Surely Dowling and Haggan had reported the incident from Friday, and Banwell already had a wariness about him that suggested he was on to him. Now things would be different. Yet if he didn't show up, what then? Would Banwell send his thugs looking for Crisp? Had Pendergast already been made aware? If so, there would be no going back.

Yet, he decided his best move was to show up to the office as if nothing had happened; if Banwell inquired about his encounter with Dowling and the others, he would simply dismiss it as a minor misunderstanding. Worst case, if Pendergast and his cronies were waiting there for Crisp's arrival, he would dispatch Percy to summon Speers, although he wasn't sure that meant anything. But he didn't make for the office immediately—there was a matter of greater urgency. Earlier that morning, one of Percy's gang of street urchins had caught sight of the giant of a man named Skahill, lumbering towards the slum district just blocks from Crisp's boardinghouse. Without delay, the boy had raced to Crisp, breathless and wide-eyed, bearing the news.

The March sky, heavy with grey clouds, cast a sullen gloom over the already bleak neighborhood known as The Patch. Home to eight hundred souls, this peculiar squatter settlement hardly qualified as a proper community, lacking even the basics of streets or alleys. The houses, dingy and stained with soot, were scattered at haphazard angles, as if tossed by a careless hand. The only semblance of order was the numbered plaques affixed to each structure. At the center of this disarray stood the McLaughlin Saloon, a dark and brooding landmark, serving as the nerve center for Hugh McLaughlin, the so-called 'King of The Patch' and the undisputed leader of its affairs. Though his domain was a mere two city blocks, McLaughlin's influence rivaled that of Jim Pendergast, albeit on a more modest scale. To the residents of The Patch, McLaughlin's word was law, and uniquely, he was the only outsider embraced by the Croatian majority, his authority unchallenged, his presence the bedrock of their community.

Crisp moved through the narrow, cluttered pathways amongst the slovenly hovels and ramshackle dwellings with a hunter's focus, his eyes scanning every doorway, every lean-to, every potential hiding spot for a sign of Denis Skahill. Amidst the desolation of the slum stood an unnoteworthy decrepit house. Neighbors had whispered of a hulking figure seen slipping through the shadows, and now Crisp was certain Skahill hid within.

As he approached the ramshackle residence, he noted broken windows patched with newspaper and a door hanging slightly ajar. He could almost feel the presence of the man lurking inside, a shadowed form just beyond the grasp of his vision. Stepping quietly toward the house, he sheltered behind a pile of refuse, as a movement caught his eye. A silhouette shifted within the shadowed interior, but the figure's features melted into the gloom, unidentifiable. His heart thudded in his chest, each beat a drum of war as he edged closer, his hand resting on the Derringer pocketed in his coat.

Just as he stepped forward, readying himself to challenge the shadow, a harsh voice cut through the silence. "What are you skulking around here for?" Patrolman Crotty emerged from around the corner of another tumbledown shack, his baton in hand, a sneer twisting his lips.

Crisp turned, frustration and urgency battling within him. "Crotty, this isn't the time. Skahill is in there, and I need to get to him before he slips away."

Crotty stepped closer; his eyes gleaming with malice. "I know all about your little chase, but you're out of your district Crisp. In fact," he said, gesturing dismissively behind Crisp with scorn, "as soon as you crossed them tracks, you entered Kansas. Seems we're both outside Speers' jurisdiction here." He removed his patrolman's overcoat, and stood leering at Crisp. It was clear Crisp no longer faced lawman Crotty, but instead looked upon a common thug interested in only one thing.

Crotty came forward, catlike on the balls of his feet, and then lunged, his baton slicing through the air with deadly intent. Crisp recoiled just in time, the baton narrowly missing him, the whoosh of it close enough to stir the hair on his neck. He was at a disadvantage with his bandaged hand, yet fueled by a surge of adrenaline, he countered with a swift movement, tackling Crotty to the ground with a force that knocked the wind out of both men. They tumbled into the muck of The Patch; their bodies entangled in a vicious ballet of violence. Mud splattered as fists and feet flew; Crisp's punches with his good hand were precise, each one imbued with the weight of his desperate quest, while Crotty's responses were crude, driven by brute strength and deep-set hatred.

The brawl escalated under the watchful eyes of the locals rapidly gathering in a tight circle around them, their voices rising in a crescendo of jeers and cheers. Each blow exchanged between the men was punctuated by the crowd's hungry shouts. As he grappled with Crotty, Crisp's mind sped through his options. His initial tactical advantage slipped away under the scrutiny of the encroaching spectators. The thought of drawing his Deringer crossed his mind, a desperate consideration dismissed swiftly; the risks of a stray bullet in such a dense crowd were too high.

Struggling to his feet, he met Crotty's next charge with a hardened gaze. They clashed again, this time against the corrugated metal of a makeshift lean-to, the tin buckling under their weight. Crisp's eyes darted around frantically, searching for anything that might serve as a weapon amid the surrounding debris, but nothing suitable caught his eye. Amidst the chaos, he spotted a dark figure observing the fight silently from the shadowed shack just out of reach, an ominous reminder of the stakes at play.

Crotty barreled into him once more, pinning him against the lean-to with the full weight of his body. Trapped and running out of options, Crisp groped desperately along the gritty surface behind him, his fingers seeking to gain leverage. But as their struggle continued, it was clear that the fight was far from over, each man driven by forces both personal and profound, and neither demonstrating an edge over his opponent.

Then Crotty went after Crisp's bandaged hand. Crisp caught his eye and read his mind before he could take hold leaving Crotty to grasp Crisp's wrist and forcing Crisp to maneuver defensively. With his free hand, Crotty snatched repeatedly at Crisp's weak spot, each attempt thwarted by Crisp's desperation. Crotty took advantage of Crisps' position and pushed him around at will. Just as it seemed he had the advantage on Crisp, a spry figure darted through the crowd. Percy, short and wiry, slipped between the onlookers and kicked Crotty hard in the side. A scruffy dog that had barked feverishly throughout the entire bout chose this moment to latch onto Crotty's pantleg. The distraction gave Crisp the moment he needed to break free.

"Come, Colonel!" Percy yelled, pulling Crisp to his feet. Together, they dashed through the muck and filth of The Patch, leaving behind both the shouts of the crowd and the venomous obscenities from Crotty. Crisp's heart pounded not just from the escape but from the burn of betrayal and mounting frustrations that seared at him with every step.

Crotty had seemed to know of Crisp's purpose, perhaps all along, and had interfered not just out of rivalry but to protect the sordid network within The Patch. As they slowed to a stop a few blocks away, hidden in the shade of a looming warehouse, Crisp clapped a hand on Percy's shoulder, grateful yet overwhelmed. "Thanks, boy. I owe you."

Percy nodded; his young face etched in determination. "Just get him, Mr. Crisp. Get him before he hurts anyone else. Let's go back now."

In between breaths, Crisp coached the boy. "Not yet, not until we have the upper hand." He caught his breath and nudged the boy onward with the weight of his task settling heavily upon him. The fight had been lost, but the battle was far from over. He needed to regroup, replan, and act swiftly. Skahill remained hidden within the confines of The Patch, but for how long. Crisp knew the path would be harder than he'd ever imagined to find the monster lurking in that foul district on his next visit.

———

Late into the night, the sterile confines of the City Hospital were cloaked in a subdued quiet that was punctuated only by the soft footsteps of nurses and the distant murmurs of uneasy patients.

Cassie drifted in and out of restless sleep, her dreams dark and suffocating. Her nightmare held her in a dark maze where shadowy figures closed in from all sides. She ran, her breath catching in her throat, legs trembling with the effort, but the labyrinth twisted endlessly. She could hear ragged breaths behind her, closing in with reaching hands.

Through the haze of terror, she saw Crisp ahead, his figure strong and sure, a beacon in the darkness. She called out to him, her voice raw with fear, but the ground beneath her began to crumble, spilling into an abyss that separated them. Crisp's eyes were wide with determination, his arms outstretched, but there was nothing he could do as the gap between them widened.

Her dependence on Crisp was complete. He was her protector. But even as she reached for him, her fingers brushed only air, the distance between them growing impossibly vast. His voice, once so steady, now seemed hollow, fading into the darkness as she realized that he, too, was powerless.

And then blackness engulfed her and she slept thoughtlessly.

Outside, a bitter wind whipped through the streets, but inside, all seemed peaceful—until violence shattered the calm.

A hulking shadow loomed within the sanctuary, moving with disturbing grace. A giant of nightmarish proportions stalked forward, his fury warping his features, driven by a single, terrifying purpose. His monstrous presence hovered over the frail and vulnerable patient below him.

A door creaked open when an unsuspecting young orderly stepped into the patient's room. Her eyes widened in horror at the sight of the giant, his enormous hands reaching for the frail form of Cassie Curtain who still slumbered uneasily. Driven by instinct, the orderly shouted for help, her voice slicing through the corridor's silence, as she lunged forward in a desperate attempt to thwart the kidnapping.

The scuffle that followed was both swift and violent. The giant, taken aback by the sudden and spirited defense, reacted with raw strength, thrusting the orderly against the wall with a thud and a crash of furniture that resonated along the hospital halls. In his other arm, he grasped Cassie, who awakened to a nightmare, screaming and struggling against his iron hold.

As the commotion escalated, nurses and other hospital staff

rushed toward the disturbance. Locked in a desperate struggle, Cassie managed a final act of defiance, clawing at the giant's face, and eliciting a guttural bellow of pain from him. With his grip loosened, she slipped from his hold, and the giant, his mission thwarted and face bloodied, shoved aside anyone in his path as he bolted into a maze of hallways, desperate to escape. The beastly man slunk into a hidden corner somewhere in the darkness; a concealed nook hidden from his pursuers.

In the chaotic minutes that followed, it seemed like order had been restored. Orderlies bustled about, straightening Cassie's room with hurried efficiency and nurses moved with practiced hands, trying to soothe her frayed nerves. But the tension still hung in the air and preyed upon staff and patient alike.

The police arrived moments later, igniting chaos once again, as they flushed their quarry and the chase intensified. Officers dashed through the labyrinth of hospital corridors, following the thunderous echoes of the giant's escape. The chase was frenetic, with the echoes of boots and shouts filling every turn and stairwell. In a desperate bid for freedom, the giant man smashed a large window at the rear of the building, disappearing into the enveloping darkness outside, and leaving behind a wake of shattered glass and shaken lives.

Inside, the hospital slowly regained its calm, but the fear and adrenaline of those harrowing moments lingered, a stark reminder of the danger that had just escaped into the night.

As first light, not more than a couple of hours later, Crisp, still battered and bruised from his earlier altercations, plodded toward the hospital. His steps were heavy with exhaustion, but his determination to check on Cassie pushed him forward.

Another restless night had left him feeling like a frayed rope about to come undone at any moment, scarcely able to hold back any amount of force or resistance. The day before, he had reported to the 520 Main office, after he'd cleaned up from his foray into The Patch. As if nothing at all had happened last week, Banwell simply greeted him indifferently and immediately piled on loads of paperwork, that kept Crisp at the office until late in the evening.

Throughout the tiresome day, Crisp had kept a wary watch for Dowling and his boys, but they did not show themselves. Likewise, Skahill had been conspicuously absent from the office, and to Crisp's surprise, he learned the man had in fact not been seen for several days. This he gathered from inquiries with Gallagher and Wyse. He hadn't planned on what he would do if he encountered Skahill at the office, but now his hopes that Skahill remained holed up in the Patch were rekindled. He also questioned other staff members in the hotel, but all he uncovered was the fact that Skahill's presence was always elusive; he seldom lingered with the others, nor remained at either office for long. More often than not, he was out 'running errands' for the boss, or so everyone presumed.

Crisp let all those thoughts tumble into the gutter as he ascended the steps to the hospital, his thoughts shifting now solely on what awaited him inside. Speers, who hung vigilantly outside Cassie's room, shot forward to intercept Crisp.

"Hello, Thomas, why all the Bobs hanging around?"

"Algernon, she was attacked again last night," Speers said, his voice tense, "But she's okay now." He tried to slow Crisp who rushed past, only to be halted by another policeman standing outside her closed door. Through the glass window of the door, he could see Cassie resting peacefully under the policeman's guard.

"Someone broke in and tried to take her. An orderly stopped the attack, thank God, but he got away," Speers continued.

Crisp's mind raced with fear and anger; he clenched his jaw as the implications settled in. "It must've been Skahill; did anyone see him? He knows I'm after him now," he muttered through gritted teeth, the reality of his situation sinking in. His pursuit of Skahill had turned personal and perilous, bringing danger not only to himself but to those he cared about.

Noticing the unyielding determination in Crisp's gaze, Speers edged closer. "Algernon, you need to be careful. This man is dangerous, and now he's desperate."

Crisp nodded, the harsh grip of reality tightening around him. "I know that. But I won't stop until I've caught him. He's made this personal, and I intend to end it."

A nurse squeezed by, and before she closed the door behind, Crisp whispered, "Let her know I am here."

Outside her room, the hospital had returned to its uneasy quiet, but for Crisp, the silence was a call to action. The stakes had been raised. The hunt was more urgent than ever. His determination was unshakable, his course was set. Skahill would be brought to justice, no matter the cost.

Speers stayed close to Crisp's side throughout the day, providing both emotional support and tactical counsel as needed. Their conversation remained intense, undisturbed by the constant clatter of orderlies, nurses, and patients bustling around them. Convincing Crisp to leave Cassie's side had taken a monumental effort, but the additional presence of Speers' men, coupled with Speers' reassurance that Skahill would now be in hiding, finally convinced him that she would be safe for the time being.

They found an unused patient room where they could speak freely and Speers ushered Crisp inside.

"I'm close Thomas... he stays in the Patch."

"Are you sure its Skahill?"

"I'm going off what the boys saw, but they have seen the man before."

Speers shook his head in doubt. "If he's holed up there, then how can we be certain he's the man who broke in last night."

"Surely someone saw him? Didn't anyone identify him? It wouldn't be hard."

"Just vague descriptions. A big man, yes, but not certain it was Skahill."

"Who else could it be?" Crisp asked, his voice laced with astonishment.

"You mentioned Carnes and Wyse. They are big men, right?"

"But why would they do this? No, it had to be him. I think he saw me there looking for him in The Patch."

Speers, his brow furrowed in concern, leaned forward in his chair. "Like I've said before, we need something definitive on Skahill before I go to Pendergast."

Crisp, his face drawn with fatigue and frustration, countered immediately. "I don't understand. What about your Bertillon

System? You've had long-standing orders with your men to abduct suspects, to hold them, or even run them out of town if necessary. How is Skahill any different?"

Speers shook his head, his expression solemn. "It's no use, Crisp. This is different. This man is one of Pendergast's. I can't move against him without something concrete—I need irrefutable evidence that even Pendergast can't ignore."

Crisp raised his voice. "What more do you need? Cassie's identified him as her attacker."

"I can't jump to any false conclusions on this one. Everything we've got is circumspect. It won't stand against him. We either have to catch him in the act, or in that lair you've discovered. We've got to tie it all together proof positive."

Crisp's good hand clenched into a fist; the frustration palpable. "And while we wait for this 'irrefutable evidence,' how many more women have to be attacked? How long until he slips through our fingers entirely?" He paused, biting back the sharp retort that had slipped out, already regretting the edge in his voice.

Speers sighed, his gaze steady on Crisp. "I understand your frustration, Algernon, I do. But my hands are tied in ways you don't fully appreciate. If I step out of line, without adequate proof, Pendergast will shut us down, and any hope of catching Skahill evaporates. We play this by the book, or we don't play it at all."

Crisp took a deep breath and calmed himself. "I saw him in that den I spoke of. I waited there, and he came. He had some sort of garment or women's hanky. He pulled it from his pocket and hung it along with his other trophies he's collected. There was blood on the ground, or what looks like blood. I'm pretty sure it was blood. Oh. And then he rummaged around until he found a large butcher knife. He left promptly, but we lost in him in the streets."

"Did you gather any of that evidence?"

"No, I was cut off from him, trapped in another room where I observed his movements unseen. It's a long story," he held his hands up in defense. "But I can go back now and get those things, and more. There's plenty of evidence there."

"That's a shame, you're a better detective than that. You should've gathered the clues right then and there." Speers shook his head in disappointment. "Those things may be gone when you go back," he added gruffly.

"Listen. The past few days have been very trying," Crisp argued. "I don't need to be reprimanded at the moment, thank you very much."

The room fell silent for a long moment, the weight of the situation settled heavily between them. Finally, Crisp leaned back in his chair, rubbing his temples wearily. He shifted strategy on Speers. "There's too many of your men here; he won't be back. What if some of your men accompany me to Pendergast's Hotel? As soon as we see Skahill, we'll tell him we want to ask him some questions. That will surely call his bluff."

Speers shook his head. "Nothing at Pendergast's. We need to catch him elsewhere."

"If only we had some way to lure him out from The Patch; something so compelling he can't resist."

A spark shown in Speers' eye and he snapped his fingers. "There's a temperance protest later this week on St. Louis

Avenue," he repeated. "It's exactly the sort of event that could draw him out. I'll have extra patrolmen there, but that's not enough. I'll need your eyes too; it's our only chance to spot Skahill."

Crisp nodded, with the conviction returning to his voice. "Yes. We can pass the word in the streets; sow discontent and drum up resistance among the locals, something he can't refuse." Speers saw a spark of ingenuity rekindled in Crisp's eyes. "I'll be there," he assured Speers. "But we can't let him get away in the meantime. We'll have to keep eyes on The Patch. If he moves, we'll try to corner him until your men can get there." Crisp paced the confines of the room, the rhythmic steps his tried-and-true method for untangling his thoughts. "I'll see if I can work from the hotel office this week, in case he turns up there, or maybe one of the others will see him. A few greenbacks in the right hands of the staff will alert me if he comes around."

Speers shook his head. "I don't think going back to Pendergast's is a good idea. I received this message today." He handed over a piece of paper.

Crisp took the note, reading the neat, precise handwriting. It said, *please stop by my office this week. I want to discuss this new man.*

"Whose writing is this?"

"I thought you'd recognize it for sure. It's Pendergast's," Speers replied, his voice laden with a mix of caution and inevitability.

The implications of the note were dire as Crisp handed the paper back to Speers. He raised his bruised hand showing it to Speers. "You're right. Maybe I shouldn't go back there. If you hadn't shown up last week when you did, who knows if I'd be standing here now."

"Exactly." Speers waved the letter, "Let me handle this. You better stay away from his offices. I think you've gathered all you can from there, no sense putting yourself in further danger."

Crisp's mind raced with the possibilities of what Pendergast wanted with Speers, and how this might change the dynamics of their investigation. His mind suddenly flashed back to Cassie. They'd said she'd be ready to leave in a day or two and he needed to find somewhere safe for her.

As if reading Crisp's mind, Speers said, "I'll make sure my men stay here until she's ready to go. You let me know where you're taking her and I'll promise to keep her safe."

It was a reassurance that told Crisp his bonds with Speers ran deep, deeper perhaps than the complicated relationship between Speers and Pendergast.

Chapter Seventeen

Spring had finally arrived in eastern Kansas bringing a gentle warmth that coaxed blossoms from their buds and filled the air with the sweet scent of new growth. The trees, once bare, now showed hints of green sprouts in their lofty boughs. Robins chirped from hedgerows and fence lines, declaring the new season's arrival, yet the morning air held a chill as Crisp stepped onto the wide porch of a boardinghouse on Summit Street.

With Moreland's help, Crisp had secured a safe haven for Cassie upon her release the day before. Speers, leaving nothing to chance, had insisted she be moved discreetly, a police carriage pulling up at the back of the hospital to shield her from watching eyes alert for her departure.

The grand Victorian structure where she now resided, with its intricate woodwork and commanding view of the city, offered a sense of safety and respectability far removed from the tenderloin district of The West Bottoms.

A patrolman paced the sidewalk in front of the boardinghouse, his steady gait a reminder of the precautions taken. He occasionally nodded at Crisp, as his eyes followed the patrolman's route along the white picket fence that enclosed the tidy lawn. In the distance, Crisp caught sight of Speers approaching, his heavy footsteps resonating on the cobblestones, a rhythmic beat that quickened Crisp's pulse. He crushed the remnants of his cheroot underfoot and slipped inside just as Speers reached the door.

The spacious parlor was filled with natural light and fresh air from a set of large windows on the western wall; the gentle breeze and invigorating air of Kansas City's West Side seemed to infuse the space with a gentle, restorative calm. Moreland, seated nearby with a newspaper in hand, folded it neatly as Speers entered the room behind Crisp, his expression grave.

Speers' voice was low, almost a murmur as he addressed Crisp, glancing briefly at Cassie before returning to his friend. "Algernon," he began, "how is she today?"

Crisp moved quickly to adjust the pillows behind her head, his movements gentle yet purposeful. "She's improving; just needs rest."

Cassie, ever resilient, spoke up with a hint of impatience. "I'm better now, I don't need all this molly coddling. And there's no need to whisper."

"Now, now, you just rest, Love," Crisp soothed, tucking the blanket more securely around her legs. He then turned to Speers, gratitude in his voice. "Thank you, Thomas, for arranging the patrol outside. It's a comfort to all of us, especially Cassie."

Speers offered a small nod. "I'm glad to hear you're feeling better, ma'am." His hand moved to his chin, rubbing it thoughtfully as a troubled expression clouded his face. His eyes, laden with unspoken concern, shifted between Crisp and

Moreland before he gestured for them to step into the adjoining room. "I found this at my office this morning," he said, his voice low, handing Crisp a folded note. Moreland leaned in to catch a glimpse as Crisp unfolded the paper:

I WARNED YOU MR. SPEARS,

CALL OFF THEM TEMPRANSS WOMEN AND TELL THE MAYOR TO KEEP OUT THE AFFAIRS BELOW THE BLUFFS AND TELL YOUR DETECTEV

TO WATCH HISSELF!

Crisp's jaw tightened as he paced to the window, his gaze sweeping across the hill in the distance. "He's taunting us. I thought he might have gone into hiding as you suggested, but it seems he's determined to provoke us further."

Moreland's voice was low, a whisper of caution. "It's like he's trying to draw you out, Algernon. Using the victims as bait to see how far you're willing to go."

"How do you think he managed to get this letter into your office without being noticed?" Crisp asked, his mind already working through the possibilities. The thought nagged at him—was Crotty working with Skahill? It didn't add up, but the possibility poked at the edges of his thoughts, even though he couldn't quite see the motive or the connection between the two men.

Speers had no answer. After a moment's hesitation, he cleared his throat, grounding the conversation in practicality. "I've increased patrols around The Patch. If he's still hiding there, it won't be easy for him to get in or out. But if he thinks we're closing in, he won't stay long."

Crisp nodded. "I believe I will venture back to that place, this time in the guise of the inhabitants of that borough. He will not set eyes upon me."

From across the room, Cassie's voice trembled with concern. "Charlie, be careful," she murmured, her voice strained. "This killer... he's not just a shadow anymore. He's real, and he's close."

Speers' expression was somber as he agreed. "She's right. We're dealing with a man who has nothing to lose."

"What if he eludes you again? Or what if he's already gone?" Moreland asked, his tone edged with worry.

Crisp turned from the window; his eyes hardening with determination as a plan began to take shape behind them. "One step at a time. Let's first determine if he is still hiding there. If not, we'll have to cast a wider net to smoke him out. Once we've determined he's still somewhere in The Bottoms, we can set a trap. He's coming after these women, in retaliation for the movements he despises. We will use that against him."

"What have you got in mind?" Speers asked.

Crisp's eyes glinted with determination. "As you suggested before, we might be able to draw him out during the parade tomorrow. If we can spread the word far enough, make sure everyone on St. Louis Avenue knows about it, we might catch his attention. Marcus, I need you to help with that. Percy and I will pass the word in The Patch. Can you spare a few men?" he asked Speers. "If he shows, it won't be easy to take him down."

Speers frowned; his skepticism evident. "Do you really think he'll take the bait?"

"I'm counting on it. Once he knows the parade is happening, he might come forward looking for his next victim."

Speers shook his head. "He's dangerous, but he's no fool. If he catches sight of my men, or you for that matter, he'll vanish."

Crisp's smile was calculating. "You're right, which is why your men will stay out of sight, but within earshot. As for me, he won't even know I'm there," he added, a hint of mischief in his tone.

Cassie's voice, soft yet insistent, cut through the tension. "You have to catch him, Charlie—for all of us."

As Speers and Moreland made their way down the steps to their respective tasks, Crisp paused on the porch, watching them go. The stakes had never been higher. He turned back inside, his determination hardening as he steeled himself for the inevitable confrontation he knew was coming.

The sun shone down with a false warmth, casting a harsh light over The Patch and intensifying the stench of rot and decay that seemed to cling to everything in the slum. The air was thick with the scent of waste and refuse, not only seeping in from the adjacent packing houses, but from garbage and other excrement dumped by the residents around their homes without care. It was as if the very ground had absorbed the misery of its inhabitants. The downtrodden residents moved about their business with an air of resignation, seemingly immune to the squalor that surrounded them.

An old man, bent under the weight of years and hardship, carried two buckets of water suspended from a yoke across his frail shoulders, the liquid sloshing over the rims as he navigated the uneven ground. Nearby, a woman dressed in a patchwork of tattered clothing scoured the dirt for sticks and firewood. Two slovenly men engaged in a heated argument over a piece of rusted tin, their voices rising in a clamor of curses and shouts as each claimed the scrap for himself. Another man precariously balanced on a rickety ladder, nailing flattened vegetable cans onto his roof, the makeshift shingles clanging as they joined the layers of metal and wood that barely kept the elements at bay. And further down the path, a woman in muddy boots shooed away three mangy cats that circled a dead animal carcass, the bloated remains blocking the narrow entrance to her tiny home. Algernon Crisp was among them.

Crisp moved through the squalor with a practiced eye, his gaze lingering on the ramshackle residence with broken windows haphazardly patched with old newspapers, the place where he'd seen the silhouette of Skahill lurking previously. It was a fleeting glimpse that haunted him now. Maneuvering around a foul-smelling cesspool that blocked the path that served as a crude thoroughfare, he edged closer to the shack, his eyes scanning the area for any sign of its elusive inhabitant. The doorway still stood ajar, just as it had when Skahill had watched him scuffle with Crotty. He moved beyond its perimeter, halting briefly to adjust the heavy yoke about his shoulders.

As he made a second pass of the structure from the opposite direction, a boy's voice rang out, loud and clear.

"Did'ya hear? There's another of them women's parades tomorrow – this time they want to get rid of The Patch."

Crisp gave a knowing wink to the lad, Percy, who moved through the area spreading discontent among anyone who would listen. He set his buckets of water down, wiping his forehead with a dirty handkerchief. He was dressed in a shabby overcoat two sizes too big, his face obscured by a stringy, unkempt beard made of horsehair affixed to his own whiskers and dirtied cheeks. His gloves were worn threadbare, with fingers poking through the fabric, and an old straw hat with a broken brim crowned his disguise.

Kneeling down as if to tie his bootlace, he carefully surveyed his surroundings. True to his word, Speers had increased patrols on the fringes of the community. He eyed two officers conversing at the intersection of State Line and Fourth not more than fifty paces from where he stooped, and he had seen another patrolman talking to a resident on the north side of the enclave just beyond a stone's throw, making his presence clearly visible to anyone in the shantytown. Percy had been present throughout the day as well, and together they had inquired among the inhabitants they encountered if any had seen a large man recently, but none could confirm sighting anyone of Skahill's description since earlier in the week.

With a nod, Crisp signaled Percy to move toward the shack. He created a ruckus, dropping his buckets and cursing at a stray dog, giving Percy an instant to move up to the doorway of the shack. As Crisp gathered his buckets and continued mumbling to himself, he watched the boy peek through a gap in the covered windows and then peer through the ajar door before shaking his head to relay to Crisp that the place was empty.

Crisp trudged along with his buckets after giving Percy a quick nod, and with a furtive glance, he quickly circled the house and joined the boy. Inside, the shack was a testament to the fleeting nature of its occupant's stay. A tiny firebox made of old brick and a flue fabricated from tin cans sat on one side of the single room. It held ashes, but after examining the charred cinders, which were cool to the touch, Crisp surmised there had not been a fire in use for some time. The sparse interior offered no clues of recent habitation other than a filthy and frayed blanket lying atop a pile of mildewing straw.

He checked the floor near the door, hoping to find large boot prints, but the packed dirt floor at the threshold and within the interior yielded no such evidence.

"Where do you think he went?" Percy asked, his voice tinged with frustration.

Crisp guessed the man had stayed briefly, moving on after observing Crisp in the confrontation with Crotty. "That's a good question," Crisp muttered. "Are you absolutely sure the man your boys saw was Skahill?"

"Yes, followed him from St. Louis Avenue they said, sir. We'd seen him before; hard to forget that one."

"Did he carry anything with him? Was he accompanied by anyone? Did he speak to anyone around here?"

The boy responded to the barrage of questions with a defensive edge, revealing nothing that hinted at the suspect's true intentions other than seeking out shelter in this tiny shack.

"I believe what you say," Crisp replied, his tone apologetic. "He must've only been here for a short stay, and once he recognized me snooping around, he decided it was time to move elsewhere." Crisp cursed himself now for his lackadaisical approach, it would've taken little effort to hide his person from Skahill, and perhaps Crotty, on that previous morning.

"Don't worry, Colonel. If he's still in The Bottoms, my boys will spot him."

"Yes," Crisp agreed, "I trust they will."

The city's hum grew steadily louder as Crisp and Percy moved away from the filth and grime of The Patch and navigated into the bustling streets of The West Bottoms. The late afternoon thrummed with activity, producing a discordant melody. The cries from street vendors hawking their wares, the clatter of horse-drawn carriages on packed earth and cobbled stones, the rattle and clang of horse carts and trolleys, all joined in a dissonant chorus against the encompassing backdrop of the continual roar of distant factories, and a steady rumble coming from the railyards. When woven together, they created a symphony of urban life.

They'd left Crisp's boardinghouse, shedding their slovenly disguises and setting their minds on a single task ahead—meeting Marcus on St. Louis Avenue to devise a plan to lure Skahill to the upcoming temperance parade. But as Crisp walked, a gnawing frustration settled in his gut. The search for Skahill in The Patch had been futile, like grasping at shadows in the murky gloom of that forsaken slum. He chided himself; Speers' men would have been enough to catch sight of the giant man had he appeared there. His own efforts would have been better spent using Percy's gang of eyes and ears to scour the streets in a four-block radius around the district. But even that may not have been enough. But no matter how many eyes he had at his disposal, none of them would catch Skahill lurking about if he had gone into hiding, and no amount of searching, watching, or tracking would amount to anything if the man was no longer in The Bottoms at all.

Pedestrians weaved through the crowded streets and sidewalks, their faces set with purpose, oblivious to the hunt Crisp and Percy were engaged in. Percy's sharp eyes roved constantly, flitting from one figure to another, searching for any sign of their quarry. As they veered southbound onto Liberty Street, then turned onto St. Louis Avenue, the two of them paused. The boy suddenly gripped Crisp's arm, his voice barely containing his excitement. "There! There! The red wagon!" he exclaimed, pointing eagerly just a block away where the street merged with Union Avenue.

Sure enough, a small and narrow boxed freight wagon painted a dull, unmistakable red with white faded lettering made its way slowly along Union Avenue, hampered by the dense traffic. A large figure sat at the reins, his broad back unmistakable. For Crisp, the sight of the wagon was like a cruel twist of fate. Finding it here, amidst the chaos of the city, felt much like the unpredictable luck that accompanied him at the gambling tables, where fortune smiled one moment only to cruelly snatch it away the next. This moment was his, but he knew all too well how swiftly it could slip through his fingers.

Without a word, Crisp and Percy sprang into action, their feet drumming against the boardwalk and thudding in the dirt as they wove through the throng of people, and narrowly avoided carriages that rattled down the street. The city's tumultuous noise blurred into a distant hum in the background, their every sense honed in on the red wagon slipping away ahead of them. The urgency gripped Crisp, a persevering force driving him forward—this was his chance, his need to apprehend Skahill burned like a fire within him. Everything hinged on this moment, and he could not afford to let it get away.

Skahill, as if sensing the chase closing in, cast a glance over his shoulder. The instant he recognized Crisp, a flash of fear crossed his face, and he lashed the reins, urging his horse to quicken its pace. His hulking frame bent low over the reins as he maneuvered through the crowded street, navigating between carts and pedestrians with a desperate urgency of his own. The city around them seemed to constrict, its busy streets now a maze of obstacles that only added to the tension of the pursuit.

For a brief, agonizing moment, a streetcar clattered in front of them, halting their advance and severing Crisp's view of Skahill just as they neared Union Depot. When the streetcar passed, Skahill had vanished from the wagon, the reins slack and abandoned. Crisp's heart lurched as he spotted the large man vaulting from the driver's box, his boots hitting the ground with a thud before he took off on foot toward the depot, swimming through the sea of chaos, lost within the ebb and flow of passengers pooling around the entrance to the grand building.

Crisp and Percy reached the abandoned wagon, their breath coming in ragged gasps as they scanned the crowd. But Skahill had vanished into the tumultuous swell of Union Avenue, slipping through the mass of travelers and locals like a shadow lost in the mist. Smoke and steam from departing locomotives hung heavy in the air, obscuring their view and lending an almost surreal quality to the scene. Crisp's chest tightened with frustration and determination—Skahill was so close, yet the city had swallowed him whole, leaving Crisp to grapple with the bitter taste of a chase thwarted at the final moment.

Percy looked up at Crisp, his young face etched with frustration. "He's gone, Colonel. What do we do now?"

He put a steady hand on the boy's shoulder, his thoughts clouded by the day's revelations and the urgency of their mission. "We think, Percy. We plan our next move carefully. He's still here, somewhere close. And we're going to find him." As the noise of Union Avenue filled the air around them, he felt the weight of their task bearing down, consuming him with uncertainty. Skahill would not escape justice—not while Crisp still had breath to pursue him.

Under the heavy cloak of afternoon shadows cast by the sprawling edifice of Union Depot, Crisp looked towards its monumental clock tower soaring more than a hundred feet into the sky. His plan was straightforward: ascend the tower for a higher vantage point to survey the sprawling railyards where he believed Skahill must be hiding.

Each heartbeat drove home the pressing need of his mission as he made his way into the interior of the busy depot, cutting through the plush waiting room, past the express offices near the center of the structure where he searched for access to the tower. Positioned strategically outside on the street below, Percy was tasked not only with watching for Skahill but also for keeping Crisp informed from his ground perspective. The street was busy with the hustle and bustle of daily commerce and travelers, yet the imposing figure of Skahill was nowhere to be seen.

Crisp climbed the narrow, creaking staircase inside the clock tower, his footsteps echoing off the worn treads that groaned underfoot. Reaching the top, he pressed his eyes to the dusty glass of the southward facing window beneath the clock face, scanning the railyard's labyrinth of tracks and freight cars. Despite the clarity of the day, Skahill's distinct form evaded detection. Likewise, searching to the east toward the bluffs, looking west over the stockyards, and peering down on the Union Avenue to the north provided no signs of the enormous man.

He darted between the four windows, his eyes sweeping every patch of ground where Skahill might emerge. It was a futile effort. With each click of the clock tower's gears, the seconds bled into minutes, the relentless clacking echoing his desperation. The mechanical sounds seemed to mock his urgency, mimicking Skahill's retreating footsteps that carried him farther away from Crisp.

Could Skahill have entered the station and even now be hiding somewhere just below the tower? Had he climbed aboard an empty freight car and was now riding the rails to the outskirts of town? Crisp refused to give up hope as he darted between windows making a hasty search.

Meanwhile, Percy noticed a familiar patrolman moving toward the depot. Recognizing the threat, he quickly devised a series of sharp, urgent whistles—the prearranged signal to warn Crisp. However, in his heightened state, Crisp misread Percy's cues, interpreting them as a sign that the boy had spotted Skahill. Crisp descended the steps swiftly, his mind racing with the possibility of finally cornering his quarry. He burst into the crowded waiting room and dashed through an exit emerging behind the depot where he stopped and stared into the chaotic network of railway lines, his eyes intensely searching for Skahill.

A flicker of movement—a shadow darting between the shifting railcars—caught his eye. Crisp held his breath, waiting for the train to clear the tracks beside the depot before he sprang into action. He rushed across the steel rails, his steps quick and measured, skirting sideways along the next empty line, running parallel to a string of parked boxcars on the next set of tracks. At the end of the row, where he had glimpsed a large figure only moments before, his heart pounded with anticipation. But as he rounded the last of the cars, ready to confront the murderer, Crisp found himself staring directly into the cold, menacing eyes of Dennis Crotty.

The patrolman's sneer twisted into a malicious grin as he recognized his adversary. "I warned you to stay away from here," Crotty taunted, stepping closer with evident intent. Crisp stood his ground, no longer haunted by the inner demons that had once tormented him. With the weight of his past lifted, his former weaknesses had been forged into a steel fortitude, ready to face all obstacles. "This ends today, Crotty," he declared, his voice calm and measured, though the adrenaline surged through him like a flood.

Crotty, ever the brute, wasted no time, lunging forward with fists clenched, eager to draw first blood. But Crisp, fueled by a determination that brooked no more harassment, met him with equal ferocity. The clash was immediate and brutal, a savage exchange of blows that sent both men reeling across the rough gravel and steel tracks of the busy railyard. They grappled with each other, there in the middle of an unoccupied set of rails, their bodies slamming into the unforgiving ground, and fists flying as they fought for dominance. The noise of the clattering railcars lumbering past, the hissing steam from parked locomotives, and somewhere close, the rhythmic clanging of a bell—all seemed to fade into the background, replaced by the raw sound of grunts and the sickening thud of flesh on flesh.

The clarity of a bell cut through their skirmish, its increasing frequency and volume signaling a warning to Crisp. Over Crotty's shoulder, he saw an oncoming steam engine creeping its way closer to where they rolled on the ground, trapped in a valley of shifting freight cars looming above them on either adjacent track to where they dueled.

Crotty too must've sensed the imminent danger, and in a desperate bid to end the fight, eyed a passing freight car on the adjacent tracks. With a snarl, he broke free from the fight looking for a safe retreat. He lunged for a slow-moving railcar passing on the adjacent track, but in his rage, he misjudged the distance, the speed, and overlooked the folly of his move. His boot slipped from a bottom rung of the boxcar ladder which snared his pantleg and pulled his feet out from under him.

Crisp saw the reckless move for what it was—suicidal. He

saw Crotty dragged alongside the moving train car, struggling in desperation to free his entangled leg and attempting to push himself clear of the approaching steam engine. Crisp too realized he needed to act quickly to avoid doom. He read the fear in Crotty's face and hastily launched his own risky leap onto a car at his back that was moving at much slower pace. He gained a foothold and looked back just in time, his eyes widening as he realized the horror about to unfold.

Crotty freed his pantleg and rolled free of the freight car dragging him through the yard, but his timing was all wrong. In an instant, his triumphant scream turned to one of terror as he collided head-on with the massive locomotive. The sickening crunch of bones and the squelching, fleshly, squish of limbs and torso reverberated through the air, barely masked by the hissing steam and screeching metal. Crisp, panting heavily, stood frozen as he watched the scene unfold in horrifying slow motion. The train, indifferent to the tragedy it had just caused, rolled on, leaving behind the mangled, unrecognizable remains of Crotty.

As the locomotive chugged past, oblivious to the life it had snuffed out, Crisp stared at what was left of Crotty, a tumult of emotions churning within him. He turned away, only to lock eyes with the horrified engineer who looked back in dread, hands still locked on the break lever that brought the train engine to a screeching stop. Several feet away, Crisp dismounted from his moving train, careful not to repeat Crotty's fatal mistake, careful not to step into oncoming rail traffic.

He stood in the center of an abandoned track struggling with the bitter satisfaction of having just ridden himself of his tormentor opposed with the sickening horror of the brutal end he had just witnessed. The triumph, if it could be named such, curdled at the back of his throat, leaving a bitter aftertaste that made him shudder as he turned away.

Skahill, had once again slipped through his grasp, as fleetingly as Lady Luck in The Climax Saloon. As he stepped from the tracks, the weight of unfinished business riding burdensomely on his shoulders, he muttered to himself as he had countless times before when faced with a losing hand, "tomorrow—perhaps tomorrow."

Chapter Eighteen

T he atmosphere on St. Louis Avenue was charged with a mixture of fervor and festivity as the Women's Temperance Union parade marched through the heart of The West Bottoms. It was the next day, and banners fluttered in the mild breeze, proclaiming messages of sobriety and reform, while the determined faces of the marching women brought a solemnity that belied the colorful spectacle. Among the twenty or more women huddled in formation, all clad in the solemn, layered garments of the era, one stood out from the rest. She was not taller, nor did her frame differ much from the others, neither drawing particular attention, yet her attire was best described as off from the others.

She was draped in a high-collared, black silk bodice that cinched tightly at her waist, cascading into a voluminous skirt that swept the ground. Her shoulders were framed by puffed sleeves, and her outfit was adorned with intricate lace trims, adding a touch of elegance despite the severity of the black. What set her apart was the ill-fitting nature of her clothes, borrowed in haste, a black veil that draped mournfully over her face, obscuring her features in shadow. Her gloved fist punched the air with fervor, her voice raised in a fervent cry, yet the falsetto tones were swallowed by the chorus of shouts that reverberated off the stone facades of St. Louis Avenue.

Amidst the crowd of spectators and hecklers Speers and Moreland stood watchful, their eyes scanning for any sign of Denis Skahill amongst the gathered crowd of spectators, their eyes occasionally locking on the mystery woman whom they recognized as Algernon Crisp in drag. Percy was on point too, and although Crisp couldn't see him in the crowd, he knew the boy wasn't far. Speers had assured him that his men were close by, but Crisp hadn't caught sight of a single one. A creeping doubt grew within him—had they quietly slipped away, leaving the three to face Skahill alone?

"Skahill's nowhere to be seen—he would stick out," Moreland muttered to Speers, frustration edging his voice as he adjusted his hat to shield his eyes from the afternoon sun. They'd positioned themselves near the center of the parade route, hoping the large gathering would flush their quarry into the open.

"Perhaps I should not have come," Speers muttered.

Crisp's attention was drawn across the street, where perched precariously atop a light post, he spotted Percy, his youthful face intent and watchful. His position gave him a clear view over the crowd, and his job was to signal Speers and Moreland if he spied anyone matching Skahill's description. Crisp's attention diverted to a large man who seemed to detach from a group of spectators and strode with determined purpose toward a nearby shop. "There," he gestured, pointing to the figure, his pulse quickening.

Speers and Moreland, quickly but careful not to draw

attention, made their way across the street, weaving through the throngs of parade-watchers. They entered the shop on the heels of the retreating figure. Crisp waited with bated breath as he marched, they finally emerged—but the sinking feeling in Crisp's stomach confirmed immediately that they were mistaken. Regretting the time wasted, they hurried back to their original post, yet, as they crossed back, their attention was drawn to Percy's animated behavior from atop his perch. They quickened their pace, hope rekindled only to find the boy's excitement the result of a minor scuffle that had broken out near him, unrelated to their hunt.

The somber black phalanx moved steadily down St. Louis Avenue, a dark wave flowing through the heart of The Bottoms, finally coming to a halt near the State Line, where the pavement met the invisible boundary. Their routine was the same all along that stretch, but none of the men had managed to sight Skahill lurking within the crowd of spectators nor hidden in the dark recesses of the street.

As the parade began to disperse, the reality of their unsuccessful day settled heavily on Crisp. The sun dipped lower in the sky, casting long shadows that seemed to mock their efforts. He rubbed the back of his neck, feeling the weight of discouragement. He rejoined the others and conversed in hushed tones.

Moreland looked at him, the lines of concern etching deeper on his face. "We'll find him," he assured, though his voice lacked its usual conviction. "We must."

"I can't help but feel he is close," Crisp said to Moreland as they stood apart from the dwindling crowd. His gaze distant, he scanned the horizon of rooftops and windows that lined St. Louis Avenue. Somewhere in that tapestry of weather-worn warehouses and shabby saloons, Skahill hid, watching, waiting, and planning his next victim. "Let's see if he's still here. Keep a close eye on me, but don't make it obvious you're following. Give me space to walk alone."

He veered away from the crowd, deliberately stepping onto a secluded byway with his face still partially hidden beneath the muslin veil which served a dual purpose—masking his identity as a man in disguise, but more so to cover the fresh bruises Crotty's fists had left the day before. He carried a handbag draped over his elbow, and walked slowly maintaining the appearance of an inconspicuous female pedestrian. Speers and Moreland separated, tailing Crisp from two blocks back, each hugging opposite sides of the street, their movements calculated and discreet. Percy signaled to a group of boys on the other side, and like rats slipping into the shadows, they dispersed in all directions, each with their own target in mind.

Crisp moved slowly, allowing others to pass until he was alone. At the head of an alleyway, he paused, rifling through his handbag with a show of indecision for any onlookers. He turned into the alley, a narrow passage just long enough to connect two streets. It was bathed in soft light, leaving a path visible and clear. It was the sort of place where a person could walk without apprehension. No one followed.

He repeated the routine at the next block, ensuring no one lingered too close, and giving off the impression of a solitary, vulnerable figure. All the while, Moreland and Speers kept their distance, careful not to betray their intent. This cautious dance continued for several minutes as Crisp methodically wove between sides streets and connecting corridors for two blocks on either side of St. Louis Avenue where the parade had taken place. He wandered down forlorn side streets and dangerous alleys; yet his ruse failed to draw Skahill from his hiding place. Finally, he signaled the others, and they regrouped at the corner of St. Louis and Mulberry, near where the parade had begun.

"It's no use. He's either onto my game or nowhere close," Crisp said, his deep voice drawing curious glances from passersby at the sight of an awkwardly dressed woman speaking with the Chief of Police.

"Maybe he's too cautious to act in broad daylight," Moreland suggested.

"I've considered that, Marcus. I have another trap in mind, one we can set tonight. Will you help?"

"Of course," Moreland replied.

Speers, clearly exasperated by the day's efforts, finally spoke up. "Gentlemen, I'm not convinced this strategy of yours will work. I think he's too clever for such tricks. I'll keep my men on high alert in case he's spotted, but I'll leave you to your own charades tonight."

"Understood. Thank you for your help today, Thomas."

Speers nodded; his jaw tightening subtly, masking the frustration simmering beneath his stoic exterior. As they turned to leave, the chilling thought that Skahill, perhaps amused by their efforts, perhaps emboldened by their failure today, lingered in Crisp's mind, propelling him forward with a renewed, desperation and determination.

Several blocks away, farther west than the team had ventured, a lone temperance woman walked along Wyoming Street. She had stayed behind after the rally, her sense of duty compelling her to visit a nearby shelter run by the Provident Association, where she intended to spread her message of sobriety to the downtrodden and homeless.

But she never arrived.

A dark figure, lurking in the shadows, overpowered her and dragged her into an alleyway just a block off of Ninth Street.

———

The twilight cast a velvet hue over the streets as Crisp and Moreland settled into the sultry confines of Madam Blackwell's assignation house. It was Thursday night, and the brothel, a gilded cage of vice and velvet, though not as busy as on a weekend was still alive with muted laughter, subtle sounds of desire, and the faint rustle of silk.

In the bawdy space that was the lounge of the brothel, they conversed in hushed tones with Eliza, one of Cassie's closest confidantes from the trade, who had agreed to assist Crisp in his plan. Crisp laid out his strategy, his voice low and urgent, convincing her that she would be safe. But as they moved to their positions, a shared tension lingered in the air, a silent acknowledgment of the danger they all faced.

In one of the lavish rooms upstairs, Moreland positioned himself behind the heavy drapery of a bay window overlooking Eighth street. He watched the street below with the eyes of a hunter, every muscle tense, knowing that Skahill could appear at any moment. Downstairs, across the street from the brothel,

Eliza lingered in the dusky glow of a streetlamp, her face half-hidden in shadow. Crisp, tucked away in the doorway of an abandoned building nearby, could feel the pulse of his own heartbeat, his hand steady on the loaded Dillinger concealed beneath his coat. Moreland, gripping his Colt Peacemaker, hoped the threat of their weapons would be enough to subdue Skahill when the moment came. Yet, they all knew that the plan was a gamble, a longshot with no guarantees.

In the alley beside the brothel, Percy kept a vigilant watch from a fire escape, his sharp eyes never leaving Eliza's position. The night air was cool, his breath forming little clouds as he shifted, his youthful energy barely containing the anxiety that buzzed through him. He listened intently; every miniscule sound magnified in the tense silence. Eliza's role was pivotal: she would act as bait to lure Skahill into the open, where Crisp and Moreland would confront and hold Skahill at bay while they secured him in bindings until Percy could summon one of Speers' men to make a formal apprehension. Chosen for her striking resemblance to one of the previous victims, they hoped her presence was enough to entice the elusive giant from hiding, but Crisp still had his doubts. It was a longshot at best.

Hours dragged by, the brothel's usual business ebbed and flowed like a tide around the tension that held the trap in place. From his vantage point, Crisp felt the weight of each passing minute, his gaze locked on the pool of soft light where Eliza waited, the fear of failure grasping at the edges of his determination. A few men approached her during the next two hours, their intentions quickly redirected toward the warmth of the lounge across the street, but Skahill remained elusive, a shadow that refused to materialize.

Just as the night seemed destined to end in disappointment, Percy's distinct whistle—a sharp, piercing sound that cut through the ambient noise—rang out from the alley. Crisp and Moreland bolted from concealment towards the side alley between the boardinghouse and its neighbor, their hearts pounding with a mix of adrenaline and dread. As they reached the fire escape, they found Percy speaking animatedly with another boy, dirty-faced and wide-eyed. "He said there's another one, Colonel," Percy explained breathlessly, gesturing towards his companion. "Just a few blocks from here!"

Crisp's jaw clenched, his face hardening with determination. "Where?" he demanded, his voice a low growl of urgency.

The smaller boy pointed down the street, his hand shaking. "By the old mill, on Fourth."

Without hesitation, Crisp bolted toward the location, his coat flaring out behind him as he moved with purpose. Moreland was right on his heels, his own determination evident in the speed of his stride. Percy and the other boy struggled to keep pace, their breaths coming in ragged gasps as they tried to match the unrelenting drive of the men ahead.

As they approached the Union Mill, the flickering glow of lanterns and the subdued murmur of a crowd confirmed their worst fears. Crisp pushed his way to the front, where a group of detectives stood huddled around a shrouded figure on the ground. He locked eyes with Speers, the unspoken question hanging between them.

"One of the women from the parade today," Speers said grimly, his voice heavy with the weight of the loss. The realization struck Crisp like a blow to the gut—another failure, another innocent life brutally taken. Speers stepped closer, his voice low and firm as he drew Crisp away from the scene. "It's time... We must go to Pendergast."

Chapter Nineteen

T he following day, an early morning rain drenched Main Street, leaving vast puddles that forced trolleys and horse carriages to proceed with caution, mindful of the pedestrians they might otherwise drench. It was afternoon before Speers could break away from other duties, and Crisp had restlessly spent most of the morning pacing the corner of Speers' office, his impatience growing with each passing minute, eager to move against Skahill.

Eventually, Speers, after insisting on a brief stop at his favorite diner, led Crisp to the familiar office at 520 Main.

"I tell you, I almost had him in the railyards," Crisp said, frustration evident in his voice. "I can't guess where he disappeared to."

"Don't worry, we'll take this up with Pendergast and get your man."

Crisp hesitated, his voice dropping as he confessed, "I regret what happened with Crotty. I never intended for it to end like that."

Speers met his gaze, his expression understanding. "I know you two had history. But I've spoken with Halpin, and I believe every word you've said. There is no fault on your part for what happened."

It was half past two when they finally stepped into Pendergast's Saloon, situated directly beneath his office. The interior was a haven of shadows, the low ceiling and narrow windows allowing only a faint, sepia-toned glow to penetrate the space. The rich mahogany bar gleamed dully under the flicker of gas lamps, casting an amber hue over the worn wooden tables and plush, deep-red velvet seats. The familiar clink of glasses and murmured conversations filled the air, but the atmosphere changed tangibly as they made their way through the crowd.

Bill Haggan and Rory Taffe leaned heavily against the bar. Their presence loomed like a dark cloud. As Crisp and Speers approached the stairs leading to Pendergast's loft, Taffe pushed off from the bar and blocked their path, his expression darkening. "Thought we made it clear; you're no longer welcome round here!" he sneered at Crisp.

Speers raised a hand authoritatively, his voice steady, "He's with me, official business—with your boss." His calm demeanor did little to soften Taffe's hostile stance, but Haggan laid a hand on his colleague's shoulder, signaling him to stand down.

With the situation momentarily diffused, Speers led Crisp up the creaking stairs to the office where Pendergast sat reviewing documents. The spacious room was quiet, in contrast to the rowdy saloon below, lined with rich wood paneling and heavy curtains that muffled the sounds of the street. Pendergast looked up; his face unreadable. "Thomas, what brings you here?"

Speers didn't waste time on pleasantries. "We need to talk

about Denis Skahill. Crisp, close the door if you please." Though Hagan and Taffe had not followed, Speers took no chances in tipping off Pendergast's men. As Crisp moved to the door, Banwell pushed past into the room. With Speers' nod of approval, Crisp shut the door behind him.

"There's been a series of murders, and all the evidence points to Skahill," Speers said bluntly. Caught off guard, Pendergast leaned back, a look of puzzled inquiry spreading across his face as he first eyed Crisp and then turned back to Speers. Crisp remained silent, letting Speers navigate the treacherous waters with Pendergast, unwilling to wade into the murkiness and risk whatever lurked beneath the surface.

"First, I owe you an explanation. Mr. Crisp here is a private detective under my employ. I apologize for the deception, but it was the only way we could get close enough to Skahill."

Banwell let out an audible gasp, his contempt barely concealed, but Pendergast remained composed. Crisp noticed a subtle tightening around the man's eyes suggesting his suspicions against Crisp. Pendergast shuffled papers on his desk, organizing them as he formulated his response. "Skahill?" he repeated, his tone revealing nothing. But in the next breath, his demeanor changed, a mix of frustration and humiliation. He swallowed hard and exhaled out his nose, "I assume you must have compelling evidence. I'm sure this accusation was difficult to bring forward. What do you need from me?"

"Where is he now, Jim? Where does he stay?" Speers pressed; his tone insistent. "We'll provide you with all the facts later, but the man must be apprehended. He is a menace and can't be left unchecked."

Pendergast sighed, exchanging furtive glances with Banwell. "He hasn't been around for days," he said flatly.

Speers tilted forward, his voice a low warning. "This isn't the time for a cover up, Jim. I just want Skahill, nothing more."

After a brief, tense moment, Pendergast gave a slight nod, and Banwell stepped forward. "Mr. Pendergast is right—Skahill hasn't been in either office for some time."

Pendergast's face betrayed a moment of deep thought, though he tried to hide it. Crisp, feeling a pang of betrayal for his previous undercover engagement, remained silent.

"Jim, you know as well as I do that being tied to a murderer would ruin you politically," Speers said, his words cutting through the tension. "I assure you; this will be handled discreetly."

Pendergast nodded slowly, resignation creeping into his expression. "I understand. Do what you must." He turned to Banwell. "Tom, help the Chief. But keep my name out of it."

Banwell offered what little information he had. "He tends our uptown wagons and horses at a lot near 5th and Grand Street. I believe he stays in the abandoned building behind this one, just there on Delaware Street," he thumbed toward the wall at his back."

Crisp, sensing an opportunity, spoke up. "Is there anything else you can tell us about his recent behavior? His whereabouts these past several days?"

Banwell, with a pointed look at Crisp, replied, "I thought you had an eye on things from the inside." But with another nod from Pendergast, he continued. "We think he's been using our wagons recently. Our regular driver reported some strange activity, but everything was always returned, put back carefully."

Speers seized on this information. "I could use your help on this one. My men have been scouring The Bottoms for this man for days, but it seems he's been right under our noses the whole time. Ask your boys to keep a look out and let us know if they see him. We'll follow up on what you've provided," this said to Banwell, and looking back to Pendergast, "Jim, we need to get this man off the streets."

With the information they needed, Speers gestured for Crisp to leave, while he lingered for a moment longer in hushed conversation with Pendergast. Banwell and Crisp descended the stairs back into the saloon and Crisp found himself immediately surrounded by Dowling, Taffe, and Haggan, their hostility barely masked, while Banwell looked on in amusement.

Speers wrapped up his private assurances to Pendergast in a few words and came down just in time to intervene. "Enough!" he barked, pulling Crisp away from the men, preventing what could have easily escalated into a brawl.

Outside, on Main Street, Speers turned to Crisp with a grave look. "Now we know where to find him.

Crisp nodded, his nerves on edge. "Thanks for everything, Chief. We're closer now than ever, we have to move quickly."

"Not too hastily," Speers cautioned. "Skahill might be too much for you and I to handle alone."

"But we can't wait another day, he may kill again. Or Pendergast's men may tip him off, and then what?"

"No, we shan't wait another day, but time is against us. We only have a few hours before it is dark. Give me an hour to gather some men. We'll do this properly."

Crisp nodded. "I will keep an eye on the place and wait for you there."

"Be careful, Algernon. these men aren't to be underestimated either," he said gesturing toward the saloon. "You need to distance yourself from this place."

As they parted ways, Crisp felt a mix of anticipation and dread. The final confrontation with Skahill was imminent, and everything hinged on what happened next.

Crisp wasted no time, rounding up Percy and rushed to the courthouse where he found Moreland. He pressed Moreland to urgently wrap up his tasks and within twenty minutes, the three of them were on their way to the corner of Fifth and Delaware. Crisp was determined to find Skahill, and urged them to move with haste, yet he feared what might be waiting for them at Skahill's downtown hideout. Nonetheless, he was ready to end Skahill's reign of fear and terror, and with the aid of Speers and his men, he was convinced they could do it—if Skahill was there.

Arriving at the intersection, they paused on the corner between the Armour Building to the west and The Delaware Hotel on the east, while their eyes swept the block to the south. Crisp pointed toward the abandoned structure that sat behind Pendergast's saloon. The building, a narrow and dilapidated four-story hulk, loomed there like a battered fortress, wedged between the C. J. Fletcher Candy Company and a nondescript liquor distributor. Its storefront was scarred by fire but the rear portion of the structure was intact, although crumbling into decay.

"The Chief and his men won't be here for a bit," Crisp said, his voice low and filled with tension. Percy and Moreland listened intently, awaiting his command. "Let's get a peek at this place before they arrive."

He sent Percy to scout the location, specifically the front entrance half way down Delaware Street. There were no sidewalks on this stretch, as most of the buildings contained warehouses and other commercial enterprises closed to the public. The street was not busy, nor well-lit, as dusk descended upon the city, and Crisp worried the boy could be easily spotted if someone were watching, yet the boy managed to blend into the shadows with practiced ease as Crisp's eyes tracked his every move.

Moments later, Percy reappeared, breathless and wary. "All boarded up from this side. No one could get in that way."

"He must have a rear entrance," Moreland murmured, the obvious truth hanging heavily in the air. Crisp suggested they investigate the alleyway that ran north to south in between Delaware and Main. They crossed the street, walking along Fifth in front of The Delaware Hotel, and half way between Delaware and Main, they found the entrance to the alley. The hotel loomed like a giant at their backs, its ten stories towering over the shorter, more sinister buildings that flanked the alley. The corridor ahead, wider than the cramped passages of The Bottoms, yet still suffocating, seemed to beckon them forward, its dimness cloaking whatever dangers lay within.

"Maybe we should wait for Speers," Moreland said

cautiously.

Crisp agreed. "Yes, it will be difficult to surround that place the way it's hemmed in on all sides." Sensing the apprehension in his friend's eyes, he suggested, "You wait here Marcus, Speers will be along any moment and can post men from all sides. In the meantime, we'll inspect the area and find the best way to get inside."

He nudged the boy forward into the alley and together they crept along its walls. The passage was cluttered with empty crates, barrels, and refuse, with the stench of decay clinging to the air. Parked wagons and scattered detritus filled the narrow path. Crisp heard vermin scurrying amongst the debris, a reminder of the filth that Speers' clean-up efforts had yet to touch.

As they moved deeper into the alley, every step fraught with fear, Crisp maintained eye contact with Moreland, lest he and the boy fall prey to the dangers lurking there.

Chapter Twenty

The sun had set over Kansas City, casting ominous shadows and an eerie pall over the city block between Delaware and Main. Percy took up his usual post on a fire escape, his focus locked on Skahill's hideout with eyes sharp and alert. Moreland stood at the mouth of the alley on Fifth Street, his gaze sweeping the area for any sign of Skahill's approach and patiently awaiting the arrival of Speers' men. Crisp ventured alone into a derelict building, every step echoing as he ascended the creaking stairs to the fourth floor. From there, he had a commanding view, able to watch over both of his companions and keep a vigilant eye on the rear of Skahill's building.

The minutes dragged on, each one marked by the ticking of his pocket watch, yet there was no sign of Speers or his men. Crisp glanced up at the darkening sky, where the evening's first star flickered faintly in the dusky mauve, and a nagging dread took hold—what could be delaying them? Leaning out of the empty window frame, he signaled to Percy below, who responded in turn with a subtle wave to Moreland letting him know they were both in position, and still within line of sight. With tension tightening like a coiled spring, all they could do was wait.

They didn't have to wait long.

The sun had slipped below the horizon, and now nightfall cloaked the city with a thin veil of clouds that drifted in from the northwest. The only light came from the scattered street lamps on Fifth and backlit windows showing from The Delaware Hotel. Crisp's gaze settled on a fenced enclosure behind the abandoned building, where he could see it connected to the alleyway not far from Percy's perch. The boy had moved to a second fire escape on a nearby building, giving himself a better vantage point. Hanging just below the landing, he waved to Crisp, who couldn't help but admire the boy's sharp instincts and fearless determination.

In the dimming light, Crisp's pulse quickened as he caught sight of a large shadow moving deliberately through the alleyway below. It was unmistakably Skahill, his hulking form ominous as he lumbered forward, carrying the limp body of a woman draped over his massive shoulder, her garments disheveled and torn. The scene was chillingly familiar—Skahill emerged from the shadowed space next to Pendergast's Saloon, where Crisp had only recently joined Wyse in a waiting carriage. A cold certainty tightened around him. The red box truck was likely parked there now, the only plausible means by which Skahill had arrived with his grisly burden.

As Crisp peered down from his vantage point, each step Skahill took toward the decrepit building sent an involuntary shudder through him, the sight of the hulking figure creeping ever closer, stirring a deep sense of dread. Skahill slipped through the fence, vanishing briefly from view before reappearing at the steps of a back door where he climbed inside.

Crisp's eyes never left Skahill, tracking his malevolent silhouette as it flitted through broken windows and gaping voids in the walls. He climbed to the third floor, his heavy tread a silent harbinger of the horrors to come. Crisp watched in mounting dread, as Skahill stopped, fully visible through a large windowless opening, and laid the woman down on a makeshift table. In the chilling silence of that place, Skahill handled the woman's clothing with an unsettling softness, his movements disturbingly deliberate and childlike. He slowly stripped them away, each action precise and unnerving in the shadowy light.

Crisp glanced at his watch. Where was Speers? He shifted to signal Percy or Moreland, but could see neither.

He turned back to the building across from him, but the dimness of the vast room swallowed Skahill's movements, casting him intermittently out of Crisp's desperate sight. Shifting anxiously to another dust-coated window, Crisp strained to catch every detail. Skahill's broad back was turned, obscuring his ghoulish acts from view, but the way he stood over the partly visible body suggested he was on the verge of something unspeakable.

Crisp hurried back to his original vantage point, his breath catching as his worst fears materialized before him. He spied the woman's exposed skin glowing ghostly white in the faint light, her body unnervingly still—yet Crisp thought he detected the faint rise and fall of her chest. Skahill's shadow loomed over her like a predator poised in chilling deliberation. Crisp felt the seconds slipping away, each one ticking closer to the horror about to unfold. His eyes were glued to the scene, the weight of the impending danger pressing down on him, as he prepared to intervene in the only way he could.

His mind raced as he calculated his next move. Time was running out; Skahill would claim the woman's life at any moment, and yet, without Speers' men, he stood little chance of subduing the giant alone. His Derringer, now tiny in his pocket, was useless at this range. With an unwavering resolve, he decided to act. Ending Skahill's reign of terror was paramount, whether he managed to capture him or not. At this critical juncture, saving a life took precedence over all else.

Crisp edged to the right of the window frame, straining for a clearer view that might reveal the quickest path to Skahill's location. As he shifted his weight, seeking leverage, the rotted flooring beneath him suddenly splintered, plunging his leg into a void below the floorboards. His right ankle twisted painfully as it became ensnared in a snarl of broken wood. He fought desperately to free himself, panic mounting. Glancing back in alarm, he caught sight of Skahill's hand emerging ominously from the shadows, the unmistakable glint of steel in his grasp.

Just then, a flicker of movement in the fenced enclosure behind the building caught Crisp's attention. Was it Speers or one of his men? He squinted into the stygian gloom and his heart sank—it was Percy, driven by reckless curiosity, completely unaware of the peril he walked into, creeping toward the steps Skahill had mounted just moments before. Crisp watched in horror as Percy vanished into the rear of the building, oblivious to the shadow of death lurking above him.

Panic surged through Crisp as he struggled to free his foot, snagged on a twisted piece of debris. He saw Percy's shadow moving upward, tracing the deadly path Skahill had taken. He had to act—now. With a desperate yank, Crisp tore his foot free, shredding his trouser leg and leaving deep gouges in his skin. He leaned out the window, his voice slicing through the stillness of the night, "Percy! Get out now!"

Skahill, startled by the shout, snapped his head toward his window, searching until his eyes locked with Crisp's. A wave of rage contorted his features, and in an instant, he abandoned the woman, rushing from Crisp's view, presumably headed towards the building where Crisp hid. Percy, hearing Crisp's warning, and realizing the peril at hand, darted away, disappearing from Crisp's view but not from danger.

Crisp abandoned his post with haste in an effort to rush toward Percy's position. Limping as he moved, he descended a flight of unstable stairs, pausing at a landing halfway between the second and third floors; the scuffling of feet somewhere below told Crisp he was not alone. He bent haphazardly over a loose railing to get a better view, and there at the foot of the steps, he saw the unmistakable colossal boots of Denis Skahill.

The thundering of his heartbeat pulsed inside his head like a relentless drum, loud and overwhelming. Skahill's heavy footsteps trounced up the rickety stairs, his giant stride taking them in twos and threes. Crisp turned to flee; his only escape up and away from the pursuing behemoth. Rounding the turn back to the fourth floor, the boards under his feet gave way. He crashed through a gaping hole that opened in the landing and fell onto the third-floor landing just below him with a crash of boards and curses.

Disoriented from the fall, he scrambled to extricate himself from the debris ensnaring his legs. The groaning of the stair treads below, burdened by the approaching sinister weight, jolted him back to the harsh reality of his predicament. As he struggled in his prone position, the looming figure of Denis Skahill ascended the stairs, his massive form creeping ominously closer. Skahill's grim face emerged over the final step, his intense, piercing eyes meeting Crisp's in a silent, terrifying challenge.

Outside, Percy's shrill whistle pierced the night, summoning help. Crisp's mind grasped at the clarion call hoping that anyone, Speers, Moreland, or the police, would hear and come to his rescue, drawn by the urgency of the signal. Crisp's hands fumbled through his pockets in a frantic search for his Derringer as Skahill stormed up the staircase. He attempted to reason with the brute's limited reasoning, his voice urgent, "Think, Denis! This doesn't have to end in more death!" But his plea was lost on Skahill, who, consumed by fury, leaped at Crisp.

In one of his enormous hands, a large blade glinted ominously, the same one Crisp had glimpsed moments before. His other hand, bare and gnarled, lashed out, clawing at the air like a monstrous talon seeking its prey. Crisp kicked frantically at Skahill's grasping hand, but the giant's fingers seized his pantleg. As Skahill hefted his blade high, its weight poised for a deadly strike, Crisp twisted to his side. The blade came sweeping down, biting hard into the wooden floorboards with a force that wrenched it from Skahill's grasp.

Crisp rolled to his back again, trying to kick free of Skahill's hold, but it was a hopeless struggle against the giant. The confrontation became a fierce tussle, both men grappling perilously on the weakened stairs, a dance of survival on the edge of destruction. Crisp fought frantically for a grip, to push himself farther from reach, but Skahill's massive hands clamped down on his legs, pinning him with terrifying strength.

In one swift motion, Skahill maneuvered his knees onto Crisp's torso, crushing the breath from his lungs. Crisp squirmed, every ounce of his strength aimed at breaking free, but the weight pressing down on him was overwhelming, threatening to suffocate him entirely. Skahill's grotesque face loomed inches from his own, with hideous yellow teeth bared in a monstrous sneer. Hot, foul breath rushed from Skahill in ragged pants, assaulting Crisp's senses and driving home the terrifying reality of the moment.

Then, in the half-light of the stairwell, Crisp's eyes locked onto deep, crimson scratches marring Skahill's cheek—they could have come from only one source: Cassie's desperate, clawing nails. The shock of recognition struck Crisp like a blow. Fury welled up inside him igniting a fire, a burning need to break free, to tear Skahill apart with his bare hands if necessary. He surged against Skahill's crushing grasp, muscles straining as he thrashed with all his strength. But it was no use. Skahill's massive hands had Crisp pinned to the ground.

Just then, the shuffle of feet further below reached Crisp's ears, heralding the arrival of help. Speers' authoritative voice cut through the chaos. "Crisp!" he bellowed, as he and his squad of policemen stormed the building. "Crisp! Hold on, we're here!", his voice a lifeline thrown in the midst of turmoil.

Under the relentless pressure of Skahill's iron grasp, Crisp struggled for breath, his resistance faltering. With a rasping voice thick with desperation, he screamed for help. At that moment, the worn and decayed stairwell, groaning under their combined weight, could no longer bear the burden. With a catastrophic groan, the staircase splintered, plunging them both into a maelstrom of flying wood and billowing dust. As they tumbled downward, the world around them disintegrated into chaos.

Descending into a cloud of splinters and debris that enveloped them, gritty particles stung Crisp's eyes and coated his tongue with an earthy paste. The sharp, pungent odor of disturbed dust thick with the building's history, filled his nostrils. Each set of steps fell collapsing on the next set below them and gaining moment until the massive pile of wood settled on the lowest concrete floor in a crashing heap. In a brutal instant, a violent shockwave coursed through Crisp's body as they smashed to the ground, plunging him into darkness.

Speers, and a contingent of officers rushed into the dilapidated building just as the catastrophic crash echoed through its halls. They dove for cover as a thick cloud of grime, dirt, and debris burst into the entryway, choking the air around them. Crouching low, they waited for the swirling chaos to subside, then cautiously began sifting through the wreckage, eyes scanning the devastation.

They found Crisp pinned under Skahill's immense inert body, both of them buried in a pile of rubble and debris. Skahill's neck was grotesquely twisted and his grey eyes bulged lifeless yet imposing. Moreland and Percy reached the scene, their eyes widening in disbelief at the sheer scale of the destruction. Seeing the wreckage sprawled before them, a jagged landscape of rubble and ruin, their hearts sank with immediate concern for Crisp's fate weighing heavily on their minds.

Speers directed his men to carefully extricate Skahill's lifeless form in order to free Crisp. Beneath the wreckage, battered and regaining consciousness, Crisp blinked open his eyes to see Speers standing over him. Through the haze of pain and confusion, Crisp's lips curled into a faint smile as he rasped, "Chief... did we get him?"

Chapter Twenty-One

I n the tranquil, sun-drenched confines of their new residence on Summit Street, Algernon Crisp reclined with his leg wrapped in gypsum plaster and supported by pillows, and his face a tapestry of bruises and cuts told tales of his recent confrontations. Beside him, Cassie Curtain, similarly marred yet further along in recovery, occupied the sofa with him.

The room was peaceful, the stillness occasionally broken by the soft turn of newspaper pages. Despite the throbbing in his leg, Crisp had dismissed the offer of opium tincture that Moreland, now acting as temporary caretaker, had procured under their doctor's orders.

"Are you certain you don't want something for the pain?" Moreland inquired.

"Quite certain, Marcus. I've found better ways to cope," he said with conviction, setting aside the paper and putting his arm around Cassie.

She too sought new ways to heal from the scars of her past. Though he'd yet to figure out the specifics, Crisp had reassured her that his newfound purpose would enable him to start over and build a business that could support their new life together. In the days following their harrowing ordeal with Skahill, they had lain together, recovering and dreaming of the future they would create.

Heavy footsteps clopping across the front porch announced the unmistakable arrival of someone at the boardinghouse. Chief Thomas Speers entered the parlor, his face a blend of relief and approval. "Good to see you both safe and recovering," he said, pulling up a chair. "I've just left the hospital. The woman Skahill had abducted is doing much better. Shaken, but thankful to be alive."

A wave of relief washed over Crisp. "That's good to hear, Chief. It was a close call. Hard to believe Skahill is dead."

"It's a miracle you're not," Moreland quipped dryly.

"His death simplifies things considerably with Pendergast. No messy trials to sully his name," Speers remarked wearily. "There are no ties between Skahill's killing spree and Pendergast—no hidden motives, no secret orders. Skahill was acting alone, a madman driven by his own darkness." He paused, allowing the weight of his words to sink in before continuing.

"What about Crotty? Was he in league with Skahill?"

"With both of them gone, we may never know. But there's another matter to investigate; Pendergast employed Skahill as a favor to Father Patrick McClary—his connection to Skahill's crimes is troubling. Skahill was McClary's son, hiding behind the fabricated name."

"Son?" Moreland's voice betrayed his shock.

"Yes, it seems there is a dark history there beyond Skahill's brutality. We need to determine just how much he knew about his son's heinous acts, and whether he's culpable as an accessory.

I may need your skills to help uncover the truth behind that."

"Interesting for sure. We will have to discuss this in more depth," Moreland responded.

Speers moved closer to Crisp's resting spot, handing him a folded copy of the latest edition of *The Kansas City Star*. "And thanks to you, the city breathes easier. Take a look."

Crisp's eyes locked on to the headline: "Local Hero Stops Killer: Algernon Crisp's Brave Confrontation Saves Lives." The story that followed detailed the account of his harrowing encounter with Skahill.

"You're a local celebrity now," Speers said with a laugh. He then nudged Crisp to turn the page. Half way down, in the center column, Speers pointed to an advertisement:

C. ALGERNON CRISP – INQUIRY AGENT
512 MAIN ST., SUITE B.
Professional Services Rendered with
Integrity and Diligence.

Crisp, astonished, looked up questioningly. "I appreciate everything you've done for me, Thomas, but what's this address?"

"That," Speers revealed, producing a key and a signed lease agreement from his coat pocket, "is your new office, a gift from the mayor. He was quite taken with your bravery and thought you deserved a proper place to continue your work."

Accepting the key, Crisp felt a profound sense of renewal. "A new office," he said reflectively. "It seems I am truly reinstated."

Speers had not seen a genuine smile on Crisp's face in a very long time. "You've more than proved your worth," Speers affirmed, rising to leave. "Look after yourself, Mr. Crisp. The city needs more men like you."

"Thomas, wait. We're to be married next Sunday, on Easter. Won't you join us after church for dinner?"

"I congratulate you with all my heart!" He shook Crisp's hand heartily, jarring his leg in the process. "I wouldn't miss it for the world. Good day to you both."

As Speers departed, Crisp exchanged a knowing glance with Cassie before turning to the boy who hovered not far from earshot. "Percy, we want you to live here with us. No more hungry nights alone, no more running the streets. It won't be easy—I expect you to get schooling, and I need your help looking after Miss Cassie. What do you say?"

Percy, taken aback, struggled to find his words. With watery eyes, he dashed over and enveloped Crisp in a bear-like hug. "Gee, Colonel! That would be swell, like a real family!" Cassie gently placed a hand on the boy's shoulder, easing him back from Crisp, who winced under the enthusiastic grip.

"Marcus, could you show the boy to his room?"

"Certainly, follow me—" but the boy was already bounding up the staircase, his excitement evident as he anticipated what awaited him.

As he watched Percy rush up the stairs, Crisp realized that, for the first time in years, he was no longer looking back—only ahead. Turning to Cassie, he smiled with renewed hope. She too seemed to sense the beginning of something new, a life far removed from her troubled past.

Outside their West Side boardinghouse, Kansas City thrummed with life, but within the quiet room, they envisioned a future bright with promise—one far removed from the shadows that had once threatened to consume them.

THE END

Historical Note

Shadow Beneath the Bluffs is a historical fiction mystery set in Kansas City, Missouri, in the winter of 1893. I need to make some comment regarding historic and cultural accuracy in the story. Although I have conducted extensive historical research—much to the thanks of the Kansas City Missouri Public Library staff—this is essentially a novel: a work of fiction. As such, I made the decision that complete historical accuracy should not overrule the need for development of character and plot, and ultimately story.

The dates of key events, and certain locations within Kansas City are as accurate as my research allows, though many names and characters are wholly fictitious. I have also taken some creative liberties with historical figures, particularly Jim Pendergast and Thomas Speers. If you find fault with my choices, I offer my apologies, but as always, the narrative comes first—sometimes at the expense of perfect historical precision.

About the Author

Shadow Beneath the Bluffs is the second release by author Ted Bolerjack. His debut novel, **The Blackbird Conspiracy**, was released in 2023 and is available in print and e-book on all major retailer platforms.

Ted has been writing poetry, historical fiction, sword and sorcery, and adventure thrillers since taking his first creative writing class in high school. Ted is an avid roleplaying gamer which lends well to his talents in character and world building, and in orchestrating tales of epic escapades and quests with his friends in the gaming community in Kansas City.

Ted lives in rural Kansas with his wife Danielle, three dogs, and two horses.

Visit Ted's website: http://www.tedbolerjack.com

www.ingramcontent.com/pod-product-compliance
Lightning Source LLC
Chambersburg PA
CBHW071229300726
48975CB00002B/342

Lux

NOCTURNAL SOULS
BOOK TWO

LANA SKY

Lux

Lux By Lana Sky

Copyright © 2024 by Lana Sky
All rights reserved.

No part of this publication may be reproduced, distributed, or transmitted in any form or by any means, including photocopying, recording, or other electronic or mechanical methods, without the prior written permission of the author.

This is a work of fiction. Names, characters, businesses, places, events and incidents are either the products of the author's imagination or used in a fictitious manner. Any resemblance to actual persons, living or dead, or actual events is purely coincidental.

Cover Design by Caoimhe Coleman
Interior Formatting by Charity Chimni
Editing and Proofreading by Katie Crum
Alpha Reading by Jessica Rita Rampersad

Acknowledgments

Thanks so much to everyone who supported this draft along the way, including the many beta readers who provided encouragement!
Please keep in mind that this story includes dark, graphic, and explicit content matter that may not be suitable for readers under the age of 18—or for readers who are uncomfortable with the following subject matter: explicit sex, and graphic depictions of violence.

Caspian

I hold the limp body of a fae in my arms, having drained her dry. My Niamh. So sweet. So innocent.

She trusted her tender throat to me--a mistake that should be her last.

I'd heard rumors of the potent benefits of fae blood; a taboo delicacy that even Cassius--a lover of sin and debauchery-- refused to let me partake in. I understand now why he was cautious.

Her taste is sinful. In every swallow, I find harmony in both body and mind that quiets the chaos and destruction left in the wake of my old master.

Unlike his, her thoughts don't consume mine. She doesn't aim to claim me. Control. Corrupt me in her image.

Staying within her pretty little trappings takes effort. Care. For I desire to be caged. There's no need to fight for the first time in decades - or centuries, I can't remember.

Like tissue paper, her will is soft and quivering. As fragile as her delicate skin is. Niamh. My Niamh. All mine.

I tell her as much, pressing my lips to her throat. Then I lick the healing mark there: two delicate little dots still weeping beautiful, luxurious crimson.

"I've tasted you," I say gruffly. "I stopped. Don't know why."

The fact that she breathes at all is a mystery. Cassius believed fae blood to be dangerously addictive. One drop alone should have aroused a mindless bloodlust. Yet another one of his many lies, it seems. Though... If I had the choice between a hoard of mortals to feed from and another drop of her blood, I would pick hers in a heartbeat. No question.

"Is that bad?" she whispers in return, those dark eyes wide and soulful. Still full of life.

"No. I still want you," I tell her.

A lie. Can't want what I already have. In every way that matters she is mine.

Yet, she isn't.

That is her one flaw. I *can't* mark her the way Cassius did me. Words alone aren't enough.

I *want* to stay.

"I need you." She clings to me, her voice a whisper, her thoughts hesitant. "I missed you. So much."

Missed me. For all the days that I sat brainless and empty. She waited for me. Pined for me. Needed me.

My hand traces a path up her ribcage, finding that quivering, thumping mass, trapped beneath layers of pink fabric and pale skin. Her heart. It yearns for me, thumping so loudly I could dance to the tune. Perhaps, I will. Slowly, I peel away the flimsy material glimpsing the flesh beneath.

A good fae would run from me.

She, instead, shudders. Her reaction to me is damn near instant. Desire erupts in our collective mind, but I can't determine who it belongs to. Only that it scorches like a stoked flame, hungry for a catalyst. Embers to feed it. Warmth to leech from.

More.

As my gaze falls on her mouth, she laces her fingers around my neck before I can claim it. Our lips meet. Then tongues. Fuck, the taste of her...

Can't get enough. Never need enough. She is an addiction I'll gladly suffer for twice as long as Cassius. An eternity, if that is what it takes to become sated.

If she survives that long. The male fae is coming for her. I can feel him, scratching and crawling on the outskirts of her skull. There are others who hunt her as well.

However, she seems unaware of the danger. In her mind, I only see and feel me. Longing for my touch. My skin on hers.

Good.

If it means she can't focus on anything else, I'll give her everything. I'm her world in this moment, and it feels so damn good. Too good.

I enjoy observing her frantic gasps when I finally pull down her dress and reveal her naked body underneath. Although she's frail, she has a beauty I cannot deny. It makes me drop to my knees, reach around to cup her delicate ass against the palms of both hands. With my head bowed, I press my forehead against her thin, trembling stomach. I inhale her scent. Breathe her in deep.

"Tell me I'm yours," I say. Command.

More wrong words—*say you're mine*, I should have demanded—but they ring true when heard out loud. A plea. Desperation personified.

"Say it."

"I'm yours," she says instead, working those slim fingers through my hair, parting the strands, grazing my scalp with greedy, grasping touches. I'm greedy for her--a hunger far beyond my lust for blood.

Though I didn't drain her dry, I can still taste her on my tongue. Sweet. Delicate. Until now, I have never had the chance to savor my prey's blood. Just one bite was all I took. Having tasted her, she then did the same, licking up my blood like a sweet treat. It has already healed and transformed her gaunt frame. My hands slide around to her front, tickling the inside of a pale, white thigh thrumming with warmth.

A low sound trickles from her mouth, but I don't need her to say a word. I'm in her head already. I know what she wants.

More.

I drive the tip of a finger inside her, and she still wants more. The need she feels ripples through my skin. I'm electrified by her heat. It stimulates this dead body more than gallons upon gallons of blood ever could. I add another finger beside the first and hear her whimper. Moan. Music to these damned ears.

The feel of her... One touch spurs on a hunger that somehow aches worse than being crushed under Cassius's thumb. I would have killed myself rather than be touched by him. Be near him.

Yet, my only goal now is to touch her as much as possible. To feel this body shiver in response to me. Ache for me. To hear that trembling mouth beg for me.

"Caspian..."

Despite being a balm to my soul, her voice is a dangerous melody. A taste of it is never enough.

"More," I rasp into the flesh of her belly. I will always need more.

And she is so eager to give it to me. Another gasp of my name as I stroke her from the inside out. More searing heat to greet the next searching plunge inside of her. My name again. A thready gasp again. Over and over until her nails threaten to pierce my skull and her head flies back, body bowed.

She is now more beautiful to me than any damn painting she could desire. Her pleasure alone is rich enough to paint with.

I slide my fingers from her, glistening with her essence. I stroke one along her skin.

There. That glistening strip is more appealing to me than blotches on canvas.

"A masterpiece," I tell her, laughing at her sharp intake of air. "Shall I tell you what I see here, little Niamh?"

In this ivory skin, I see myself reflected. When I look into her ebony eyes, I see heaven. In my hands, I hold her world. While I draw mindless patterns into her skin, I have her full attention. My desire is written on her body with these grazing nails and probing fingertips.

It's a tragedy, this artwork of ours.

A beautiful damn tragedy.

Nevertheless, I will endure every minute. Pushing her into a wall, I drag her down to me and endure her. Hard, with a thrust that takes her breath away. Harder still as her body envelopes me in a molten fist. Then deeper still. So deep that I can feel me through her.

Her awe.

Her greedy need.

Her hunger for more.

I take her and take her. Even when she cries out my name and I spill my seed inside of her, I barely let her breathe before hardening again. Thrusting inside her. Hearing my name rip from that throat.

Damn Cassius to hell, but he was worth it.

To feel this sin in his place, any torture was worth it.

But for how long?

How long?

Even now, others pound on the door of our figurative minds, howling to be let in.

Don't want to. I bury my mouth against her shoulder to shut them out. Ignore. Ignore.

"Caspian." Her hand cradles my cheek, her tone worried. "Someone's... Someone's here."

A real-life intruder, then. They knock on the door of this hovel, hesitant and unsure. Not the male fae. He would barge in and claim her.

So, who?

"He betrayed us," she says, her voice thready, eyes blazing. "Altaris—"

"He didn't," I snap. Don't know how I know that. Then I smell it. Hear it. An unfamiliar yet familiar smell. Frantic, unsteady breaths coming from behind a metal door.

Not human. Something else. Not a threat, either. Their mousy scent reeks of unease and fear. Altaris sent them, but he scared them well.

I look down at my fae as she reaches for her dress.

"No." I want her naked. I want her to wait for me. I'm not done being inside that body. I'm not done with her peace. "Stay here."

Before she can reply, I have my clothing on. I cross the wide space—this looming building Altaris sent us to. It's old and abandoned. The air reeks of mildew and musk, but there is plumbing. Electricity. Appliances. Those things mortals crave and need.

Things she needs. There is also food for her in a metal case in the corner. Heat to warm her trickling in through looming vents overhead.

And there is a heavy metal door to provide her protection. I wrench it open. Stare down the figure on the other side.

A man, with dark hair and a scar across his right cheek. His brown eyes are watery and bloodshot. His breath smells of alcohol, but he isn't drunk. For now.

As soon as he can slither away to some corner, he will be.

"Hey," he says, his frown wary. "The name's Daven. Uh, Daven Wick. I'm ah, Colleen's dad."

The name of the mortal with the strange healing magic. This man is her sire. Don't care. I can sense my fae, moving despite my objections. Tugging on her dress.

No. I begin to turn toward her. A tendril of her thoughts reaches out to me then like a trembling finger. So damn hesitant. Gentle. I feel her penetrate my skull and make herself at home. In response, I decide that killing this man would solve nothing.

She's curious of him. Because of Colleen; the smiling blonde with the leather case. She likes her. Aims to appease her.

"Um, Altaris sent me over to check out the..." The man trails off as his eyes widen. "Holy shit." His hand flutters across his face as though the motion might adjust his vision. It's a ghost he sees behind me. Some horrific figure from a long, long memory. In a trembling voice, he says the name of this horrifying specter, "Aurelia."

Not a name. One of the houses of fae. Her house.

Yet he does not mean to refer to her as one of many. No. There is a specific woman in mind. A specific creature whom he sees in her black eyes.

He blinks. Shakes his head to clear it. Places his face in the palm of his hand. Through gaps in his fingers, he eyes her. He stares at her for so long she's forced to clear her throat, inching toward me.

"I... I'm not," she says gently, her tone pained. The same pain in her voice that I recall from those days sitting empty in that room.

"Bloody hell. I'm sorry," the man says, letting his hand fall. "I'm Daven Wick at your service." He extends his hand for her to take.

I step in front of her before she can.

There is something wrong about this mundane. A stench beneath the booze. Beneath the shock and alarm at the sight of Niamh. A darkness shrouds him, barely visible in his gaze, but there none the less.

Like a vamryre trapped in the hive mind of our masters, he too belongs to another creature. Several perhaps. They yank his leash and keep him chained, only to be used for their ends. Not Altaris. The vamryre is too lazy to exert his will on a mortal.

Others. Powerful ones.

Through him, they seek to achieve an aim. What it is? I don't know, but it has to do with her. My fae. They want her for themselves.

"I, uh, well Altaris sent me over to check on you two. Make sure you found the place ok—"

"Lie," I snap. "Spit out the truth mortal or I will send you to Altaris without a head."

A fair exchange for wasted time. Time I could spend with her. Near her. In her.

Time to try to reclaim what I've lost. Thoughts. Memories. Humanity perhaps. If only to satisfy my curiosity. If only to prove that Cassius isn't the only one with answers.

"Altaris wanted me to see her for myself," the mortal says, cutting to the point. He is a smart one, recognizing a threat when he hears it. Yet he isn't afraid. Beneath the air of booze and exhaustion and sadness is confidence. He is protected by his unseen brethren.

He trusts in them completely. Safe in their web he fears nothing.

Not even me.

"Explain," I demand.

He sighs. "It's nothing... I'm sorry by the way—" He looks over my shoulder. "I don't mean to be rude, talking over you like you don't exist."

I don't even need to see her face to sense her shock and alarm. Her awe. Her entire life has been spent being ignored. Overlooked. Neglected.

Interest by anyone thrills and shocks her. Unsettles.

I take a step closer, toward the man. Watch him swallow. Ah, now he is afraid.

Good.

"I'm not going to hurt you two, if that's what you're worried about," he says. "Altaris just wanted me to swing by and drop some things off. Food and the like. And he wanted me to ask *you* if you've read his book."

The fae nods, her breath against my shoulder. She's inched closer, seeking out my hand, entwining our fingers. A useless gesture.

One I return with an even harder grip.

Lines are being drawn. Claims are being staked. Somewhere, unseen figures are plotting and scheming. They want her badly. Badly enough to coddle us both and ply us with lies to keep us still.

All to better rope us in their snare. Just like fucking Cassius.

"Say what you want," I spit.

The mortal raises an eyebrow. Doesn't even flinch. "Nothing. Yet. But Altaris is transactional. I'm sure that, as a vamryer, you know that better than anyone. He'll help you both for a price. I wouldn't tout his expertise, but in your case, you will need it. He is the only one powerful enough to shield you on the outside. My bet is that they have half of the Citadel out looking for you."

Because of a bounty. Because of Cassius. Because of the supposedly dead male fae who lurks and lingers in the distance.

Too many mysteries to solve. Too many crises I don't give a damn about fixing.

I only want her. Need her. I'll keep her, no matter the risk.

I dare anyone to come and take her.

"Aurelia. Night Aurelia," Niamh says, her voice furtive. Soothing on the soul. The anger in me quiets down. How the hell is that possible? Her nearness makes anything a reality. "You've met her?" Her eyes are on the mortal man, and they widen as he nods.

"You could say that," he admits, his mouth twisted into a frown. "But that's a story for another time. It's getting late. I'll unload the truck, show you guys around the place. I'll be out of town for the next few days on an...um, business trip, but when I get back, we can have a chat. I'll tell you anything you want to know."

Which is everything. Her hunger for knowledge suits her like bloodlust does a vamryre, but it's just as volatile. She'll seek out answers to her own detriment. To her own destruction.

The answers glinting behind this human's eyes won't soothe her. If anything, they'll serve to torment her more.

But I want to know. Her thoughts are fleeting and quick. It's like she's afraid to voice it even in her own skull. Her own will has been beaten down by stupid fae rules and expectations.

Damn her.

"Fine," I say.

"I just got to get the crap from my truck. I'll be right back."

I watch the mortal leave, only to creep inside minutes later. A black bag is slung over one shoulder. It rustles with all matter of objects. Some food, as he claimed. Others...

Not.

"Altaris wanted me to bring a few other things as well." He shrugs as though in a nonchalant manner. As though his mind isn't busy with unease and regrets. As though he isn't still staring at my fae as though he knew her in another life. Or her mother, this Aurelia.

"Col also sent some clothes for the lady, and I added some of my old things as well." He sets the bag down. Opens it and withdraws a handful of items one by one. Neat piles of clothing. Bags of food. A dangerous book.

When she sees the cover of it, the fae goes silent. Pale. Those black eyes darken to an unnatural hue. It scares her, whatever knowledge is contained within that black cover.

She hates it.

Altaris knew. He sent it along as a reminder, meant to trigger some secret looming between them.

That she is not fae. Not a pure, special creature she spent her entire life admiring.

No, she is something else.

A corrupted, unknowable thing.

Mine alone.

CHAPTER 2

Niamh

Any darkness can be dispelled by the smallest light. Life among the archives taught me that. No matter how dark or neglected a corner seemed, the glow of a lantern was all I needed to reveal what was hidden.

I remind myself of that fact. I repeat it over and over. Silly Niamh, even the smallest light can dispel the deepest dark.

But what if you *are* the darkness? For I feel it lurk within me, festering and growing. Fear. Doubt. Unease.

Despite leeching off Caspian's strength, I can't escape the dread. His thoughts are an impenetrable fortress, like a candle held too far away for its light to reach me. Even so, a few observations split through the cracks.

Like wariness.

My mind is alien to him. To everyone. Only Altaris has the answers as to why—him and the mortal man who knew my mother. In my brain I can call her that. Night Aurelia.

Though I've never met her, I know she possesses the hall-mark characteristics of house Aurelius: red hair the color of sunset and green eyes like wet moss. They are said to be renowned for their beauty and revered for their grace.

Even so, with one glance, this man mistakenly thought I was her. Despite my wrong coloring. Despite my wrong nature.

It doesn't matter how many times I was told that I was different, he still sees her in me.

And for the first time, I start to wonder...

Greedy, resentful things I have no right to question. Such as...*why*? Why did she leave me without a word? Without so much as an explanation. I had to hear it from the Lord Master or infer it from the Citadel workers who avoided me: I was different. Unnatural. Abomination.

I look like her--though the memories she evokes in this mortal seemingly aren't pleasant. He gapes at me the way I eyed Day when he kissed me. Fearful. No, *terrified*.

No. I shake my head. Not here. Not now. Those thoughts are in the past. Caspian is my future. Inhaling his coldness, I lean into him. It must be evident to him that I am uneasy, because he stiffens.

"Get out," he tells the man. "Now."

"I was just going," he replies, raising his hands in a placating gesture. He walks to the door. Stands there. Hesi-tates. "He hasn't told you, has he? Altaris. *How* I know your mother.." He frowns. "He didn't. I knew the man could be shrewd, but damn." He laughs, but the smile shaping his mouth doesn't reach his eyes. Instead, anger burns within them.

"What truth?" I ask. It feels as if my heart has grown wings, fluttering up my throat. His words seem more than a harmless taunt. They imply something, but what?

"I can't say. I'm *contractually obligated* not to--" He shakes his head "But, if you're interested in your mother and her past, I could show you better than I can tell you."

"No," Caspian says.

At the same time, I say, "Please."

I spent my entire life refusing to question, even once, but now? I'd go to the ends of the earth to find answers.

The man blinks. Then he nods, his eyes on Caspian. "Maybe another day, but I will say this: Altaris's protection always comes with a price. Make sure you think long and hard before making a deal him. The bastard has his secrets. I bet they won't take too much effort to find--" He scans the wide space around us and then meets my gaze. "Good night."

After walking through the metal door, he turns around. Slams it shut.

"No," Caspian growls. His back is to me, his body tense. Yet he doesn't shrug me off. Doesn't release my hand. Though I know he wants to, he doesn't pry into my thoughts either.

It's like he's forgotten how to reach into another's soul and take what he desires. Those torturous days of silence changed him forever.

They still are.

As is the blood I give him. Our mental connection gives me an insight into him I didn't have before. For instance, I feel his irritation ripple through me before I even hear it in his voice.

"He aims to hurt you," he tells me, his voice ice cold. "Sell you. Chop you into little pieces. Can't you see that?"

I can.

But so did he. So does everyone, even Day. Especially Altaris. They want to chop me. Control me. Own me. Destroy. Throw away the pieces of Niamh and act as though she never existed.

My mother didn't. She left me behind. Never looked upon my face. Maybe if she had. Maybe if she did…

She would want to know me.

He doesn't understand. Irritated, his thoughts slither and ram against mine. Probing but not penetrating.

"Tell me what you are thinking," he snaps. While facing away from me, he continues to support my body without even trying. Without wanting to.

"You have no family," I say, pressing my chin to his shoulder blade.

He doesn't. None he remembers or cares to recall. The others in his hive mind—especially Cassius—he does not miss. Despises. He would rather die than call them family ever.

But I...

"I need to know," I say. "I need to know what I am. I need to know why she didn't want me."

I know the reason. The rules didn't allow it. The rules deemed me different.

Yet, I broke them. For a simple wish, I went another way. I left.

I wanted to see a museum badly enough to escape from decorum.

She birthed me. Gave life to me.

Shouldn't she have been equally compelled? But she wasn't. Instead, she left me alone to die.

"I need to know why," I croak, my mouth against Caspian's shoulder. "I need to know what I am. I need to hear her say... I want her to tell me why she didn't want me."

I'd comforted myself so long with the Lord Master's lies. But there is more to it. Altaris taunts me with the truth. I am more than a dirty thing. I am a hybrid.

A half-breed, though mixed with what?

"We don't need them," Caspian hisses. "I know who you are. You are mine—" He wrenches me around to face him. His fingers grip my hair, bringing my mouth closer to his. "My fae. We belong to no one. We are beholden to *no one!*"

But he is wrong. There is a fear that lurks at the back of his mind. One he refuses to acknowledge. Can't hide from.

Cassius is near. He is hunting for him. Pining for him. Craving him.

"I will never go back," he tells me, his voice the embodiment of sin—yet his touch is softer than any heaven. He brushes the hair from my face. Cups my cheek. Bores those red, angry eyes into my own. "I will kill him first," he says. "I will go back and kill him. I will go back and kill your mother as well. They will cease to control us. Never again."

"No," I say. I have no right to decide his path regarding his old master. As for mine... "I want to see her. I only want to see her. To know her. That is all."

I want it badly enough to consider an idea I loathe: returning to the other realm so soon after my flight for freedom.

His eyes flash but he nods. "Fine. Tomorrow night, we will return to kill Cassius and see the Aurelia. Then we will be free. We will be together."

I nod, leaning into his embrace. "Together."

But for how long?

He wants to shred his past. Burn it to ash.

I am not sure if I wish to do the same. I know, though, that when he is near me, I can do things I never thought possible. No realm can hold me with him by my side.

But how long will he want to be?

I can't escape the nagging thoughts.

Altaris's lies.

The secrets written down in his book.

How long before I destroy my Caspian like I seem to destroy everything else?

"Sleep," he tells me, pressing his mouth to mine to seal off the thought. That one he heard.

And it unnerved him.

Caspian

Oh, how she torments me. My damned fae.

Damn her for waking me from that mental prison. Damn her for making me remember...

What food smells like; fresh milk on the verge of spoiling. Eggs rotting in their fragile shells. The hiss of warmth creeping in through rusted vents.

Worst of all, she commands my senses and makes me see everything Cassius blinded me to. Beauty. Smiles. Laughter.

I could content myself with watching her for eternity--yet she yearns for more than me. Other things. Other thoughts. Other beings.

In Cassius's enclosed, false world, any other desire was snuffed out. Crushed out. He never tolerated straying thoughts and longing whispers.

It's why he hates her so.

It's why he craves me so.

To me, he extended a choice. Choose him. Want him.

Never. Never.

So, he hunts me still.

I could do the same to her. Mold her and manipulate. Give her an ultimatum and enforce it. Slip into her thoughts and make me the only thing she will ever want to see.

But even in her skull, she evades me. There are parts of her coiled like a snake—a rarer breed of viper than Cassius. Her anger is a slow-acting poison. Should I harm her, she will come to hate me. Those others in her life—the stupid elder fae, and the ones who ignored her—she hates them all. Just doesn't know it.

Her hate doesn't fester in her soul like mine does. Those she hates are reduced to dust in her mind. They cease to matter.

If I bend her to my will I will cease to matter.

So, I will coddle her. I will feed her and dress her and wipe her clean. I will swat away those who seek to harm her.

As a result, I will be the only one she can see.

Caring for a mortal, however, requires more skill than I thought. I must store her food before it rots. Unfurl the clothing sent for her. Set aside the ugly bits.

The building itself has more to it than the bottom level. There is an upstairs with a rickety floor and narrow, empty rooms. One has a dusty mattress and dirty, old sheets.

I make her sleep downstairs instead. I sit on the floor with my back to the wall. Pull her toward me. Marvel at how naturally she fits, coiled into my side. A puzzle piece that went missing.

A strange thought. Silly thought. It's something that Cassius would have sorted away through his sieve of filth, never letting anything too sentimental in.

I hate it.

I...

I sigh and lean into her. She smells nice. Feels nicer. A warmth emanates from her that goes beyond that little mortal heart. One touch, and she sets even this dank, dark place ablaze.

If I'm not careful, she'll set the world alight.

They'll all want her then.

And she will have no need for me.

CHAPTER 4
Niamh

When I wake up, I am both burning alive and freezing cold. Limbs of ice encase my body. Warm air trickles through the gaps, trying to coax life into this frigid form.

The truth is I would rather freeze to death like this in his arms, safe from all who seek to harm us.

Because there are plenty. Unease taints the air as the unseen heat does. Prickling and looming. A constant reminder of the threats that haunt us.

A bounty lies on both our heads. Retribution for Day's death—a pain I will endure later. Address later.

For now, Caspian is a prison that binds my body tightly to his. He doesn't sleep, I know that much about the vamryre. True to his nature, he is still and quiet in the dark. He scarcely makes a sound. Yet his mind is wondrous and teeming with life.

I love to explore it, for his mind is so alien from mine. My thoughts are orderly, beaten into submission. For years, all I had in my skull was a secret, tiny space to store a few precious things. Just a few.

Caspian's mind is a garden, scorched and stripped raw, but now overrun with seedlings long since buried in the dirt. It is beautiful, terrifying chaos. A maze of new recollections and old memories. Like a valley of ice, glass, and stone, it is a frightening, twisted place. He has yet to navigate it all himself. I doubt he even wants to.

I do. I would scale the highest mountain and crawl to the ends of the earth for him. For him, I will tiptoe through the mess his master made of his mind and help him salvage whatever is left.

I will do this all somehow while avoiding the council and helping him silence Cassius forever.

Maybe...if I do so, he will want to help me.

He will stay.

Yes. I nod to myself and peel my eyes open to the room we've found ourselves in. The bottom floor of Altaris's supposed new Safe House. One inhabited by just a vamryre and a wayward not-fae.

Compared to my small room in the Citadel tower, it is massive. Every sound echoes. My breaths scrape on the air. Large windows scale the walls, letting sunlight in.

Poor Caspian. He must be careful not to step into one of the many puddles of golden sun. Were we in the other realm, the rays could not harm him. Here, they are painful. Perhaps deadly.

We will need to cover the windows.

For now, we need to clean. There is too much dust in here. Too much clutter that reminds me of Altaris. He must store things here in boxes that are piled in the corners and block most of the open space.

If I could, I would destroy everything he owns. I hate him. The Lord Master was indifferent to me, but Altaris is cruel. He cloaks his malicious ways with kindness and fake smiles, but one day, I will make him pay for toying with me. I will rip out his throat—

"Naughty little fae," Caspian scolds against my ear. He was never asleep, of course. The crisp, mocking voice still startles me. "Creeping into my mind, stealing my anger from me. You are delicate and soft. Hands like these couldn't kill if they tried." He holds one up for inspection.

His thumb runs along my palm as he watches pale fingers flex, with nails too frail to rip out any throats. At least, not yet.

You stole from me, he implied. The anger. His glorious rage. It's in my head, seeping through me, making me think naughty thoughts.

I laugh. Then, bare my teeth as though they were fangs like his. There is something appealing about his anger. I enjoy the power that comes from picturing myself biting and tearing.

There is nothing like feeling powerful-it is so damn different from fearful, meek submission.

"I like you submissive and meek," Caspian tells me, but there is amusement in his voice. He likes that he's infected me.

Perhaps, in some way I have infected him.

"You heal me," he says, so quietly I could have imagined it. Thought the words in my own mind and pretended he uttered them.

Before I can be sure, he stands, tugging me along with him. He steers me to a metal square against the wall. Opens it, revealing a light and several shelves and a few strange items scattered across them. He takes out a bottle of white liquid and makes me drink from it. Milk. Then he opens a clear sack and pulls out a slice of pillowy soft bread.

I eat as he watches me. Awe flits across those red eyes before his thumb shoots out to trail the length of my chewing mouth.

"I need to remember," he says, almost as if reminding himself out loud. "You require sustenance."

Sustenance and comforts that he doesn't. Like more milk to ease the dryness in my throat. Then water to wash the blood from my hands. More blood stains my beautiful pink dress and Caspian strips it, tossing it aside. He leads me to a new room with a porcelain basin that he fills with water from a metal tap. I climb inside and it's blissfully warm. Far better than bathing with a bucket of lukewarm water and an old rag.

Yet, it must have been a while since Caspian needed to bathe as a mortal does. His body is perfect, even when streaked with blood. Awkwardly, he stands, watching me.

"I need soap," I say.

He frowns and I swear he mutters "ah, ha," like a historian making some revolutionary realization. He leaves, returns. I stare. Giggle.

Wait. It's a noise I've only heard from the Citadel workers, or mortals walking outside of Altaris's shop. Even Poppy would do so for no reason, as if her thoughts alone were entertaining enough.

But I bring a finger to my lips as if to trap the sound inside me. Feel it. Relish in it. Try to remember how to make it again.

And Caspian...

He is more determined than I am. He stares at me and then lowers his gaze to the bottle in his hand. He raises it as if it alone was the source.

But it wasn't. It was...

"The look on your face," I say, trying to explain. How his red eyes had narrowed then. I can't put it into words. More noises slip out of me. A giggle, a gasp. A sigh as he stalks forward and upends the bottle, pouring liquid directly into the water around me.

Then he crouches. His pale hands slip beneath the water's surface. He stills. Looks up at me, dark eyes questioning. He wants to know something but won't ever ask it out loud. It lingers in his mind, and he lets the thought drift over into mine.

Why that noise? That laugh. What made me do it?

I suck in air and try again to explain. "You looked so... confused. You know everything, but you'd forgotten this: baths need soap to wash the body clean. You'd forgotten..." My lips twitch, and I can't contain another giggle. Another louder, lingering bit of sound. It startles him. He stiffens, then lowers his head, still testing the water's warmth with his fingertips.

I think I've offended him. Then I hear it: a single thought floating amid his chaos. *Beautiful noise.*

My heart thumps. The air in here feels tight again. Stifling. Perfect. Suffocating.

I could die like this here, with him. But then I wouldn't be able to experience new things. New observations about him, my Caspian. Like the fact that once he recalls that water needs soap to clean, he snaps into action with clinical efficiency. With a rag fished from Daven Wick's borrowed things, he helps me wash with more care than even I utilized while performing my chores around the Citadel.

I slaved over those floors. I strived to ensure that every last inch gleamed and shone.

Compared to the way he treats my body, I woefully failed. He worships this pale, gaunt frame. He utilizes a care that leaves me breathless. Yet I can tell from his expression alone that he doesn't intend to treat me any differently than what comes to him naturally. So studious he looks. How I would imagine an artist would, slaving over their artwork.

Or so I assume.

Eventually he looks up and notices me staring. His hand grips the rag tighter, leaving it pressed into my lower back.

"You are laughing," he warns, still cautious. Am I mocking him?

Never.

"I am happy," I say. It sounds so strange on my tongue. A foreign word I've never spoken. A mind state that requires near-constant giggles and laughter.

A word that makes him frown and eye me in a new, unsettling way. It's like he's noticing my appearance for the first time. The face atop the body he's washed with utter reverence. Too-big eyes. Dark hair, clinging to me like a cape. Twitching pink lips and crooked, broken smile.

He looks at me, this abominable creature. This half-something, half-fae thing. He looks at me and for the first time in my life I don't feel unworthy of being seen.

In his eyes, I am something beautiful. Something worthy of being touched.

And he is worthy, too. Worthy of laughter and giggles and anything else I could possibly give him. I'd offer him the world if I could. He could have my tears too if he wanted them.

"I like your laugh," he says, his expression stern, his voice brusque. Business-like. He then stands and extends his hand to me. I take it and step out of the tub into the suddenly chilly air. I stand still as he wraps me in a fuzzy strip of cloth and then helps me into the clothing Daven Wick provided.

A big, bright shirt like Colleen's in sunflower yellow. A long, green skirt that swishes as I walk. I love them. Soft and warm and bright.

He picked them for me due to their color alone. It inspired a thought he couldn't shake: how would I look draped in fabric sunlight? I can't tell what he thinks of his creation in person. He merely tilts his head while those red eyes roam my body from head to toe.

Watching him, I note all of the ways the mortal realm has affected him as well. He's more alert, and constantly on edge. Bathed in dried blood, he somehow seems less intimidating than he did when he cornered me in the archives. He seems lost here. Unsure.

"I should wash you," I say, steering him to the bathtub.

He doesn't resist, and I take my time to inspect him in every way I can. He's so tall that even though he sits on the rim of the tub, he still towers over me as I crouch beside him. He doesn't seem to care or notice the water temperature I bathe him with. He just watches me, his gaze stoic, limbs rigid and unmoving.

But beneath my touch... He stirs to life, adjusting himself to my cleansing swipes. It is necessary for me to remove some of his clothing, and with every part of him bared, my throat tightens. The weight of my heart grows heavier, and my tongue becomes damp, so that I have to swallow repeatedly. After I wipe him down, I can't keep myself from lingering, tracing my fingers along his muscular chest. His skin is porcelain, unblemished by any flaw. Not a single scar, not even a pimple or birthmark. He is perfect. In a trembling voice, I tell him so. Perfection in living form.

That compliment doesn't seem to offend him. He merely nods, his voice a low, rumbling rasp. "I am."

All vamryre are taught to think so, and embrace their physical perfection. Yet, I can't risk asking him next, "How long? How long have you been a vamryre?" He remains silent as my fingers traipse over his breastbone and ghost across a pale nipple.

As I approach the crest of his ribcage, however, he gently bats my hand aside and stands.

In no time, he redresses himself without requiring my assistance. Then dons a leather jacket with a low hood. Wearing it, he can navigate the warehouse fully and in silence, we fall into the task of moving Altaris's boxes out of sight and opening up this space.

Our space.

I've never had one to call my own before. I'll accept such a gift even from someone like Altaris. A whole space to call my own. A winding room with echoing floors and beautiful windows that display swathes of the outside city. A shadowy alley. A flat, gray yard overgrown with weeds. The brick of a nearby building.

Even if we travel to the other realm, we will come back. We must. I will promise myself that much at least.

In silence, Caspian and I continue to wander, and look and inspect.

But in contrast to my awe, he is brooding. Impatient. Unimpressed.

"Too many points of entry," he says, scowling at a window. His hood protects him from the worst of the sunlight, not that it seems to bother him. The amount of glass does.

"Too much space," he adds while standing in the center of the room. "Too many obstacles."

The observation gives me a glimpse into the way his mind works and how he thinks. The awe of his own space does not faze him: as a vamryre, ownership was not a question. They could take what they wanted from whomever—except their master. Belongings were interchangeable, and nothing held their interest for long.

Until him.

Until me.

Having something to protect is new to him. An uncanny, unfamiliar feeling. Any bad actor can use various avenues or routes to get to us, and he notes them all.

How differently we both see this space. I view it as the epitome of freedom, while he sees it as a fortress that must be defended.

How can I not? In this realm, I am not regulated by a single bell tower. I can go where I'd like. Do what I want. Even with the risk of danger looming overhead, it is…

Perfect. Beyond any dream I could have ever dreamed.

I'm smiling again. It is only from Caspian's gaze, the way he clenches his jaw, that I know.

"Your anger is intoxicating," he explains without prompting. "Your happiness is vibrant. You feel emotions differently than others." He doesn't know what to make of it. Slowly, his lips curl downward into a disapproving frown. "You are a contradiction."

"What does that mean?" I ask, hoping he will tell me. I don't feel insulted. No. He could never intentionally hurt me. Instead, I am curious. Compared to the straightforward texts I grew up reading, his way with words is so different. Sprinkled with hidden meanings and unusual phrases, he is a language unto himself.

One I desperately want to learn.

He eyes me for a long while, his head cocked. "You do not make sense. Even your tears are beautiful. You shouldn't exist."

I was wrong before. He can hurt me. With gutting, tiny stabs of an invisible knife. All the air has left my lungs, and I am unable to breathe. My vision turns blurry.

"No!" He is beside me in an instant, swiping at my face with a hiss of annoyance. I'm crying again, those infernal tears he called beautiful.

"You wail and I want you to stop," he snaps, bringing his mouth low to brush my jaw. "The mere sight of your tears irritates. I don't want to provoke them. I hate it. I speak to you as I would anyone else. You have me, wrapped around your little fingertips, at your beck and call. You repulse me in your pain," he adds, raising a finger toward my chin. It shakes. With rage, he shakes. "I should enjoy your meaningless sobbing. I should *want* to hurt you."

The fact that he can't frustrates him.

It thrills me.

Pain has been the one gift I have so freely received since the day I was born. My own mother didn't hesitate to give me it in spades. Yet, a monster who kills—heartlessly, he kills— can't bring himself to deliver that same gift to me alone.

I like this feeling. What is it? Power?

I feel powerful near him.

I feel...

"I feel safe with you," I tell him, meeting those soulless eyes directly.

Safe enough to return with him to the other realm if it means setting his mind at ease.

Safe enough to withstand any enemy.

Safe enough to indulge in greedy desires I shouldn't.

I could offer him up any and everything to stay. My heart. My soul.

All the blood I have in me to take.

Caspian

In comparison to Cassius, she is a more demanding master. He would issue his commands. Expect that they be followed. What I wanted or needed never factored into the equation. His will superseded all.

It's different with her.

The wants and needs she has are fleeting, but persistent. Rather than dwelling on them, she avoids them. Her neglected desires flit across her mind like a caged bird with two broken wings. It takes another person to rescue the poor creature.

My frustration with her comes from that; she makes me *want* to serve her. Want to keep her happy and smiling. Seeing her makes me want to repair those sad little dreams.

Not so that I can break them later, as I should. As I *should*.

I want to make them whole because of her. To please her. Keep her.

Cassius' rage could be enjoyed if I failed him.

I fail her, and the tears fall. I'd rather rip out my fucking eyes than see her tears fall.

I will collect those broken little dreams of hers. For now, I will fulfill them, if only to plot and scheme how to use her gratitude for my benefit. That is how I will punish her.

Her desire for me will outweigh mine.

Taking her hand in mine, I embrace her. I help her put on those silly shoes she wears to protect her feet from the elements outside. Then I step with her out into the sun.

And once again, she confounds me. Her hand frees itself from mine and she steps forward, skin glowing, eyes so damn wide. When she throws her head back, her dark hair spills untamed down her back.

I blink. I've never seen a fae fly. Never cared to. As they lorded over us all with their magic, they jealously guarded their secrets. As if, with just one glance, they could lose all their specialness. Vamryre are not so daunted by our power. Our skills are the embodiment of what we were.

What I was. A superior race of being, united by a collective mind, containing more knowledge within our skulls than the fae could ever amass--or so the lie went. Perhaps Nataniel and Pol upheld that lofty ideal. Not Cassius.

It is rumored, however, that fae wings are thin, glistening things that sparkle and hold their slender bodies aloft with little effort. The ability to fly is what makes them stand out.

It is their sole advantage on a battlefield, more powerful than even their fae magic.

Watching a fae fly is said to be a horrible, woeful experience.

Lies. She is terrible and woeful while standing on two feet, with the sun gleaming off her hair and her lips stretched wide. Her laughter guts me. I remember what it feels like to have a beating heart in my chest when I see her smile. How it can ache at the slightest damn provocation. How it can rebel against its owner's wishes and crave things. Long for them.

I see her and I long to make her smile last as long as I fucking can.

I crave to make her laughter ring on the air for all eternity.

In that empty place where my mortal heart once sat, she seeps into my soul.

She is poisoning me through and through.

I would gladly spurn any antidote.

"Where are we going?" She spins around, her arms outstretched, pink lips spread taut to reveal white teeth beneath. "It isn't dark yet, so..."

She trails off, her unease apparent. To sneak back through the portal, the cover of darkness is needed. For now, there is daylight to waste. Time to stall.

"Where do you want to go?" I ask her.

A tilt of her head indicates she is thinking, but her thoughts are clouded to me--not that she tries to hide them. Even in her skull, she smothers and tucks away that which she yearns for most.

Finally, she shrugs. "Anywhere."

She reaches for me.

I take her hand.

I will lead her anywhere.

CHAPTER 6

Niamh

For now, our return to the other realm seems eons away. Our pace is relaxed and unhurried as we walk through the mortal city. As a reward for agreeing to his request, Caspian humors me. Seething, and quiet, and vigilant, he humors me.

I am grateful. Despite his relentless navigation, he lets me gape and stare to my heart's content. Oh, this world is so very beautiful. Vibrant, that term he used for me: it fits better applied to this realm. The walls of this city are vibrant, the buildings looming yet without blocking the sunlight. The streets are drenched in shadow and sun. Light and dark.

It makes me wonder how it would look as a painting. What colors would an artist choose to depict it all? There aren't enough hues in the world.

There aren't enough sounds to compile the cacophony of chaos that swarms around us. Moving cars. Trucks. Tolling bells. Voices. Laughter. Everything.

I am in a maze of beautiful, violent, perfect noise and I hope to never find my way out.

With Caspian by my side, I will never need to. He knows the way. He's never lost track of every road and turn we've taken. Every twist and alleyway we pass through. He notes it all.

Yet he lets me wander and follow whatever shiny new fancy I spy. Oh, there is a park here! Lush green and ripening flowers. There is a stream cutting through it. Then a path where mortals race by, balanced atop metal wheels.

"Bikes," Caspian explains.

He knows so much. A wealth of knowledge sits in his mind, waiting to be accessed. Unlike Day, I don't have to beg him to share it with me.

I merely have to point, and he explains. So patient, yet indifferent. This knowledge means little to him. He doesn't care that "kites, airplanes, shopping buggies," are all so alien to me. So very interesting.

It is only when we pass a monument of stone that he tenses. It depicts a man, wearing heavy armor. Strange armor, but the garments of war, nonetheless. They have the same air to them as the chainmail and enchanted armor described in the old histories in the archives.

I imagined Caspian to be the sort to bare his teeth at the mention of violence. Relish in it.

He doesn't. Silent and contemplative, he stares instead. His fingers loosen their grip on me, and he steps forward, alone, both physically and in his mind. His thoughts are closed off, his expression unreadable.

Even when I reach out and touch him, he doesn't react.

My heart pounds painfully in my chest. "Caspian?" I picture those horrible days when he sat silent and empty. I can't relive that. I can't lose him again. "Caspian!"

He blinks. Turns his head. Looks at me from beneath his hood.

"Come." He continues onward as if he never stopped, leaving the monument in our wake. I can't stop staring at it. *First World War* makes up lettering carved into the top of the stone upon which the soldier stands. There is a placard on the wall that reads, "A memorial to the fallen."

Vamryre do not participate in mortal wars, at least not after they become one of their collective mind. Perhaps he survived the wars between the races in the years prior to the last thousand of peace? I don't know. Looking at his face alone, one could never tell his age.

Even his thoughts don't reveal an answer. They are shrouded. Hidden. Dustier than the items Altaris surrounds himself with.

The fact that Caspian dislikes me looking is even stranger. His mind cringes from mine. Anger builds. Like a creature on the defensive, he's aching to retaliate. Shift my focus.

Thus, he does so by the only means he knows.

He leads me down an alley darkened in shadow where the rays of the sun don't reach. It's cold here. There is a rotting smell in the air, and the road is narrow and winding. Even so, I breathe it in. I take in the brick walls covered in layers of faded paint. They are sloppier than the neat paintings in my stolen sketchbook, yet no less appealing. Intoxicating. I stare and stare and find new ways that mortals can express the simplest and most complex of things.

Indecipherable words are written in white ink. Faded portraits depict solemn faces of the dead. Meaningless symbols. Faceless names.

It's here that Caspian refuses to narrate. No matter how many times I point and question him, he remains silent. This is his punishment for whatever transgression I committed by upsetting him.

I'd deserve it.

However, we soon leave this alley behind and turn onto a street that seems familiar. A set of marble steps and gleaming columns appear...

I gasp with recognition. The museum is the one place he knows I will be too distracted to pester him, so he brought me here. How naughty. How cruel. Oh, how this hurts.

"I upset you," I whisper to his back as he walks without me, resolutely forward. "You should be angry with me."

Yet he rewards me. Despite his resentment, he rewards me.

"Come," he commands, still moving, letting wandering mortals drift in between us as I stand and stare at him. Then I remember how to move, putting one foot before the other. I race to catch up with him. Seize his wrist and grasp it tight.

Retaliation I could stomach.

Not this. Not kindness. Not ruthless selflessness.

He is too perfect for words. Too precious to keep. A monster would be mine only until he grew bored, but Caspian? He can't grow bored. I won't let him.

I won't lose him ever again.

Should anyone take him from me...

I will rip out their throat.

Caspian

Boring walls. Empty halls. Paint splotches on canvas with no meaning. The first time was a novelty. I could forgive her, then, for her reaction. So awestruck. She's seen little outside of her stone prison. Of course, the mortal world impressed her, shiny and new.

By now, the sparkle has worn off, the shine dulled. She should inspect these artworks with a sigh and smother yawn into the pale hand that flies to her mouth. Then we will go to the portal and she can leave here content for now. During her pursuit of Night Aurelia, I will hunt Cassius down. We will be free.

All in all, she should beg me to take her from this place *now*.

Not gasp. Another wide-eyed expression shapes those plain features of hers, giving them light. *Depth. Dimension*--words that suddenly take on a whole new meaning in this fucking fractured brain. You could sculpt those cheeks with charcoal and soot, but it would take decades of color matching to depict those eyes. The darkness in them. The worry, the pain, the fear and the hope.

Her hope is stifling. I see it, glimpse it, taste it and it breeds a festering ache within me. Something too dangerous to linger upon.

In my mind, she is a viper, and I feel an instinctive need to push her away. Shove her if I have to. Off a cliff if I must.

She is dangerous to me.

She makes me remember...

Things I don't want to.

Like...

How rain smells on damp skin. What blood tastes like—long before the taste of it grew to sate me. When it was bitter on the tongue. When I had to wade through gallons of it. Once upon a time. Sometime in the distant past. Or the future?

Can't tell. Can't remember.

The air has changed in here. In these dank, dusty hallways lined with skeptical mortals and prowling guards. They don't seem to pick up on the change. Don't notice what their little eyes and dull senses can't acknowledge.

I can feel it. Sense it.

The darkness unfurling in this sprawling space. There is evil here. A malicious entity.

I should leave now. Seek only to protect my fae. Reaching out my hand towards her pale form, I approach her. Her attention is focused on another painting, oblivious to everything else around her.

Like the damned smell. Sulfur and ink. Dust and mustiness. An itchy, crawling, choking, goddamned familiar scent. It calls to me. It lures me away from her, through a crowd of aimless mortals and deeper into this rickety, rotting, old building.

Despite the pretty veneer, this place is much older than it appears. Its very foundation stinks of centuries of mortal filth. I sniff, hating the stench of it. Old paint. Older dust. Decades and centuries of mortal odors caked into the walls.

But one scent does not belong.

It is familiar. Too familiar. It draws me deeper, down a set of stairs and into a rarely used corridor. The scent of neglect and decay is thicker down here. So heavy I want to choke.

Still, I'm propelled forward, closer. Relentlessly drawn toward the source of the odor.

A painting: a series of them in a tiny little display festooned with a sign I don't bother to read. There are twelve of them, displayed in a neat little row. Ugly little visions of things. Nothing like the jaunty, happy portraits upstairs.

These are the demented figments of a very disturbed mind.

A familiar mind...

How?

I try to remember. For once, I *want* to remember. What sick mind created these visions, so unlike the other mortal-made images?

A twisted soul.

With globs of oil and pigment, they depicted vile things that remind me of Cassius. Pale creatures reminiscent of my fae.

Moreover, they depicted this world as burning.

All of it burning.

And she, my Niamh, stands at the center of the destruction, dark eyes blazing, fixed straight ahead, glaring at me through space and time.

I failed her and she hates me.

It's me she's burning.

Me she's trying to kill.

CHAPTER 8

Niamh

In front of me is a painting of a woman with hazel eyes. With her head partially turned, she gazes longingly at the viewer, her eyes wistful, soulful, and beautiful. How I wish to give her whatever it is she seeks so forlornly. It must be more precious to her than a visit to a museum or a wayward mother. Something she fears she may never find again.

I wish I could reach out and touch her cheek and tell her that all isn't lost. Sometimes dreams can be delivered in the darkest of places by the unlikeliest of deliverers.

And some dreams become dashed horribly by unforeseen circumstances.

I hear the cries of startled viewers around me, like a piercing siren. Someone shouts. Screams.

A man in blue storms forward, waving a blunt, black instrument toward the nearest exit. "Everyone! Attention, everyone! We're issuing an evacuation. Please file calmly and quietly out of the nearest exits—"

Panic.

Pandemonium.

People scream. Women grab the hands of children and all rush to one of the doors with gleaming green words portraying the way to safety.

Safety. Because there is danger in this beautiful, sacred place. Distant shouts rise from the distance. "Move, move, move. West Gallery!"

Something is wrong.

But where is Caspian?

Reaching out, I expect him to appear from nowhere and take my hand. He doesn't. Neither is he over my shoulder, or anywhere nearby as I spin around.

"Miss?" The man in black waves his device menacingly in my direction. "Please, leave. This is an evacuation."

There is no argument. No discussion. The press of mortals around me swells and expands, jostling me among them toward the doorway. Out, only a busy street swarmed with masses of scared, terrified people.

Their emotions slam into me. Jar and disrupt.

I look for Caspian. I need to find him.

He isn't here. In his black hood, he stands out, even with his features obscured. With it down, he is undeniable: a star among stone. I look and look, trying my best to resist the flow and press of the crowd.

"Move!" Another guard points down the block. "Keep moving, please! An orderly line."

Orderly. Orderly.

But where is Caspian? The back of my neck prickles with sweat. My heart races. I spin around, craning my neck, looking, and looking. I see him nowhere.

I reach out and feel him nowhere.

Even in my head. It is empty, with only my own thoughts circling around.

"Caspian?" My voice rings out, swallowed by nearby murmurs and questions. I try again. Can't hear myself. I can't even hear myself think.

The museum is too far away, getting further with every forced step.

"Detour. Detour," someone mutters, another guard. They point and shout. Point and shout. The crowd thins and spreads. I need to go back. I try to, only to be shouted at and pushed back. Further away.

No.

I resist the press of the crowd. Try to slip to the outskirts, ducking around bodies. The only way out is through a darkened gap in between two buildings. There are no other people in there. No shouting, yelling, pushing. I race toward it and gasp once I'm finally free.

I can think again. Caspian. Caspian. Where is he? I try calling for him out loud. "Caspian? Cas..."

A noise sounds nearby, making me jump. A smattering of footsteps, quick and light. My heart lurches, hope surges. I rush toward it: a corner of the alley further in where the light doesn't reach. Makes sense for him to hide here. Lurk here.

It makes sense.

But the figure who detached themselves from the shadows— the figure I reach out for—isn't Caspian. They are too tall and willowy. Too cruel. Their skin reeks of cologne and sourness. I stagger back, out of their reach.

And right into the grasp of another figure I didn't even notice closing in on me from behind.

Their hot breath tickles my throat as they chuckle, "Gotcha."

Caspian

Memories aren't always worth recalling. Some emerge from your subconscious, from the muck of your mind. The one place I didn't mind having Cassius snuff out of me and spoil.

Weak things. Pointless recollections. Thoughts of a stupid mortal.

Like guilt. As hard as I try to smother it, it festers inside me. I was meant to do something, once. Something important.

I failed.

Failed. Failed.

And someone has mocked me for it. They smeared the proof over the canvas. Made a spectacle out of the reality I once lived. I don't remember how or why the sight makes me angry.

It just does. I want to rip and tear apart every last painting. Try to. Will.

Can't.

There are forces at play beyond me. Beyond the fingers I lash at the canvas with. Beyond the hands that struggle to restrain me. Beyond the voice in my head, whispering a niggling whisper: *you've seen this before...done this. You did this!*

A warning. A warning. Remember. Before it is too late, REMEMBER!

"Niamh!" I shout her name as I lash at the painted figure resembling her. I need her here. Need her to explain.

Explain why her image is here.

Why someone painted her.

Why she looks so damn happy amongst all that chaos and destruction.

Happier than she has ever been with me.

CHAPTER 10
Niamh

As I wake up, I find myself in a dank, dark, enclosed space. It isn't the peaceful arousal I've come to expect since I entered the mortal realm: stirring awake in Caspian's arms.

This place is colder than he could ever be. So cold my breath paints the air before me white. I'm shivering, my teeth chattering together. Pitch-black darkness cloaks everything else. All I can hear is the distant hum of what sounds like music. And...

Voices. Loud, raucous voices.

My head aches. I reach up to touch my forehead and my fingers brush a dried, crusty substance caked to the skin. A searing pain pulses above my left eye. It hurts to blink.

Where am I?

Tentatively, I reach out. Try to speak. "Caspian?"

Nothing.

Not even a mocking laughter in answer.

Because a possible reason for this predicament has already entered my mind. It's always been there. A small, hidden fear that my reliance on him was a lie. On his end, devotion was a burden. He left me.

And this time a wayward truck wasn't what found me.

Predators. Their auras betray them. A strange word, one I think I stole from Caspian's mind. He liked to catalog people while working under the sway of his master. Easy prey. Not prey. Worthless. Predator.

Given that he was a vamryre, mortal predators were a game to him. He loved pretending to be weak, and then turning the tables. Going for their throats right when they thought they had the upper hand.

Cassius didn't command him to enjoy those moments. He did, anyway. He enjoyed taking the power from those who abused it, even if he didn't know it then.

In the absence of him, these thoughts seem to fester. The old ones. The things he left stuffed in mental boxes and never bothered to sort. The parts of him that Cassius severed from his soul and discarded as useless at various intervals.

Poor Caspian. I can see those shattered bits of him. Visualize them. Yet, if I try to seek out anything more—any actual thoughts—it's like I hit a blank wall. He's cut me out. Closed himself up.

Because a part of me insists, *he left you here to die, of course.*

He left you to be gobbled up.

Eager to do so, three monsters lurk nearby. I can tell from the cadence of their footsteps and—eventually—the tone of voice. Among the trio, one has a deep, raspy baritone and a heavy, resonant step.

"You bet your ass, Cyrus," he rumbles. "It's our lucky day. An honest to God, fucking fae! We just stumbled across her while tracking the little Lunarian minx—"

"Who you let prance away. To capture a fae, you say? I'll be the judge of that," a softer voice cuts in. Slick and oily like Altaris's purr, but darker. Somehow gruffer. His voice inspires more unease than that of the first man. It's like, with one whisper, he can penetrate skulls and corrupt minds. He reminds me, in a way, of the Lord Master. Some powerful, elder fae. "You dumb sons of bitches wouldn't know a goddamn pixy from your own arsehole."

"Take a look! She's the real deal, Cyrus," a third man pitches in. His voice is a mix of the two, yet somehow the least offensive. "Pretty as a fucking picture. The spitting image of the one in the ledger—"

"She isn't fae, and I'll tell you why, you fucking idiots—"

Suddenly, a bright light explodes into being, blinding me. I shift back, striking a firm surface that rattles in a chilling echo. Ice-cold bars kiss the back of my neck. I'm in a cage. It is tall, made of black metal that clangs with the slightest movement. A circular space surrounds it, with a wooden pillar reaching up to the ceiling. Except there isn't a ceiling in the normal sense: just swaths of dark, scarlet fabric suspended by ropes and cord.

Crowded around the wooden pillar, three men stand before me. One is dressed in vibrant red that reflects off the bars of my cage as he approaches. His suit is as elegant as one Altaris wore, but small details diminish its grandeur. There are subtle stains here and there. Wayward wrinkles. Even his black hat, trimmed with crimson string, seems slightly askew on his head of dark hair. With a sigh, he kicks the metal, sending a clang throughout the narrow space.

"I'll tell you why," he repeats, scanning my face with two intense gray eyes. "Take a good look at her. No fae stone around her neck. No glimmers in her skin. Most important of all, and listen closely now, boys... Do you see any fucking wings?"

"Well, uh..." A shorter man tiptoes into view, rubbing his balding head. "She's got a sweater on, don't she? Besides, look at her! If she ain't fae, then I'm the fucking queen. Here, let's take her top off and see if she--"

The slender man shifts, raising his arm. A sharp sound pierces the air. Flesh on flesh. The second man howls.

"Well, your bloody highness! I don't give a damn what she looks like. No wings, no fae. No fae, means no high price. You dumbasses have never seen a real damn fairy, but I have. Ain't no shirt that can hide those wings. At least the mundane brat has something to show for her heritage. This one is pretty, but she'll fetch the price of a mere human. Nothing special about her."

I blink as my eyes adjust to the harsh brightness. Slowly it fades to a dull yellow coming from a lamp dangling above. This entire room is not quite a room at all. The walls are fabric instead of wood or stone. A bright, gaudy red, they sway and buckle with the lightest movement, yet they are thick. Impenetrable. The floor beyond my cage isn't a floor at all but grass and dirt. Crates upon crates fill nearly every available space in here, but there is an order to the chaos, unlike in Altaris's domain.

These men are not vamryre either. Their eyes do not glow an unholy red or green or silver. Their skin is flushed pink, and everything about them seems mortal. Except there is an air about the one in red. Something Caspian would deem abnormal. He moves with a jerky, brutal grace and looks at me with a sense of practiced boredom rather than awe.

He knows of the fae. He's seen one. More than one.

But how? How?

I need to know. So, I listen, head bowed, vision obscured by my falling hair. I curl into a ball and watch them all watch me.

"She ain't no mere human," the deeper-voiced man rasps. He wears black from head to toe and sports a long, forked beard awkwardly balanced on a narrow chin. "I mean, look at her, Cyrus! Maybe she's one of those vamryre—"

"She isn't vamryre, either," the man in scarlet claims. He stalks forward and crouches before me, his head cocked, brown eyes bright with interest. They scan my face and limbs with calculated glee.

As the seconds pass, my heart flinches at what I see in that gaze. He's lied to his two companions. He is interested in me for some reason. A skin crawling, hair-raising reason. I am a piece of meat to him, but one he does not want to devour himself. A darkness flickers in his gaze. As faint and chilling as a lingering shadow.

Caspian knew such looks well. As a predator, it was how he assessed his prey. How he measured their worth for Cassius. Those with the rarest attributes garnered him the most praise. A sated Cassius loosened his leash, and poor Caspian desired nothing more than freedom from him.

This man's intentions are not so basic and not so noble.

He looks at me, and he sees silver. Piles upon piles of silver. Wealth that he does not intend to share.

"You two clear out," he commands without looking to see if his orders are followed—they will be. "Go muck out the goblin pens. I'll see what we can salvage out of this so-called fairy."

The other two leave through a gap in the fabric walls, muttering between them.

Which just leaves the man in red, eyeing me skeptically. Without his cohorts near, he lets more of his real emotions peek through. Avid interest. Marked concern. Something else. Fear?

Not of me. Can't be of me. Fae are peaceful creatures.

Yet, he is cautious. Perhaps like Altaris, he thinks me something else, beyond my true heritage.

A monster.

"What's your name?" he demands. When I don't answer fast enough, he raps on the metal bars with a fist, making them jangle. "Come on! Is it sunrise, or daylight or whatever the fuck your kind call themselves. Oh, that's right, darling—" He chuckles and raises a dark eyebrow. "I know damn well where you're from. The stink of the other realm is all over you. But I also know that whatever you are…it isn't fae, even if they raised you. *So, tell me your name.*" His voice breaks then, almost as if his true manner of speaking is far different to the poise and polished words.

He reminds me of Altaris—yet different. Altaris, if the man were trying to pretend to be anything but what he is. A powerful creature.

A creature not to be trifled with.

He wants my name, but Niamh is for me alone. Only Caspian is worthy to utter it, and perhaps Poppy and Colleen. Not him, this creature lurking before me.

Lying is a sin, but only there. Out here, there are no rules. Just games to be played. So, I swallow, and eye him fearfully through my lashes.

"Aurelia," I say.

He whistles. His eyes widen. Somehow, I have said the right thing.

The wrong thing.

The piles of silver he envisioned before are morphing as his smile widens. They've become gold. Platinum, even.

"Oh, holy fuck. You stupid little bird. How the hell have you wandered out here and fallen right into my lap? No worries." He rises to his feet, still chuckling low. "Old Uncle Cyrus will take good care of you from here on out. Good fucking care!"

He stares into space and laughs and laughs. It's not just my appearance that amuses him so. He is remembering something. Recalling someone. Another fae perhaps, that he had in his capture once upon a time. He looked at her and saw silver and gold. She had two wings. A fae name.

"Who?" I croak. Too many questions within me attempt to break free at once. Only disjointed fragments spill out. "Another fae? Who was she? Tell me!"

He cocks his head at my tone. Too loud. Too demanding.

Oh no. I went too far and dropped my ruse. Caspian's insights are all I have to draw from and even in his absence, he has taught me well. Predators react best to docile prey. Those they can toy with. Hunt. Those who they know won't ever fight back.

For a second, he saw me as something else. He didn't like that glimpse of her, naughty Niamh.

I bow my head again. Cower again. I'll do anything to make him speak. I need him to speak.

Because a part of me already knows the answers he may give, even if they are impossible. Even if they are fantastical.

"A pushy little thing, aren't you?" he wonders, stalking back toward this cage. "Not a smartass like the other one. That one. I wonder if she ever made it back, the little bitch. I gave her fame and fortune. She gave me this—" He pulls back the sleeve of his right forearm, revealing a scar etched into tanned flesh. It's silvery white, shaped in the form of a crescent moon. Bite marks.

"Yeah, a tricky little bitch. Made me a fucking fortune, though." He lowers his sleeve with a grisly smile. "I gave her sumthin to remember me by, too. Should be about your age by now. I wonder if you've seen it. What?" he questions in response to my gasp. "You didn't think I could tell you all apart? It's in the eyes."

He points at his own with those spindly fingers. "All you little bitches wear your age right in the eyes. Pretty and shiny until the light goes out. Right before they grind your kind into dust and use what's left of yous to power that little hidden city. Ah, I bet you all think you're so damn smart. That we haven't figured it out by now. We have." He reaches up and taps the rim of his black hat. "Luckily, we use our brains for what they're meant for. Not hiding like rats in a cage, but for making money. You, sweetheart, are going to be my new main attraction."

He spins on his heel and lifts a corner of the heavy fabric, revealing a gap. "Minchae, get your sweet lil' ass in here! Say hello to your new lil' sister."

A slender figure appears, slipping past him. Though she walks on two feet, it would be a crime to call her movements with such a crude, simple term. She floats. Practically flies, though—like me—she has no wings. Grace imbues every inch of her tall, delicate frame. Even Day didn't carry himself with half her poise.

Her posture isn't due to elegance alone. Heavy, rusted chains encircle her ankles, threatening to weigh her down. She must work twice as hard to counteract them, keeping her head high in the air, gaze fixed ahead. As a result, her lean frame is all muscle, visible beneath milky white skin. Her clothing is unlike anything I've ever seen—even on the mortals that wander the city streets, or the strange figures who frequented Altaris's shop. Shiny green fabric encircles her breasts and winds down to her hips, covering little else. Leather sandals protect her feet from the harsh ground. Even so, she is more regal than the Lord Master, cloaked in their robes of pristine white.

Then she looks at me, and I am more confused than ever. She isn't fae, I know that. Yet, she could be one. Her face is as beautiful as a sculpted doll's. The only minor flaw is that one of her eyes is a brilliant blue and the other green—anomaly, the Lord Master would declare, even if she were born of fae. Her features alone would bar her from belonging to any sole house.

Then she approaches and a shimmering glow catches my attention, emanating from her left side.

"Where did you find this one?" Her voice is whisper-soft, yet the man in red flinches in response as though she shouted.

"Never you mind that," the man snaps. "Just clean her up and get her ready. You two will go on tomorrow night as the new star attraction. The Fae Twins." He raises his hands and paints the letters onto the air, beaming as he does so. "Teach her the routines and get her ready. Simple preening and waving stuff. And Minchae?"

An expression of disgust washes over the woman's face. Instead of responding, she simply tilts her head in acknowledgment.

"If I sniff even a hint of funny business out of you both, I'll cut you to pieces and make a pair of wings out of you. I only need one bloody fae."

Again, she doesn't reply, but her strange eyes meet mine and I shiver. Something passes between us. Not thoughts or words, but a shared sentiment.

A quiet longing.

We are both creatures cast aside as strange and unwanted, made to feel unique in our wickedness.

Lo' and behold, we are not the only ones after all. There is solace to be found in that lie.

Whatever demented creature I am, so is she.

A not-fae with one painted wing.

CHAPTER 11

Caspian

I bash my skull against anything available. Beat these brains out of the bones and flesh. It feels good to watch my own blood drip down. Onto my face and dry into a crust. I need to feel muscle and tendons meld, and flesh become whole, driven to knit together again by the vamryre curse.

Then I bash, bash, bash it all out again.

It's only amid the pain that I can think. Try to remember...

Something. Why the fuck can't I remember?

I try again. Endure again. Bash and break and barrel this stupid brain into submission. I will recall it all, no matter the cost. Why those paintings were so goddamn familiar. Why *she* was in them. Why my fingers tingle and ache as though itching to perform some vital task? Something I forgot how to do. Remnants of it tease the edges of my broken mind.

Canvas and oil.

83

Oil and Pigment.

"Caspian—"

Canvas and pigment.

Pigment. Oil.

Bash.

"Caspian!" That voice itches in my mind, but it isn't Cassius's sly murmur, so I don't need to let it in. Not that I'd want to let *him* in. Damn him. Damn him.

But he knew. Those things I forgot and want to remember. Cassius knew them all. He would taunt me with them.

What a naughty little sadist of a mortal you were, my Caspian. I plucked you from obscurity. Saved you. You were always meant to be mine. You came to me, willingly—

"If you want to track down your little, morbid, fae toy before she's chopped to pieces and sold on the black market, I suggest you cut out this ruckus, Caspian. Listen to me!"

Listen. Fae. Toy. Mine.

I see her. Beautiful, fragile little Niamh, chopped to pieces. Sold.

I stop, even though I still want to bash. I think of her, and I stop. Then I blink away the blood and try to see. Focus.

I'm in a room. A room with chains dangling from the concrete walls and a harsh light above. A room that reeks of blood and bodily muck that isn't mine. Piss. Shit. So many men and women alike have been herded in here and left to rot. Their stink has collected in the metal drains carved into the floor. It's never been cleaned properly, just hosed down with water that smells like sulfur. A naughty room this is. Meant for containment.

Not of mortal or vamryre, or lunaria alike—but all.

All kinds of races have been stored here.

Butchered in here.

I want someone to try to butcher me. Oh, what fun we will have—

"You need to focus, Caspian," that stern voice cuts in. Nags. "I don't much care for the little creature, but I shudder at the damage she can do while unleashed upon the population unsupervised, even for a moment. You need to help me find her. Damn, what was its name again? Eve? Neel—"

"Niamh," I say. Her name is a spell that snaps me back. Clarity returns with icy precision. My Niamh is out there alone. Beyond this butchering room.

Because I left her. I wandered off into that museum and saw those damned paintings.

Or is it a lie? This creature is keeping her from me. He aims to take her.

I turn on him, blinking more of his body into view. Tall, slender. Piercing green eyes and a sly grin. What did Niamh call him? Altaris, the one she hates.

"Where is she?" I demand, my hands in fists, fangs drawn. My skull is melding together again, and my vision is clearing by the second. Should he lie to me, I'll have more than enough strength to kill him.

"I was hoping you could tell me," he says without fear. "You've mated with her. Use your little mental connection thing and tell me. Or were my suspicions of her wrong? Perhaps, she's merely a powerless abomination? It doesn't seem that her blood melted your body, at least." He strokes his chin as if seriously questioning an answer.

"Can't hear her," I snap, not that he is worthy to know any inch of her thoughts. There is too much chaos in my head. Too many whispering murmurs. Despite my best efforts, I am unable to find her thread—the connection to her mind. That realm of perfect peace.

"Ah, a coherent response. Finally, it seems you have regained some of your senses," the man, Altaris remarks with a sniff. "It appears that over a century in Cassius's little mind dungeon hasn't tamed that temper of yours. Still impulsive, as always. Still prone to stubborn resolve when you don't get your way."

"Don't speak as if you know me," I snap. He doesn't. Not who I was before or after. No one does—except Cassius. One day, I will make the bastard tell me. I'll rip the answers from his skull.

"Of course, I would never presume," Altaris replies, but his tone is light. He is mocking me.

Any other time, I'd care. Not now.

"Niamh. Where is she?"

"While you were getting yourself wrangled by a whole squadron of mortal police before the boneys showed up, she skipped away. Vanished. Perhaps the fae retrieved their creature, but I would hear if their agents came through the portals. They are a noisy, dramatic sort." He sighs in disgust. "However, it's been dead silent on that end. Someone else must have her. Unfortunately, that does not narrow it down. There are quite a few unsavory characters on the prowl who would dream of coming across a wayward, unprotected fae. For nefarious reasons, as I am sure you can imagine."

They would sell her.

Whore her.

Destroy her.

"Not so fast," Altaris warns as I lunge toward him, aiming for the doorway at his back. "There is the little detail of you having been placed in boney holding to deal with," he tries to explain. "I suggest you listen, because those chains around your limbs are not for mere decoration. They are more than capable of restraining—and severing the limbs of—vamryre and lunaria alike, so I suggest you *calm yourself.*"

He uses that tone again. The stern, authoritative one. In some ways, it reminds me of fucking Cassius, but in other ways, it doesn't. Altaris is stern, but he can't punish me if I resist him. He can't torment my brain. He can't make me see what only he wants me to see.

Yet, he is just as dangerous as the entire vamryre horde. Perhaps more so. He hides his true nature well behind his frilly clothes and polished manners. Bullshit. Lies. Underneath his exterior, he is worse than I am. Rages more than me. Hates far more fervently than I ever could.

He is intriguing, so I listen, even if the chains are thin enough to shatter. Some might take an arm or leg in retribution, but so be it. I'll crawl limbless to find her.

Suddenly, it feels vital to.

I remember her standing in the gallery, hair alight by the sun, eyes wide and expressive. It wouldn't take a callus actor to harm her. A bus. A car. A fucking motorbike.

"I need to find her," I say. If she isn't dead already, smashed to bits by her own infernal curiosity.

"Finally, you are beginning to see reason," Altaris remarks. He threads his fingers together and eyes me from across the peak they make. "We must discuss a matter before I can secure your release. The bond on your head is very high, my friend. Two-point-one million arun. That's practically astronomical. Being a fugitive and wanted for several unsolved mortal murders, and now mangling and disfiguring seven hapless mortal security guards and four boneys, I am surprised they granted you a bond at all. That must be Anna Greeves's doing, trying so desperately to bring civil order to this haphazard place. In any case, I happen to have exactly two-point-one million arun lying around that I could lend you. Two million will come with no strings attached—"

"Why?" I snap, sensing bullshit. Everything has a price. Nothing is for free. Two million arun must be stupid mundane money. Play money. Doesn't matter. No one gives away the lint in their pockets for nothing.

"We can consider it settling an old debt between you and me. Don't worry yourself about the particulars."

"Particulars?" There are none. "Don't know you. Don't owe you."

"All very well and good." He unlaces his hands and waves me off with one. It's a practiced gesture. He pretends to mingle with the mortal riffraff now, but once, this creature was powerful. Once, he commanded millions with the slightest wave of his hand. He hides it now, but his body remembers. "The point is, you will owe me the remaining arun. You may make your own arrangements to pay it off, but frankly listening doesn't seem to be your strong suit. Before we see your fae, we need to visit a friend of mine first. Someone who will help us tie up any loose ends when it comes to my repayment. Then we will find your fae. Agreed?"

"No," I hiss, rattling the chains that bind me. "I will find her first! I must find her now!"

Without me, she's lost, vulnerable to any monster with eyes. Oh yes, they will hunt her. Sink their teeth in and feast on my pretty fae. I won't let them. I'll kill them all.

"Frankly, my dear, this isn't negotiable. Unless you plan on staying in boney prison until some sham trial that Jack will use to flaunt his authority, I really am your only option."

Him. Lying bastard. He lies to me still. There is something lurking in his gaze, slipping away as I try to find it. He knows something. He is afraid of something, but it isn't me or my fae. He reeks of guilt. Pathetic. Repulsive.

However, it makes him different from Cassius. His guilt implies that he means what he says. Repayment for payment.

"Fine," I say. "Just take me to her. Before..."

Before she's hurt again. Killed. Before I lose her good.

Altaris nods. "Give me a minute or two to track down the riff raff, ah. Speak of the devil and they shall appear." His tone is a hiss as a woman enters the room through the partially opened door behind him.

She is tall, dressed in black leather with a silver stick in hand. It is long, nearly the length of her willowy frame. Paired with her stiff posture, I assume it is a weapon of some kind. One she desperately wants to use on me. Her dark eyes scan my body with a swipe, cold and appraising.

To her, I am a beast on display. She'd request more than two million arun—whatever the fuck that is—for me. Twice as much. Perhaps far more.

"I knew this one had to be one of yours," she sneers to Altaris, returning his derision with her own harsh tone. "How many times must we warn you, shopkeeper? Watch your little vermin or we will shut down your sleazy operation and send every one of those monsters to the pits where they belong."

The pits. A place that makes Altaris flinch, though he scoffs. This mortal doesn't scare him, even with her threats. She amuses him. He toys with her, flashing a gleeful smile.

"Boney Marin, ah. I thought I'd smelled your presence when I arrived. Still on the *Lys*, I see. I heard in the papers about that awful incident your crew investigated the other day—that awful Black Fang nonsense. I'm sure the stress must be driving you to many a sleepless night. Is Jack aware?"

The woman pales, her dark eyes flashing. "Mind your fucking business, vamp. Are you here to pay his bond or run your mouth?"

"Both," Altaris replies. "Frankly, I'm surprised you're here in the station, babysitting one of my little monsters while a serial killer is on the loose. How is the hunt for the Black Fang going?" He pauses.

Marin says nothing.

"Unless, of course," Altaris continues, *"you* are the one being punished with a day of desk work. Tsk. Tsk. Now, will you file his bond work, or shall I?"

"Bloodsucking prick." The woman storms from the room, her posture defensive. As he watches her go, Altaris is beaming.

"Must have been something I said," he replies innocently before following her out. "Should be only a minute or two, Caspian."

A minute or two. Long enough for Niamh to get swallowed up. Chewed into pieces. Spit back out.

I left her. I left her. How could I?

Because of them. Those paintings. I try to remember them— recall what they looked like—but I can't. They are blank, black squares devoid of meaning. I need to go back to that damn museum and find them again.

After I find her.

"Well, that is done with." Altaris reappears near the open door, and two men follow him inside. They're dressed in the same black leather as the woman, sporting similar sticks that dangle from belts at their waists.

They approach me. Hesitate and share worried glances. "Are you sure he's properly sedated?" one of them wonders of the other. "This little bastard took out two of our best men. I hear he nearly ripped poor Joel's bloody arm off!"

"I will vouch for him, my darlings," Altaris says. "Dear Caspian won't do anything naughty, now will he? Naughtiness will result in your bond being revoked, all my money being poured down the drain and more time wasted. We don't want that, do we?"

"No," I hiss. "We don't."

"Good. Now, hurry to it, boys! We have other business to attend to!" Altaris claps his hands, and the men jump to attention. They fear me, yet they fear him more. They scurry around, trading fearful glances between us both as they wrangle their chains and use silver keys to set me free.

When they do, I finally notice the state of me. The mess I've made. So much blood, both mine and that of others. Oh dear. I've made such a mess.

I'll make a much larger one if Niamh isn't found. If she is harmed. If she is dead? I will tear this world to shreds.

"Hold on--" The female returns, stick in hand, held at the ready. She stares past me, straight at Altaris. Her smile alone is smug. "Looks like this one won't be going anywhere."

"And, pray tell, why is that?" Altaris counters.

He takes a single step, placing himself in between us. As if he--slender and tall--would be a match for several muscular men, and a woman at that. Yet he is. All three mortals tremble. Only the woman looks willing to take him on.

She swishes her stick impatiently through the air, then lowers it. "There's an envoy from the other side here to take him back. Looks like this vamryre is here illegally. Even your smooth-talking and false paperwork can't get him out of this mess."

"Is that so?"Altaris swipes a thumb along his chin. He hides it well, but he is uneasy.

Because 'envoy' or not, this has all the hallmarks of Cassius. My old master has come for me already. Not directly, of course; he wouldn't bother his pompous ass with such a demeaning task.

But he's sent one of his pawns, for sure.

I can smell them, even if their thoughts are blissfully absent from my skull. Somewhere nearby.

"Now, now, Caspian. There is no time for theatrics," Altaris tells me. As he approaches Marin, he shrugs. "Show us the way to this envoy. I will negotiate on Caspian's behalf."

The woman laughs. Then scoffs. "Right this way."

"I think we may have to add onto your contract, my friend. Come," Altaris prods, nodding toward the doorway. "Let's hurry before Marin comes up with something else to charge you with out of spite."

I stalk forward, surprised to feel more blood dripping from me. My own. My skull is slow to heal. I'm still bleeding. My vision is still partially blurred. I laugh. Away from Cassius, I must not heal the way I used to. Not lightning quick with barely any pain to feel.

Here, I suffer.

Oh fun.

Swiping away the blood, I follow Altaris from the chain room and into a narrow hallway. Mortals mill around here, all dressed in variations of black leather. Most of them sport silver sticks. The ones that don't lurk behind heavy desks that line the space at varying intervals.

We enter a plain room adorned with only a long metal table in the center. At one end sits a figure, dressed in white. Not one of my old siblings. Not Cassius himself.

Another. Two guards dressed in green robes loom behind the figure, ready to defend at a moment's notice. I sniff the air and frown. Spicy. Like Niamh, yet harsher, with none of her floral notes that mark her scent. Still, they are fae.

And they are here, far from their den of safety.

"Oh my," Altaris says, stepping forward. He inclines his head, but there is no respect in the gesture. Instead, the jerky movements seem insulting. "To what do we owe this great honor?"

The figure cocks their head. Long, white hair frames an impassive face, composed of indiscernible features. The sharp eyes and harsh bone structure are the hallmarks of an elder fae--and not just any. A name comes to me, stolen from Niamh's thoughts.

Lord Master. The one she feared. The one who mutilated her body with numerous scars. In contrast, their body seems whole beneath their white robes. A subtle lump at the base of their neck alludes to the presence of the appendages Niamh lacks: wings.

"This vamryre is a fugitive from the laws of the Citadel," the figure says. "To maintain the established order, we request that it is returned, along with the creature it fled with." Their voice is low and even-pitched. In spite of that, there is a power resonating through it that puts even Altaris's to shame. Their body may be old--yet, still a child to any vamryre--but their mind... It is incredibly ancient.

Almost as if they alone contain their own private hive mind.

Perhaps they do. Among the many reasons why my old master hated them was their love of mystery and secrets. They knew things that even vamryre did not.

Such as how to circumvent the rules of the realm they created. Altaris told Niamh that no fae can enter this world. A lie, it seems.

Yet, when I eye the vamryre, he does not seem surprised, *per se*. His eyes scan the envoy's front, honing on a silver chain draped around their slender neck. I soon notice that the guards also sport a similar, gaudy piece of jewelry: silvery chains supporting a small, blue stone. Is that the answer, perhaps?

"Ah, well, I am afraid that any vamryre who enters this realm and is rejected by their master, falls under *my* domain," Altaris says, drawing all attention to him. "It must be an oversight the boneys didn't convey. I apologize for the inconvenience. I am sure you travelled quite the distance." He doesn't move to sit, leaving himself and the table as a makeshift barrier between me and the fae.

As if he thinks *they* need protecting.

The Lord Master creature blinks. "The fae is not under your purview. We request its return--"

"I'm sorry!" The door behind me opens, and a woman stumbles in. Her long brown hair obscures her features; she sputters, and she tries to bat most of it out of her eyes. She's slight, average height, wearing a brown jacket and matching skirt--not the black that seems the chosen color of the other mortals who inhabit this building. She runs a trembling hand down her front and smiles warily. "I am Anna Greeves, the newly elected mayor. I wasn't expecting an official delegation or I would have--"

"It doesn't seem that there is much to discuss," Altaris says, clasping his hands together. "Caspian is now under my protection, no longer a member of his collective. As for the other... She is not my concern--"

"No," I snarl. My gaze is on the Lord Master. The fae are rumored to have powerful magic, but I'll take my chances. Its figure is thin and lithe, liable to snap under my strength. I'd rip their throat out before they could utter any incantations.

"There is no need for theatrics, Caspian," Altaris warns in his authoritative tone.

"Oh, of course not," the mortal woman interjects. "There is a bureaucratic answer to this, I think." She sways, rocking from one foot to the other. A ball of energy, she exudes a nervous quality that Cassius would scorn.

Yet, Altaris doesn't wrinkle his nostrils at her as he did to the other woman, Marin. He holds himself rigid, his posture almost... Deferential. As if she, this fragile mortal, holds power of her own that I cannot see.

The Lord Master, does not seem of the same opinion. "I do not understand," they say. "On behalf of the council, I--"

"I am afraid that any official extradition requests must be submitted in writing and argued before an official hearing. I am sure you understand." The woman, Anna Greeves, nods and nearly trips in her haste. "The soonest we could schedule one would be...oh, a week, I believe. There is a horrific murder investigation underway at the moment, and the boneys are stretched thin. In a few days, I am sure there will be plenty of time to hear these arguments."

"Is that a denial?" The Lord Master raises a white eyebrow. Behind them, the guards step forward, their expressions unreadable. The twitching of their robes indicates the presence of wings. In such a setting, would they dare to reveal them? I hope so.

"We exercise our right to reclaim our citizens by any means necessary," the Lord Master insists.

They don't draw weapons, but I recognize their stances: prepared to fight.

So am I. I lower my head and curl my hands into fists. Cassius, the bastard, trained me well. He preferred his toys always on alert, waiting for his command. To bite. Tear. Destroy.

"Well, out here, we must do things by our laws," the woman mayor explains, her cheeks flaming. "It is in the official charter. To go against that, I would need a writ signed by the entire council. Unless you have one..."

"It seems this is a conversation well beyond us, Caspian." Altaris practically shoves me to the door. "We should take our leave--"

"No." The Lord Master's voice rings out, firm and echoing. In their path, the mortal woman practically curls in on herself. "We demand that our fugitives be returned--"

"Well, there is one option," the woman says meekly. Some part of me bristles at her display as she trembles from head to toe. Perhaps it is the look in her eye, barely visible behind her wayward mass of hair. Stern, steely, unwavering. "I will put them under my direct observation. They will be tracked at all times, until you can arrange for an official summons. It is the least I can do." She bows again, but when she rises, her beaming smile reminds me of Altaris' dismissive wave. "I happen to have one on me, in fact--" she rummages through her pockets in a drawn-out display. Finally, she withdraws a small object that she cradles in her hand: a red gem no larger than her little finger. "Altaris, will you do the honors?"

He approaches her warily and takes the gem in hand. Then he turns to me. "Don't resist, Caspian," he mutters. "For your own good."

My own good--the reason why he raises the gem to my forearm. Then, with reflexes too quick to resist, he jams the gem against the inside of my elbow. The gem melds into the flesh in an instant, becoming a red, circular patch of flesh. I dig my nails against it, but it doesn't budge.

"Thank you so much for your visit," the mortal woman says cheerfully to the envoys. "Altaris, you may handle the arrangements to ensure this fugitive is given our utmost surveillance."

"Of course. Come, Caspian." Altaris heads for the door, and I follow. Before the Lord Master could argue, we escape the room together.

I sense it is a fragile victory. Red tape will not be enough to keep Cassius at bay for long. He will come for me. The fae will come for Niamh.

The ceremony will commence, and she will die. I feel it in my soul.

Just like I feel the burning itch of whatever the hell he placed into my arm.

I stop short, my gaze on his neck. "What did you--"

"A minor inconvenience," he explains, once again deploying that commanding tone of voice. "Trust me. It is merely a pesky little tracking device to mark your whereabouts, nothing less, nothing more. Be thankful your bond was upheld. That whole incident was, as the mundane say, 'by the skin of our teeth.' This way--" He advances toward one of the green desks, staffed by a woman dressed in gray. "Let us hope this damn bond has been taken care of. Hello, dear, Elsie!"

"You're all paid up, Altaris," the smiling woman replies.

He nods to her, his smile gallant. "As expected, Elsie. You may forward all notices for his court appearances to my address, should there be any changes."

"Will do!" She looks at me and pales. Her pretty smile falls. "Your first appearance is on the ninth," she says tremblingly. "It will be an official extradition hearing as well. You are to come in through the court entrance and wait there—"

"Never mind the details," Altaris says, waving me along like I was a dog on a leash. "I will make sure dear Caspian makes all his appointments. Don't you worry."

"There is one other thing," Elsie calls out. "His permits aren't in order. He has some expired temporary visas, but I can't find anything recent. If there is an immigration issue, I'll have to send the case straight to Jack—"

"Oh, don't you worry yourself about that," Altaris says, still moving me along. "I am on my way to visit dearest Mrs. Willtze now. We will get all his immigration paperwork squared away. Do give your future husband my regards, darling. I just knew you two would make the perfect couple."

Elsie giggles. "Oh yes. That was so nice of you to introduce us—"

"Altaris Ipsum." The booming voice rings out from the end of the hall. There a man stands. Tall, his dark skin glistens. So does his bald head. He wears the same clothing and sports the same stick as everyone else in this damn place—yet every head swivels to him. Every nearby mortal stands at attention. Fear isn't what guides them but something else. An emotion that Cassius could never, in all his centuries of living, convey from another being willingly.

Respect.

They all respect him here. Everyone, it seems, but Altaris.

"What the fuck are you doing in my domain, vamp?" the man questions. "From what I recall, the last time you were here to pick up one of your crazy, little vamp bitches after she tried to drain an entire family dry, I warned you then. Stay the fuck out of my station. I said then if I caught one more of your vermin, I'd toss them into the pits myself—"

"And yet here we stand," Altaris says, his smile wide. He folds his hands together in front of him and inclines his head. "Boney Jack, looking as strapping as always. Do give my regards to dear Marin. It seems that the recent increase in workload isn't agreeing with her delicate sensibilities. You might want to check that contraband locker of yours and see if any Elysium is missing."

Boney Jack clenches his jaw—the only indication of anger he gives. Unlike me, he doesn't rant, tear, and brutalize in his rage. He is cold, quiet, and calculating. "Mention her again and I'll toss you into the pits my fucking self," he warns.

"Well, as marvelous a time as that sounds, I really have other business to attend to. So, you'd best get out of my way." While Altaris's tone is polite, his eyes blaze.

Boney Jack resists for merely a second before stepping aside. Then his gaze drifts to me.

"Holy fuck, who let this one out? I thought you were here for the blonde bitch again. You can bond her out, but not this one! A whole fucking squadron out of commission because of this twisted motherfucker. That shitstorm at the museum took a whole day to clear and disrupted an active murder investigation—"

"My Daisy darling," Altaris says, his voice alarmingly flat. "Who, courtesy of Poppy is no longer blond. Has she been arrested again?"

Jack laughs. "Don't tell me you didn't fucking know. Your kind know everything. She got spotted trying to go after a crowd of bloody Girl Scouts this time. The day she kills someone, vamp, is the day I have your balls in a vice."

"And what a marvelous day that will be," Altaris snaps. "You will call your men and have them reroute Daisy to her home. Since she *almost* killed someone, she should get what? Probation? A fine? Poppy will arrange to pay the fee from my accounts. As for this one, the bond was set and paid. Take it up with your wonderful mayor if you'd like. She's still on the premises, I believe, dealing with another mess."

He stalks forward. Beckons me with a nod of his head.

I follow.

There is a strange stench in this place. An overcrowding of beings, along with their blood and sweat and tears. I'd been wrong before. They aren't all mortal. They just keep the others segregated in some dank, dark space below. A prison. The term comes to me as I follow Altaris into the night and look back to see a sign perched above the bright green door. *Boney Headquarters.*

They keep the rules here. Accept bribes to let the naughty voyeurs from the other realm come to play with mortals and watch them suffer. Those who disobey their orders wind up in cages deep below. A prison.

While under Cassius's protection, I've never been here, but I wanted to. Once...

Once, I desperately tried to come here, to find this place. But why? For whom? Who?

I'll cause a ruckus. They'll take me to prison, a woman told me once. *Find me there. You have to find me there. Caspian!*

"Caspian?" Altaris is watching me, his expression bathed in shadow. "Come along, dear, we have a contract to discuss, you and I. Quickly, before there are any more delays. We can thank our lucky stars that Mayor Greeves intervened, but she is a shrewd one. She won't keep the hounds at bay for long. We must find your fae before *they* do. Come!"

I shouldn't follow him. I should find Niamh. Crawl into that peace hidden in her mind. Shut out these bothersome memories and nagging thoughts.

I forgot something.

Someone.

Someone important.

Long before Niamh, I left her behind...

No. I shake my head to clear it and fixate on the smiling vamryre before me. He holds the answers to finding my fae, and she is all who matters to me now.

Without her, I can't give a damn about anyone else.

Not even myself.

There simply isn't enough space in my mind to care.

CHAPTER 12

Niamh

She is beautiful in name only. To call her that is a crime. An insult.

There is so much more to her than meets the eye. So much mystery contained in her thin, frail frame. I have never been jealous of anyone for their beauty before. Not even Day.

Minchae is everything I want to be. She is poise and grace, but most of all... She is powerful. It drips from her, hidden but no less undeniable than Caspian's bared fangs. She cloaks herself in delicate movements and a quiet voice, but I can see through the act to what lurks beneath.

She is not fae. They are taught to hide themselves. Shield their specialness.

She merely toys with those who think her weak. One day—a day that only she decides—she will punish them for insolence.

Yet she looks at me and smiles sweetly. "You're an odd one. You can talk to me here. Those bastards won't barge in. I've trained them well."

Trained them not to enter this room of fabric—a tent, she called it. Her realm, made of purple fabric and lamps that glow a hellish green. She crouches before a tall, clear mirror while I stand. The grime and muck on me have been washed away, but her touch is nothing like Caspian's. Colder. Indifferent. To her, I am a doll, but one she strives to dress well.

For I am part of her plan, whatever it may be. There is a role she would like me to play that has nothing to do with what Cyrus has planned for us.

To suit her needs, I must be pretty and soft. The rosy red contrast to her vibrant green. In an outfit like hers, I seem half-naked. Unseemly. Wrong.

"Where the hell did they find you?" Minchae asks, continuing to tug my thin, silken shirt into place. "From one of the enclaves up north? I hear they go further than the ones down south do. Breed brother to sister like the fucking fae. Sick bastards. Is that where you're from? Can't you speak?"

"I can speak," I say, my voice halting and broken. "I don't know what you mean."

Enclaves. North. South. She speaks almost as if...

"I'm from the Desinan complex," she explains, her eyes downcast, voice low. "Been established for a few generations now, and they think we're bloody fae royalty. We don't get married to our blood siblings, but they don't frown upon first cousin relations. Just as sick in my opinion. Don't know how my Ma was related to my Da thank God. Yet, this is the result."

She gestures sadly to herself, as if her beauty and grace alone is a shameful outcome of whatever horror she implies. I don't understand her derision. To the fae, blood is everything. Siblings are married and that is the only way. Cousins are a foreign concept. I think about asking her to elaborate. Then I see her face and say nothing. This topic hurts her more deeply than I can ever know. The pain in her eyes is sharp and real and...

Do I look this way? To others? To Caspian? Is that why...

"Well, wherever you came from, it's rotten luck that you wound up here. Cyrus is a right prick, but if you toe the line, he'll ignore you. His other two minions are pure dumbasses, too stupid to know their cock from their arseholes. It's the clients you've got to watch out for." She meets my gaze over the mirror's surface, her expression stone. "Especially the VIPs. Cyrus warns them to only look but not touch, but you get enough pricks with money in one place, and they believe they can do as they please. Just heed my advice: stay above, on your toes and you'll be fine."

She rises to her feet and stretches her arms above her head. "It's almost show time. I'll just freshen up my makeup and then we'll head out to the main stage."

She crosses over to a small desk laden with vials and tubes of colored powders and liquid. She raises one to her lips; like magic, they transform from a dull pink to a luscious red. I watch in awe as she dabbles powder around her eyes next, giving them an ethereal purple shimmer.

"You want some?" she asks, catching me staring. She nods to her pots of powder. "Frankly, you're so damn pretty makeup would just be overdoing it. I, on the other hand, have to play up my 'exotic features.'" She scoffs at her appearance, narrowing her different-colored eyes. "It's my only appeal. Otherwise, the customers would just tune out. You, however, don't need it. You're right pretty. Too pretty," she decides, eyeing me from over her shoulder. "Anymore and we'd have to beat the brutes off you with a stick. Come here." She crooks a finger, festooned with long, bright blue nails.

As I approach, she stands to allow me to sit on the small stool she vacated. I stare blankly at the features splayed over yet another mirror. Pretty, she says. Perhaps to the mundane. Perhaps to mortals. Perhaps...even to Caspian, I am as such.

But to the fae?

I am nothing. These black eyes reflect only emptiness and sorrow, even as Minchae carefully dusts the lids in a coating of gold powder.

"Damn," she says, reaching for a rag. "Let's get this off of you before someone sees. You most definitely do not *ever* need makeup. If I were free and had the money, I'd want to buy you myself." She smiles warmly. I think she believes it. In her world, that is a compliment: to be bought and sold.

Or so she pretends. There is a calculatedness to her words. Everything she says has a double meaning, decipherable only to her. Even now, she looks at me and schemes and plots.

Something about my face, festooned with makeup pleases her. Yet another piece to her ultimate plan.

If I were like her, I'd have a plan of my own. I would act on the thoughts bothering and prickling on my mind. I wouldn't hesitate for fear of rejection or violence. I would trust in my allure the same way she seems to trust in hers.

"They said there was another fae," I say, my voice thick. It trembles. Oh, how it trembles even at the mere mention of her. Night Aurelia. Was she truly... No, she couldn't have been. Even Altaris claimed it to be so, and for whatever reason I am inclined to believe him. On that point at least.

Fae can't leave the other realm.

So then how...

"I've been here for three years, and I'm the only 'fae' I've seen," she says with a shrug. "I heard the Crowley boys claimed to have one a while back, but they're the sort to stick fake teeth on a piece of shit and call it a goblin, so who knows. Besides, we're all fakes anyway. Never the real deal." She spins and contorts herself to view her back in the mirror.

I have never seen fae wings before, not even Day's. His robes were specifically designed to conceal them, and he kept them hidden at all times.

But... if I had to guess, his might look something like the beautiful design etched onto Minchae's skin. Spanning from her shoulder down to her hip, it is an amalgamation of pigment and skin. Shimmering greens and blue seem to swirl against her flesh, as if it could peel away at any moment. Unfurl and become a real wing with which to fly with.

She only has one. Just one.

Yet...

I'd give anything to have something similar.

"It is so beautiful," I say, reaching out. I don't mean to. I can't help it. At the last minute, I ball my hand into fists before so much as a finger can come in contact with her.

"It doesn't hurt," she says, spinning back around. "You can touch it if you'd like. I don't mind."

I shake my head. "I couldn't."

It would be unseemly and rude. As if I asked to touch her eyes or stick my fingers in her nose. As beautiful as they are, I must content myself with watching the shimmering almost-wing. All while longing I had something even remotely close to the same.

"I'm guessing you don't have a mark," she says, frowning. "I didn't check before. Do you mind?"

She gestures for me to spin in a circle. I do, and she gingerly peels back the silk custom from my skin, peering at the flesh beneath.

She doesn't gasp in awe, shock, or remark sadly at my lack of wings. She hisses through her teeth instead.

"Fucking monsters! Oh honey, I'm so sorry." Her voice is choked. She's genuinely disgusted, but not because of my deformity. Something else makes her breathing hitch and her hands shake. What is it?

I don't realize I've asked out loud until she raises an eyebrow at me, her eyes wide. "You mean you've never seen what they did to you?"

Did?

"Here. Look—" She takes hold of my shoulders and gingerly steers me back before the tall mirror. Then she makes me contort my neck much like she had, so I can view my back in detail.

Caspian viewed me in this way once. I will never be able to forget it. The shock in his tone. The subtle disgust he couldn't hide. I'd always assumed...

I'd assumed it was me. My abominable deformity. Perhaps the scars left by the Lord Master from my punishments. It didn't matter.

Whatever he saw that disturbed him so, didn't matter to me.

Minchae's pity reveals a darker truth. One that slowly starts to creep in as I make out pale flesh and a ropey spine. Under icy, pale skin, bluish veins creep and crawl, but that is not the alarming visual.

Neither are the scars, though they are numerous: several neat lines from years and years of accumulated sin.

The sight of them isn't what makes my stomach turn. I can feel something raw and cruel clawing across my chest and burning my eyes. It's shame. Regret.

Regret for never looking before. For never being curious. Maybe if I had, if I was...

I would have left much sooner.

Seeing what they did to me, I would have rebelled without a trace of painful guilt. My sins were not enough to justify their lies. A horrible, twisted lie.

Once, I had wings.

So long ago that very little remains of them but shorn nubs on my shoulders. I know it instinctively, the way I know my heart beats in my chest. After cutting them out, they left wicked wounds behind.

Then, year after year after year, they punished me. Nothing can hide their work, not even scar tissue. Through blurring, searing tears, I can see now. I can remember... Something that scratches at my soul and makes me sob openly without caring for who sees or hears.

I was whole once. My true nature was not an abomination, but a *fae*.

I was robbed of that right.

They stripped me bare.

Then punished me for their crime.

Caspian

"Altaris Ipsum," a woman sneers from behind a partially opened door. "Don't you know how late it is? I stop seeing clients after six, you see."

The vamryre beside me grins. He is all charm and smiles. "Ellarika, my darling. As young and spry as always. I know it's late, but could you squeeze me in for a teensy, weensy little contract? Then I'll be out of your hair in a jiffy."

The woman scoffs and sighs. The door she holds is pulled wider to reveal her plump frame, dark eyes, and round mass of coiled black hair. She eyes the vamryre in my shadow warily and shakes her head at what she sees. "Fine," she mutters, stepping back into a dull, drafty room. "But just this once."

"Of course, my darling," Altaris trills, leading the way inside.

As a lamp flickers on, the woman shuffles to a desk piled high with paperwork. This room is small and square, with no windows. The desk alone takes up most of the space, and the woman has to squeeze behind it just to claim a leather seat. Then, she sighs again, more loudly. "What is it this time?"

"Oh, just a minor little arrangement between the two of us." Altaris gestures to me. "My friend needs to amend his contract."

As she looks over me, the woman scoffs. In her gaze, however, I don't find surprise. Her lips press together into a thin line. Recognition? "Bollocks," she hisses, "I know of this one. Tons of unpaid fees and debt to his name. So very many expired visas. Yet he isn't one of yours." Her dark eyes continue to probe at mine, like buzzing flies seeking a way in.

"No, this one is a special case," Altaris says, folding his hands together. "He will need all the required immigration work, as well as his little friend—we shall discuss her case later. Right now, all we need to do is draft a little repayment contract. A few pesky arun. Caspian here has agreed to work it off. There also is a matter of rent for my other home across the city. We can charge him the usual rate, my darling. If I could pester you to expedite—"

"I can have it for you in three days." The woman grabs a pair of spectacles from her desk and balances them on the bridge of her nose. Instantly, her eyes are three times their size. She is much more than a buzzing fly, but a patient, hungry frog. "No more no less."

"Tonight, I am afraid," Altaris insists in a pleasant tone. "I will reward you handsomely, as you know."

"Blast you to hell, Altaris! I am busy." She makes a show of rustling her papers and prodding her glasses.

All for show.

It is all just for show.

She's had a contract ready with my name on it long before this moment. For years, even. The ink on the parchment is decades old and bone dry. I somehow know it before she pulls it from a desk drawer, safely coiled, sealed with red string.

I've seen it before.

Signed it before.

Many, many, many times.

"Mill about for a minute and let me work," the woman harrumphs before pouring over the document. As if it isn't ready.

As if she hasn't already prepared every single detail.

This is how they work, the two of them. Herding wayward sheep into traps already rigged to be sprung. They think me stupid and gullible like the rest.

I laugh. Then I march to that desk and snatch away the contract.

It's as expected, but the name is all wrong. Not Caspian. Two letters. C.W.

C.W.

C.W.

"Ah, ah, ah!" Altaris wrestles the document away as if it is made from gold. He cradles it to his chest and strokes the parchment with soothing fingers. "No need to wrinkle the damned thing. Just sign your name on the dotted line, darling. So, to speak. There isn't a line. Just scribble your name at the very bottom."

I look at him. Then I smile and chuckle. Or growl. Nothing like Niamh's pretty fucking noises.

"You think I am an idiot?" I ask him. "I am not. You are a liar. A fucking liar." I feel it in my gut—in the pit of my very soul. Even though the details aren't clear to me, deep down a feeling of betrayal stirs inside me whenever I look at him.

I think I'm meant to hate him almost as much as *she* did.

Until he blinks. Sorrow floods those cat-like, green eyes and he nods. Just once. "I know," he says. "You are right. But there is a deal to be struck. So please sign."

"No." I storm off to another corner of the room. I want to rant and rave and break. There is nothing valuable here to smash, however. Just pages upon pages shoved into filing cabinets and wooden drawers. So many fucking contracts he owns. The bastard must own the goddamn city.

Yet...

He isn't gloating over his possessions and triumphant over them. As he sighs, he sounds exhausted by the burden. A strange thought.

"You are toying with me," I tell him. "I don't know how, but you are playing me like a puppet."

He's silent. Then, "Please, Caspian, darling—"

"Don't call me that," I hiss. My hands curl in and out of fists. I want to strike him. Need to kill, pummel, and beat something into submission. A bloody pulp.

"She will not last long on her own," he warns, persistent. "You two picked a dangerous time to visit this city. There are murderers on the loose. A gang of wayward lunaria. Traffickers. Those who ply black magic as their trade. As you saw for yourself, the boneys are stretched thin as it is. Let me help you find her, before it is too late."

"Liar," I tell him. "You have your own reasons. Tell me what they are!"

"Fae do not last long in this realm. Their blood is valuable, and as a novelty they are prized by traffickers. Not to mention the fae. If they sent one of their corrupted elders here, it can only mean danger for her. They will stop at nothing to find her."

The imagery is purposefully cruel, meant to goad me into giving in to him. "You don't care about her."

"I don't," he admits. But he does care about me. He is sorry. Very, very sorry. Sorrow and regret coat him like stinking perfume. He reeks of both. I can't take the smell. My nostrils itch. I'd sign over my soul just to get him far away from me.

"Fine," I snarl. "I'll sign it—"

"Here." He reaches into the pocket of his purple coat and retrieves a silver pen. Extends it to me.

The parchment, however, he holds aloft and partially rolled so I can only see the very bottom of the page.

Regardless, I wield the pen and slash at the parchment. A single bold line is my signature. It's all the bastard seems to need.

"A pleasure doing business, really. Ellarika, darling, please file this away—" He hands the scroll to the woman, who accepts it with practiced reverence. Carefully she rolls it and reties the string. Once it's safely hidden in her drawer, she folds her hands over her desk and raises an eyebrow. "Anything else?"

Altaris chuckles. "Well, well we shall need those visas prepared. Make them air-tight in case the boneys get antsy. The other realm will want these two, so we must jump through all the bureaucratic hoops." He claps.

Ellarika nods. "Done and done. When I'm through, even Jack won't be able to turn down his nose at these."

"That's my darling." Altaris beams. One could almost miss the pain still lurking in his eyes. That term cut him deep. *Liar. Liar.* But to what end? He betrayed me somehow, someway. I just don't remember.

Even so, he gives me a wide berth as he beckons me back out into the night-shrouded street, where streetlights fail to displace the impenetrable sheath of darkness.

"I know you've had a very busy day already," Altaris says as he starts down the road in some random direction. "But there is one last detour we must make. Before we can find your little creature, thing."

"Niamh," I hiss. Her name. She went through all that trouble to steal it from her books—I can still taste those memories of hers, how she hunted through pages of text for the right one. How she practiced sounding it out loud as if waiting for the one day when she might say it to another person. *Niamh.* She fought for that name. Bled for it in vicious scars carved into her back that seemed to never heal. The least he can do is fucking use it.

"Yes, yes." He waves me off. "Before we can rescue your little darling one, there is one little stop we must make first. Unfortunately, Ginni is a stickler for time, and I am not allowed to bother her during business hours. We must see her only in her 'off time,' after sunrise. I suppose it's what I get for letting my darling ones make their own schedules—"

"No," I snarl. "No more delays! You said they will come for her."

And alone, she makes for easy prey. Perhaps they've found her already?

"Patience," Altaris warns. As if he knows me. As if he can see into the chaos of my mind and make sense of the anger and hatred there. As if he knows what it feels like to have a hole in your soul where a monster squatted and pissed in for decades upon decades. Only to one day have that reeking spot empty and vacant. Niamh alone can fill it with sweet words and gentle touches.

I need her back.

I'll...

I'll lose what little is left of my goddamn mind without her here.

"I promise I will get her to you," Altaris says. "Safe and sound. You have my word on that."

His word. What use is a fucking word? I want to scoff. Refuse. Then I look him in the eye and see the truth lingering there. The power lurking there. He means it, this one promise.

In this boring, mundane world, his word is law, worth more than Cassius's piles of silver.

Worth enough to wait.

For now.

CHAPTER 14

Niamh

"... The beautiful, the mesmerizing, the indescribable Minchae!"

Until now, I hadn't experienced such emotions. What jealousy can do to your soul and make parts of you sting and burn. How it can sit like poison in your chest, weighing down your heart with every breath. It can corrupt and change everything you thought about yourself.

At the same time, it instills within you a hunger. One I never felt in the archives while I watched the other fae interact or while I saw Day wander the halls unchallenged, with his head held high. I looked at them and felt shame for what I lacked.

Never once, did I stare in seething envy and wonder...

How do I do this?

How do I unfurl myself from a strip of painted wood hanging from two strings above a massive, cavernous space filled with spectators? How do I move as though their gasps and thrilled murmurs don't affect me? How do I manipulate my body through the air, as though in flight, without ever needing a pair of wings?

I watch Minchae, wide-eyed, open-mouthed and shame or guilt isn't what I feel. A burning, itchy need takes root in my limbs instead. I need to move like that. Carry myself the way she does. I want to fly in a way that no one can ever bring me down to earth again.

"Found wandering the jungles of the far east, this beauty is a creature unknown to this realm, whispered about in legends and rumors. The spawn of myths. A siren of incomparable grace. I give you..."

A thudding sound comes from nearby—the result of a man dressed in bright orange clothing beating on a round object with a taut end.

As Cyrus stands in the center of the ring, Minchae slowly undulates her hips until only her bent knees bind her to the wooden bar above.

My heart stops as a cold sweat prickles up and down my spine. There has never been a time when I have been so captivated. Not even as Day told me rare stories of his day-to-day life in the fae section of the Citadel. The story intrigued me, but I didn't sit glued to my seat, waiting for the next twist with bated breath.

Then...

"I give you a breathing, flying, real, live fae!"

Suddenly, Minchae comes to life. Wings spring from her costume—delicate ones made of wire and fabric. As a result, her glowing eyes and shimmering skin are every bit as captivating as the sight of a true fae in flight.

In this moment, as she glides through the air, leaping effortlessly from wooden rod to wooden rod, she is flying. No one could tell her otherwise.

And I...

I will not stop until I am able to do so myself.

Yet, as enraptured as I am, the novelty has worn off for most of this crowd. Some boo. Some snicker and make snide remarks as to the body of the woman above them. What other ways could she "use those knees," they wonder.

Such careless sentiments make me angry and bitter. How dare they? Don't they know...

Don't they know that some souls spent their whole lives merely dreaming of witnessing something so remarkable? Souls who could never even imagine what it could feel like to be so damn free?

My heart aches the longer I watch her. When she is finally lowered to the floor of the arena and takes a bow before Cyrus, I am in tears.

"The incredible, Minchae, everyone!" he bellows.

Despite their loud clapping and hollering, the crowd's accolades ring hollow. As Cyrus proclaims, "And next, a spectacle

sure to dazzle your senses...I bring you, the fighting goblins!"
The reaction is much more ecstatic.

Fools.

Idiots.

Dumbasses.

Caspian would declare them all worthless imbeciles and worse.

I am not so inclined. These people are spoiled and rotten. They know nothing of beauty when they see it. Most of them would stand in a museum and yawn. Or see a fae grace the sky with real wings and crave bloodshed instead.

"Was I really that bad?" an amused woman wonders.

Minchae. I didn't even notice her come up beside me, draped in a purple robe that obscures her costume. "It's not a matinee night, and I've done that particular performance a million bloody times, but the bastard insists. Perhaps I can use your advice to get him to let me change it?"

"Oh no!" I stammer, nearly biting my tongue in my rush to add, "You were amazing! Incredible! I can't even imagine—"

"Enough." Smiling, she raises a hand to render me silent. A faint flush paints her cheeks. Her gaze is clouded. Confused.

"I'm sorry if I offended you," I croak. "Truly. It's just that you were..."

Magnificent.

She sighs. "Don't worry yourself. I know you mean well. It's been a while since I've come across anyone so green. They really didn't let you out of their commune, did they?"

She doesn't mean the other realm and the fae. Her disdain is for a "settlement" where they marry sister to brother. To what ends? Something that results in beings like her. Like me. Half-formed creatures deemed different by most.

Yet, the sentiment is all the same, no matter what place she refers to.

"Yes," I say with a nod. "I was not allowed out."

Her eyes widen and another emotion flits across her face too quickly to name. A shudder runs through her as she drops the edges of her robe tighter together, then crosses her arms around herself. The gesture is universal, as naive and sheltered as I may be, she is unnerved by me. I make her uncomfortable.

Shame creeps in, eating away my thrilling excitement. I am that creature again, who lurked within the halls of the archives, forgotten and unwanted. I am unworthy of notice and shiny, beautiful things.

I deserve nothing.

"Come on." Minchae has turned her attention from me, and frowns as Cyrus continues his rambling speech. "Let's get out of here before the bastard makes me do an encore."

She leads me back to her tent but holds up a hand before I can follow her inside. "Just a moment." She darts between the fabric and reappears a moment later with a silk robe nearly identical to hers, but a vibrant, emerald green.

"Put this on. No use in giving these sick bastards a free show."

She gestures to my red costume, and I tug on the edge of the short skirt. As I slip the robe around me, I marvel at its softness and comfortable length. Some greedy part of me recognizes it as the same color the fae wear in their robes in the other realm. Like Day.

I may never wear clothing of the same status, but this is just as good. In this smooth, watery silk I feel as regal as the Lord Master ever could.

"Frankly, I'm surprised that anyone managed to pay attention to me with you gaping like you were. I looked down at you and nearly slipped off my trapeze."

She laughs.

I feel my face turn bloody red.

"Oh, I am so sorry! So sorry!" Perhaps I should hide my face like Caspian does in the sun. Rather than for my own protection, it would be for those around me. If my excitement can cause such disruption to others, how dare I express it so openly.

Yet, a niggling doubt creeps in. Caspian saw me just as excited as this, if not more. He thought me beautiful then, worthy of devouring. He wanted me more.

"Goodness, you are a strange little thing," Minchae says, still smiling. Another laugh escapes her, but it is strained. Exasperated. "I thought it was an act at first. I know plenty of beautiful girls who pretend like they don't notice. It's an act they put on to make the men around them swoon and drool. I've worked with countless vain, spoiled, greedy bitches. Frankly, I'm jaded. But you..." She spins to face me, her gaze thoughtful. Inquisitive. "You are the real deal. You have no idea, do you? The effect you have on people?" She gestures around us with a wave.

I follow her stare, confused. Around us are tents and cages of creatures and beings of all sizes and shapes. There are noises and smells and sounds. There are crowds of people milling to and from the main stage and random bursts of gasps and laughter.

Minchae has led me away from the chaos. Even so, people gather here. Staring. Lurking. They pretend as if they aren't enthralled by one sight, yet it draws their interest over and over.

Me?

No, her. Obviously, her.

I look back to her, questioning.

She laughs. "You're an odd one, alright. Very, very odd. Cyrus is probably counting up the gold he plans to make off you as we speak."

She leans against a nearby cage and sticks her fingers between the bars. Inside of it is a strange creature. It resembles a goat of some sort, but with too-large eyes the color of moonlight.

"It's called a Grivet," Minchae explains, reaching out to stroke the creature's dark fur. "Supposedly they can tell the future, but it's one of those 'at midnight, on a full moon after you bleed a chicken dry and stand on your head ritual type things.'" She sighs as the Grivet leans into her touch. Then she pulls away and continues drifting toward the outskirts of the cluster of tents and chaos.

"You aren't from a commune, are you?" she wonders, turning back to stare at me with a long, searching glance. "You can't be. They would have eaten you alive or kept you for themselves. One look at those eyes and they'd never let you out of their sight. I used to think I was the closest they'd come to recreating some mythical fucking fae. Ta-da!" She gestures to her body with a sad, forlorn expression. "I was wrong. I was wrong about so many things, and now I'm stuck here, rotting away on a high wire. Cyrus will never let me leave. Never."

She tilts her head back and laughs, letting the flame of a nearby torch illuminate the streaks of blue in her hair. I can't imagine her feeling shame or guilt at her appearance. Even stranger is the thought that... She could be comparing herself to me.

I shake my head to banish the thought. No. Never.

"You're fucking perfect, aren't you," she says, eyeing me once more. "Cyrus can count his lucky damn stars. He certainly doesn't need me anymore. He'll never come across anyone who looks half as fae as you do."

"But he has," I croak, staggering toward her. My fingers twitch. I want so badly to rip off my robe and show her my back again. I am not fae, not even close. They mutilated me to make it so. I would give anything—anything!—to have even one beautiful, half-formed wing. Anything at all...

Except Caspian. He is my hope in the darkness, and I cling to his memory. Even if he left me behind, the memory of him is all I need. I'll hang onto it until I die.

For now, another being who abandoned me takes his place. Suddenly, she seems closer than ever, within my reach.

"There was another fae," I say in response to Minchae's puzzled expression. "More than twenty years ago. He taunted me about her. Do you remember?"

She shakes her head. "I've only been with the bastard for three years. Before that, his main act was a three-headed hydra, so I doubt he had his hands on a real fairy. But..." She pauses and strokes her chin. The blue tips of her nails sparkle in the firelight as she muses quietly to herself.

Suspense builds. It's rude, but I can't help it. I must ask.

"But?"

"Hmm?" She looks up as if she'd forgotten I was even here. "Well, if Cyrus did have another fae, he'd have marked her in his ledger. I'm sure you saw it?"

"Ledger?" I shake my head.

Minchae frowns. "It's where he catalogs all his creatures. Where he bought them from. Who he sells them to. It's his entire business right there. I think he even lists his suppliers in there. Not everyone his goons find winds up in this shit-show. He has buyers of all sorts. Information like that would fetch a pretty penny on the black market. Enough to purchase a nice future far away from this shithole. Besides, if he ever did have a fae in his collection, she'll be in there. You could at least see if you recognize her—"

"See?" I feel my heart stop and then flutter back to life. I can't hide it. Disguise it. Just how badly I want that possibility: to see her for myself. An image. A snippet. I'll take anything.

Minchae eyes me warily, an eyebrow raised. "He catalogues all of us," she says with obvious disgust. "I guess he hasn't gotten around to you yet. He's probably waiting to see how big of a crowd you draw in tomorrow night. Or, tonight, I guess..." She sighs and looks up at the dark sky above. "I suppose it's already past midnight. The show will die down. He'll have one of his lackeys do the send-off while he counts his hoard of coin. Come." She beckons me onward with a wave of her head. Voice a whisper, she adds, "we'll need to be quiet. Stealthy. Think you can manage?"

I nod and make my steps soft as I creep in the shadow of hers. Stealth was the only way of life for me in the other realm. There was no choice but to avoid being seen. Stay hidden. Be meek, modest, and ashamed of my being.

Here, as I follow Minchae around cages of strange beasts and a thinning crowd, my heart races. This is a feeling I never felt while scurrying through the archives. Like my heart might burst out of my chest with one wrong movement. As if pure electricity prickles beneath my skin—a lightning storm of nerves and anxious energy.

I'm excited, I realize. This is fun, in the strangest, most complicated sense of the word. Fun to keep quiet and hide. Fun to crawl behind a massive yellow tent and peek inside through a gap in the fabric.

Validating, to spy Cyrus the Ringmaster, hunched over a desk, flipping through an old book with worn, yellow pages.

"That's it," Minchae whispers into my ear. "We'll never be able to get it, though. He watches it closely and has wards guarding the desk he keeps it in. We'd need a distraction to get to it. Something to keep him busy..."

Keep him busy. I nod along as I watch the man paw aimlessly through his book. Was he lying? Is my mother really captured within those pages? A memory. A photograph. I'd take anything.

It hurts. Only now can I realize just how badly it hurts, to have her so close. To know that someone somewhere—make that two someones, here in the mortal realm alone—have seen her. Glimpsed her. Enough to recognize her form in me.

I hate myself for never questioning Day about her before. It seemed so rude then to question. So greedy.

But now those regrets are all I can dwell upon. Feast upon. Day, my beautiful, poor, confused Day, may be the closest to her I may ever come.

My eyes burn. Tears spill out. Minchae taps me gently on the shoulder and we crawl away back to her tent. Only there does she see my face and notice the glistening wetness.

"Oh, honey..." She reaches out. Thinks better of it. Instead, she grabs the rag left discarded among her makeup and gingerly dabs at my eyes with it. "I'm sorry. I guess this means a lot to you. Whoever you're looking for."

I nod. It's all I can do. Nod and nod. My mother is a creature always on the verge of my existence. In the other realm, it was easy to forget her. Easy to ignore the pain festering in my chest from the day I was born. I wanted her then, but I had to content myself with my meaningless, worthless existence.

Here...

The world brims with possibilities. I can wonder about things I couldn't even dream of before. I can think dangerous thoughts, and I can yearn for that which has always been beyond my reach. My mother may hate and despise me—that is her right.

But I want to see her, at least. To know in which ways I am like her. Is it our eyes? The way we smile? I need something. Anything.

"Okay, hear me out." Minchae tosses her rag aside and pulls her stool toward me. She perches herself on the edge of it and draws her knees up to her chest—a beautiful, effortless display of balance. "I have a plan. I've been toying it around in my head for years. It's time I blow this joint and move on to greener pastures."

Blow? I struggle to keep up with her terms, but I nod regardless.

"Cyrus guards that book with his fucking life, but I think if we work together, we can devise a plan just devious enough to work. Are you in?"

In? I nod.

She smiles. "Good. Luckily for us, your new performance will give us the perfect cover. I'll go over your role. Memorize it as best you can, then leave the rest to me."

I nod.

I will.

I will scheme and plot and plan.

I will see my mother's face, any way I can.

At least then...

It might be enough.

Caspian

The bastard makes us wait in his 'home.' There, he crowds us into a narrow room piled high with gaudy, worthless trinkets. He pours two delicate cups of gross-smelling liquid. I assume it to be perfume until he raises one of the cups to his mouth. Drinks.

Meeting my disgusted stare, he shrugs. "Vamryre can partake in some mortal niceties," he says dryly. "Tea. Try some. It might calm your nerves."

"No," I hiss. Then I pace, balling my hands into fists, thinking of her alone out there. My fae.

How badly is she injured this time?

Is some monster feasting on her delicate remains...

"Please sit," Altaris says. "You're going to work up my darlings. We aren't the only ones here, you know. I'm sure you remember how important it is to have peace and quiet while one regains one's mind. And while you seem immune to bloodlust for now, not all of us are so lucky. Some of my darlings are irritable as they adjust to their new diet, so do be considerate."

I stop. Cross to a chair. Sit.

The bastard annoys me, but he has a point. I do remember what it was like in my shattered mind. Unless I had her voice to cling to, the darkness was endless. My Niamh. She spoke to me, then. She guided me back. She shielded me in her twisted little mind.

Why can't I hear her now?

I try to seek out those delicate thoughts. I find nothing. In my chest, something vile and disgusting stirs to life. It is an old friend, I think. From before Cassius. After Cassius.

Fear.

Imagining her gone forever fills me with fear. Cassius, I could live without. Survive without. Thrive without...

But Niamh...

"I need to find her," I say, my voice grated and rough. "I need her back."

"And we shall," Altaris says after another sip of his tea. "It won't be long now. Just an hour or so. In the meantime, I should remind you that your court appearance is in two days."

He eyes a clock on the wall. Dark with two spindly legs drifting around a stylized full moon. It's gaudy and garish like everything else in this place. Tarnished by time, valuable only to one who owns it.

"I will accompany you, but I hope you have enough sense not to get yourself into more trouble. I have enough tension with Jack to contend with already, thank you."

He sets his cup down onto the matching saucer. They are chipped, yet gleam, barely used.

This vamryre has so many useless, pointless things, but I can tell he values them all. A sense of care is evident in the neglect. How the dust protects them with a shallow coating. As long as they remain untouched, left behind, he is the only one who can enjoy them. Cassius craved gold and glitter, but this vamryre prizes dusty, valueless things.

"You are staring," he sniffs, setting his cup aside. Staring at him, I am. Those cold, green eyes observe me with an intensity a mortal could never possess. Most vamryre don't view the world as he does: through contracts and payments, but also some small shred of kindness—twisted though it may be. After all, he chose to help me despite his master's wishes. I still can't fully understand why..

"What are you?" I ask him.

He chuckles. Nods. "I am what you are. A creature of the night, sustained by blood, damned by the mortal world—"

"Liar," I say. "You are something else."

Something that lurks beyond most mortal's grasp of time—mine even. I only caught a glimpse of the broad expanse of Cassius's real mind—the one he kept us away from. He is older than dirt, as some mortals might quip. So old the meaning of life was lost upon him, and he collected his pretty trinkets to distract from that fact. To hide from the emptiness that threatened to consume him day in and day out.

Until...

Until he met me.

No. Don't want to remember. I shake my head to clear it.

"Tell me," I demand of the vamryre before me. I remember the way he was in the face of the fae Lord Master. Unafraid. Mocking, even. "You do not fear them. You have no master to call you back. How?"

Altaris laughs. It's a sad, broken sound as if he didn't mean to make such a noise at all. It comes from deep in his throat, past the bravado and lies and pretty clothing. Deep down, he is far different from Cassius.

Where my old master shunned his humanity, Altaris clings to it. Just a small, teeny tiny sliver he's kept tucked in that expansive mind for centuries upon centuries. He hoards it. Values it.

That humanity is what makes him so dangerous.

"There is something else you want to ask me," he says, his voice soft and haunting. Broken.

The vulnerability itches and scratches at my soul. Don't like it. Don't. Only Niamh can reveal this side of herself to me. I want to coddle that weak flame—her humanity. Maybe one day I will snuff it out. Maybe never. It is mine to tame and keep safe.

Altaris's pity is a different creature entirely. I don't like it. It reminds me...

It reminds me of something I'd long since forgotten.

"I know you," I say. "From before."

Before I came to the mortal realm this time?

Or even before then?

Before this twisted remnant of my soul was all that remained of who I once was?

Before Cassius, even...

I look at the vamryre, expecting answers, but he just nods. Merely once.

"I did," he says. "I know you, still. You are Caspian, once as a toy of Cassius. Any more, and I think you may not like the answer. Ask me about the fae instead. Your fae. How I know her true nature."

I grunt.

He smooths his fingers over his lap, his expression pensive. "I've seen it before," he admits. "The damage done when those fae breed with the wrong kind. The children they make. Wretched creatures who belong to no one."

He's broached this topic on purpose. He wants me to think of something. The biological reason for sex and mating, beyond pleasing one's master and bringing new victims into his fold. Children. Procreation.

I've done so with Niamh more than once already. Therefore, I take his words as a threat.

"Are you saying that if she carries my seed, you'll kill her?"

"Oh darling, gross!" He fishes a square of white fabric from his suit jacket and presses it to his nose. "What vile imagery. Luckily for you, *that* one cannot reproduce. None of the fae can until they reach their Night status. Thirty or so, I believe is their ripened age. The time when they usually want to run from that realm. Your dear one is technically, still in her Day era."

"So then why mention it," I snap.

"For a damn good reason." He raises an eyebrow, his gaze sharp. "Hybrids are a dangerous sort, my darling. Their blood is wild and untested. They are prone to foul rages, and they attract each other like moths to light. You should know full well the heritage of one, before mingling with it."

He turns his head, looking away from me. Hiding something.

I frown. "What aren't you saying?"

"Her mother is fae," he replies, lowering his strip of fabric to reveal that his mouth is set in a hard line. "We must quickly find out who her father is, between you and me. I have some suspicions, none of them comforting. Has she told you? A hint of her bloodline, perhaps?"

"Don't know," I say. Even in her own mind, she doesn't like to think of it. It scares her, in fact. "She believes she is fae."

"But she isn't," Altaris remarks. "That much I know. We must find out the truth. It is vital, Caspian. Do that, and I will cancel all of your remaining debt to me. You have my word."

"Why?" I look him up and down. A creature such as him would never willingly walk away from ownership, not if it is tied to his precious paper scrolls. "Why do you even care?"

His gaze flits back to me as he purses his lips into a flat line. "Because your safety is at stake. I care about that."

Liar. He is afraid.

"You care about who I *was*," I say.

He nods.

Then tell me, I mean to say. I open my mouth to choke the words out—

"Altaris!" A panting woman races into the room and leans against the doorway. For show, of course. She is a vamryre and has no need for breathing or baited ones at that. Still, she is distressed.

So distressed, in fact, that Altaris rises instantly and approaches her.

"Poppy, darling," he warns, his tone stern. "Indoor voices. Tell me calmly and quietly what happened—"

"Daisy's gone again! And it's all my fault!" The redhead, Poppy, buries her face in her hands and cries--as if we, superior beings, could ever feel guilt or shame.

Then I remember. I felt it once. In that motel, after I tore my own siblings apart. I held their bloodied, broken bits in my hands. I sobbed and wept.

And, before my mind shattered in two, she comforted me, my Niamh. With a soft voice and gentle words, she tried her best to bring me back.

Altaris is not of the same mind. He sniffs in irritation and brings a hand to his nose as if to ward off the stench of female crying. "What happened, my dear?" he tries again. "Poppy, speak clearly, my darling. Darling—WHERE IS DAISY?"

An uproar goes up from beyond these splintering walls. Cries and moans and other whimpers of the like. There are many vamryre here with sore, broken minds. They wince at the slightest noise. Cringe in pain at the tiniest whisper.

To them, Altaris's bellow is a sledgehammer on fractured, shallow glass.

"Damn it," he hisses. "I must see to... Caspian." He snaps his fingers at me, as though calling a dog to heel. "Help Poppy track down Daisy. Then we shall all find Ginni and give her a good, bloody talking to. That's the fifth time in nearly a week that she slipped out under her watch! At this rate, the damn boneys will own us all, house and home." He raised his voice without realizing it.

More cries ring out than before. Some screams. Wails.

"Oh blast!" Altaris races off, leaving me alone with the strange one.

Poppy. Despite the color of her hair, she could have been one of Cassius's. She's pretty enough to have been.

Despite her thin veneer of beauty, however, her intellect is unmistakable. She hides it well with her too-loud voice and simpering sniffles. But, ah, she is wise. Wise enough to have been plucked from mortality by only Nataniel himself.

She notices me staring and makes a show of wiping at her eyes. There are no tears. "Poor Daisy. It's my fault she got out," she laments. "I thought she wanted to go on one of my morning walks. To do some calisthenics. I turned my back for one second and she ran off."

She blinks as if expecting me to say something. Give a damn.

I say nothing. Instead, I barrel past her and try to find the way out. The sooner I track down this foolish wayward vamryre, the sooner I can find my fae. The need for her is growing, turning into an itch I can't scratch. A constant ache. She's an addiction with no cure.

Not that I would ever want one.

Without her, Cassius lurks and looms desperate to regain entry to this soul he had slip from his grasp.

"Where?" I snap at the redhead. We're on the street, but she just stands on the sidewalk, peering from one direction to the next.

"I'm not sure. She usually sticks close to the... Your face is burning."

I blink. Fuck. I forgot to pull the hood of this jacket low. When I do, the prickling burn eases somewhat, but not as quickly as I'd like. I need to be careful out here. Without the collective mind, I don't heal as fast. Can't risk too much damage.

To find my fae, I need all my working limbs.

"Um, let us go this way!" After rearranging her own hood, Poppy takes off down the block, her steps light, practically skipping. Despite her very real concern for the other vamryre, she enjoys this. The chase. The tracking of another creature.

Oh yes, she was one of Nataniel's. I've never met his sliver of our hoard. Just heard their thoughts sometimes, reflected through Cassius. They were an alien sort. Cold. Callous. They treated those in the other realm as prey—even the others in the collective hoard. Their minds were icy and reptilian. Cassius prized beauty but Nataniel quashed all humanity from his collected toys.

Compared to me, they were truly monstrous.

Yet, she pretends well. She puts on the faux mortal act and seems to truly care about this lost one. This Daisy.

I don't. I don't give a damn about anyone or anything, except for myself. Except for my fae. And once... Maybe...

Cassiopeia. My poor one, trapped in Cassius's hovel. A true brother would have freed her sooner. She would have done the same for me.

And I will.

Once I retrieve my fae, I will return to the other realm. I will drive a knife through Cassius's fucking heart. I will find Cassiopeia no matter what it takes.

I will.

I will.

If I say it enough times, I might start to believe it.

"This way!" Poppy turns down a narrow street that opens onto a familiar road.

I brought her here once, Niamh. She begged to go to the park. She ooh'd in awe at the various scenic mortal things but didn't attract the wrong attention.

Such as a crowd of terrified children watching her lick blood from her fingers.

Oh dear. How naughty. It's the kind of behavior Cassius would encourage. To make a spectacle. A scene. To inspire fear in their little hearts and relish in their screams.

Except for one minor detail. Children were not allowed to be our target. They were too messy. Their deaths drew too much attention. Too much scrutiny.

Which was why Cassiopeia loved to skirt that little rule as much as she could. She loved to lead a wayward child away here and there, to make Cassius rage and scream. Oh, what fun we used to have, in those days.

She never went too far, however. Fed from one. Maybe a little scratch here and there. Just enough to provoke a reaction.

It was our game, her and I. To provoke a response. To press as many of our master's buttons as we could. To push and push until the bastard had no choice but to accept that we would never be fully his.

Never bow.

But here there is no master to play for, and I see the act of toying with children for the morbid diversion it truly is. How cliche. How droll. To make the little ones cry for their mommies and daddies in broad fucking daylight. She must have come here when the school bus would arrive and drop them off to frolic in the morning sun.

This one must be freshly freed. One of Cassius's. Some long lost sister from years ago whose name he erased from our memory.

With a sigh I stalk toward her, leaving Poppy behind. What a foolish distraction. What a silly, stupid fool.

She isn't even feeding. Just playing. She turns to face me, her eyes blank, her expression dazed and empty.

But...

No. That isn't right. Her face isn't right—like how I remember. A mocking smile, eyes like scarlet. Like mine. Long white hair that kissed the curve of her lower back.

We spoke the same, in our own unique cadence. It was the only way to set ourselves apart. The only way to separate from him.

Me and my Cassiopeia. My dear heart. My other half. My sister in name if not by blood.

I missed her so fucking much. So much he had to smother it out of me. He nearly smothered my soul to do it.

But I remember.

I see her and I remember how badly I failed her.

The Boney prison, she told me. *I'll cause a ruckus, and they'll send me there. You'll come for me. You'll free yourself from him and come for me. Caspian! You must come for me!*

But I never did.

I failed her.

I failed her.

I failed her.

And she bares her teeth at me angrily. Life slowly begins to creep into those haunted, dull eyes as the children around her scream and scatter. She sees me, my dear one, and she curls her lips back from her teeth.

"I waited for you!" she wails at me. "I waited and waited! Where were you?"

I was here.

And nowhere.

She and our devious, twisted rebellion plans had slipped my mind.

The day he took her from me, part of my soul was lost. Getting it back isn't a painless melding of two shorn halves. It hurts. It fucking burns. As I run to her with no regard for anyone, I am rendered boneless and stumbling.

Pulling her into my arms, I hold her so tight. "I'm sorry," I say. I'm sobbing the words into her neck, gripping her body to the point of cracking bones. "I'm so sorry."

"Where were you?" she demands, her voice broken and hoarse. "Caspian... I needed you. Where were you?"

I owe her more than just an answer.

Such a betrayal requires atonement. Retribution.

She sacrificed her soul for me.

I owe her far more than mine in return.

CHAPTER 16

Niamh

Preparation for a show begins with blood and sweat. Hours upon hours of practice. There is more to it than meets the eye. Balance is required on what Minchae calls a trapeze. So much strength is necessary to sustain the required movements. So much grace.

To fall is to rattle bone and batter skin. To fly is to fling yourself at nothing and pray that your grip alone can save you from falling. It is like jumping off a roof on command but there is no Caspian to catch me.

No stone floor to fall to, either.

If I slip from this height, a skinned knee might be the least of my worries. I must close my eyes just to gather up the nerve to swing my weight forward, allowing gravity to guide me.

All in all, it is the most thrilling, exhilarating, exciting thing I have ever done. Second, perhaps, only to escaping from the other realm hand-in-hand with a vamryer.

"You're catching on quick," Minchae chides from below. "Just watch your posture. Keep your grip nice and clean. Feet pointed! Ok, now let's see if you can fly."

Fly. Or in this case, swing myself in the right rhythm and catch the bar she'll swing to me. It seems dangerous. Too dangerous and risky to be the regular pace of any training.

Nevertheless, she has a plan to implement. If I can't perform my role, there is no point in trying. I might as well get used to being a pretty bird in gaudy clothes.

Because Caspian isn't coming for me. I don't know how I know, I just do. It's a pain I don't even have the space in my mind to process just yet. So, I ignore it. I blot it out by swinging on a wooden bar as though I don't have a care in the world.

As though I'm not dying on the inside.

As though it doesn't gut me to the core of my being to realize that he left me again. He isn't coming. He would have been here, otherwise. He would have tracked me down. Kept me safe.

But it doesn't matter.

I can ignore the pain as long as I open my eyes to spy the dirt floor of the arena down below. As long as I wait for Minchae's cue to "Go!"

I release my grip on the bar. Fling myself forward.

Feel nothing but ice-cold air and falling, falling, falling.

I can't rely on anyone. Not the Lord Master. Not Day. Not Caspian. Not even Night Aurelia.

But...

These bones have been honed over years of sneaking onto rooftops to find their footing. Having scurried and hidden for years, I can rely on my reflexes as well. When others fail to catch me, I can trust these hands, skilled at handling any book.

Suddenly, my fall is halted. My fingers curl around a firm surface and I let my body do the work to propel me forward.

I fly, devoid of wings or true fae heritage.

I fly without my Caspian there to catch me.

For a heart-shattering moment, I fly and it's more than enough to fill my heart and erase the painful jagged edges. For a second at least.

Until my body stops moving under its own accord and the cold reality bites back into my consciousness. My muscles are cramping. My sweaty fingers tremble with exertion, fighting to maintain their grip. I'm slipping.

Down below, Minchae claps. "Bravo!"

Suddenly, a newcomer enters our rehearsal, his red coat billowing out behind him. "Minchae, what in the hell? You trying to get her killed? I said teach her the ropes, not try to break her fucking neck. Get her down from there!" he snaps, Cyrus.

With an exaggerated sigh, Minchae stands and crosses to the lever that controls the height of the trapeze bars. Slowly, slowly, the one I'm clinging to is lowered until my bare feet hit the dusty earth.

Surprisingly, I don't feel relieved. Break my neck? It would be worth breaking every bone if it meant tasting even a second longer of freedom. Devoid of wings, I flew.

I don't expect to taste that freedom again for a very long time. Despair grips me. I choke back tears. The burning pain creeps down my throat and sears my eyes. Still, I grit my teeth rather than give in. I won't cry. I won't—

"Bloody hell, look at her. The poor thing is scared to death! You, missy, better watch yourself." He jabs a finger angrily in Minchae's direction. "You may have gotten used to being the main attraction around here, but sabotage of your co-performer isn't very 'fae' like." He makes it sound like some mocking, playful thing. A mask one wears to play pretend. "Just get her to sit there and look pretty. No flying or jumping—"

"I want to fly," I say. I meet his skeptical gaze and I don't know what he finds in me. His expression changes. He swallows. Frowns.

"I want to," I insist. "I can learn. I can try."

"See?" Minchae appears by my side and slips her arm around my shoulders. "She's fine. Together we will put on a show the audience will never forget. That I promise you."

"Why does that sound less like you being a good girl, and more like a threat?" Smirking, Cyrus glances at the chains which encircle her ankles. "Don't forget what happened the last time you tried to pull off one of your slick little schemes." His voice is harsh, scorching hot against my cheek. "Did you tell her all about how you sold out the last little slut we had you perform with? Got her sold to save your own skin. A naughty girl, this one is. You'd do good to watch your back," he says to me. "Before she slips a knife into it."

Minchae does not even flinch. "I don't know what you mean," she murmurs, her voice the picture of innocence.

"Next time, I won't leave your bruises in discrete places where you can hide them. I'll beat you to a pulp, you fucking half-breed. With your new replacement, I no longer need you. So watch yourself."

As Minchae stares blankly into the distance, her expression remains unchanged. Emotionless. "Of course," she intones.

When Cyrus finally storms off, she scoffs and spits on the dirt at her feet. "That blasted, puffed-up son of a bitch! Ugh!" Her hands curl in and out of fists as she paces. There are goons still around, mucking out cages and carrying equipment around the arena—not that she seems to care if they witness her anger. Cyrus is the one she cares to maintain her calm around. It's the only shred of power she has over him.

I know the feeling.

"God damned bastard!" A cloud of dust rises from her feet as she spins around and sighs. "Are you sure you're ready tonight?" she asks, with her back to me. "You won't chicken out? You're okay on the trapeze?"

There is a hidden meaning to her words. At night, huddled in her tent, we barely slept on the pile of ratty blankets that seemed to be her makeshift bed. Instead, we plotted and schemed. Or, at least, she did. I listened. Rapt at attention, I listened. She made rebellion sound so beautiful in her husky voice. More than mindless rebellion. A carefully constructed plan with little left to chance.

The role I played was simple, but pivotal.

I nod. "Yes, I am ready."

"Good—" She turns to face me and takes my hands in hers. "We're in this together, for better or for worse. Got it?"

I nod again. "Yes."

"Good." A sudden shadow appears over her beautiful features, dimming her expression. She seems lost. A ghost that forgot their tie to the corporeal realm. Fae, especially, were prone to lingering long after death. It's why they as a whole devised fae stones to make use of those wayward souls yearning for a purpose.

Or so they tell us.

Now I am not so sure. If they were just a sacred end, then why did they litter the walls of the portal? Neglected. Haphazardly shoved into black stone.

It doesn't make sense.

"I can't last another second in this wretched place," Minchae hisses, hugging herself tight. She appears so small in this yawning space. A speck of glistening green amid an ocean of red and yellow.

I stand out as well, wearing my borrowed robe, but I am not sure what picture I make. Not glistening and pretty. A hollow spot, perhaps. One too barren for anything but moss and neglect to take root. A dead tree in an endless forest, covered in overgrowth.

"Oh, sorry. I didn't mean to bring you down too." With a heavy sigh, Minchae collapses right there on the dusty floor and sits with her legs splayed out before her. "I get so wrapped up in myself sometimes. It's how you had to be, growing up in the Desinan. They snuff out all weakness there. Brainwash this stupid 'obedient' bullshit into our heads. Damn. Growing up, I couldn't wait to get the hell out of that place. But sometimes..." She looks back at me, both colored eyes reflective. "Sometimes, I do miss it. Having a bunch of people tell you what to do can be a hell of a lot more comforting than trying to wing it alone. Here—" She pats the space beside her and draws the edge of her robe aside. "Come sit."

A giddy feeling fills me as I do so. It isn't the excitement or freedom I felt while 'flying.' It isn't the desperate, anxious need I felt around Caspian. There was no thought then, in those moments. Just reacting to whatever my body wanted.

This requires thought. Tact. Skill. Navigating a conversation with someone when there is no clear end. No real aim. Their problems weigh heavily on their minds, and speaking them out into the open is the only way to find relief. Mortals do the same. They flutter and fret about certain subjects, never landing on them. Like butterflies avoiding a flower they desperately want.

"I think she is my mother," I say, voicing my problem for all to hear. In my head, it sounded pathetic. Out loud, the longing is clear. The pain is clear. There is no denying it. "My mother...who abandoned me in the Citadel. I've never even seen her face. I don't know what she smells like or looks like. I don't even know who my father is. Or if my father is..."

Someone other than Night Aurelius, the only man it possibly could be.

"She left me without a second thought, and I know why," I admit. "She had a purpose to attend to. Other children to produce. I was an abomination. I wasn't meant to exist. Even so... It hurts to be abandoned." I hug my arms to myself as she did, but I don't find comfort in the meaningless embrace. I miss Caspian. I miss his strength, and his voice hissed into my ear, telling me what I was, daring me to question and challenge. With him, there was always a challenge. That was the point.

He called me 'It'.

I demanded he know me as Niamh.

So, he did. Mockingly, derisively, he did so without question.

I told him not to leave me.

He said he wouldn't.

So why hasn't he come?

"He won't come," I say out loud. "Caspian has abandoned me too. At least... I hope he has."

It would be a betrayal worse than that of Night Aurelia, the woman who gave birth to me. The prospect hurts so damn much—almost as much as the prospect that he is in danger himself does. In any case I need to find him. Somehow...

"Oh dear, I've done it now," Minchae murmurs. "I'm sorry, honey. I sometimes forget that I'm not the only one in the world with problems. Here." She fishes something from the inner pocket of her robe and offers it to me. A delicate square of white fabric that she uses to dab away my falling tears. "Trust me, I know the feeling," she says, once my face is patted dry. "I've been abandoned my fair share. Done plenty of abandoning too, on my end. I know how it feels. I know how utterly worthless the people you're supposed to trust can make you feel."

There is more she wants to say, but the words won't come. They stick in her throat, as unvoiced intakes of air. Yet, she doesn't cry. She bites her lip rather than let herself.

I try to embody the same determination. Enough tears. Enough wallowing. I am so very tired of wallowing. Caspian left me, yes. Night Aurelia left me. Day left me. Everyone, eventually, will leave me.

Except for Niamh. I can never leave me. That should be comfort enough.

Maybe it is.

"There is... There is something I should have told you before," Minchae admits, fingering the dusty hem of her robe. "It's awful of me, I know. I thought... I thought you were just like all the other girls. The other riffraff. They blow through here a dime a dozen, thinking they can charm their way from rags to riches. I've seen girls far uglier than you are charm those around them, get everyone to eat out of the palm of their hand to get benefits and special privileges the lot of us don't." She scoffs, scowling at the memories. "I thought you were like that too. Girls that like... Like me. We know better than to trust anyone else. We scheme and plot and stab each other in the back. It's how we are. I thought you were like that too. Which is why..." She swallows hard and inclines her head, meeting my gaze through a fringe of black hair. "Which is why I was planning from the start to sell you out. Cyrus doesn't leave his ledger in that fucking desk like an idiot. If that were the case, I would have stolen it a long time ago."

She smiles a sad smile.

"No, he has it guarded by two jackdaws. I don't know how the bastard came across them, but one jackdaw is vicious enough to take on, let alone two. The only way I feasibly saw a way around it was to find some stupid patsy to use as bait. Have them grab the journal, and while the jackdaws feast, take the blasted ledger for myself and run. It sounds like murder, I know it does." Her face turns white as she shakes her head. "But if you were the kind of girl I thought you were, you'd have seen right through my act. You'd *know*. You would come up with a scheme of your own and we'd stab each other in the back. We might both end up bloodied and busted for it, but alive at least. I thought you were like that."

I sit quietly, taking in every word she said. The picture they paint is surreal. I may not know what a jackdaw is, but I recognize her barely suppressed shudder for what it is: utter terror. The creatures scare her. They 'feast' on victims, and she would have gladly served me up to save her own skin.

I should be angry.

I should feel even more pain.

More and more tears should fall down my face and I should curl into a ball of agonized loathing, never to move again.

Perhaps I will.

But...

I need to know.

"Who are you looking for?" I ask. More than once, she has referred to the ledger. Mentioned how valuable the information contained inside is—but she thought I was like her. Cunning and devious. Money alone would appeal to someone like that, and they would never stop to think what truth could actually be hiding underneath.

"I betrayed someone a long time ago," Minchae says, her voice hoarse. "Someone I thought was a conner, but she was like you. She trusted me instantly like you do. I watched her be sold to the wolves. I owe her. I spent three damn years trying to find her, to make it right. I've been after that ledger for three whole fucking years!" She laughs, and an unfathomable sadness floods her gaze. "Her name is in it, and where she was sold to. I should want to find her badly enough to take on a whole fucking pack of jackdaws. She would do it for me, I know she would. But I've been scared to act for three fucking years..." She's crying. Tears spill down her face more elegantly than they could ever adorn my own.

I reach toward her with her strip of fabric in hand. Carefully, I dab at her tears.

She laughs, frowning. "You know, it's hard to believe this isn't all an act. But it isn't. Is it? You aren't from..." She breaks off and inhales as if trying to find the right words. Then she leans closer, making her voice soft for only me to hear. "You aren't a mundane, are you? You're a pure-blooded fae."

"Not pure," I reply woodenly. "A half-breed. A hybrid of some sort."

Or a monster, as Altaris claimed.

But Minchae doesn't recoil in disgust and derision. "Holy fucking hell," she rasps, her eyes wide. "You're the real deal. In this place!" She glances around and leans in even closer. "If Cyrus finds out, he won't just have you performing in his shows, honey. He'll sell you off to the highest bidder. You should have gotten out of this place yesterday. There's no telling what he'd do with an honest to God fae in his grasp. Forget the ledger. I'll cause a distraction right now and you run. The bastard hasn't chained you yet. They think you're too weak. Go, now!" She lurches to her feet. "I'll call the guards over and—"

"Wait!" I reach out and brush my hand along her shoulder. I don't know what else to do. Interacting with other beings at all is still so new to me. Even so, she pauses, her head cocked, body radiating nervous energy.

"What? Honey, we've got to get you out of here. It's one thing if you were a mundane, but I would rather die than see that greedy bastard have a real payday fall into his lap."

"I... I want the ledger," I say. "I need it."

More than anything else. More than the way I ache for Caspian, even. I need to see my mother's face so badly it hurts. Even if it's a sketch in a ledger. Even if it's just her name.

Even a scrap of paper is something to cling to.

Minchae scoffs. "Honey, do you even know what a jackdaw is? What they do? They're hellhounds with wings! They guard an object to the death. Once they get a taste of your blood, they don't stop until you're dead. I don't know how the bastard came across them, but he has two—two! Just one was enough to haunt our nightmares in the Desinan. They claimed it guarded the High Master, but I never saw it for myself." She shudders and holds herself so tightly her knuckles whiten. "My plan was to let the brutes go at you and somehow sneak the ledger away, but that's done and over with now. It was wishful thinking anyway. It would have never worked."

Feed me to the jackdaws. Me with dirty, corrupted blood. An abomination Altaris can't even stand the sight of. I've never heard of those creatures before. Don't know if they are magic or mortal creations.

In either case...

I'm willing to try. I survived being torn apart by a monster once. Twice.

Perhaps I can do so again. If it means seeing my mother—a fragment, a sliver—I'll suffer anything. What else do I have?

"Oh no!" Minchae shakes her head and jabs a finger at me. "I know that look. Fuck, you're just like Dabne. I said no! No! Don't make me regret growing a conscience. Maybe I was never gonna do it anyway. There was a guy once. Who tried to run from the enclave. They displayed him for us, and he was in pieces. Literally, neat little pieces! They said the jackdaw did it, and we never fucking questioned after that." Her voice trembles. She's speaking too quickly to enunciate every word properly. Her eyes are wide and stuck in the past. She's horrified.

Like my Caspian, there is a nightmare world inside her head that she's desperate to avoid reliving. Perhaps...

In the same way she aimed to use me, I can use this to my benefit. To help us both. To get us both what we want.

"I think our plan will work," I say, curling my fingers tight. "It will. It must. We must trust each other."

Only for now.

Only until then.

I'm holding my breath as I wait for her reaction. I'm so anxious, my belly churns and throbs. I feel sick. At the same time, I feel electric all over again. Plotting and scheming is almost as fun as flying.

"You're serious," Minchae rasps. "Oh, fuck! What have I gotten myself into?"

"A plan," I say with a stern nod. "We have a plan."

A plan as seemingly hopeless as running away to the mortal realm with a vamryre in tow, all to see a museum. Crazy. Reckless. Stupid.

I lived it once.

I aim to achieve one more success again.

Even if the face of Night Aurelia is the last thing I see.

I'll try.

Whatever it takes, I will try.

CHAPTER 17

Caspian

Cassius worked so hard to damage my memory, and now I know why. To shatter any recollection of her, my dear one. My sister, my heart. My other half.

With her, I was always stronger. She helped me remember. As his angry, sadistic, monstrous Caspian, I was a monster he could not control.

Together, we shielded each other from his corrupt influence.

All we had was each other.

Still...

She was taken from me without a second thought, and I rarely questioned him. I rarely asked him why. I forgot her at times, my dearest one. I forgot her face. Her smile. Her coldly mocking voice as we plotted against him in secret. She was snuffed out of my skull far more easily than she should have been.

In the end, Cassius got what he wanted.

I left her behind.

"I waited and waited and waited," she tells me. Over and over until her voice breaks. "I waited and you never came. I tried everything, Caspian. Everything! Where were you? Where?"

"I was... in the dark," I say. In that dark, wretched hive mind. In that twisted collective brain.

It's no excuse.

"No excuse!" she hisses, beating against my chest with two delicate fists. Slam. Slam. Slam. I barely feel the pain, but I let her hit me. If that is what it takes, I'll let her break me into pieces like she was.

"We only had each other. Just us! It was JUST US! How could you endure him without me? That disgusting, fucking shithead! How could you survive him without me? Oh, Caspian, I'm so sorry. I told you to follow. I told you to come! WHY DIDN'T YOU LISTEN?"

"Darlings—" The voice cuts into our jaded reunion.

We aren't alone, I remember. There are others about. Fragile, sensitive creatures huddling in rooms both above and below where we stand now. In Altaris's strange domain of empty vamryer. He stands in the doorway of some narrow room piled high with a table draped in purple cloth, with even more material shielding the two large windows.

"I hate to interrupt, but the noise level... Can we just keep it to a minimum, please? The other darlings are already upset, and I frankly cannot afford more *incidents*—" His tone is deliberately cutting, his gaze on my Cassiopeia. "In one day. Indoor voices, darling ones. Indoor voices."

He slips from the room and gently closes the black door.

Slam. SLAM! Cassiopeia pummels me with her fists. It is starting to hurt. Starting to feel. Starting to remind me of another slender creature with grasping hands and a persistent voice.

Niamh. My Niamh. Lost. Alone. Needing to be found—

"I'm so sorry." Cassiopeia collapses into me. Her arms scratch around my waist—a physical embrace. In all the years we dwelled in Cassius's demented playground, we rarely touched. A holding of hands there. A hug here. We didn't need physical contact in the same way we needed our minds. Our thoughts. We'd let them mingle and merge until we couldn't tell which belonged to the other. We were one. A hateful duality fixated on one purpose.

Kill Cassius.

Make him suffer.

Make him pay.

"He's still there," Cassiopeia says, her voice muffled by my coat, her face pressed to my chest. "Still thriving and living. That sick piece of shit! I hate what he's done to you. I can see it on your face. Sick bastard. He tormented you. Why didn't you come for me? You promised."

I promised. That I did. We had a plan. An elaborate and carefully devised scheme, once we knew we'd gone too far and escape was our only option.

We ran together into the mortal realm.

Cassius followed. Personally, he followed. But why?

It hurts to remember.

"We should go now," Cassiopeia laments, still striking me. Bang. Bang. "Go now when he least expects it. Stab him in the bloody eyes. Rip them out. Eat them in front of him. We should go now. Kill him now—"

"We can't," I say. Then I grasp her wrist before she can hit me again. I step back and watch her fist flail in my grip, striking nothing. "I need to stay. I need to find..."

"You need. You need!" Her eyes blaze, a dull hue of red. Out here, they've lost that scarlet sheen. They're more amber. Her hair...

I reach for a strand with my free hand and frown. It's been desecrated. Someone painted over the silvery white with a garish pink. Until now, I didn't even notice.

"What have they done to you?" I ask her. Demand an answer.

She shakes her head. "Not important. We are. We must leave. We must. We must. We must—ah!" She sinks into a crouch cradling her face in her hands. "It hurts. This stupid, fractured, lone mind hurts. I need you, Caspian. I need your thoughts. Your voice."

"I am here," I say, moving toward her, ready to touch. Provide comfort. A pat on her shoulder to mimic the way our minds would collide. I reach for her hand. She snatches it away.

"No! No! I can't think! It hurts! Can't think. Can't think..." Her voice devolves into a moan as she rocks her body back and forth, her eyes squeezed shut.

"It's okay." A delicate voice. Falsely delicate.

I turn to see the wise one standing in the doorway, peeking inside. "It takes us all time to adjust. Poor Daisy. I've never heard her speak before..." She trails off and sighs. Then she meets my gaze directly with her strange, probing eyes. "Altaris said you have business with Ginni in the basement. You can go. I'll watch over her. It is alright."

Her kind, sweet naivety is an act, that much I know. A lie. False. Yet her words ring true. Still, I should refuse. Deny. I should take my dear one to the portal and together, we can kill Cassius once and for all. The sight of his blood will heal her brain, the same way Niamh's screams healed mine.

Wait...

Her screams. They tugged on me then, but the world is silent now. Wherever she is, she is not in pain. I would know, and I would come for her. She is lost but not in pain.

Yet, I do not want her to be. Those screams do not appeal to me like they used to. Her laugh is prettier. As if I care for pretty things. I don't. But her laugh...

It's the most beautiful thing in the world to me.

"Go." The strange one, Poppy, fully enters this space and crouches down beside Cassiopeia. She pats her back and shushes her in gentle tones. Fake of course. She is wise beneath it all, and she knows far better than I do. My dear one's pain isn't normal. Those eyes reveal the truth—she is afraid.

I try to banish the thought as I leave. Go. Then I stop in the middle of a dark hallway and try to remember where I'm supposed to go. Basement. Ginni.

No. I need to go out. Into the city. Before she can scream for me, I must find Niamh. I need to find her. Grip her tight and hold her close. In her peace, I may remember more. I may recall more about my life with Cassiopeia before the pain. Before the bastard tore her out of my brain.

Before I failed her, too.

But I must find her first. Find a way out of this hovel. I storm forward into another narrow room. Find a door. Reach for it.

A man appears from nowhere to block the doorknob from my grasp. Not nowhere. He is stealth incarnate. Dark, soulless eyes. Bright blue hair that was once golden. I know who he belonged to without much thought. He reeks of violence and sin. A violence well beyond what Cassius enjoyed.

This is one of Pol's. She of blood and war. She who led the vamryre's response to the fae and lunaria in the old wars. How do I know this? My Niamh. She read to me in her precious archives, a book she thought I didn't ingest. That paired with older knowledge floating around my skull. Probably that of my old master.

He despised Nataniel, his wise brother, but dear Cassius feared Pol. Only the strongest and most brutal pets were chosen for her brood. Known to have an iron fist, I'm surprised she allowed any of her past spawn to wander off. Cassius always thought she ate those she became bored with. Bored. Because unlike what they shoved down our throats, becoming one with the collective was not for eternity. Not always. They would pick and choose their pets and grow disgusted with those they deemed useless.

How do I know this?

I am not sure. Being with Cassiopeia jarred another memory free. One that we hoarded and protected for when the time came for it to be of use. To leave the collective was not to die. We knew it beforehand. He made me forget.

And now the wayward spawn of him and his brothers seek to plague me still.

"Move, brother," I hiss at the Pol-spawn.

He doesn't flinch. He nods his head, indicating another doorway. Then he approaches it first, expecting me to follow.

Bastard.

I dig my heels in, intending to watch him go. Then slip out while his back is turned. I am done with Altaris and his games. Done with this house of broken toys. I need my fae and she needs me. The itch for her grows stronger. Impatient. Irritating.

Niamh. Niamh. Niamh. Her name plays on my skull in a haunting melody. A part of me fears her screams will be the crescendo of it. Her agonized, pained cries.

And I will have failed her again.

A door is opened. The Pol-spawn stands beside it. Once again, he nods toward the darkened space beyond.

My response is to clench my fists. "I need to leave."

He says nothing. Another firm and stern nod. Grunts and jerky movements are all he speaks in. Yet, I understand completely. I try to leave, and he will stop me.

More time wasted.

So, I storm in the direction he indicated. Down the stairs, into a gray room with bulbs dangling from the ceiling casting a greenish light. It's only mortal magic, nothing fae. Still, the light is softer to vamryre eyes. It enhances the appearance of finer details. For instance, I can see every angle and plane of the Pol-one's face. His disgust.

He does not like this place, but he goes where he is told. Moving past me, he raps his knuckles hard on a battered metal door.

"Coming!" trills a voice from the other side. A humming sound emanates. The door is shoved open. A tiny figure darts away without bothering to see who steps inside.

"Ah, at last." Altaris stands at the back of the room, a piece of black fabric pressed to his nose. "I trust you helped dear Daisy get settled in?"

Daisy. A fake name. A lie.

"Her name is Cassiopeia," I snap. "We were spawn of Cassius. You kept her here, broken, and desecrated. Why?"

"Kept her." Altaris scoffs at the term. "Call it what you will, but we strive to keep poor Daisy contained until her mind is healed. Away from any tender mortal necks she may chew upon. As important as our individual work is," he adds, his tone scolding, his gaze fixed on a far corner, "protecting one another is our *most* important task. I haven't seen a vamryre die at boney hands for over one hundred and fifty years, and I prefer to keep it that way."

"Sorry!" The voice is anything but contrite. It belongs to a tiny woman—barely as tall as my elbow. She scurries into a darkened corner of the room wearing an oversized, white coat and silver-rimmed glasses. There are a set of large, metal drawers there. She opens one, and peers inside. Opens another. Beams.

A thick stench wafts from both. Decay. Death. In the dim lighting, I can make out body parts--an arm here. A leg. Beneath the acrid decay is a scent I recognize: Niamh's. It appears that this dank basement is the final resting place of those who attacked her.

"I was very busy," the female chirps as she slams a drawer shut. "Poor Daisy. It is my fault!" Yet she is still smiling as she spins to face us.

Similarly to Cassiopeia, she has also been desecrated by time spent in this realm. Although her hair is reddish brown now, I know it was once white. As the greenish light illuminates her eyes, they reflect a dark, amber gleam. Like mine, they used to be red.

She is one of Cassius's. An old one, well before my time. In essence, she represents everything the bastard desires in a prey. Tiny. Beautiful. Young and ripe.

Yet, she is not simpering and sweet. She is sharp, moving like a furtive mouse, always hunting for something. A mind that easily diverted wouldn't do well in a collective cage. I bet this one wasn't discarded as useless. It is likely that she wandered away on her own, distracted by something shiny.

"I apologized," she reminds Altaris sweetly. "You say apologies show contriteness. Therefore, I am contrite. My work is important. Very important. I keep us from starving—"

"I know," Altaris insists, rolling his green eyes. They have played out this conversation between themselves before. Many, many times. "But Ginni, darling, when I ask you to look after a young one, you should at least *try* to. Especially when you were the only one of us she seems to respond to. One of Cassius's, you say?" He asks, looking at me. "I suppose it makes sense."

Of course it does. He knew, all along, which monster each wayward spawn belonged to. He can tell with far more precision than I can. Yet, he is feigning ignorance. Why?

Because of me. His eyes flicker with that fleeting guilt again. Maybe Cassiopeia was the reason all along? The explanation for why he seems so damn guilty around me. Always sighing. Always casting his pitying looks. My dear one was locked away in his hovel.

Yet…

He knew me even before then. He said so. *Caspian, one of Cassius's toys.* It sounded mocking to me then. Viewed from another lens, the words sound sad instead. A punishment to himself. A cruel reminder.

Caspian, toy of Cassius.

Why?

Why?

I can't remember.

Wait… Something comes to mind; two letters scribbled over and over on a decades old contract. Another name.

This vamryre knew me as another name, once. C.W.

I could ask him. When our eyes meet, I see a yearning in his empty gaze. Longing. Hope. Hope like Niamh's when she begged me to take her to the mortal realm. As if with one single question, I could ease his mind. Free him of some terrible burden. One word.

I open my mouth.

"Your noises are bothering me," Ginni snaps, rubbing at her forehead with a slim, pale hand. "So many noises. Angry and seething. Get out. All of you, get out!"

"Ginni, darling," Altaris starts without moving an inch, "We are here for a reason, remember? Try to think, my darling. Any news on the black-market sites? We are trying to find someone."

"Yes," I hiss, turning on the smaller woman. "A fae. Where is she?"

She blinks. "Don't know. Don't know. No news of fae. I wish there was. Fae blood is rumored to be sweet and nice. Magical. Oh, how I would long to chop, chop, chop delicate fae limbs and see the bones underneath—"

"Caspian, darling." Altaris's tone is sharp. It hooks into me, locking my body into place. "We do not fight here, among fellow darling ones. That is a rule and it is one I take great pains to enforce. Don't we, Scythe?" He looks to the blue-haired one of Pol. The bastard nods and flexes his limbs.

So that is why he is here. To protect the tiny one, Ginni. Her work is important, it seems. The work of death and decay. It reeks in this wide room. Traces of blood stain the floors. Those metal drawers contain more than paper or trinkets.

Body parts.

Body parts for this insane, demented lost one to chop to her heart's content.

She catches me staring. Winces. "I don't like this one. Everyone out. Out!"

"We will leave soon, my dearest. Just as soon as you tell us one more thing."

Ginni shakes her head, nearly sending her glasses flying off her nose. "Don't want to. Don't want! Don't!"

"Careful now, darling one. Listen to me carefully. I need you to use your contacts now. For me. Ask them about a fae. A frail-looking creature, long, dark hair. Pale and gaunt. Beady little eyes—"

"Beautiful," I snap. "Niamh is beautiful."

Altaris waves the material he once held to his nose dismissively. "In any case, Ginni dear, we need to find her soon. Remember how we don't like it when the boneys show up on our doorstep?"

Ginni shudders. "Nosey boneys! Pestering. They take my bones and bits away. All my bloodied bits!"

"Yes, my darling." Altaris nods. "They also confiscate our very important blood supply. If we don't find this fae creature before they do, there will be dozens upon dozens of boneys on our doorsteps, dear one. They will shut us down for weeks, if that. No new supply of blood for our darling housemates. They may close down our operation entirely and we don't need that, do we?"

Ginni cringes, horrified. "No! No!"

"Good. So go into your quiet place and ask those contacts of yours about a fae."

"Oh!" Ginni reaches up, grasping fistfuls of her hair. Then she nods. "Yes. Yes. A moment, please." She scurries to a door at the back of the room. It leads to a closet. She clambers inside and slams the door in her wake.

"It won't be long now," Altaris says, unfazed. "Scythe, darling, why don't you go out and scout a path for us? Make sure there are no unsavory characters about."

The blue-haired one nods and fades into the shadows.

"And you, Caspian..." Altaris eyes me warily, his gaze unreadable. "We need to discuss that girl of yours, you and I. She is dangerous. I have told you that. Her mind is a warped little hive. There are ways to free yourself from her, should you choose. You merely have to ask—"

"Noises!" Ginni shrieks from behind the door of her closet. "Noises! Noises! I require silence!"

With another sigh, Altaris presses a finger to his mouth.

For what seems like hours, we stand and fucking wait.

Finally, the door to the closet opens. Ginni reappears, tugging at her hair with trembling fingers. "My contacts are restless, yes," she says gravely. Her eyes gleam behind her glasses as she looks up. She is ecstatic. "So many naughty thoughts on the wind. So much impending murder. So many new bodies to chop and chop!" She rubs her hands together and spins in a gleeful circle.

"Ah-hem." Altaris clears his throat. "Ginni, darling..."

"Ah, yes. The fae one is here, nearby. A circus of freaks and sideshows. Somewhere on the outskirts of town. You should find her soon," she adds, smiling longingly, staring at nothing. "So very many want to chop her up. They've seen her, yes."

"Boneys?" Altaris questions.

Ginni shakes her head. "Oh no. Worse. Far, far worse. Oh dear! An ancient being--like you. He is very naughty." She giggles and squeals like a fucking child craving a delicious sweet. She is odd. Disturbing. The way she smiles while surrounded by death and decay is disturbing.

Yet... So did I once.

"There are other monsters on the prowl," she declares happily. "So very many. They seek to take and eat and loom in her shadow. You must find her quickly now. Or don't. How I would love to have a fae to chop and chop—"

"Thank you, darling." Altaris stands tall and tucks his fabric scrap into his pocket. "It seems as though we should be on our way."

"Yes, yes," Ginni says, appearing behind him. With her tiny hands, she practically shoves him toward the door. "It is almost business hours. Opening time. Sunset is opening time, the start of business time. You promised. No bothering me then. It is a rule."

"Yes, dear one," the older vamryre says gently. He lets her push him from her room as I follow. Not because she threatens me. It would be easy for me to break her and rip those delicate limbs off one by one.

She is creepy, though. Something is wrong with that one, a brokenness in her brain.

It makes her strange. Dangerous in a way that Cassiopeia and I never were.

We had a sense of self-preservation.

When it comes to her strange, creepy interests, she is fearless.

"Oh, and one other thing," she says before slamming the door in our faces. From behind it, her next words are muffled, broken by cackling laughter. "The fae one. Her blood is naughty and wicked. You mustn't let her be bitten. Only chopped. Those who bite her will meet a cruel fate! Bye bye!"

Her words ring out in a haunting echo. I try to ignore them. Try to.

That was something I already knew.

Fae blood—Niamh's blood—is the key recipe to a dangerous fate.

It makes one care for her.

Crave her.

To the ends of the earth, I will crave her.

CHAPTER 18

Niamh

I feel as if my entire life has been a performance. An elaborate rehearsal for an event that never took place. In the grand finale, I would perform, then the curtain would fall, and my moment would come to an end.

Maybe that day was meant to be the centennial celebration. My moment to shine. To be paraded before all the fae—before all the realm, even—and displayed in full before a violent, dramatic end.

I tell myself it would have been a fitting death regardless. I should have been honored to be shown and displayed. Honored that some lone vamryre knew of my wickedness and wanted to exploit my death for his own unknown purpose. Certainly a far better end than the one I'd always imagined, alone, in obscurity, with nothing but dust and cobwebs to bury me.

Perhaps.

Perhaps...

A real stage, however, is contained and small. Only the rapt attention of the audience matters. Their oohs and ahs of wild acclaim. Their enjoyment.

After all, that's the point of a performance. It is for the viewer's and performer's enjoyment.

Atop a strip of wood, dangling above an arena made of metal pillars and striped fabric, I realize something that guts me. Tears fall down my face unnoticed – down, down, down, but I don't bother to wipe them away.

In order for a performance to be enjoyable, the performers must enjoy it themselves. Even Minchae, as much as she hates Cyrus and this work, lives for the moments she preens upon the stage, bathed in the glow of spotlight.

I can't recall any other moment--prior to entering the mortal realm--when I felt as I do now. Afraid. Excited. Terrified. Undaunted. At peace. Compelled to act regardless of my fear.

I sit on a swing, high above the earth, with death just a fall away, and I feel happier than I ever did in the bell tower. More at peace than I ever have in the archives. I was numb and dumb, ignorant of anything beyond my narrow courtyard then.

Here, I am angry. The lies of the past twenty-four years are piling up. The damage done to me—both in mind and body—is piling up. As are the horrific crimes inflicted upon me by those I once trusted.

However, I can let go now and die, shattered into a million pieces, and feel more at peace than ever before. Death didn't scare me before. I would have gladly welcomed it.

But now?

Death is a cat hungry to give chase, and I am a mouse, scurrying just beyond its reach. A terrifying experience, far beyond my sheltered, safe environment.

But, oh, is it fun. As if Caspian himself is on my heels, ready to spill my blood once and for all--only he can't hurt me here. He can't leave me here.

All I have to do is lower my body until only my trembling fingers keep me aloft. Then I let go. I leap into the void!

"I give you, the magnificent wild fae!" The voice explodes against my eardrums along with the roar of a full crowd. I didn't notice until now. It's only when the spotlight falls on me that I see the rest of the arena beyond Cyrus' little circle of dirt.

So many people sit below. Blank, expressionless, staring faces. I can't make any of them out. Which is a good thing. Oh, how is it a good thing! There is no judgment up this high. No whispers to avoid. No gazes to hide from.

It doesn't matter who gapes or stares, or who looks at my odd, abominable frame in disgust.

This high up, no one can touch me. No one.

Fae or not, I can fly. My reflexes allow me to soar through the air. Catch myself. Let go. Spin. Jump. Sit on a swing and smile at no one.

However, there is a role to remember. There is more to this performance than just fun. I must be a distraction. A damn good one. So I stand, bracing my weight gingerly on the balls of my feet. I finger the edge of my red costume. I pull a string tucked into my waist.

Then I rock forward to nudge the wing beneath me into motion. Then I jump.

And I sprout wings.

They aren't real, but that is beside the point. They spring from my shoulders, made of wire and sparkly red material.

The audience gasps in shock and awe.

Then, I perform my role. It is simple in theory, but oh so complicated when done. There are careful movements of muscles required. Intakes of air to propel me forward. Stamina to grip the bar long after my grip threatens to fail.

There is a point to it all, I know that.

Yet...

I simply forget. I move and react and let my body fly. I forget Minchae's careful instructions and go painstakingly slow through the motions. Every movement. I make it last. This diversion. This distraction.

I draw it out until the last possible second when I'm finally lowered to the floor of the arena. Cyrus's words bellow into my eardrums, a meaningless murmur. Belatedly, I remember that I am supposed to bow. Preen. Wave and smile for the crowd as Minchae does.

I can't. I'm crying, and it isn't fair. I truly don't mean to. The tears spill down my face regardless. Through a blurred, hazy screen, blinded by the spotlight, I can't make out any details of the figures seated before me. I can't hear their voices or their shouts.

I can't hear anything but my own heartbeat, playing a mournful rhythm. Thump. Thump. Go back. Go back.

Fly some more.

That entire routine couldn't have lasted more than minutes, but I wish I could have stayed up there for an eternity. If given the choice...

I would never come back down.

"Again, we have the lovely fairy girl! Ladies and gentlemen, she will be accepting donations in the buckets being circled by our lovely volunteers."

I blink. That voice. It isn't Cyrus's—a flaw in our plan. Perform. Distract. Minchae would sneak into his tent. Make an opening. Hide. I would come as he was busy closing up the show.

Something is wrong.

I spin on my heel and attempt to slip out of the arena. A stern hand comes from nowhere and seizes my arm. "Where the hell do you think you're going? You hear them out there? They want a bloody encore!"

An encore. Only now do I finally hear. The screams. The shouts. Demanding. Pleading.

"Encore! Encore! Give us the damn fairy!"

Another performance. My heart soars. But then I remember —it would waste time. The plan is already derailed. Something is very, horribly wrong.

"No!" I try to wrench away from the man.

His grip tightens. His upper lip curls back from his teeth, his arm tensing. I know he will hit me. My body is already tensing in anticipation of the blow.

But then I remember something Caspian said—no, not quite like that. It was something he did. I was hungry and he went up to a food vendor. Give me, he demanded sweetly, his voice sin. So the man did.

"Let me go," I say, copying his confident demeanor, making my voice sweet. But then I go further. Girls like you who bat their eyelashes, Minchae had said. I look him in the eye. I try to look meek and appealing. "Please," I say sweetly. "Let me go."

He does. He lunges from me as if burned. Struck. Dumbly he blinks and stares at his hand. "Um... You sick or something? Just go to the loo, then come back."

I leave. Then I race, panting and sweating as I head for Cyrus's tent. There is no need for stealth. I can hear the shouts from here. As I wrench aside the entrance to the tent, I hear Minchae's scream.

"You think you could trick me, you little bitch?" Cyrus has her pinned flat against this desk. His hat is askew, his teeth bared, eyes blazing. His fingers are clenched tightly around her throat and he aims to kill her.

I can feel his intentions wafting through the air. He doesn't need her anymore. Not with an honest to god, real, damn fae in his clutches. He knew what I was from the second he saw me. It's why he didn't bother to chain me. Without wings, as weak and frail as I am, I pose no threat to him. No chance I could ever escape.

Not like the other one. Not like her.

But the name that pops into my head is wrong. Not Aurelia.

Parna.

But I am being silly. My brain conjured that name from nowhere. Fae cannot read thoughts, even though Caspian's... Caspian is different. We shared body, mind, and blood. He is different.

Yet...

I can look at his man and see his fears and hatred spill out onto the air. He hates Minchae in a way beyond pure annoyance. She needles him. Challenges him. He hates her because she has never ceased to remind him just how weak and powerless he truly is.

"Let her go!"

"N-No!" Her multicolored eyes fixated on me, blazing with anger. "Run!" she chokes out. "Get the hell out of—"

"Did you really think this fucking stupid plan would work?" Cyrus laughs and shoves Minchae aside. "That you could waltz in here, steal from me and then take your new little companion away? She's planning on selling you to the black market," he says to me with another cold bark of laughter. "I bet she spotted you the same way I fucking did. A broken, distorted fae, but fae all the same. You're gonna make me so much fucking money once the boneys hear. They'll have no choice but to extend their protection. Now get the fuck back on stage—"

So intent on me he was, he didn't see Minchae clamor to her feet. Didn't see her grab a long wooden stick from the corner of the room. Never even saw her wind up and slam it into his skull.

He isn't dead. Not yet. But she's bought us minutes, at least.

Panting, Minchae tosses the stick aside and meets my gaze. "Help me find the ledger."

I nod. Then, without a word spoken between us, we both lunge toward different sections of the tent. She moves to a bookshelf, I approach the desk. I open a drawer and find nothing but parchment. Open another. Another.

"Here," I say, spying a leather book. Somehow I know instantly what it is. Cyrus's ledger. His most prized position, lying unattended in an unlocked drawer.

"Wait!" I hear Minchae cry out as I start to reach for it. "Let me do it! The jackdaws!"

Too late. My fingers brush the leather surface and a cold, rustling wind rushes past my ears. It seems like a breeze—as though someone left the tent flaps open and a gale storm has blown in.

Knocked me back.

Off my feet.

A storm of swirling knives.

CAW!

CAW!

CAW!

The shrieking noise deafens me. Sharp, stabbing pains rip through me. Everything is a blur of pain and ice and agony. I'm being torn to pieces. Slice, by slice, by slice...

"That's enough boys," a cold, cruel voice calls out. "Leave her body intact. The stupid, little bitch."

I blink as Cyrus appears, hovering above. He crouches low, his gaze cold, his voice unnaturally hot against my skin.

"You stupid, little bitch. You know, I thought you were defective. Different from the other one, that little cunt. I guess not!"

His foot swings out, slams into my side. A scream rises in my throat, but I bite it back. Fight it down. I am done screaming and crying.

I force myself to meet his gaze. I won't huddle and cower any longer.

I got to fly.

I can die happy.

Die even at his hands.

I got to fly.

In death, maybe I can fly again...

"...Just like that other bitch," he says, chuckling. "Maybe you need to be taught a lesson too? A long-term lesson." He moves for the buckle of his pants. I know the threat—what it entails.

Long-term lesson. Too.

Long-term.

Too.

Is that what he did to Night Aurelia if she was the fae he held captive? Gave her a long-term lesson? No. He gave that lesson to me. That torment to me.

The reason for everything--my existence and my pain--may lie with some bastard I never knew existed.

He is the reason.

And I want him dead.

I want him in bloody, bleeding pieces.

I want to rip out his throat with my bare hands.

I want to—

"What the hell? Get back!" Cyrus is moving, inching back, back. Away from me. Two large, black creatures fly at him, with nipping beaks of unnatural sharpness. Their red eyes blaze.

We hear you, sister, they sing to me, whispering in my skull.

We will do as you ask.

We will rip and tear into bloody chunks.

Tear his throat out.

I watch them do so. I watch...

And I smile.

Caspian

The Pol-spawn is quick and efficient. In response to the strange one's odd ramblings, he nods once. Then he turns on his heel and leads us through the winding, darkened streets. The street lamps in this part of the city are broken and flickering. No light reaches this deep into the shadows.

It is a night realm. A quiet corner where creatures, mortal and immortal alike, thrive in the dank darkness. This is a black market. Somehow, I know the term. A roving collection of alleys and shops that spring up after nightfall, meant only for mundane eyes.

They do not hoard their strange, faded magic like the fae do. They do not obscure and hide their weirdness like the lunaria, and they do not retreat from view like we vamryre.

They trade their magic and shove it into boxes and trinkets. They haggle and shout and fight over it. They ply their trade right in the open as boneys patrol between them. They think themselves civilized.

They are—the way rats and pigs are civilized. Rutting and fucking and stewing in their own shit.

Yet, my Niamh is here among them. In search of her, I scan the face of every mortal we pass. I pay close attention to their meaningless words and mindless chatter. I sniff the air, testing it for her. Tasting for her.

Not yet.

Not here.

She isn't here.

"Ginni said something about a circus, darling," Altaris remarks while gazing in disgust at a woman who hawks goods from a wooden box. "The same term could be applied to whatever the hell this is, of course, but I think she meant something a bit more literal."

The Pol-spawn nods. Keeps moving, barreling his way through an aimless crowd. He is quick and assured in his steps. His gaze is narrowed and focused. He is a hunter on a mission, determined to track down his prey.

So am I.

I try to grasp her thoughts again. As I pass a woman with long dark hair and a lanky frame, I try to say her name. It isn't her. I knew it from the start. Some part of me needed to say it though. Throw her name into the air and see what answers back.

"This way." Altaris inclines his head as the Pol-spawn changes direction, cutting through another alley. "It seems we might have made headway, at least."

Headway.

Right to a dead end.

There is a brick wall at the end of the alley. There is no escape. No path to continue but to go back.

Yet Altaris marches forward. "Oh dear. I was hoping Ginni meant some mortal playground. Not one of these wretched... I thought I shut this down ages ago." He snarls. Raps on the brick with his bare knuckles.

The brick he struck moves, folding inward, as do several others until a doorway is created. Beyond it, the alley stretches on as if never interrupted and the city gives way abruptly to a wide, massive field where a crowd of tents blaze in lantern light.

The *Circus of Souls,* reads a sign.

Plastered on a poster is a crude creature with haphazardly drawn wings.

"Oh dear," Altaris hisses, but there is none of his mocking sweetness. No polite air. He is furious, his tone flat as ice. "This establishment, I most definitely shut down. Come. We must be vigilant. The creatures here may seem like harmless attractions, but I assure you that some are very, very real."

"Attractions," I snarl. Is she here, my fae? As an attraction? Shoved into a cage, meant to be gawked at.

"Now, now, Caspian," Altaris warns. "I hate to take this tone with you, truly I do, *but I command that you listen!*"

I stop short, paces away, fists at my sides, foot in the air. Undeniable power laced that command far more than Cassius could ever compel. Altaris, despite his pretentious appearance, is not like other spawn.

I can't move. Can't resist. Even if I wanted to. But I don't. There is wisdom lurking in his tone. A plea. *Be patient. Let me handle this. I will get your fae back if you are patient.*

As though I were a dog to him, gnawing at my leash. But for her? I will be. I will be patient. I will bite my tongue and nod in response.

To get one step closer to Niamh, I will heed Altaris's wishes.

Because she is here. I can smell her, faint and crisp in the air. My tongue dampens. I can taste her. I ache for her.

In a way I have never once craved blood, I ache for her.

"Now, we must handle this tactfully," Altaris says, moving to stand before me, his fingers laced together, brows knitted. "If this shitshow is run by who I think it is... We must tread very, very carefully. Oh bloody hell, what is it now!"

His eyes are beyond me, toward the alley we came from.

A trio of black-clad figures stands there now. Boneys, I suspect. One of them was the female he taunted at the prison. Marin.

"Well, well, well." She taps her silver stick against her palm with a wicked smile. "Who the fuck but you would show up at a murder scene? What I wouldn't give you to arrest you."

"Arrest away," Altaris says, raising his hands innocently. "I beg you to. In fact... I dare you."

Marin laughs. "We aren't here for you, unfortunately. Looks like another creature has run amok that isn't one of your little pets. This area is now a crime scene, so run along."

"Crime?" Altaris wonders in a skeptical tone. "Oh pray tell?"

"Nothing you're fucking privy to know," Marin snaps. "Now clear out, or I will arrest you—"

"Oh dear, Caspian—"

I run. I run before he can order me back and close my ears. Fuck him. Fuck them. Fuck.

I can smell her. I can hear her now, my fae. My poor, poor fae. Not sobbing or crying. No, she is dead silent. Too quiet. Her breaths rasp in and out of that delicate throat, but strained. As if she's suffocating. Dying. Frozen.

I run. Through milling crowds and cages of stinking, howling animals. I run until I feel her presence. Until I taste her nearness on my tongue.

I run directly through a cloud of red fabric and into a large room. There she sits, my Niamh, staring blankly, covered in blood. As dead to the world as I was when Cassius severed my mind from his, she sits there.

I call out her name. She does not answer. I take her into my arms and she is still.

"...bloody crime scene! Get back or I'll have your fucking head on a spike, vamryre—"

"You will do no such thing." Altaris's voice ushers in a deadly quiet. Even the mortals heed his power. They, with their false authority and silver sticks. Though they pretend to hold power, they know who *really* makes the rules.

As Altaris speaks, they are compelled to listen.

But I don't. As I hold Niamh in my arms, I feel the warmth of her. Her bloodied hair is brushed away from her face as I stroke it. Staring into those black, blank eyes, I am speechless.

Her mind isn't damaged. It has not been severed, cut, and allowed to rot. Angry and raging, she's in there. She is in shock.

"I said get back! Do you not see the fucking mess around here. Hey! That is evidence!"

Evidence. The robe I use to cover her gaunt frame. Evidence. The blood I smear over her skin in my attempts to wash it away. It doesn't belong to her. Odd blood. Rotten blood...

Vamryre blood?

"Bloody hell, Altaris! I know you think you run this damn city, but you and your little pets can't waltz all over a crime scene. And that one certainly isn't one of yours. She's being arrested on suspicion of murder—"

"You are speaking," Altaris snaps. "Yet I hear nothing of value. Hush. I shall only speak to Jack."

"This is my crime scene," the woman interjects. "You vile, fucking vamryre. One would think you'd want to get justice for your own kind. This bastard was a black market seller. Do you see what the fuck she's done?"

Done. My Niamh, pale, and frail, bundled in bright green silk. She sits amid a pile of blood. Surrounded by a neat collection of body parts. Limbs. An eye. A bloodied, naked torso.

In the center of it...

"Oh dear," Altaris says, and genuine dread creeps into his tone. He's worried. No, beyond worried. He is afraid. "This certainly complicates things."

"That it does, you vamp prick," the woman, Marin, snarls with glee. "This is a capital murder case with all the hallmarks of dark magic being at play. Boys, arrest the girl and get these damn bats out of my fucking face!"

A silence falls, but Altaris isn't the cause.

I was.

"Touch her," I said. "And I will kill you all."

When I am not prodding at my Niamh testing her for damage and danger. When I am not calling out her name repeatedly to no response. When there isn't vamryre blood that isn't mine smeared all over that pretty, crooked mouth.

"Oh dear," Altaris says, his tone hard again. "This will cost me a pretty penny. A capital murder charge is not cheap. She will be denied bond, which means I will have to pull many a string to keep her out of boney custody. Do you hear me, Caspian?"

I nod. I hear him. He wants another signature. Another mark on his contract. What exactly is it I'm selling away, who knows?

Once she's in my arms again, I don't care about anything but keeping her safe. Waking her up. Getting her to speak to me. Blink at me. Anything!

"Boys, clear out," Marin hisses, sounding distant. Her anger is a show. She is more afraid than Altaris is. Her voice quivers. Her pulse is racing. The result is a distracting hum that calls to my predatory instincts.

No, wait. Not mine.

"I need to get her out of here," I say, still stroking her black hair. Those black eyes stay fixated straight ahead, watching nothing. But I can hear something within her rustle and stir to life. Its only musing is base and cruel: *hungry, so hungry.*

My voice rises. "Altaris!"

"Oh blast! Enough! Will everyone just let me think for a bloody minute!" He paces into view, stroking his chin, those green eyes darting to the bloody mess my fae made. The torso draws his particular interest—namely, the hole in the center of it.

A hole where a heart is meant to be.

"What the fuck is this, Altaris?" Marin hisses. "Those bloody vamps you swore to keep on a leash, but a bloody fucking fae! That is beyond all the codes and ordinances. You'll have that council come down on our fucking heads—"

"Oh poppycock!" Altaris waves her off, still frowning. Her mewling words mean little to him. He has the means to smooth this over. Even this—bloody murder and missing hearts—he has the means to smooth over. It is the details that startle him. This place. This body. This crime scene in particular.

It unnerves him.

Unsettles.

He's seen it before.

"You know," I say. What exactly am I implying? I don't know. Can't say. But he knows something that has him restless and pacing and muttering to himself aimlessly and bitterly.

"Damn," he mutters. "Bloody damn. Blast."

"What am I? Fucking invisible?" Marin marches toward him, flashing her silver stick. She stops short, frozen in place.

Because I growled at her. I whirled on her, teeth bared, vision turning red.

"Touch her and I will kill you—"

"Now, now, Caspian, it is alright," Altaris warns, using his commanding tone, keeping me from lunging at the mortal and ripping out her throat. "Take your little darling one home, hmm? The other house, not the one where my precious ones live. *Take her home and only there.* Understood? Scythe will accompany you."

"Altaris! We're in the middle of a bloody murder investigation and you want to traipse off with the prime suspect. No. I refuse. Not on my watch—"

"What in the hell is going on here?" The voice is different from the rest. Deeper, more assured. This boney is not like others, playing pretend. He means business.

"Ah, finally," Altaris says, turning to face him. The dark-skinned man. Jack. "Some real authority. We have a few minor details to work out, you and I."

"Jack!" Marin's voice is an agonized rush. "This bloody bastard wants to take a stray fae suspected of murder to God knows where! You can't let it happen! Arrest them all—"

"That would be a very bad idea," Altaris says sweetly as I lift my fae into my arms. Her head lolls. She is so weak. She's so light, she could float away.

I move toward the door.

In an attempt to stop me, the woman blocks my path.

"Jack," she insists, like a child pleading for the punishment of another.

"Yes, Jack," Altaris interjects. "Let them go and you and I can make arrangements to salvage this mess. There will be no arresting of anyone. These two are under my protection."

"Two stray other-realmers," Jack begins, his voice deep. "I think that's beyond even your meddling, Altaris. I heard about that visiting envoy. This is an immigration issue. That makes it boney business."

"Ah yes, well it seems you need some convincing. Marin, I suggest you corral the witnesses or whatever it is you do." He waves her off.

She scoffs.

The man, Jack, nods with a sigh. "Marin, please."

In a huff, she storms off and the second she's gone Altaris drops the act. "Now, then. We can talk plainly." His true age seeps into his words, making everything around him feel heavier. He is ageless. Not to be trifled with. "I will give you three reasons why you will let my new darlings go unaccosted."

Jack crosses his arms, a black eyebrow raised. "They better be good bloody reasons—"

"Oh, they are." Altaris smiles, baring his fangs for all to see. "Yelim, Yarrow, Max—"

"Fucking..." Jack's voice breaks. His will shatters. Wide-eyed and stoic, Altaris has his full attention. "You sick son of a bitch. How did you even—"

"Clear the scene, darling," Altaris says, his charming self once again. "I suggest you do so now. Caspian, why don't you run along as well. Take the fae with you."

Run.

I cradle Niamh in my arms and leave the room—no, a filthy tent. Filth and rancid creatures abound in this place. Too many noises, sounds and sights itch at my senses. Scratch at my psyche. It is a destitute place for exploitation and sin.

Yet she wound up here, because of me.

"I'm sorry," I tell her, my mouth near her ear, voice low and soothing. "I am so sorry."

She doesn't say anything. There is nothing on her mind but blank space. As I take her through the enchanted alleyway and back into the city proper, she flinches. Just once, nothing more.

So I run. I move blindly in the direction of Altaris's domain and I barely notice the creature relentlessly keeping pace. It isn't until we arrive at the decrepit warehouse that he comes from nowhere to open the heavy front door.

"Stay out," I tell him.

Out. Out.

It's her domain, not mine. The place where she gaped at the windows unrestrainedly and danced away the cobwebs. Her place with its food rotting away in a refrigerator and persistent heat crawling through rusted vents.

I set her down in our corner, against the wall, at the far end of the room. Then I strip off the gaudy robe and stare at her in full. Underneath, she is shaking. Blood coats her delicate skin. There are bruises all over her body.

Despite this, her skin remains unbroken. I find a rag and wet it with lukewarm water. I clean her limbs meticulously and find her arms unblemished. Her perfect torso, devoid of wounds. Her throat. The scalp beneath her thick cape of hair. I nudge her around. Eye her back.

Rip the rag in two. Don't mean to. It happens as I inspect a mass of black on her back that shouldn't be there.

It looks like ink, but it isn't. In shimmering black lines, two birds are etched into her flesh. When I try to wipe them away, the marks don't budge.

Nevertheless, she flinches. It hurts her. I can feel her pain. Good. Good. She's still in there, that shocked brain. She just needs time to come out again. Coaxing.

As if I know how.

Hands like mine are made for killing and tearing. Ripping. Gentleness is unknown to them. They can't stroke soft, silky skin without breaking bones underneath. This voice is incapable of maintaining a soothing hum.

I try to talk to her. I'm growling at her.

"Niamh, wake up. Look at me!"

But she is looking. Staring into some infinite void right past me. It isn't natural, I know as much. Something has her mind captured, dangling on a string. When I reach for her, she's yanked further away.

Bringing her back will require drastic measures.

Searching, hunting, I scan the room. Near the door, I see a pile of things on a wooden table. The mortal's things. Daven Wick. He brought her clothing. Food. A book.

One of Altaris's, dark and foreboding, reeking of unseemly truths and forbidden histories. This book frightened her. Alarmed.

I try reading from it. "...hybrid creatures are..."

Her body flinches inward as if she is in pain.

I throw the book aside. Crouch down beside her. Stroke her.

"Come back to me, dear one," I say, using words that this murderous tongue stumbles over. It's new to me. I'm not good at this. The fake one, Poppy, would be. I should ask her to come. Beg her to coax Niamh back from this dark, far place.

No.

Only she was able to bring me back from an internal hell that I had retreated to after being cast out of Cassius's mind. I alone will save her. It's just a matter of finding the right method for me. The right language.

But what?

Not speaking. My words aren't beautiful like hers are, my voice isn't liquid sin. Every grated, grumbled word I speak will harm her more.

But what?

What?

I pace again. Stalk toward that pile of items. Tear through it. There is nothing. Just clothing with parchment shoved into the pockets. In one I find a crumbled nib of wood and lead no longer than my littlest finger.

Pencil, a part of me declares, recognizing the shape. A tool. Utensil.

But not to stab with. Jab with. Kill with.

Something else...

But WHAT?

I pace. Growl into the air. Slash the pencil at nothing.

Wait. That motion. Movement. It is familiar.

Still holding the thing aloft, I crouch down low and flip open that infernal book to the very back page.

Little lines here and there. Scritch scratch.

Magic. It flows through me as it does in her voice when she reads. Only it is in my hands. Magic that makes me drag the pencil across the paper. Magic that makes me shape and mold a creature from thin air.

Magic that resembles her in the end when all is said and done.

No, not magic. An imitation of that which she is so impressed by. A sloppy excuse for a painting with no pigments. No oil. No canvas.

It is ugly.

No...

Even in these unseemly, murderous hands, her beauty shines through. She makes this ugly, forbidden book whole once more with her image.

I rip it out, my defaced page. I shove it into her hands. Wait.

Were she in her right mind, she would wail and rage. How dare I desecrate a book, even one she despises?

I wait.

She doesn't stir.

Her pale hands clutch at my page, but her eyes gaze right past it.

She is stubborn, my fae. A stubborn wretch. A stubborn, beautiful wretch.

But I will wait her out.

For I am a vamryre, and all I have is time.

Niamh

Oh dear, I have done it now. The ultimate sin. A bloody sin.

I enjoyed it. Killed and killed. I killed and...

It was fun for me. To watch him struggle and wriggle. To watch him gasp and writhe in pain. That man was evil. That creature was sinful.

He deserved to die.

But did he?

What haunts me is the fact that I don't know. I can't know. There are so many memories and truths beyond my reach. Things denied to me, both my fate and other actors. My own mother—her visage, her memory, the sound of her voice—was denied to me.

My father, too. My father, who may have been a monster of a creature, broken and vile. He may have preyed upon poor Aurelia and taught her a 'lesson' she would never forget. I was not conceived in duty or even in love—but act. Violence. A twisted, cruel act.

It is what I deserve.

A fitting beginning to the life I so wretchedly deserve.

But...

There is a small matter of reliving the murder I am supposed to have committed. I see him writhing. I see sharp beaks and claws snapping and biting. But I hear him too, his voice very much alive.

You little bitch!

I'll gut you!

Tear to you little pieces!

You think you can find her, that fae bitch? She's already dead...

Then I said something. To him. To them—the creatures carrying out that massacre for me. I said...

I can't remember.

They spoke to me in return, little voices whispering into my skull. They said "We do this for you, sister. We will bite, rip and tear. We will stop—"

Wait.

I told them to stop. I think. I told them to stop so that I could stand over him, bloody Cyrus, bleeding and broken on the floor of his tent. I crouched down low on top of him. I reached for his throat. I demanded.

"Tell me..."

Something.

Tell me something! I screamed at him. Demanded.

Then the world went dark. Blank. Just like that I can't remember anything else. What I asked him. What I said.

I only remember the voices, quiet and cowed. *We will stay with you, sister. Hide within you. We will be good to you, mistress. Oh good, yes.*

The jackdaws. They go by that name, but it isn't really theirs. In the past, they were something else. Virile and living. Something called...

My heart hurts too much to think. I can't remember. It's better to sit here in the dark. To wallow and wither. To breathe and dream.

I dream of icy coldness. Of gentle touches and delicate kisses pressed to my temple. I dream of a voice, murmuring into my ear, "Come back to me, my dear one. Come back."

I hear...

Him, Caspian. I hear him inhaling my scent into those withered, useless vamryre lungs. I hear him sigh. I hear his footsteps pace and pace and then I hear him whisper to me. I can feel him stroking his fingers through my hair as he does so. Carefully. Cautiously.

He is oh so gentle, and it hurts. What did I do to deserve such gentleness? If I am the product of violence and hatred, then why do I deserve such calming, soothing touches?

Why do I deserve a voice that breaks against my ear as it repeats for the millionth time, "Come back to me, Niamh."

Why?

There isn't an answer.

One good enough will never come.

And yet, I don't need a reason. He asks me to stay, so I will stay. He begs me to return, so I will. Bit by bit, I will life into these withered limbs. I try to speak. Speak. Say anything.

My lips twitch, I know that much.

Caspian sighs and sighs. "Come back, Niamh," he demands more forcefully. "Come back! Come back or... I will burn your book."

No. My eyes open instantly. They burn as hot sunlight trickles in and warms my skin. It is so blindly hot. He's kept the heat running. He's bundled me in blankets that smell like dank mildew, but are somehow still warm. He has made food for me. It is a mass of various things crammed onto a plate, shoved onto my lap.

I am hungry. I swipe a finger through a mass of white and gray substances. Eat. I gag. It tastes awful. I swallow it anyway. My Caspian made it for me, so I will eat it anyway.

I eat and eat until the plate is wiped clean.

Then I look up.

He is watching me with those intent scarlet eyes. He is patiently waiting for something—which is odd. Caspian is never patient. He does not wait. Yet for me...

He hesitates.

Then he crouches low onto one knee and gingerly swipes at the corner of my mouth with the pad of his thumb.

"You were gone for three days," he says.

Gone. Not physically. Most of the time I was here, with him, I know that much. Yet, my mind was gone. Somewhere strange. Somewhere that I can't remember. I learned something. Something vital and awful and spine-tingling.

Something about myself.

What is it?

I can't remember. The harder I try, the more my skull aches, as if it was once fractured into pieces and crudely made whole again. I wince and cradle it against my palm with my messy hands.

Caspian tsks, sucking his tongue against the roof of his mouth. "Let me," he insists, commands. Let him clean me. Let him gently wipe my hands clean with a rag. Let him smooth the hair back from my face. Let him look at me.

His beautiful features are beyond description. Captivating. Even when he kills and is covered in blood, oh my, is he mesmerizing.

I am not.

He looks at me like I am a sad, lost thing. Lost because he left me. Found because he wants me again. Lost and found. Found and lost.

How long before he loses me and never comes back?

"I took my eyes off you for one minute," he says, his voice a deep, unsettling rasp. "One minute."

It's my fault. He took his eyes off me, and chaos erupted. He took his eyes off me, and I was shoved and pushed along with a crowd and taken by vultures.

He took his eyes off me. For what reason?

He doesn't say. I wait for an answer. Seconds pass before I realize he has no intention of providing me with one.

Because I am not worth an answer.

No...

Because he is hesitating to give me one, the real one. Uncertainty on him is a glimpse of heaven. It peeks through those red eyes like a ray of sun piercing through a storm cloud. Just for a moment. Just one.

Still, I will treasure the sight for the rest of my life. He didn't leave me on purpose. He was compelled to. By what?

"Tell me," I ask. Demand. My voice is pleading and soft.

Still...

He takes my hand in his and brings it to his mouth. He presses his lips there, to the fragile skin. He inhales my scent and then raises those beautiful, sinful eyes to mine again.

"I saw paintings," he admits in a rasp. "In the museum. They were in a forgotten room. They made me feel...angry." He hates this. Admitting things to me out in the open. Revealing that he is more than a monster driven by his master's orders and blood. He saw a painting too. Enough to become distracted by it. He saw something in the artwork, just like I do.

My heart sings!

Until he frowns. Until a desperate, confused pain flits across his face, and I am confounded. Whatever he found, whatever he saw, it didn't set him free or inspire happy, wondrous thoughts. It terrified him, my Caspian.

It puzzles him still.

"Oh." I reach out for him, and he leans in close, letting me hold him and comfort him. Soon, I am the one seeking comfort from him, pressing my face against this chest, and inhaling deeply. I was angry at him, I realize that now. Angry and bitter and tormented by him leaving me.

But now I know the reason. The truth.

That space inside my heart doesn't sting anymore. I feel whole again. Whole and safe and wanted by him. It is a delicious, most dangerous feeling. I curl into him and savor it. I bask in it.

And I feel him bask in me.

Our thoughts mingle again. Hesitant and cautious. One of us pulled away from the other, though I'm unsure who or why. It happened in the museum. Perhaps when he saw the paintings that distracted him so, and the chaos that happened after startled me. We were apart, then...

I am quickly realizing that I don't like being apart. He is not like my Day, my dear one, my brother in blood. I could tolerate his absences. Bask in his fleeting attention. Even when he hurt me, I would have accepted another visit from him again.

With Caspian, there is no option. No feeling. No cautious want.

I need him like I need air to breathe. Without him, I suffocate. I can survive but suffocate. It hurts to breathe without him there. It hurts to think and talk and act normally.

Unless I am flying...

"You flew." His confusion is marked by the curious, gentle way he prods into my thoughts. So gentle he is, always. I sigh and lean into his touch, both physical and mental.

"I flew," I tell him. "With paper wings and silk. It was wondrous. Wonderful."

I may never get to do so again.

"I can make you fly," Caspian says. He means so in a crude way. In a sexual, deviant, naughty way.

I don't care.

His promise is music to my ears. With him, I can fly, some-how. Anyway, I'll take it.

I press my mouth to his jaw. I linger there, feeling the muscle flex against me. He is discomforted by this, nearness. Yet, a part of him is unsure whether he likes it or not. Whether he needs more or not.

He spent so long in that mental prison, doling out pleasure as a punishment to his master. He doesn't even remember what it is he wants, or enjoys, or likes.

"I will make you enjoy," I say. A fair enough trade. His gift of flight for my touch.

We tangle into one another, a mass of limbs and prodding mouths. Our kisses are open and tentative, placed against patches of skin. I kiss him along his collar bone. Then peel the material of his shirt aside to see what lies beneath.

He kisses me along my throat, then lower, nosing aside the red material of my circus costume. He never took it off. Didn't want to disturb me. It's why he piled me high beneath so many blankets, to shield me from the imagined cold.

Those blankets shroud us both now and become our own kingdom. A private realm. One in which we rule supreme with no other lords to bow to.

Bathed in the darkness here, Caspian bows to me. His kisses become more urgent. Frantic. A lapping tongue and raking teeth that pull at pieces of me as if he aims to swallow them whole. But he doesn't. He doesn't so much as bite. Just licks and tastes and beats my body into submission with his hunger and lust.

My heart pounds. My breaths grow heavy and slowed. I can't describe how he feels. The weight of him pins me down. I am stripped bare by his groping fingers and laid before him like a banquet table.

If he took me like this, I wouldn't know any better. I wouldn't want anything more.

But he doesn't.

He pulls back, flips me over, and makes me mount him. Our pelvises collide with a collective groan. My hands brace against his bare chest for leverage. Those red eyes glare up at me, daring me to take the gift he's offered.

Power over him, body, mind, and soul.

It is a gift more precious than that of flight.

I can touch him unrestrained and trail my fingers across that chest, rippling with muscle as hard as marble. He is perfection in every sense of the word. Nothing—no manmade piece of art—compares to him. Not now. Not ever.

I lean forward and press my lips to the base of his throat. A low grumble resonates there in response. He isn't used to being touched. Worshiped. The terms are alien to him. Savoring contact is unfamiliar to him. He bucks with every inch I explore.

One of his thoughts slips into my mind, unbidden: *can't remember.* What he looks like, before his current form. What the mortal who once wore this very flesh felt like. Tasted like with warmth and sun on his skin. It haunts him, deep down in the fragmented chaos of his mind, where he doesn't let himself dwell.

It terrifies him to question what sort of person he was like. What drew Cassius to him and vice versa. That is the truth about becoming a vamryre. One they don't like to let slip out: it is a willing gift that can only be bestowed upon those who ask.

Once, the human mortal he used to be went to Cassius and asked to be turned. He asked that bastard to consume him, body, and mind. He hates himself for that.

But I could never hate him.

"You are beautiful to me," I murmur against his skin. My lips trace a path down his breastbone and hover over where his heart should be. Where it is still. I see it there, a fragile, neglected thing, yet there nevertheless. "You are art to me," I tell him, kissing him there. Once. Twice. "When I am with you..." My fingers shake as I spread them out, tracing him, memorizing every bit of bone, muscle, and flesh. "I forget that I cannot fly."

Whenever I am around him, the ache in my soul goes away for a moment. Not because of his gift for persuasion. It is in moments like this, when he takes one of my hands gently in his own and watches the slim fingers hover, bathed in shadow.

"You are artwork to me," he echoes, his voice deep and rasping, eyes blazing. "In this body, I remember what I am. I think. What I was." He frowns and trails off, then he copies me, contouring himself to press his lips to my forehead.

That kiss is the most intimate of any we have shared before. It is strange for him. To react on a desire merely for his own benefit. Not because Cassius was in his head urging him to. Not because Cassius commanded him *not* to.

He wants to kiss me on the forehead like this. On the lips. Against my throat. Lower still. After that, he stops and listens to the cadence of my breathing. In and out. It is magical to him.

This is magical to him. Silence and nearness and grasping hands that hold each other tightly. There is no need for any more. He could listen to my heartbeat for an eternity.

And I could endure his listening for an eternity more.

"Sex was a chore I undertook for him," he admits, his voice low. I hold myself still, giving him the space to mull over the words before he speaks them. "A duty. I never enjoyed it. Never wanted the bodies I claimed for him. *He* wanted them, not me. But with you..." He looks up, gazing at me through wayward strands of white hair. I'm captivated. Riveted. Heartbroken. "I saw you, and I wanted you. For myself. Me alone. I ached to be inside of you. Does that scare you, little fae?"

It should. I feel my cheeks flame and my heart race--telltale signs of fear. Or something else. A dangerous, primal emotion I've only ever felt with him. With his hands on my body and inside of it. In the most intimate way possible, we embraced each other with our bodies.

I feel my throat dampen and my tongue thicken at the thought of him. Maybe...

"From the moment I first saw you," I say, fumbling over the words, "I wanted you too."

Although I am sure he has heard those words before from far more impressive people than myself, he doesn't laugh. Over the years, he has held bodies much more ample and appealing than the thin hips he currently cradles.

He has taken more people than I want to acknowledge. A wealth of carnal expertise floats around that closed-off brain. Yet...

I can't deny that when he looks at me, his jaw clenched, fangs peeking beneath his lower lip, his hunger for me isn't fake. Neither is the desperate way he rocks his hips into mine. Caught off guard, I shift my body in response, bringing myself into contact with the dangerous part of him.

In a choked grunt, he arches himself into me, watching me writhe and my eyes flutter shut. It's so different from how I grew up thinking mating should be--an act I never was meant to take part in. It was described in the archives as another task to endure, another purpose to fulfill.

Not vital.

It is he who makes this moment crucial. I can't breathe without him inside me. I can't think outside of his thrusts' slow, steady rhythm. My only words are frantic chants of his name.

In return, he is silent, ruthless, and endless. He lets me keep a semblance of control until he simply can't. A predator takes over, flipping me over, pinning me down, and slamming his length into me. All of it, no mercy given.

None required.

The friction blinds me. As his fingers glide along my flesh, sending sparks shooting down my spine, I am rendered senseless. There is no reprieve until we both cry out and collapse, his body on top of mine.

Only then can I remember myself again. Who I am apart from him.

Someone I never want to be again.

THERE ARE BAD, BAD THOUGHTS ON THE HORIZON in both of our minds. Things that happened in the time we spent apart. We both are hesitant of the other's new secrets, afraid to prod and poke. Yet our curiosity gets the better of us.

He asks first. "Tell me what happened to you. When I left."

I nod and bury my face against his shoulder. Rather than speak, I shove the requisite thoughts into his mind. I let him see it all. Feel everything I felt. Everything.

As a result, he tenses with hatred, anger, and pity.

"They hurt you," he growls, moving his hands to my waist,

and gripping me tight. "Made you bleed. You didn't scream. If you had screamed, I would have found you."

Part of his anger is directed at me. For not needing him. For suffering in silence without him there.

I press a kiss to his chest. Then another along his jawline. "I am tired of screaming," I say. "Tired of crying."

He nods. His frown deepens. Those eyes are deep, dark red as he mulls over my thoughts in greater detail. Minchae unnerves him. Cyrus infuriates him, and the mention of my mother...

His fingers run through my hair as he sighs. "I will take you back. Soon. Now," he says, reiterating his earlier promise. "I will kill Cassius and you will find the Aurelia, to kill or not as you please. I will take you and Cassiopeia—"

Her name. It has lurked in his mind always, but with few concrete thoughts to tether it. Not now. It is a vibrant section of his mind, brought to life by a chance meeting. A beautiful female vamryre with white skin, pink hair, and reddish eyes. Daisy—yet he knew her as a different name. There is no way to describe how intimately he knew her: as his sister, his other half and his partner in bondage.

Cassiopeia. Part of him is so happy to have found her again. Thrilled. It sings as I did when I got my taste of almost-flight. He is at peace.

Yet, he is unsettled. Agitated. Cassius must be confronted. He promised both me and Cassiopeia that he would.

But...

He doesn't want to. He thrives on violence and revenge, but he fears facing Cassius. Not the man himself, but the creature he made him once. Might make him become again.

"No," I say. "You will not take me back. Not now. Not until you are ready."

He scoffs, still petting through my hair. "Ready."

As if he needs to be ready. He of unmatched bravery, ferocity, and strength.

His refusal to admit it even to himself is a testament to his pride. No one else holds sway over him like Cassius. He brings out the worst in him. Rather than being a mere vamryre, he transforms him into a monstrous creature.

"You will not," I insist before planting another kiss on him. As he grunts in response, I feel my stomach flutter.

Although he may have more expertise in the carnal arts, I am learning quickly from him. Kisses that are violent, hungry, and bruising are his favorite. These small, quick, tasting ones, however, mark him deep, deep beneath the skin. After years of being ruthlessly devoured by the mind of another, he loves to be savored. Cherished. Treated like porcelain and glass.

He will never admit it out loud, no, never.

But I kiss him once. Twice. Thrice.

He rumbles in pleasure.

"You'll go back when you want to," I tell him.

It is clear that he is seething and spinning in his mind, even though he says nothing. His troubles are far greater than Cassius. Mostly to do with me. Something terrible happened at the circus that will need to be dealt with. By all appearances, I did a very, very bad thing.

By all appearances, I am just as cruel a monster as he is.

But Cyrus deserved it. He deserved to die and be poked apart. He deserved to be attacked by his own jackdaws. But did he deserve what came after?

Violence I don't remember inflicting. As soon as he stood over me, everything around me went black.

I shift away from Caspian. Suddenly I need distance from him. I need to feel the cold air, and smell the remnants of food, and dank musk and remember what it's like to feel shame.

I did a bad, bad thing. I don't deserve to bask in peace and happiness. I don't deserve him.

"Your back." Caspian has drawn our blanket aside, exposing us to the rest of this open space. Our space. His eyes are on my spine. On that mass of scars and damage.

Yet, in his mind, I can tell that something new spans this part of me. Something that itches and scratches. Something I don't want to remember. Not yet.

"I don't know," I say, shifting away from him. I hug myself tight and blink, fighting back any hint of tears. No more tears. "I don't know. I don't care."

He is silent. I feel his mind pull away from my own, but not out of disgust. He's hiding his recollections. Hiding how he stares at me, his gaze tracing a path down my spine. Suppressing his urge to reach out and touch. To notice what he didn't before.

Like the deliberate damage beneath the scars.

"I... I had wings," I say. With bitterness and so much anguish, my voice breaks. Then I'm shouting. "I had wings! I did. I did and they took them from me. They lied to me. I had wings. I did!"

He is silent. But in the fragile seconds that pass, his body comes to envelop mine. His mind becomes a possessive, reassuring pressure that shuts the doubts, fears, and pain out. I feel so much pain all the time, but around him, it is banished. He holds me tight, and I find peace in him again.

It isn't fair.

It isn't right.

If he leaves me again...how will I survive the loss of this?

"I will not leave you," he growls into my hair. "I won't."

But he doesn't promise. He knows that he may not be able to keep a promise.

Still, it is enough. I relent to his contact and let him hold me tight. For hours we must stay like this.

It's nearly dark out when someone bangs on the door.

Caspian is up first. He already took the time to dress us both in the clothing Daven Wick supplied: him in a black shirt, brown leather jacket with a hood and dark parts. For me, he chose an orange dress with short sleeves and large round brown buttons going down the front. He likes dresses on me. He likes the way they swish around my legs as I move. Almost like wings.

For now he warns me back as he approaches the door alone. He wrenches it open. Three men stand behind it. One of them is tall, with dark skin and piercing brown eyes that seek me out.

"Niamh the fae," he intones in a deep, booming voice. "You are hereby under arrest for the ritualistic murder of Cyrus Triarc. You have the right to remain silent. Everything you say can and will be held against you in the court of law. You have the right to an attorney—"

"Right, right," a figure beside him sniffs. "That is all very well and good. You said your little spiel. Let's get on with it. Not to worry, my darlings," he says, his gaze on Caspian. "We will escort dear Niamh to the station where the boneys will book her in as they are wont to do. Then she will be released on her own recognizance under my guardianship. All is well that ends well. Now come along."

Caspian stiffens, his eyes flashing from the tall man to Altaris and back again. Slowly, he nods. Then he extends his hand out to me.

I take it, and step forward, following him out into the descending night.

The tall man watches me exit. His clothing is so dark, he almost blends seamlessly into the shadows, save for a bright metal object that hangs from a loop in his belt. It looks like a silver rod of some sort. A bashing weapon. Yet...

A faint outline cloaks it. Magic, a voice in my head proclaims. Not mine. Not Caspian's.

I shiver. Then I keep moving, walking past Altaris and the third figure I recognize as Scythe. He is silent but as our gazes meet, he nods once. A polite greeting.

"Well, on with it," Altaris snaps, his eyes on the tall man. "The only good thing about traveling with a boney is your goddamn gift for quick and efficient travel. It almost makes up for the many areas in which you lack."

"You're already on thin ice, Altaris," the man warns, but he frees his stick from his belt and waves it through the air.

There is a crackling. A sudden tension of energy and air—as though the very life is being squeezed from my lungs. Then, just as quickly, the strange force eases. I gasp, swaying on my feet as Caspian's grip on me tightens.

"A warning would have been nice," Altaris remarks, his green eyes shimmering. "My guests are not familiar with this realm and boney ways. You'll startle them. As we are quickly finding out, these two do not react well to being startled."

The tall man is already walking away, returning his stick to his belt. "Wait here," he snaps, before retreating down a long winding hallway. We are suddenly inside of a building I don't recognize. The walls are an old, faded green. The floors are dark, polished wood. The air in here radiates authority, much like the halls of the Citadel archives do.

But there is a key difference.

In the archives, no one looked at me, directly. No one except Caspian and Day.

Here, the very many people milling about all stop to stare. They gape at me. Some in horror. Some in abject curiosity. Their attention burns and stings. I feel too exposed. There are too many eyes here, and unlike the Circus of Souls, I can't launch myself through the air, festooned with silken wings to ignore them.

"Patience, my dear ones," Altaris says, clasping his hands together. "It took a mighty great deal of strings being pulled to get you *both* out on bond. How lucky for you that I am a generous and kind benefactor."

But he is not generous. Not kind. His help comes with a price tag attached. He is transactional in everything, even the dealings in his shop. I hate him. Despise him.

I hate even more that Caspian does not.

He listens to him. Maybe in some way, he trusts him. They are vamryre at their core and speak the same language: collateral, debt, ownership. Contracts and dealings are comforts to them.

Not to me. I loathe the idea of owing anything to Altaris. I should face my punishment alone.

"No," Caspian snaps out loud, his back to me, his gaze still on Altaris. "You will not. You will not."

He is warning me, and deep down I know I should heed this one wish. Not for my sake but his. He is afraid for me, I can see that now. Afraid of what I am capable of.

Afraid of what I may have done in his absence.

So am I.

"We will accept your protection," he tells Altaris. "For now."

"Oh goody. It appears Marin will be the one to process her paperwork. What fun," Altaris remarks dryly.

As the woman approaches, he sneers. If she notices, she doesn't react. She holds her head high, wearing an outfit identical to the other man's down to the silver stick at her hip. I can't stop staring at her. Her eyes are wide-set and strangely shaped--almost cat-like, with dark brown irises. Paired with her pale skin, she is as beautiful as any fae.

That is, if her expression wasn't contorted in utter disgust.

"This way," she says before turning on her heel and marching across the hallway. The room we enter next is small and cramped. The silver desk in the center of the room is cluttered with paperwork, and the black walls add a sense of mystery. The offices of the council of elders might look like this, if I had to guess.

Though, perhaps, not quite as small.

"Barely a week in the mortal realm and the both of you have wracked up one hell of a rap sheet," the woman,

Marin says, leaning over the desk. She makes a show of flipping through paperwork, but her eyes remain focused on Altaris. He is the sole target of her irritation, no one else. "Who first?"

"Dear Caspian's matter has already been squared away," Altaris explains with a smile. "We are merely awaiting his court date. You can commence with dear Niamh."

"Niamh, is it?" Marin turns her gaze to me, but I notice it is markedly softer. She even speaks in a different tone, stern but nowhere near as cold. "You will need to be questioned. Cyrus Triarc was no saint, but that was some grisly business. Too grisly, in fact, to be explained away as self-defense. We need to know what happened from the start."

"Unfortunately, dear Niamh cannot remember," Altaris explains, approaching the desk. He drags his finger along the edge of it and sniffs in disgust. "She is in shock and will not be answering anything without her lawyer present. Seeing as how her lawyer is now Silas Appleby, and he is currently away on business, the soonest she can be questioned is...hmm, Monday."

"Three days?" Marin slams her fist on the table, making it lurch across the floor. "You arrogant prick, vampire! You think you run this city just because you have more money than God and the scruples to match. Hell no. If we can't question her tonight, then I'll throw her in lockup until Mr. Appleby *decides* to arrive."

"Temper, temper, Marin." Altaris wags an admonishing finger. "It's the lys that does it, you know. That sweet, rich powder induces calm and happiness, with a lingering aftereffect of uncontrolled rage and irritation—"

"You don't know what the fuck you're talking about," Marin hisses. She turns toward the doorway and yells out, "Jack!"

"Jack and I have already discussed these details," Altaris says sweetly to Marin's immense aggravation. The redder she turns, the more pleased he seems. "It's all settled. However there is one matter you can assist with. The body. It seems your new medical examiner may not be as well-versed in mundane lore as most. I have arranged for Ginni to assist her down at my clinic—"

"You mean your chop shop?" Marin hisses. "It isn't like we don't know what you do down there. You and that creepy, demented, little vamryre. Selling body parts. Draining them of blood to feed your fucked up brood. If I had my way, you would have been shut down ages ago--"

"Ginni has kindly offered her assistance in this despicable matter," Altaris says over her. "I would suggest you not insult her, or my 'brood,' in front of me."

Marin swallows hard, heeding the warning. "I'll have Aleska find you on your way out. As for Niamh. We'll need a booking photo, fingerprints, a blood sample, and her visa paperwork."

"We will arrange for everything but the blood work," Altaris says. "It's a fae thing. A cultural exemption, you understand."

Marin hisses. "And let me guess, you cleared that with Jack too? If she's the one that envoy was here about, even you won't be able to sweet talk your way out of this."

"Oh, Jack was very understanding. And you are right, seeing as how the council will be after her, a simple visa will not be necessary—"

Caspian whirls on him. "What?"

My heart stops. At the thought of going back, I can't breathe. Can't think. I need to run. My back prickles and the pain distracts me enough from what Altaris says next.

I only know that he holds up his hand, stopping Caspian in his tracks.

"Calm down, both of you," he warns, his tone stern. "Allow me to explain the particularly complicated status of Niamh's immigration. She will be applying for full citizenship, given that her heritage is part mundane."

I blink.

Caspian flinches.

"Really?" Marin scoffs, an eyebrow raised. "You want me to believe that she—" she looks me head to toe and laughs, "Is part mundane?"

"Yes, Ellarika Willtze is drawing up her application as we speak. Given the circumstances, she is not eligible for extradition or free travel between the realms. Therefore, she is completely suitable to be released upon her own recognizance. If you are having trouble understanding, my dear, Jack may be able to fill you in."

"Oh, I bet he can. One day, I hope you rot in hell, Altaris," Marin hisses.

Laughing, he waves his hand at our surroundings. "My darling, where do you think we are? Honestly."

He chuckles as she storms from the room, but the second she's gone, he falls silent. "I know you have questions," he says, though I'm not sure if he's speaking to me or Caspian. "But now isn't the time. That was a powerful creature you may have killed, my darling. Very powerful indeed. You must trust that I know best. Keep your mouth shut in boney halls. We will discuss the finer points later. For now, be patient."

I nod.

So does Caspian.

An odd tension permeates the air. Something is wrong, and it goes far beyond what happened at the circus. Caspian feels it too. As he approaches, he takes hold of my hand.

Some of the feeling goes away, just enough to breathe normally again.

Marin returns with a folder that she hurls onto the table. "Just one more thing. Then I suppose we're done here."

"I suppose we shall be," Altaris remarks in a smug tone.

"This girl." Marin opens the folder and slams an index finger against a glistening square. "Do you recognize her?"

I do. With far more detail, the image is as colorful as a painting. A photograph, Caspian remarks. He knows the term but doesn't remember how. Whatever it is, the person depicted, with shorter black hair is unmistakable.

"Minchae," I say. In retrospect, I recall Altaris' advice, but when I look at him, his expression is unreadable. So I tentatively add, "She worked at the Circus, as a performer."

And now she's taken the ledger with any hope of seeing my mother along with her. The strange part is I'm not angry with her—

I am, Caspian interjects. *She betrayed you. Abandoned.*

She didn't hide her intentions, however. Even though it makes little difference to him, that means something to me.

"Minchae Almony. She's got a rap sheet about as long as your memory, Altaris." Marin's tone implies she doesn't mean it as a compliment. "Larceny. Theft. Assault with a deadly weapon. As far as we know, she's our only witness. Unless you killed her too, in which case that would make it two capital murders. Serial killers are denied bond, per the latest ordinances."

"Speculation doesn't suit you, Marin," Altaris warns. He crosses over to the desk and snatches up the folder. "Since Ginni is already handling the autopsy, I will take it upon myself to do the rest of your work and find this 'witness' to get her statement. No sense in risking a shoddy investigation, is there? I hear that lys addiction can make those who suffer from it a tad forgetful."

As Marin looks at him, she smiles. "Fuck you."

"Well, if that is done, let us get her paperwork underway. Snap. Snap. The sooner we can leave this place the better."

"Fine." A frown crosses Marin's face but she doesn't give Altaris a response this time. "You there. Fae. This way." As she turns back to the hallway, I follow behind her. "She doesn't need an escort," she snaps, without looking at Caspian. Ignoring her, he holds my hand as we trail in her footsteps. The second room we enter is wider and longer than the first.

"Stand there." She gestures to a wall adorned with neat, black lines. From a nearby table, she raises an electronic device to her eye level. There is a blinding flash. Then she sighs. "Now for the fingerprints and blood sample—"

"No blood," Caspian snaps, his fangs bared.

Marin doesn't even flinch. Taking an item from the drawers on the desk, she approaches me. With stern commands she makes me dip my finger into ink. Presses it against a smooth page. Left behind is a beautiful mass of tangled lines.

"All done." Marin returns to the table, inspecting my fingerprint. Then she stops. Frowns. "That's odd. What the hell?"

Once again, she reaches for my finger. When I look down, I see that the mark I left before has disappeared.

Frowning, Marin tries again. A beautiful mark speckles the page, as impressive as the first. But...

As if it never existed, it vanishes within a heartbeat.

"What in the world? Did we order some faulty ink or something?"

"Well, we cannot be blamed in that case, can we," Altaris remarks from the doorway. Unlike Marin, he doesn't seem surprised. In response to her puzzled expression, he smiles warmly. "If you would just direct us to the medical examiner, then we may be on our way."

With a growl of disgust, Marin storms into the hallway and bellows "Aleska!" She vanishes into another room and the door slams behind her.

Meanwhile, another woman pokes her head through a nearby doorway. She is beautiful, with long, dark hair and golden skin that seems to glow from within. "Um... I was summoned?"

Altaris looks at her, an eyebrow raised. Then he shrugs. "This way, dear one. A mortal? Not even a mundane? Strange. I am told that you are to assist with the autopsy? In any case, watch your fingers around poor Ginni. She sometimes gets too excited."

The woman, Aleska, nods, unfazed. "I just need my supplies."

Minutes later, she reappears, dressed in a black coat with a black bag slung over one arm. "Aleska Fraterani at your service."

"Altaris Ipsum, at your service." Though he bows his head elegantly, his eyes reveal skepticism. "I do hope you've worked here long enough to qualify for medical. I honestly don't know how my Ginni will respond to... Well, if you would prefer, she can do the procedure alone—"

"Oh no!" Aleska's hazel eyes glisten with excitement. "I've always wanted to study a murder up close. This is my first one. Even if I get bitten, I won't press charges or file a claim. I have my own private insurance anyway."

Altaris shrugs. "Well, onwards."

Through a pair of green doors, he steps onto the street. I'm unfamiliar with this part of the city. The streets are narrow here, the buildings towering and gangly. It isn't like the neat row of establishments near the museum. In some aspects, I prefer this wild place.

It is as far from home as one could get, the polar opposite to the orderly Citadel.

With Caspian's hand in mine, it is easy to let the rest of the world melt away. To forget any and everyone else that could intrude. Our minds are linked, entwined as tightly as our fingers are. No one else can invade our world without permission.

And here, in this stoic silence, Caspian lets himself wonder things he would never give voice to. How beautiful he thinks I look in the glow of the streetlight. How the hum of electricity—what the mundane use to power their homes and magic—reminds him of a time he can't place. A calming time. He wracks his memory to find the answer but one eludes him.

Even so, he enjoys this time with me, in a way he didn't think it was possible to enjoy anything after Cassius. His world had become narrowed to a single, driving purpose.

Resent.

Disrupt.

Rebel.

Without that burning hatred to drive him, he felt lost.

So do I.

In any case, this feels...nice, walking with him along a darkened street in the mortal realm I once thought I'd never see.

In some ways, it's better than flying.

CHAPTER 21

Caspian

There is something wrong in Niamh's brain. A dark spot she doesn't seem aware of. Sometimes, I can hear it whispering things only she can hear.

And her back. I should ask Altaris about her back.

I want to—but I sense she won't let me. There is something she is hiding from me even if she doesn't know it. Hiding it from herself.

A secret. A wound of some kind. It is hurting her. I can feel it. Taste the corruption coiling beneath my skin.

Yet...

She smiles as though unaffected. She views the world still with just hopeful, innocent eyes. A world she's already seen at its worst, stinking and violent. A word that's harmed her already far more than our old realm ever did.

A world that despises her and sees her only as a disturbing

thing or something shiny to exploit. She doesn't see it. She pretends not to see it.

As long as there is good, she ignores the bad. Her ease of doing so annoys me. A desire to see the world in only the best light. To view dangling on a swing with false wings as excitedly as genuine flight.

To look at a vamryre who gleefully described his plans to murder her and see only a savior. A lover. Someone worthy of protection.

She makes me feel weak—her of frail limbs and gaunt flesh, with a scarred back and wings cut from their stalks.

She makes me envy that strength of hers. Were she a slave of Cassius, she would not dread facing him again. She would do so with her head held high and...

She would forgive him, with all her heart. With genuine, sickening honesty. She would look that monster in the eye and forgive him.

And Cassius, that sick bastard, he would crumble.

I am not so weak as her.

Not as strong.

I feed upon my anger and plan to wield it to its fullest extent. I will find my old master, and I will gladly drive his soul from his skull. I will rip out his eyes and eat them before him as Cassiopeia boasted. We will drink his blood together.

But Niamh will not understand. She does not speak the language of wrath and hatred.

So I will hide that desire from her as she hides her secret pain for me. A fair trade. An honest one.

We will both lie to each other in one small way, with none the wiser.

Yet, why, when I look into her eyes, sparkling and ebony, do I feel a twinge of something in my chest. A part of me claims it is guilt. Perhaps not.

Perhaps it is dread for the war I know is coming. One of minds and spirits. One of bodies and souls. Cassius is coming for me, I can fucking feel him.

Her creepy fae brother is coming for her, looming ever closer.

We both will have a choice on whether to forgive or kill.

I, for one, will happily kill.

"Well, here we are," Altaris announces, gesturing to the black building before us.

The mortal beside him cranes her neck to get a better look, her expression is wide-eyed, obviously impressed. "So this is the clinic's entrance?"

Altaris laughs. "Oh no, darling. That would be the basement entrance. Scythe, could you show her the way?"

The Pol-spawn obeys without question while the mortal beside him excitedly asks him questions he doesn't answer. "Oh, where do you source your specimens? Is there a delivery system? Can I see the..."

"Well, now, there is one small matter we must discuss," Altaris says, turning his focus to Niamh. "You, my darling, will not be allowed inside my dwelling. Not any time soon. To repay your contract, either Poppy or myself will retrieve you from the other house. Do you understand?"

"Why?" I demand, gripping her hand so tightly she gasps.

Altaris looks at me and sighs. "If she hasn't explained it, I won't. But she is a risk to my darlings, and that cannot stand—"

"Why?" she asked, her voice pained. Constricted.

Anger rises in me. I'd rip out Altaris's throat if I thought I could.

But he is not Cassius, and is one not to be trifled with. So I hold back. For now.

Altaris blinks. "So you haven't realized. You don't know. Tell me, dear one, have you noticed any strange marks on your body since your return? Any strange, little voices in your skull, other than your own?"

She stiffens, but I answer for her. "On her back," I say. "There are two birds."

She frees her hand from mine and steps away. Not out of shock or shame. Just surprise. She didn't realize. It scares her to know that yet another change has taken place on her abominable form. Another sign that marks her as different.

"Those would be jackdaws," Altaris murmurs, his green eyes glittering in the dark. "The result of very, very dark magic.

Very twisted. To attract their attention, you must have witnessed something terrible. It will take yet more of my resources and contacts to find out what."

"So then why punish her?" I snap.

He shakes his head. "You misunderstand. Jackdaws are reactive by nature, driven to protect. As you have seen, my darling ones can be a tad skittish. There is no telling if someone may stumble across her and have an accident. Jackdaws do not play nicely and they do not stop until their prey is dead. I'd rather not take that risk, I am sure you understand."

She doesn't, but she nods along anyway. Standing alone, on this winding street, she seems so small, nearly swallowed alive by shadows. I reach for her. She doesn't seem to see my hand.

"What does it mean?" she asks Altaris, her voice soft. "What does it mean?"

"It means, my darling, that we need to figure out what really happened to Cyrus Triarc. As interestingly demented as you may be, I know for a fact you didn't kill him."

Of course she didn't. I eye her hands, delicate and slim. When provoked, she wants to fight and bite, but she couldn't if she tried. She'd break her bones the second she tried to drive a blade into another creature.

That is what I am for.

"That wasn't the work of jackdaws, either," Altaris remarks. "Oh no. Only a very powerful and very twisted being could be capable of such violence."

"I've ripped out hearts," I say. As if it is hard. As if it isn't easy. As if mortal and mundane limbs don't squish and give to the slightest pressure.

"Ah, but that is the problem. Several creatures enjoy employing similar methods," Altaris murmurs, his head cocked, brows drawn. "I would like to wait until our autopsy confirms it, but I have my suspicions as to the culprit. I have seen such a shoddy little circus before. I thought I had ensured that such a creature could never dare to stalk this city again."

I frown at his words, sensing a mystery cloaked within a riddle.

Niamh, however, gasps. "The fae. You've seen her. You know who she was!"

A strange thing happens. Altaris's eyes remain blank, his expression blank—but it is an act. A lie. He schools his expression into a mask to hide the real emotion flitting underneath. A fae, she said. Had he seen her?

If I had to guess, the answer would be yes. He has. Yet, he doesn't seem inclined to say.

"You should go back to the other home, darling," he says, waving his hand dismissively. "The jackdaws will protect you from harm. They are useful in that aspect at least. Caspian, you will attend the autopsy with me. I suspect we will need the assistance—"

"No," I growl. Then I reach for Niamh and snatch her hand whether she wants me to or not. Let her walk alone?

Leave her fate to demented, magic birds etched into her skin?

Hell no.

"Hell no," I tell him directly. "She comes with me, or I don't go at all."

"You do have a contract to pay off," Altaris remarks, but there is no real authority in his voice. The mentioning of some fae has bothered him. To the point he can no longer hide it. His eyes are distracted, his attention fixated on something far away. In the past, perhaps. "Fine. She may come in if you watch out for her. I'd rather you break the bones of a darling one than have them torn to pieces by jackdaws, but I warn you. If my darlings get upset, you will make her leave. It is for her own protection."

I nod. For her protection, I'll rip his house of broken, insane vamryre apart.

Except for...

Cassiopeia. She is here, lingering somewhere above, still wallowing in pain and lost memories.

"Well now, let's be on our way. Goodness gracious, I just hope Ginni hasn't taken a bite out of that mortal. The last thing I need is to give the boneys another reason to flaunt their high and mighty noses around these parts. Times will be hard enough with not one but *two* investigations taking place on our literal doorstep. Come."

Rather than head in through the main black doors, he leads us to the side of the building instead. There is a metal railing surrounding a staircase that goes down, down to a metal door. It is rigid. No sound from within slips out. After Altaris knocks, a series of sliding, slamming mechanisms indicate various bolts and chains have been unlocked.

When it finally opens, the Pol-spawn stands behind it. He wears a black mask around his nose and heavy rubber gloves that extend up to his arms. A curt nod beckons us inside.

"Ginni, darling?" Altaris calls out.

"No! No! You are not meant to visit during business hours! THAT IS A RULE!"

The insane one's voice echoes through the large chamber, but she is hunched over a massive metal slab in the middle. The mortal beside her doesn't seem to react much to the shrieking. She watches in fascination as the insane one peels a bloodied torso open with a sharpened blade. "You promised me," Ginni mutters without looking up from her "work." "No bothering me during business—"

"I *am* here on business, dear one. I would like to observe and watch. I want to see if a hunch I have will be proven or not."

"Oh." Ginni shrugs, suddenly calm. Then she jabs her knife toward the mortal. "See the serrated edges," she says, her voice as giddy as a child's. "It is nice for slice-slicing when neatness is not required. Such a mess. A mess." She continues to cut into the torso.

Beside her, the mortal nods. "Ah, a unique technique. One would think not to use a serrated edge for excavation, but when time is of the essence I could see how practicality would take precedence over skill."

"Yes, yes!" Ginni nods excitedly. "But when skill is called for, I have nice, sharp scalpel blades. Altaris got them for me special."

"Oh I would love to see them," the mortal coos. It's strange, but she sounds genuinely interested, the way Niamh does when she speaks of her books.

Even mortals can be afflicted with addled minds.

My fae, however, seems uninterested in blood and knives. In the greenish light, she appears pale. Like she might faint. Suddenly, she begins to sway.

Pulling her against me, I hold her tightly.

"It is the smell, I suppose," Altaris remarks from across the room, well beyond the reach of Ginni's jabbing blade. "I forget that mortals can sometimes be squeamish when it comes to these things."

Squeamish. From over the insane vamryre's shoulder, the human is practically cackling with glee. They speak continuously as they cut and slice. It seems they are having fun.

"Take her home," Altaris tells me. "I suppose she's had a long day indeed. I shall visit you tomorrow with the results. Now go—"

"Yes, go now," Ginni snaps. "ENOUGH NOISES!"

I do not need to be told twice. Lifting my fae into my arms, I head for the door.

"It will be faster," I tell her out loud.

Faster.

And it will ensure that I can hold her tight against the darkness and protect her from any and all shadows.

I've failed her twice already.

I won't do so again.

I'll kill anyone who stands in my way.

CHAPTER 22

Niamh

My mind keeps replaying that moment with Cyrus over and over again. I remember writhing in agony. Being pecked at by sharp, nipping knives. Or beaks. Or...

I can't remember.

I do, however, recall him taunting me with knowledge of my mother—the fae he once 'possessed.' The lesson he taught her was something she would never forget. Long-term consequences. A consequence that he hinted would be around my age.

The more I relive those words, the more my heart breaks. I can't help it. I can't stop the darkness from creeping in the doubt from taking root.

I am a hybrid forged in violence. My father may have been a monster, and I might have been the one to kill him.

No, a voice in my head insists. *You did not kill. That we know.*

We. Not Caspian's strong, confident assurances. Not my own egocentric, internal thoughts. No. Something else is in my brain: we. They speak to me in soft, harsh whispers that grow louder the more I seek them out.

You did not kill. The bad thing did. We watched. We hid. Inside of you, we hide.

Inside of me.

Flinching, I twist myself around to see my back. I can't see through my orange dress' material. I strip it off and toss it aside. Then I spin. Arch my hips. I go around in circles, trying so desperately to see.

Caspian watches me from the corner of our private space. He doesn't move. Doesn't react. He doesn't even speak—in our combined mind or out loud.

No mirror is available here, nor do I have enough strength to approach the one in the bathroom. Slumping to my knees, I cup my face in my hands. Sobs rip from my throat. Soon, I won't be able to keep the tears at bay.

From nowhere, a gentle touch sweeps across my shoulder blades, gathering my hand in a fist. That same figure crouches beside me, their body ice-cold, their voice stern but cautious.

"Tell me what you need me to see."

What I need him to?

The tone of his question was soft and soothing. It's not one he's used to using. Still, he tries.

I clear my throat and blink any wayward tears back. "Just tell me...everything," I rasp.

Everything from the time I was in the Citadel. Everything that happened after. I've spent so long ignoring my wounds and pretending my scars didn't exist. So damn long.

All along, I was wearing proof of their lies in plain sight. Once upon a time, I had wings. Someone—the Lord Master perhaps—took them from me. They tore them out.

"I see..." Caspian tucks my hair over my shoulders and fans his fingers along my lower back. His touch sends shivers down my spine. There is something so intimate about it. We've been joined together in more ways than one and yet having him touch me and describe my body in a low, haunting tone feels the most penetrating of all. I can't breathe as he traces a path up and down my spine. As his thumb ghosts over the line of a scar, I suffocate.

"I see beautiful ivory," he says to me. "Lines of ebony and scarlet. Your scars seem fresh, as though they've barely begun to heal." His fingers tremble as he traces the length of one.

It's horrific, what he is describing, yet his voice is awed. He means every word he says.

"I can see marks here," he says next, caressing around one shoulder blade. "Harsh, slicing lines. There are marks, round and identical on either side--"

My wings. Wings that existed once. That grew from me. I was born with them.

It hurts to acknowledge that. It hurts so much I can't hold back the tears any longer. What aches most of all is the way Caspian so delicately avoids those aching, empty spots. He turns his attention higher up, to my shoulder instead.

"These are new," he explains, stroking to indicate a patch of skin from spine to shoulder, extending halfway down my ribcage. "Tattoos, they seem like."

In his thoughts, I catch a glimpse of the marks: two ebony birds with feathery wings that mock the loss of my own.

"Altaris said you could hear them," he wonders out loud. "In your head. Do you?"

"No," I lie to him. I don't know why. I can't explain it. I don't even feel guilty.

To be a hybrid—and now a hybrid, murderer with fake wings made of ink and dark magic in her skull... It is too much. Too many abominations to deal with all at once.

I squeeze my eyes shut.

Caspian relents. Although he knows I am lying, he has not challenged me yet. Rather, he lets his hands fall away, and I feel a chill from the lack of his touch.

"You should get dressed," he says. Then he stands and hands me my dress.

Huddled on the floor, I pull it over my head. I stay there, even as Caspian begins to pace the space around me. He fiddles with a set of knobs in the corner to adjust the heat. He goes to the fridge. Rummages around. Pulls out the remaining slices of bread. Then he places two on a plate and sets it down just within my reach.

I sense him retreat to a far corner after that, watching me still.

It's so strange. In contrast to Day, he isn't prone to outbursts when ignored. The only thing he does is wait. He waits for the mood to pass. He waits for me to stop crying. He waits for me to speak.

He knows I will eventually speak again.

"I need to find her," I say. "The woman in the ledger. Whether she is my mother or not. I need to know what happened. The truth. I can't go back until I do."

Regardless of whether the fae is Night Aurelia or someone else, the implication remains the same: yet another lie they told us will be proven false. This one even Altaris believed. Real fae can and do enter the mortal realm. They can linger.

In addition, they are capable of procreating with creatures other than fae.

This fact complicates matters, provoking a concern I had never considered before. Caspian has been with me unbidden and without protection. No safeguard against what mating is meant for.

What if...

"You can't," he says, helping himself to these thoughts, which include him. "Fae can only breed once they become Night."

How does he know?

He shakes his head before I can ask. "It is how they keep them controlled. Otherwise that creepy fae Day of yours would have sown plenty of spawn."

The hatred he has for him seeps into me. Day's arrogance enraged him. It bothered him how he spoke to me. In fact, Caspian had every intention of killing him when he tried to kiss me.

It was only after he saw my face that he restrained himself long enough for me to have the opportunity to act.

I swallow hard at the realization. Restraint is a new skill for him, one he is still learning to grasp. He made himself try, even then, for me.

In the same way, I will try to embody aspects of him. No more sniveling and weakness for me.

"Day would know," I rasp. "He would know if our mother ever left. What she looks like. Why my wings were stolen. He knew everything."

Sometimes, he hinted at things, daring me to ask. Good, sweet, honest, and obedient Niamh never would.

"There is a bounty on you," Caspian replies. "For his death. You killed him and stole me according to them." He laughs at that.

I sigh. There is something else apart from my scars that I haven't let myself acknowledge. A sinking sensation. A feeling. An omen.

"I do not think he is dead," I say thickly. "I think he is alive. I... I think I can feel him somehow."

A bad taste in my mouth.

A chill constantly running down my spine.

A creaking in the darkness that draws me closer to Caspian without realizing it.

He has known all along. I can tell even before I look up to see him nod just once.

"He lives," he says. "He will come for you. Don't know why he hasn't yet."

Perhaps he'd gotten lost. The mortal realm is so loud and wild and expansive compared to ours. Without Caspian to lead the way, I would have never made it this far. I might still be in those woods, huddling in on myself.

"I should find him," I say. Not for revenge. Not out of hatred. I should find him simply because... He is blood to me. That means something. Even if he saw me as an abominable thing he merely humored.

I will not treat him the same way. I will not leave him behind.

I can't ignore him so completely.

And Caspian seethes. Through clenched teeth, he warns, "The creeping fae. He wanted to hurt you. Still does."

"I know," I admit, facing him. "But if I fear him, he will have control over me always. I won't be able to stop running."

He flinches at that, my Caspian. Too late do I realize that the same words could apply to him and his master.

"Fine." He pulls away from the wall and stalks toward me, his hands flexing in and out of fists. "Find the stupid, creeping fae. Let him hurt you. Use you. Take advantage of you. Would you have me watch?"

"No," I say. "Never. But if I need you to intervene you would trust me to ask you to."

He stops short. Cocks his head. Hisses. Sighs.

"You aggravate me," he snaps. "So many rules when it comes to you. Too much emotion. You must think with a clear mind. Like a predator. You must not be seen as weak!"

"I do not want to be weak," I say after a hard swallow. "I don't. I want to be strong, but in my own way. I do not want to be a monster."

Like Cyrus.

Like Cassius.

A similar argument could be made for the Lord Master as well.

Not Caspian. He thinks I mean to include him on that list. Pain flashes in his eyes, raw and real and unhidden from me. He turns on his heel, aiming to run. Leave. Think.

I lurch forward and take his hand. "Don't. I didn't mean you. Never you. You are... unique. I could never fear you."

He lets my touch linger for a moment. Then he shrugs me off. "It is late. You should sleep."

But it is morning. The sun is so bright he must lower his hood to protect him, even while inside. So bright, that splotches of light paint the space between us as he approaches the far side of the room and begins to lift boxes of old things Altaris left behind. He lifts a heavy crate. Storms upstairs with it. I hear it slam down somewhere on the second floor.

Again, he repeats the same task.

Thud.

Stomp.

Slam!

Eventually, I can't watch him any longer. I move to organize the pile of Daven Wick's things instead. I fold our clothing. I set Altaris's book in some dark corner where I don't have to look at it. On my way back, I step on a bawled bit of parchment.

I stoop for it, intending to put it in the section of the room designated for trash. My fingers twitch. I find myself turning the page over and peeking at what's written inside.

No, drawn.

Created.

A masterpiece.

I stare. Long after Caspian's stomps and slamming crates fades to a distant murmur I can't tear my eyes from this piece of paper, for it is the most beautiful thing in all of existence. Beautiful beyond anything else. More precious than wings or flying.

More precious than being in the mortal realm, even.

Someone captured me. They drew me on a page, in lines of soft gray. I stand on the roof of the Citadel belltower, my face half-turned, my eyes in the distance.

The view point is of someone who would have watched me from below. Watched me and memorized this moment. Internalized it. He hoarded every last detail away in his mind to depict onto paper later.

He drew me in the most perfect work of art.

It heals any ache I felt until now.

It chases all my fears and doubts away.

It has me riveted, heart, mind, and soul.

He drew me perfectly, and in his eyes, I seem beautiful.

Caspian

It is not in a vamryre's nature to feel guilt. Why should we? For we are superior beings, far beyond any mortal. To regret our strength and ruthlessness is to regret our very inception. Our creation.

I am a vamryre, and there is no one on this earth who can question that. Who should be able to make me question. Make me wonder. Make me think...

What if?

What if?

Damn her, for making me wonder what if. What if I could think like her? Forgive. Forget. Move through life sweetly, gazing at every single damn thing with wide-eyed wonder?

I cannot.

Even if I wanted to, I could not. No one should force such things upon me, for if they cannot deal with the mind of a predator, they cannot deal with me.

Yet, her mind is a paradise. I don't want to leave it so soon. Not yet. I cling to her thoughts, even now.

Damn her.

I seethe in frustration and irritation, yet she makes me cling to her. Prod her mind state. Test that pretty brain for any wayward thoughts. Any crack or crevice I may slip inside of.

I want to be in more than just her skin. I want to burrow into that tiny soul. I want her to feel me resonate in her from the inside out. I want to make her acknowledge my darkness. Internalize it.

Lo and behold, I am here to stay.

But she has no right to do the same to me. I am the one who saw her that day, flitting about her in her little tower. I decided to hunt her. Chase her. Claim her.

Me. She should belong only to me.

Yet, she is already staking her claim on bits of me that even Cassius never touched. I can feel her there, scratching and clawing at my insides. Warping me around her. Changing me to suit her needs.

There's a sick, twisted part of me that wants to be perfect for her. It covets the way she stares at me when in awe. When I surprise her in an unexpected way. Instead of seeing a monster in me, she sees a savior.

Yet, a monster is all I am.

All I will be.

The alternative would be to give in to Cassius's wishes for me. To stop resisting. Stop fighting. Be owned. Could I let her own me?

No.

Never.

I won't.

Even so, I can feel her grasping fingers. I can feel her marking me, nonetheless. I can't shake her grip as easily as I could Cassius.

I don't hate her in the same way.

Damn her.

Damn.

I want to shout at her. Seethe. Make her cower and feel shame. Something that proves she hasn't won. I am not a pet on her leash, she is mine.

I think about pinning her there, against the brick wall. Reminding her who and what I am.

I am Caspian, toy of Cassius. Monster. Murderer. Sadist.

I think about it.

I linger among boxes and crates instead. I move them all upstairs and out of the way. I stomp. Storm. I rage in silence.

I try to ignore her.

She hasn't come for me. The itch for me isn't as volatile as my itch for her. I crave to see her face. To see if I hurt her with my actions. If I did...

I should smile.

Laugh.

No. A part of me wants to stroke her hair instead.

So I stomp. Lift. Toss. Lift. Toss. Throw. A crate launches from my grip and slams into the wall, shattering to pieces. Objects fall out. More worthless crap and junk that Altaris has kept, hidden away to surround his empty mind with. I turn, aiming to leave them there.

A glimmer catches my eye. It is blue and round with a faint, weak glow. It is warm when I touch it. A slight vibration resonates from it into my palm. As though it is alive. Pulsating.

Then I remember: I've seen one before. Many, in fact, embedded in the wall of the underground tunnel.

A fae stone, Niamh called them. Magic to her. Fae magic. She would be shocked to see one here. Those black eyes might fall out of her skull. She would be happy, oh so happy. She would be pleased with me.

But I don't want nor need her pleasure. I need a reminder of what I am. What I stand to lose if I fail in my task and forget my true nature. Cassius will come crawling to me. He will seek to devour me.

I cannot become lost in a fae's black, doe eyes. I must remember who and what I am.

Caspian. A monster: nothing more, nothing less.

Monsters do not gripe and wallow. They do not crave happy, hopeful fae eyes.

I take the fae stone in my grasp and slip it into my pocket.

I will not tell her that I found it ever.

This bit of knowledge, I will hoard for myself alone.

Though, why Altaris had it?

That is a question for another time.

CHAPTER 24

Niamh

Someone knocks on the door just after sunset. Only then does Caspian come down from the upper levels of the warehouse. I've been sitting here this whole time, waiting. Thinking. Staring at this portrait of me and trying to find myself in this familiar, unfamiliar being.

The similarities to the reflection I've glimpsed in the mirror are many.

Yet so are the differences. I don't recall smiling like this, so peaceful. Serene. My hair isn't so thick it floats around me like a cloud. My skin doesn't gleam, visible even in ruddy shading and scratching lines.

I wish...

I wish I saw myself like this. Back then. If I had...

No one could have told me I was an ugly, abominable thing. I wouldn't have believed them. No one could have told me those lies and made me believe them.

This image, this beautiful, flawless being, would have been in my head. I could think of her and I would know. I am Niamh, and someone finds me beautiful. Ethereal. As majestic as any fae could ever be.

Yet, though I knew Caspian drew this, it seems his opinion of me has changed. He is cold when he returns downstairs. His gaze is ice, his mind closed off and distant. He barely even looks at me. Doesn't notice the page I have in my grasp. Doesn't seem to care as I slip it into a pocket in the skirt of my dress and watch him march toward the door.

He throws it open.

Behind it, Altaris blinks. He is different today. Something has unsettled him, and on him, unease expresses as pure irritation. His hair sticks out at odd angles. His suit jacket is slightly askew, and his green eyes blaze as though he hasn't slept in eons.

Which makes sense. Vamryre don't sleep.

"I cannot stay long," he warns before strolling inside, his hand tugging at his usually crisp, purple collar. Today, his clothing is a muted shade, nearly black. There are no polished, crisp lines. Even his shoes seem wrinkled and disorderly. "Scythe is on his way. You two must make yourselves useful and track down that blasted little mundane, half-fae. She has that ledger, and that, I believe, will solve at least one part of this mystery."

"Explain," Caspian snaps.

Altaris flinches at his tone. "You seem testy. I suppose all is not bliss during your little lover's honeymoon." His eyes dart to me, more narrowed than ever. "Try not to kill each other now. I already have my hands tied cleaning up your goddamn immigration messes, not to mention the impending court appearance, and murder charges. In any case, if you did kill that wretched piece of dung, I will knock a million arun off your bill. That, my darlings, was not a mundane."

Cyrus.

Cyrus the monster who implied that he violated a fae.

Of course, he was not mundane or mortal.

He was something far worse.

"That was a creature I had castrated myself long ago. Using a proxy since the lack of a heart. His modus operandi was the same, however. Lure fae creatures into his circus. Sell them to the highest bidder. At least, that is the front he maintained. The truth is worse. We must find this half-fae and see what she knows."

"Minchae," I say, picturing her. Was she too harmed by this creature? Did she know the truth?

"Scythe is tracking this creature," Altaris continues. "Ah, there he is now. Go with him. Find the fae being and bring her back. Then allow me alone to question her. Understood?"

Caspian says nothing. He draws his hood low despite the nightfall and leaves, heading toward a distant figure whose blue hair blazes against the dark sky. Scythe.

"Trouble in paradise," Altaris mutters as I follow. "It was bound to happen sooner or later. Good." He looks me dead in the eye, his expression cold. "You do not deserve him."

He blows past me into the warehouse—the space he provided—and slams the door in his wake. What is he doing in there? I do not know.

Caspian's mood, coupled with this, makes one thing clear.

I don't belong here.

And there is nothing, or no one—not even a neglected, dusty space or a conflicted vamryre—that I can call my own.

CHAPTER 25

Caspian

Anger and rage. I dwell among those emotions and embody them the most. Not softness. Not fleeting niceness, and soft, lingering glances. Not savoring kisses and gentle caresses.

I require none of those things.

I can ignore them.

Ignore her.

Focus on what I do best: enjoy the hunt.

The Pol-spawn, silent and strange, suits one purpose best of all. He, too, enjoys the hunt. He is skilled at it, tracking this mortal mundane with a skill honed over vast centuries. Eons. Pol was rumored to let her toys loose on the population in droves. Killing for them was a sport, not a game. The winner would be praised by her, the loser torn to pieces.

A cruel mistress, but she trained her spawn well. They do not question. Do not hesitate.

They would not see a fae and deign to play with her rather than kill her.

Even now, her thoughts distract me. As does her body. Her scent. My hand twitches at my side, itching to grab her. Hold her close and tight. My thoughts spin, aching to worm their way into hers. See her hurt and pain. Relish in it.

Or not.

Damn her.

There isn't time for her. As we near a busy street blocks from Altaris's dwelling, I notice the Pol-spawn stiffen. He raises his head, nostrils twitching as if scent alone is how he tracks this mundane.

But it isn't.

The Poppy one has a skill for knowledge. The Ginni one is insane enough to pick apart bodies and know how. This one's gift is for tracking. Pinning down a piece of prey with surgical precision.

He glances at me and nods toward a building up ahead. I follow his gaze. Hiss.

Not this place. That wretched motel. The Bleeding Hearts.

Fortunately, it's not where we're led by the Pol-spawn, but to a smaller building next to it. It looks like a laundromat— where mortals wash their filthy clothing in large, square machines.

Or so it appears to the uneducated mundane. There is a secret here. A flickering around the edges of the boring store facade. As the Pol-spawn approaches, the illusion blinks and gives way.

There is another establishment here, hidden behind the fake. Not a laundromat, but something else. A place for dark and seedy mundane. A place that Cassius would never let me wander unattended.

There are too many distractions in this place: once you slip inside the glass doors and into the real world beyond. Mortals must not be able to see it: a yawning space at the back of the room, behind a row of machines. Step behind them and enter a world of lights and brick and wood.

A city within a city.

A black market for mundane magic. Cassius knew of it. For a dark, hidden reason he knew of it and tucked the secret into my brain. Maybe I have been here once, but I don't remember.

Or...

Perhaps it was before him?

I don't remember.

In any case, I navigate these narrow paths, impatient and restless. As the Pol-spawn takes the lead, I stay within his shadow. My attention is drawn to the thin, fragile fae lurking behind us both.

I try to ignore her, but others are watching. Their eyes are drawn to her as if she is a wayward doe in a den of predators, bleeding. Fresh. An easy kill.

I am angry with her, unwilling to be owned.

But...

I am the only one who owns *her*. Stopping short, I let her catch up. The Pol-spawn continues, too intent on his tracking to notice that we do not follow. Still, when she nears I forget everything. Altaris's request. My purpose. My sole, fucking reason for being.

I look at her, and nothing else makes sense in the face of her pain. I've hurt her—I'm hurting her still. Good, a part of me sings, gleeful. Let her hate me. Let her remember. I am a monster. A monster. A...

I reach out my hand. Her eyes find it, but she fidgets with the skirt of her orange dress rather than take it. That dress makes her seem like a flame. A burst of starlight in the dark. These seedy mundane see her and they can't take their eyes away from this being. This unnatural creature in their midst.

It's the pain in her eyes. Pain I put there.

It makes her far more enticing to those with evil in their hearts.

"Come," I tell her, extending my hand again.

Nodding, she stares past me, still moving toward the Pol-spawn. I watch her go, seething. Restless.

I should be angry with her, but she's angry with me. My eyes roam along that slender frame, tracing every inch. I could break her so easily. Chase her down. Rip her limb from limb.

Dangle her disembodied hand in mine if she will not offer it willingly.

Within seconds, I gain on her. One of those pale hands catches my eye.

I don't move. Something won't let me, and I glower, teeth clenched, a growl caught in my throat.

She is angry with me.

Hurt and angry.

Were she Cassius I would savor the emotion with glee. Yes. Hate me. Wretched, miserable Cassius.

"I am sorry," I tell her instead. "I do not want to change who I am. You are changing me."

A chill shoots through her. She hugs herself, still walking. Limping. Wading through quicksand as if every step hurts.

I don't understand.

Then I remembered what Altaris taunts her with. The same words they hissed at her in the other realm. Evil. Corrupting everything she touches. Unworthy.

The words to fix this don't come to me. I am at a loss. Violence is my specialty, not this.

So, I watch her and follow. I keep my head low and lose sight of everything else. The winding alleyways. The sellers hawking illegal goods.

The Pol-spawn lurking nearby.

I watch her, my wayward little fae. I imagine leaving her again. Letting her get picked off by another dark, demented thing.

I wince. The thought hurts. Stings. Irritates.

I try again. "Niamh—"

"That's her." Her gaze wanders across the haphazard arrangement of stalls and mundane items. An unknown pale woman emerges from the shadows, wearing a green jacket with its hood drawn low. She is not vamryre, and it isn't the light she shields herself from.

Niamh surges toward her, nimble and quick. It takes effort to keep up with her, weaving around the bodies she easily slips past. Effort to draw level with her. Effort still to keep from grasping the hand she reaches out. "Minchae!"

The woman looks up with different-colored eyes, one green and one blue. She sees Niamh. Her face pales even more. She tries to run.

From the shadows, the Pol-spawn descends, capturing her arm in a firm grip.

"Let go of me!" She swings at him. Then shouts. "Help me! Help! This sick fucker is after me!"

The Pol-spawn blinks as a man in black leather shouts and approaches. He must be a boney, and there seems to be no love lost between them and Altaris's spawn.

He loosens his grip. The woman flees.

"Minchae, wait!" Niamh takes off and I follow. It should be easy, but she is fast. How the fuck is she so fast?

I run harder. Faster. She manages to stay just beyond my grasp until she suddenly stops.

"Something is wrong," I hear her say. "Look."

The mundane is slowing. She trips, sinking to her knees and doesn't get up again. Approaching her now is child's play. Still, she frees something from her pocket and waves it.

"Stay the hell away from me! Stay! ...Niamh?"

She looks at my fae, her eyes clouded with pain. Feverish. A damp sweat cloaks her forehead, gluing down the black strands.

"Stay back," I warn Niamh.

She doesn't listen. She crouches low before the woman and extends her hand. "What happened? Are you okay?"

"Am I okay?" The woman scoffs. "You were dead! I watched it! I watched him kill you and..." She breaks off, her shoulders heaving beneath wracking sobs. "It bit me and I'm dying. I can't find a healer. I'm dying. Dying."

Niamh murmurs something, but I move past her and snatch the woman by the sleeve of her coat. I wrench it up.

I see the proof of something I sensed from the second I saw her. The stench of sickness. The pallor of death.

"She's been bitten," I say, eyeing the vicious wound marring the flesh of her wrist. "By a lunaria."

CHAPTER 26

Niamh

It isn't fair. There are so many things I want. Things I need. Requirements I want to demand from others. Things I deserve.

But patience is an overarching lesson, more persistent than even the honesty I was taught to maintain while in the Citadel. I am constantly reminded of it, no matter where I am or what I need. When entering the mortal realm. When trusting Caspian. When it comes to finding the truth of my mother.

I must wait and wait and linger. I must stand aside patiently and bite my tongue.

But no more. I am so very tired of waiting.

No more!

I want to scream and storm and rant. I want to be like Caspian and enforce my will upon the world, no matter what it asks of me.

I see him now, leaning against the wall of our space. Our once quiet space, now invaded by many bodies and clashing voices. They struggle to save Minchae who has been bitten by a creature I have never seen in person. Yet another forbidden being from my old life. A lunaria.

A creature who can phase by moonlight into any beast which takes their fancy. Their bite is harmless—unless they prime their fangs with poison. Unless they aim to kill.

Unless they hunt mundane with the hopes of tracking them later.

All of this is explained by Altaris who is speaking to Colleen. With her blonde hair in a coiled bun and a pink sweater with the sleeves rolled up, she leans over Minchae who lays spread over the floor. Her face is a mask of concentration, her hands outstretched, fingers splayed. She is so intent on utilizing her magic, she barely seems to notice anything else.

Unlike me, she is useful. Her odd traits are her advantage. Her magic is powerful, and adept at healing. But in this instance, she struggles. Sweat drips down her brow and she mutters to herself under her breath.

While Altaris watches, his normally closed expression becomes readable the first time. He is worried. So very worried, but not for Minchae, or me, or even Caspian. His concern is for Colleen. There is a protectiveness in how he speaks to her, coaxing her onward.

"That is it, my darling," he says. "Pace yourself. If you die, your father will never forgive me, and we both know what a raging drunk he can be."

Despite the fact that Colleen does not speak, she listens intently. It comforts her in some small way to hear his voice. Like a teacher would for a student, he gives her the strength to keep going. The scene feels too intimate to watch.

A parent might encourage a child in this way. I wouldn't know. I will never know.

I turn and move blindly in search of fresh air. Silence is what I need. I can't think. Not until I'm standing out on a patch of concrete, surrounded by brick and creeping, crawling weeds. I suck in a breath. Release it slowly.

I can barely hear the footsteps behind me, as silent as the wind.

"Come," he says, my Caspian. "I want... I want to show you something."

My stomach churns. When I turn to face him, I can't see his expression. Those red eyes blaze through the shadows but seem more unreadable than the sky up above.

For the first time since coming here, I am wary of him. My heart aches. If he pushes away, I don't know what may happen. I just might break.

"Please."

The sound of his voice entices me toward him without me having made a conscious decision to move. He leads me back inside, past the chaos on the downstairs floor. Up. Up. Up. Past the second floor and onto a third. Here there is just a small landing and a rusted door leading out.

Into the open air where the sky looms above and the ground lurks down below.

"It isn't flying," he murmurs against my ear. "But close enough. For now."

Nodding in agreement, I am stunned to see the city spread before me, a barrage of lights and sounds. It isn't flying, yet...

As long as he's behind me, it might as well be. Despite having been in this realm a few days, he points out things I hadn't even noticed. A blinking, moving star in the sky—a plane. Drifting spotlights. A photo like the one I saw of Minchae but depicting a crowd of people in beautiful clothing. A billboard, he says.

It's the quiet peace that creeps back in between us that I most appreciate. Something happened before. Something that drove and drifted us apart.

Someday it will need to be addressed.

For now, I can breathe, think, and try to remember what it is like to feel this fragile, fleeting peace. Only with him can I ever achieve it.

I'd be a fool to let it go without a fight. Without demanding that he face me. Unlike Day, his anger and moods shouldn't cow me. I shouldn't be afraid to ask him...

"Why?" I say, my voice rasping. "What happened?"

"You called me a monster," he replies, but there is more to it than that. He hesitates. Takes his time to turn and twist his words over in his mind. Then he sighs. "I am a monster. I need to be a monster. To survive him, I had to become one."

In a way, I understand him. At the same time, I don't.

"I never wanted you to change," I insist. "Never. Not once. But I need to be... I can't be like you. A monster is what *they* want me to be—" The Lord Master, Altaris, everyone. "I refuse to do so. I will not be what they tell me I am."

I simply want to be Niamh. Someone else, apart from the frightened, sheltered being I was in the Citadel.

"I like you as Niamh," Caspian admits. "But people will use your kindness against you. Exploit it. Wield it as a weapon."

Like Minchae wanted to.

Like Day did.

Like Cyrus.

Certainly, he has a point.

"I still want to find my own weapon," I tell him, reaching back.

His hand instantly finds mine. Our fingers interlock. As time passes, that delicate peace grows stronger. I enjoy basking in his protection, but this feels better. Speaking on equal terms. Telling him my fears and hearing him answer back. Yet another, new form of intimacy.

Which feels more intrusive to me?

Having him in my body.

On my skin.

Or in my head.

In my soul.

I feel a shiver run through me as he steps closer. His chill is more comforting than any heat. Any fire. Any new thrill the mortal world could offer me.

Except...

For one thing.

"I found this," I say, reaching into my pocket. I still gasp in awe when I unfold the drawing. In faded light and glimmering shadow, it's even more beautiful. An image created for me.

One that he created.

"It's beautiful," I say, aware of him leaning over my shoulder, staring intently. "So beautiful. Thank you."

He says nothing, but lets the silence linger. He does not know how to react to this: creating something beautiful and watching someone enjoy it. It causes a strain in him—like an old muscle being stretched taut, long after it's atrophied with disuse.

It is a greater gift than any I ever deserved.

Great enough to sacrifice a piece of myself in return.

"When you go to kill Cassius... I will come with you."

"No," he says, but we both know he doesn't mean it. He is relieved, so relieved. Cassius can't crawl inside his skull if I am there, and I will be.

"I promise you, I will be."

"There is something I found," he says next, but his tone is wrong. Too serious for this bright happy moment. Our reunion of souls and minds. There is something weighing on his. Something heavy, and dark that threatens to usher in a wave of turmoil.

Something that will usher in far too many questions.

But this is a game that I started. One of honesty and sharing.

I gave to him.

So, he will give to me. A small blue stone that glows brilliantly when clasped in his fist.

A fae stone, so small and lonely all the way out here.

But why?

Who brought it here?

My heart flutters. "It was a necklace," I say thickly, fingering the delicate chain attached to it. "Someone wore it."

A young fae, perhaps, who stole a piece of fae magic to enter the mortal realm. She found a way to skirt the rule Altaris warned me about.

She truly was here.

Yet she left her only way out behind.

CHAPTER 27

Caspian

ltaris may want his toy back. He may regret my giving away such a valuable tool to one he despises. Don't care. As I see the look on her face, once she has that stone in her hands, I don't give a damn about anything the vamryre could do to me.

Hope is a painful thing when it dwells into those black eyes. She seems to fear it, that volatile emotion. It makes her feel greedy and reckless, all those naughty things the fae would tell her not to indulge in.

But I like her this way. I like seeing her gaze glow with interest, and I love hearing bits of knowledge churn through her fathomless mind. She takes the stone and tucks it gingerly into her pocket, along with that drawing I'd forgotten about. The one of her. She treats both with the same reverent curiosity.

And suddenly, I am the one struck dumb with awe.

"You will find her," I say. "The Aurelia. I will help you."

She nods, and a shy smile shapes those lips. It's too tempting up here in this dark, quiet space. I can't resist. I grab her wrist, pull her into me and press that mouth to mine.

A kiss is a fleeting thing. A stupid, customary act the mortals liked to be placated with. A rare glimpse of intimacy that Cassius craved. He loved to be kissed by me.

With her, there is no gloating obsession. There is savoring and vital contact. There is no choice but to kiss her harder in return. To grip her tighter as she relents to the embrace.

I kiss her and I forget myself. Sometimes, it's a fucking gift to forget. I could drown in her if I wanted to. Never to resurface.

But unlike me, she needs to breathe. I pull back, let her suck in air. She sways on her feet, still dangerously close to the roof's edge.

I grab her hand and pull her back inside.

The noise has died down somewhat—but it seems the mundane creature hasn't. She gasps for air, writhing on a pile of blankets in the corner. The blonde woman, Colleen, crouches over her, holding her hand. Altaris stands near the opposite corner. He is surrounded by two newcomers who must have arrived in our absence.

One of them I recognize as Daven Wick. The other is a woman. Her scent immediately identifies her. Awful. Musk. *Lunaria.*

"Is this the whelp that caused the bite?" I wonder aloud.

Altaris winces.

The woman scoffs, her eyes narrowed. "Watch your fucking mouth, vamp. In that pretty realm of yours, your kind do as they please. Here, your bigotry isn't tolerated. You so much as think about calling me whelp or dog or whatever fucking terms you pricks use, and I'll give you a bite of my own—"

"Now, now, Sylvie, dear," Altaris interjects—but verbally and physically. Standing between us, he raises both hands in a placating gesture. "There is no need for that. You two are on the same side. In fact, I insist you two work together."

"Cut the shit, Altaris," the whelp snaps. With her head cocked, she steps toward him. Her display might have been intimidating if she weren't half his size. It is odd to see a lunarian with such a petite structure.

Strong and robust bodies make it easy for them to morph into their beast forms. In this case, it appears that the only form she could master is that of a bird. Or a rat.

Her dark hair is streaked with gold, her eyes a flashing brown.

Lunaria were confined to the main city and rural outposts in the other realm. Cassius didn't let me mingle with them too much. Their blood was far too gamey for his tastes, and their manners were lacking. In every way, he preferred mortals. The only complementary trait he would ever extend to a wolf whelp might be admiration for their loyalty.

They were known to be willing to die for their clan leaders. To take their own lives if they had to.

Yet, this one stands alone without the safety of a pack behind her. She has no other litter mates mingled with her scent. She is solitary.

An easy mark.

"Now, Caspian, play nice," Altaris warns in his authoritative tone. "We need to find that ledger. The little fae-spawn does not have it. We must move quickly, my dears. Especially if you are sure about who made that bite—" He looks at the whelp, Sylvie.

She nods. "That's Black Fang poison," she admits. "I'd know it anywhere, but it's stronger than what we used. More potent—" She sniffs and shudders. "I can smell it from over here."

"Yes, it seems to have been augmented with some kind of enhancing property," Daven Wick remarks, stroking his chin. "I can't think of what could have been added to make it lethal. An extract of some kind. A venom."

"Or blood," Altaris remarks, his eyes on my fae. "Fae blood mixed with something else. Something unnatural."

"Killing wasn't our style," Sylvie says, but her expression is strained, her gaze distant. "At least not then."

"In any case, we need that ledger—"

"She's awake!" says the blonde, her voice rasping.

Her father approaches her in an instant. Altaris beats him there, bending low to place his hand on the blonde's shoulder.

"Can she speak, my darling?" he asks.

"I don't know." Colleen sighs, her brows knitted, brow drenched with sweat. "She's weak. I don't know how much longer I can keep her conscious though—"

"Don't you worry yourself about that," Altaris says with a wave of his hand. "Just get her to speak. Where did she put the ledger."

In a gentle tone, the woman asks... I don't care. The topic of this conversation does not interest me. It is not clear to me why I am even approaching them, coming close enough to observe the mundane's tormented face. Then I notice Niamh standing before me, still clasping my hand. She's the one who led me to this corner.

Without question, I followed.

"...sold it," the mundane says, her eyes fluttering, limbs thrashing. "Sold it to a grifter. Don't know who."

"Well, that is unfortunate," Altaris snaps. "Ask her if—"

"Take it easy, Col." Daven Wick appears on the other side of the blonde, his voice low and soothing. "Don't overdo it. Pull back if you need to. It's okay."

"A little longer, my darling," Altaris insists. "We need to know if—"

"Don't you see she's exhausted! You just keep pushing her. You don't give a damn, do you? Colleen, baby, if it's too much, you can let go."

"Do not," Altaris snaps. Despite his level tone, his gaze is cold and unmistakably authoritative. His grip on the blonde one tightens until she visibly winces, not that he notices. He is greedily fixated on his goal.

Even though she is weakening. Her veins are bulging. Quickly, she is tiring.

Yet the vamryer is not totally selfish. He is plotting and scheming even now. He has an aim in mind. What is it?

"You..." The dying mundane spies my fae, her gaze clear for once. "I... I looked. Name... Aur"

Niamh sucks in a breath. She's on her knees in an instant, leaning in close. "Aurelia?"

The mundane nods. Then shakes her head. She is too delirious to make sense. "Parna... Aurelia... Parna. Aurelia."

"Altaris!" Daven Wick is on his feet, his hands clenched, eyes blazing. "Enough is enough."

The vamryre doesn't even look up at him. "No," he insists. "Keep going, my dear one. Just a little longer..."

"I... I can't." The blonde one trembles, her eyelids fluttering. "I..."

"Colleen, baby, just let go!"

"Not yet," Altaris says, louder than them both. "Caspian, darling, could you get the door?"

I raise an eyebrow, but move forward to obey. Upon opening the door, yet another figure rushes in, racing past me. She has a bag at her hip and rummages around, withdrawing a vial of liquid in one hand. A syringe in the other.

"I'm here!" she rasps in between panting breaths. "I'm so sorry I'm late. I couldn't find—"

"Finally. Just administer the sedative, please," Altaris says, cutting over the male mortal before he can say a word otherwise.

The mortal nods and Niamh steps aside so she can take her place. She injects the mundane with the syringe.

The girl shudders. Stills. Yet, she is not dead.

"Good. Now you may relax, my darling." Altaris strokes the blonde one's arm, and she nearly collapses into his arms. "There, there. You did well."

"I need some fucking air." Daven storms off, radiating anger.

The blonde is too exhausted to notice. She slumps against Altaris as the vamryer gently helps her to her feet. "I'll take you back to the house, darling. You can get some rest there, hmm? Sylvie, I will trust you to stay here. Get well acquainted with my new guests. Keep Daven away from any bottles. I shall return."

As he nears the door, blonde in tow, the mortal doctor calls out, "I will stay and monitor her, if that's okay?"

"Of course, darling," Altaris replies before leading the blonde outside. "Caspian should be a bit more well-mannered than dear Ginni. Try not to attack each other while I am gone."

"Fucking vamp," the lunaria hisses. Crossing her arms, she paces. As she turns her attention to Niamh, she pauses. While her gaze lingers, it is not in an accusatory or fearful way, as those in the other realm would view her. She notes her eyes. That sloping mouth. Her delicate limbs swathed in orange fabric.

Her stare irritates me.

"I'm Sylvie, by the way," she says, extending her hand. "Altaris didn't tell me your name. He can be thoughtless like that. You certainly aren't from around here, that much I know."

My fae takes her hand and forces a faint smile. "I am Niamh," she says. "This is Caspian—"

"And I'm Aleska Fraterani," the mortal on the floor explains with a nervous laugh. "Medical examiner. I... I'll just try to get her stabilized. Don't mind me!"

"I've heard about you." The lunaria whelp crosses her arms and inclines her head. I noticed she was far more interested in the mortal than she was in my fae. Her eyes linger over her face, especially. "The mortal morgue-y. How in the hell did you stumble upon the mundane world in the first place?"

Shrugging, the mortal smiles widely. "I'm not sure, but I find this all very interesting. I'll try to be as unobtrusive as possible, but I would like to stay and observe her overnight, if possible?"

Niamh nods. "Of course."

"Poor thing." The mortal takes the mundane's hand and strokes the pale fingers. "Do you know her name?"

"Minchae," Niamh says.

The one who wanted to feed her to jackdaws. I eye the creature, lying in our space, on our dusty, musty blankets. She writhes in agony. Without an antidote, she will die soon.

Everyone in this room knows it but Niamh. Hope blazes in her eyes, revealing her innocence. In this case, her hope stings rather than entices. It will be broken.

Just as she is used to her hopes always being broken.

"I'll try to do the best I can to keep her stabilized," the mortal explains. "When Altaris called me, I wasn't even sure this would work. We've seen an increase in bites like this just over the span of the last few days. It's been a nightmare."

"Is this the work of you and your pack, whelp?" I ask of the lunarian.

She hisses and curls her hands into fists. "Fuck off, vampire. I'm sure your kind wouldn't be above masquerading as a lun to get your kicks. If you were smart enough to make it convincing."

"You are lunarian?" The mortal's eyes widen. "Oh my, I have so many questions. I've barely been out of boney headquarters, and I've met a vamryer and a grimoirer but never a—"

"I ain't really in the mood to star in my own personal freakshow right now," the whelp replies, turning on her heel.

"Altaris wanted me to confirm the bite in person. I have. Call me when he gets back. I have shit to do."

She storms out, slamming the door behind her.

"Well," the mortal swallows. "I'll just make myself comfortable over here. Sorry to intrude."

Intrude. She has.

There is more for Niamh and me to discuss. A deadline to our mutual goal. Kill Cassius. Find the Aurelia. We could go tonight...

I look at her. I meet her gaze with every intention of taking her there, back through the portal. We will face our demons together.

But not tonight. I see her expression, bathed in the glow of the flickering lights above. Far too innocent for pain and fear. Not tonight. I take her hand and pull her with me up the stairs, out into the night. There, under the stars, I pull her close. We settle into a corner against the wall of the doorway, and I know she will easily fall asleep here.

Right where I can protect her from the many forces drawing nearer.

CHAPTER 28

Niamh

Minchae does not die by the time morning comes. There is the expectation, heavy in the air, that she will. Caspian seems to think so. Contrary to his violent nature, it is an impending demise that unsettles him. I can guess why. With his senses, he can hear the victim's ragged breathing. Listen to their heart struggle to beat. He can taste the inevitable decay on the air, like a rainstorm about the fall.

I do not know how I feel. How I am meant to feel.

There is something else in the air that threatens to distract me from this horrific situation. A feeling. A suspicion. A niggling tingle at the back of my mind.

I am forgetting something. Something important, but what?

After checking on Minchae and Aleska, I return to the roof and pace while Caspian watches. He will know when Altaris arrives or if anything changes. That is why I tune the rest of the world out. Why I don't feel guilty for sinking inside my skull and blinding myself to everything.

Everything but the voices in my head I've been desperate to ignore until now.

They chatter, there in a corner of my mind only I can reach. Like living beings, they speak amongst themselves in hushed whispers that I must overhear.

"...our mistress isn't ready. We mustn't make noise until then. Mustn't say—"

The thoughts don't belong to Caspian. They are far more alien than even his are. Distorted and high-pitched. Unnatural. Yet, there are two distinct tones. One is soft and lilting, the other deep and rasping.

"Hush. She has noticed your chittering. Hush."

The voices go quiet while I stare at the city awakening around me and try to breathe. Monster, Altaris called me. Hybrid. Abominable.

Perhaps another term should be added to that list. Insane. I'm hearing voices. Even among the fae, it is not a promising sign.

I shift closer to the edge of the roof, hiding my face from Caspian. Despite my best efforts, I can't hide my nerves from him. My thoughts.

I can sense his interest stirring. His steps advance on me, purposefully noisy.

"What is wrong?" he asks.

"Nothing," I say quickly, wrapping my arms around my front. "I am cold, is all."

"Cold." He repeats it like a foreign term. Then he inclines his head toward the door. "Altaris has returned. Come."

"Coming," I say. Then I listen to him open the door and step inside. Hesitate. "I am coming," I insist.

So, go.

He does, but I don't know if his absence provides the peace I thought it would. It is easier to think. Easier to prod those lingering, hazy thoughts, and question what they mean.

Something happened back at the circus. Someone attacked Minchae. Who?

Who?

"We know..." The two strange voices reply in unison, their voices faint, beyond Caspian's notice. He has gone downstairs to greet Altaris. His unease ignites our connection like a candle wick caught aflame. Something is wrong.

And yet...

I can't move. I can't tear my gaze away from the view below and I can't stop myself from asking, of those disembodied voices.

"Who?"

They reply in a whisper that triggers a rushing of blood through my eardrums. A whisper that makes the entire world fall away. But this sudden drop isn't the thrilling excitement I felt while 'flying.'

It is terrifying, as though—for a horrific moment—I cease being Niamh. I cease being weak and meek and malleable.

I become something unknowable and terrifying.

A stranger within my own skin.

I stumble back and catch myself against the door to the warehouse, rattling it loudly. From down below, Caspian hears. He is worried, racing back upstairs. I can't let him know. Can't let him hear the word echoing around and around in my mind.

I wrench the door open and stagger inside. The heat hits me like an invisible wall, searing over my chilled skin. Then Caspian's icy hand clamps over my wrist, trapping me between two extremes.

"What is wrong." He isn't asking this time. He tugs me inside and slams the door behind us both. Then he pulls me down a flight of stairs and into a room on the second floor. It is long and narrow. One large window at the far end lets in silvery light—that gray dawn that creeps in before the sun fully rises.

It makes my skin look sallow, and it makes my Caspian glow. Like marble. He guides me closer, his palm against my chin. "Tell me." He growls the words.

I can't answer him. The words won't come. I can't find the right ones. So, I say nothing.

I close my eyes and relent to his touch.

I close my eyes and try to forget the answer to a question I should have never asked.

"I'm fine!" I pull away from him and head downstairs. I practically run, with him easily keeping pace behind me. His fingers lash at mine again, but I don't have the strength to return the gesture.

As I trip down the last few steps, I spy Altaris standing in the middle of the main room, his back to me, his voice mid-sentence. "And then we shall pay an old friend a visit—Ah!" He turns his head and looks me up and down. There is a coldness in his gaze that wasn't there the other day.

Almost as if...

"He knows," the voices whisper. "He has confirmed it. His own means. Ancient methods."

The same lie they told me. A lie, it has to be.

"Not a lie," they counter. "We saw for ourselves. The truth. Who attacked the fae-blooded one. Who killed the vamryre. We saw—"

"It seems our darling one is distracted this morning," Altaris snaps. "Caspian, perhaps you can fill her in when time isn't of the essence and lives aren't on the line. I shall be waiting outside."

He storms to the door. For the first time I realize that his clothing isn't a bright shade of purple. It is a deep, dark black that sets off his alabaster skin. He is more vamryre than ever. Dangerous. All-knowing.

A threat to me.

"I'll stay here." I'd forgotten the mortal woman, Aleska. She sits beside Minchae, holding her hand. From the dark shadows beneath her eyes, I can tell she hasn't slept. Yet she smiles, her eyes bright. "Don't worry about me. Altaris said he'll send over some of my things. How thoughtful."

"He wants us to come with him," Caspian explains. "To a someone who can find the ledger."

A ledger containing secrets. Supposedly of my mother's identity. Supposedly not.

Suddenly, I am not as eager to find those answers as I was before.

Answers can be more dangerous than the mysteries they resolve.

Such as the one provided to me by imaginary voices whispered inside my skull.

Who did all of those horrible things?

You did, they replied.

You.

You.

You.

CHAPTER 29

Caspian

Altaris is a liar. He plies his trade, peddling sin and lies. Creating falsehoods. In another life, I might have deemed him evil. A creature devoid of empathy or respect.

But I know differently. Deep down, he exudes pity and guilt. They both compose his true nature. The true beast lurking beneath the mask. They are his real weapons—what makes him the most dangerous monster in this shitty realm.

For he knows answers to the questions few would seek an answer to. He is desperate—or foolish enough—to try and change them. He alone has the will to challenge fate.

But he is not naive like Niamh. He knows what awaits him at the end of every attempt. Defeat. Yet, he persists.

And in me, he seems some quest yet unfulfilled. I can feel it. I can sense his fingerprints on some untouched part of my soul. The one that recognized those paintings. The one who signed those old contracts. CW.

Altaris knew him once, of that, I am sure. Perhaps it was he who offered me on a platter to Cassius? Plied me with lies. Seduced and supplicated. Perhaps I fell for his pretty face the way countless others have submitted to mine. I cannot remember what this mortal body may have preferred: male or female? Neither sex matters to vamryre. A mind is a mind is a mind, one in the same. That was what attracted Cassius. He shaped us to think the same. To view our prey as a summation of parts. Thin. Thick. Pretty. Beautiful. Old. Young. An attractive body. A pliable mind.

Then I think of Niamh, and she is none of those things. At the same time, she is all of them. My personal blend of ebony and ivory. Harsh and soft. I look in her eyes and I remember something fleeting, long forgotten.

Perhaps it is the same thing Altaris seeks?

A reminder of humanity. Of what it is like to think and feel stupid, meaningless things. To wonder and gaze at the world in awe. To see new things about this monotonous, morbid gray landscape.

She adds color I'd forgotten existed. Beautiful, bright, and captivating.

But she is more dangerous than even Altaris is. For she holds that light in the palm of her hand.

And at her will, she can snuff it out.

She is worried. Her mind recoils from mine when I try to find out what. It's a freedom I was never allowed with

Cassius. He peeled my thoughts and flayed them from my scalp. Hiding from him was futile, but I tried anyway.

And from him, I learned all sorts of tricks to try. How to corner someone in their mind and lure them into a trap they least suspected. How to deploy cunning and cruelty to achieve an aim. How to twist and turn your victim's own thoughts against them.

I could try those methods on her now. Make a crack to slip inside her mind and demand she tell me all. I want to. My hands twitch at my sides. I stare intently at her profile, as those black eyes scan the city blocks we pass.

I catch a glimpse of her curiosity and I could latch onto it. Ram and tear and break into that delicate skull.

But I don't. I focus on Altaris instead and keep moving, chasing his figure through the city. This area differs from the shadowy parts where the mundane congregate and dwell. Mortals live here, on this nice, neat street, organized in a grid. It reminds me of those fae archives. A place for everything, and every lie within its place. I look closer and sense the facade. Mortals live here, yes, but the mundane are cleverer at camouflage. They blend in nicely, refusing to stand out. They cloak themselves in their magic and their wealth.

All in all, it looks like a place Altaris should feel quite at home in.

But he doesn't. He is furtive, sticking to the shadows between buildings, as if—despite his hood drawn low over his head—he still fears the sun.

"This way," he calls, once we crest a hill festooned with neat, square buildings composed of black brick. This is a business quarter. I can smell the money and ink. I can feel the fortunes changing hands like the tides of the winds. A place that vamryre would scoff at, for we have no need of mortal money.

Yet, tucked amongst these offices are establishments that mundane and all races alike find appealing. Knowledge—that rare and far more complex than that which the fae kept trapped in their books.

I know this place. Once upon a time, I've been here before—though it was different then. Less buildings. Less grandeur. A heavy, anxious atmosphere tinged the air in those days. Something horrific had weighed on the horizon. An event that enveloped the world and turned it upside down.

An event that would make becoming a vamryre seem like a mercy in comparison.

"We are here." Altaris stops short, his gaze on a building ahead. It is smaller than the rest, composed of white and gray marble, in addition to black brick trim. A title engraved in gold sits above a set of black doors. D. Moure and Associates.

"I haven't been here in a while," Altaris remarks, wrinkling his nostrils. "I'd forgotten how nosy these mortals can be and how strict their rules for decorum are. You two will simply not do, dressed as you are. Wait here while I devise some scheme to get you in unannounced."

He starts forward, his head held high, drawing glances from the few mortals he passes on the streets. This time of day the world is still quiet. There are few here to notice us, though the ones that do gape and stare. Then quickly look away again.

We are unseemly, my fae and I. Our dirty clothes draw notice. As does the muck and grime on my skin, not to mention her beauty. Even her pain cannot dim it. For she is in pain. I can smell it as any predator can, seeping through those delicate limbs.

"Where are you hurt?" I ask her.

She shakes her head. I can feel her thoughts trying to shut me out. Hide from me.

"I don't like... I don't like when you hide from me." They are the wrong words. Cassius would demand and seethe. Never hide from me, he would command. He'd burrow into her mind so that she would never dare to make the same mistake again.

I could so easily do so. A part of me craves to cut inside her thoughts and dare her to keep me out.

"You don't need to hide from me." I mean it. I do not want to inspire fear like Cassius. Softness is strange to me. Unnatural. But I can utilize honesty to my benefit. There is no shame in that. To look her in the eye and tell her, "I will tell you what is on my mind if you will tell me what is on yours in return."

That draws her interest. She turns to me, her gaze hesitant. Hopeful. The way she looks at me stings. It is a trust that a creature like me should never be given.

For we can only break it in the end. Still, I will try anyway. For her, I will try.

"I saw paintings in the museum," I say, turning away from her. It makes the truth easier to say. To dwell in those dark, twisted feelings. Feelings I've shied from voicing, though I know Altaris knows the answers. "They showed...images. Things that shouldn't be possible. Things that have yet to come. They made me angry—"

I break off as her hand slips into mine. I didn't realize her moving towards me. My fingers twitch in her grip, but I don't pull away. I bear down harder in return.

"They distracted me from you. I left you behind."

She nods, that much she knew. But there is more.

"I saw you in one," I admit. I let the image enter my mind, and for the first time, I inspect it in detail. Her, splayed on canvas, standing amid a swath of destruction. There is a smile on her face, and an excited gleam in her eye. She looked happier than I have ever seen her. At home, in the middle of violence.

The thought makes her sick—literally. She gags, her face pale. I have to grip her shoulder and hold her tight. I have to resist pulling her into my arms completely.

She won't let me. I can sense her hesitation and fear. Her entire sanity is riding on my answer to a question she issues in a trembling whisper.

"What if I am a monster? What if... What if I killed? What will you do?"

What will I do?

There is no thought. No time is needed to come up with an answer.

"I will stay with you. No matter what you become. I will stay with you."

Because if she is a monster, then I am a creature far, far worse.

I will become whatever it takes to keep her from those flames. To stop the destruction revealed in those paintings.

Even if it costs me my soul, I'll give it.

Even if I don't know why.

Though...

It could be the magic of her blood, corrupting me. Consuming me. Melding my thoughts into hers.

So be it.

CHAPTER 30

Niamh

How can I be responsible for so many sins if I don't remember committing them? That's what makes this whole ordeal so terrifying. It is the reason why Caspian's instant acceptance strikes me as so odd. Because it is instant. He doesn't think. Doesn't doubt. Not even once.

If I am a monster, then so be it. He will stay near me.

But will Minchae?

Or Altaris?

Or Colleen?

Of course not. To them, I am a danger. A risk. If anything, I should return to the other realm for their sake. To accept my punishment. To keep from harming anyone else.

For if I committed murder without any memory of it, what else am I capable of?

And if I am a creature that Caspian glimpsed in the painting that upset him so, then what does it mean?

Nothing good. I weigh the possibilities over and over in my mind, and I barely notice when Altaris returns. Not until he loudly clears his throat and inclines his head toward the nearest building. "I am to take you around the back. Come now and be quick about it."

Around the back, through an alley that is as neat and pristine as the main street and across a small, stone courtyard containing a fountain in the center and a row of benches. There, he leads us inside through a small door, far away from any prying eyes. A narrow hallway extends beyond it. It takes us up a flight of stairs and down another corridor, into an office.

There, a woman sits behind a stately glass desk. A pair of gold-rimmed spectacles are perched on her nose, and not a strand of her white-blonde hair is out of place. She could be a vamryre, sired by Caspian's master, but her eyes are a soft shade of green. Not red or glowing.

"This is the specimen?" she questions, her gaze on me as she pokes her spectacles further up her nose. They magnify her eyes, making them seem enormous. Yet, there is a quiet undercurrent to her interest. It is unnerving.

It makes me uncomfortable.

"Yes," Altaris explains, taking a black leather chair positioned near the desk—one of three placed in a row. "Darlings, this is Dinara Amaz. Formal introductions later. For now, come forward. Yes you, fae one."

I stiffen at the sudden scrutiny cast onto me by both Altaris and the strange woman. Dinara. She eyes me, not like I am a piece of meat or a tool at her disposal to make a pile of coin. She looks at me as though I am a specimen. A book in the archive, but one with no cover, or title visible. The only way to decipher its contents is to peel them apart and scan them page by page.

"Yes, my dear. Do come closer." Dinara waves me closer with a slim hand. She is small, barely able to see above the surface of her desk, but I am not fooled. There is a hidden grace in her posture that even Caspian picks up on. He inches closer to me, his thoughts guarded and on-edge.

Still, I approach the desk and sit on the chair she gestures to.

"Good." She inspects me, her expression unreadable. Then she turns to Altaris. "You were right. This one is odd indeed, but I am afraid my price remains the same."

"Non-negotiable," Altaris snaps. Gone is the polish and poise. He is a haggling salesman, but for once he has met a price he is not willing to pay. A sum beyond any money, I suspect. Beyond any minor trinket, or heirloom he has gathering dust in his store. Something vital to him. Though he is a vamryer, he would rather die than part with it.

"Then we have nothing to discuss." The woman folds her hands and plasters on a false smile. "Thank you for visiting D. Moure and Associates. Please take a complimentary mint on your way out." She gestures to a bowl on a table near the door. Piled inside it are numerous small, white squares in clear wrappings.

Altaris scoffs. "Dinara, dear, I beg you to reconsider. Do you even realize what is at stake?" He sounds serious. This matters to him more than collecting contracts or shepherding his wayward vamryre does. Whatever he and this woman are bartering over, he wants badly.

So badly, he is willing to beg. Yet not badly enough…

"Either you have reconsidered, or there is no deal. Frankly, Altaris, you are wasting my time, and you more than anyone know how valuable my time is."

The vamryre hisses. "You stubborn, selfish grimorer. The fate of the world could be at stake—"

"You don't give a damn about the world," Dinara replies, smiling sweetly. "Neither do I. Now show yourselves out."

Altaris stands, his chin in the air, eyes blazing. "You will regret this, Dinara. I hope for both of our sakes, you come to your senses before it is too late."

He storms to the door.

I start to follow.

"Wait!" The woman's voice has changed. Gone is her polite boredom. Her tone practically trembles with excitement and when I turn to face her, she's leaning over her desk, her hand outstretched.

"Change your mind already, have you?" Altaris sniffs.

"This agreement will not be with you," the woman says, her eyes swollen with interest from behind their golden rims. "She, however, has something interesting. Something I may take as payment. In your pocket. Let me see it, please. Yes, that one…"

My pocket? I reach inside the front of my dress and stiffen as my fingers brush a hard object. In the turmoil of the past night, I'd forgotten all about it. The fae stone dangling from a delicate golden chain. The one Caspian found for me.

"Someone has been snooping through items that do not belong to them," Altaris remarks as I extend the object for Dinara's inspection. He isn't pleased, but Dinara nearly squeals with glee as she lunges for the stone, tugging it from my grasp. "Oh yes. Oh yes! This will do nicely. Nicely indeed. We may have a deal, after all, Altaris, do you agree?"

The vamryre grunts.

Dinara grins and raises her gaze to me. "Then we may begin. Take a seat, my dear." She clasps the fae stone to her desk and shuffles from around it. I realize then that her already lacking height was aided by a cushion balanced on her black chair. She is even smaller than she first seemed. An adult woman in the slender, compact body of a fae Dawn.

"Face forward," she tells me. "Close your eyes. This should be quick, I suspect. You talk in such terms of drama, Altaris, but she seems no less intriguing than any other fae."

"I'll be the judge of that," Altaris snipes. "Just scry her mind and tell me what you see. I need to know all of the naughty bits. Every nook and cranny—"

"Scry?" Caspian is at my side instantly.

"Don't worry, darling," Altaris remarks. "It is a simple proce-dure. Dinara will only tell me any information that could be of use toward discerning her heritage, nothing more. No grisly, boring details about anything else. Just the important bits."

Important bits. I can't help thinking, as Dinara moves to stand beside me, that there is another descriptor Altaris left out. He wants to know what happened at the circus. If I killed Cyrus, the ringmaster. If I am a danger to them all.

My heart races. I feel a wave of bile creeping up my throat. "I don't... I don't want—"

"Just relax, darling." Dinara takes one of my hands and the suggestion suddenly lands with the weight of an army of Lord Masters, urging the same. Relax. Relent. It will be okay.

For I am happy and calm. There is no danger here. No risk.

Other than a sharp, sudden tearing agony that threatens to rip my skull in two. I can't scream. I can't even flinch or react. In a sudden wave of darkness, the neat, orderly office vanishes. I'm in a dark, cold space. A woman is screaming, and screaming...

A child is crying. A baby, with pale skin, dark hair, and haunting black eyes. Yet, that is not all she was born with. Extending from her naked body, glistening, and trembling with effort, are two black structures, made of thin, glistening flesh. Wings.

The poor baby seems tormented as they unfurl from her and extend beside her. They are so large on her tiny frame. Enormous, but beautiful, more than capable of sustaining flight...

The vision drifts and suddenly, I'm standing over a woman's shoulder. Her back is to me, her face and features obscured. It's as though a black shadow covers everything about her. Except her voice. I can hear it clearly.

"Don't cry, little one. Don't cry," she whispers. Then she adjusts the baby resting on her lap, cradling the infant so it lies on its stomach, its dry, fully extended wings now visible. In the other hand, she raises a knife...

Another shift. I'm wandering a winding corridor. Running. Chasing something. Someone. They're drawing nearer, nearer... I round a corner, and they are gone.

I'm in the archives, standing before a row of books. A boy speaks to me, his voice radiating arrogance and confidence. "I can teach you to read them," he claims. "They say you cannot learn. You are too simple, but I am smart enough to teach you..."

A series of scenes pass in a frantic, overwhelming rush. Countless visits with the Lord Master. The biting of the blade against my lower back. Cutting. Hurting. Bleeding.

Then Caspian...

He is a bright light in this shadow of memory. From the moment I saw him, that was clear. He was a flame, meant to sear and burn. He tore my world to shreds, but it was a welcomed destruction. A necessary one.

We entered the mortal realm.

We avoided his brethren.

Met Altaris.

Then the museum.

The chaos.

The running.

Cyrus.

Sudden quiet. Like a truck screeching to a halt, the world goes silent, fixated on this one moment: Cyrus looming above me with murderous intent. His jackdaws attacked me —only I'm not seeing it from my own point of view, huddled on the ground.

I view it all from above. I see a thing, a gangly creature resembling me, lying in a pool of blood. Her wounds are numerous, her life hanging on by a thread. She doesn't scream, though she knows it could bring salvation. She doesn't want to. She would rather die.

Because to do so would put Caspian in danger...

Because Cyrus the ringmaster, was not a ringmaster at all. A monster lurked inside him, puppeting the mundane's body as though it dangled from a string. It waited until that moment to reveal itself.

To strike.

For it was a monster, who sustained itself not on selling or buying creatures. Not on violating fae. On pure blood. Rare blood.

It was a vamryre, but a strange one. Demented. Wrong. It reeked of a cloying, horrific stench of decay and when it opened its mouth, its fangs were elongated. Extended.

It would bite into the body of Niamh before its jackdaws could finish her off. It would drain her dry. Extend its life. Feed.

For it had waited for this moment for twenty years. Not out of hunger or necessity, but...

Revenge.

"I'll filet your body, little whelp," the creature told me. "Leave it for your sire to see. That bastard. That fucking prick. He must think himself so smart." The creature laughed at me. Then it kicked me hard in the stomach, tormenting me. "So godly. But he failed. He failed to sniff you. Suss you. He let you out of his sight. Despite the little dog he saddled you with, hand-picked. Perfectly placed. All a waste, for I will drain you dry." He moved, and there was no denying that the fae curled on the ground would soon be dead. She was too weak.

Suddenly, the vision shifts yet again. A new figure emerges from the shadows of the room. She throws herself at the monster though she knows she is no match. Minchae.

Easily, the creature tosses her aside. She lands in a crumbled heap across the tent, lifeless, broken.

But in that moment, something changed. It happened the second he touched her. A bright light emanated. A figure appeared as if summoned from the shadows themselves. Like the woman from before, their shape was obscured, covered in shadow. Only their voice gave them any sense of definition. Lilting. Soft. Female.

"It has been a long time," they say to the creature. "Decades for you to become sloppy. What a shame."

The creature snarled something in return, but it is too garbled to make out. Whatever it said devolves into a shout. Then a scream as the shadow lunches. Ripping, tearing noises betray the scene I don't remember. A heart being devoured right out of a chest. Body parts tearing. Ripping. Becoming strewn about.

Then a moan from Minchae. She is still alive. Finished with the creature that once was Cyrus, the figure cloaked in shadow approaches the part-fae. They crouch down beside her and gingerly extend her forearm for their inspection. Then they bite.

I wince at the sound. Bone cracks with the force of it. Flesh sizzles, dissolved by venom. Yet, the figure does not tear into her. They do not kill her then. They incline their head toward the ceiling as if knowing a disembodied figure watches them.

"Hello," they say. "Give Altaris my regards. Tell him his bloodling remains, for she is his punishment. His doom. He shall be seeing us soon."

The vision fades. The pressure relents and I find myself gasping on a cold hard floor. My stomach roils. I fell sick. Without caring for decorum, I hunch over and vomit then and there. Too many thoughts and recollections swirl in my brain. I can't tell what is mine. What is another's. Something went rampant in my brain and left a mess behind.

Even Caspian's comfort can't soothe the ache.

Because his comfort is a lie. He is a lie. A dog. A plant, meant to retrain me. Manipulate.

All as a part of someone's plan.

Altaris's plan. He knows something—more than he let on. He is a liar. A villain. A monster.

He wanted this from the start: me, a wingless, lonely abomination.

All in a game of revenge.

There is no time to process these recollections. No place to think. I need to think. I need to breathe. I can't. I can't.

"We can help you, mistress," those voices tell me, surging to the forefront of my mind, louder than ever. The jackdaws that hid inside of me, so fearful of the figure draped in shadow that they had no choice. "Trust us. Come. Come!"

I stand. As if from miles away I hear Altaris and Dinara converse as though I don't exist. As though I don't matter. Somewhere, beyond the wreckage of my mind, I can sense Caspian, demanding to be let in. He is calling for me.

But I can't answer.

There is too much shame, and guilt, and hatred. I drag myself upright. I spy a window and I run toward it without thinking. I listen to those greedy little voices urging me forward.

"Go! Go! We shall catch you!"

The glass gives way as though it was made of tissue paper. An illusion that shatters into a million sparkling shards. I fall in a sudden, terrifying motion. There is no audience below. No series of movements to perform.

I just fall.

Then lurch upward as if tugged by a hand clenched around my spine. Caspian's? No. For this strange, gripping contact yanks me higher. and higher still.

Then I feel a rush of air, rhythmic fluttering against my skin. I hear a strange, whooshing sound.

Then I look down and see the entire city at a glance.

There is no other explanation for it.

Somehow, I am flying.

With borrowed wings.

CHAPTER 31

Caspian

Some games require a long-term strategy in order to win. How did I come across that phrase? I remember it from somewhere. Once upon a time, someone said it to me.

"A long-term strategy, Collin," they insisted. "For that is the ultimate weapon sure to win any war: patience. Incredible, steely patience. You are too impulsive. Too strayed by the whims of your temper. Trust me in this and you will learn soon enough. No other weapon comes close to the strategy of patience..."

Altaris--only his voice was different then. Softer then, less wistful. His brand of charm was the same: over the top and overbearing. Yet, his tone seemed lighter, lacking the heaviness that has crept into that baritone sense. Years...no, centuries, have made him an entirely different person.

One whose sadness laces every word spoken. No longer can he hide his shame or guilt behind pretty words.

"Well, this is quite a dilemma," he says, but there is a lack of passion in those words. "Dinara, please explain again in detail. What the hell did you see?"

"Her mind is a jumble," the woman explains, her voice faint, as if she's on the verge of passing out. Or perhaps diving through the now broken window behind her, as Niamh did. She sways and braces her hand against the nearby desk for balance. "Such a confusing swirl of recollections. So very intriguing. Oh, Altaris, you were right. I should have accepted any price. Any. She is very intriguing indeed."

"Nice to know," the vamryre, snaps. "Care to tell me why she might have gone leaping out of the building?" He sounds strained, grunting with effort, as though he is grappling with something heavy.

Not that I care. My eyes are on the space where Niamh stood. Where she jumped through a wall of glass. Where she sprouted wings and took off through the sky, a beautiful mass of ebony and ivory.

"Dinara, my dear, I know scrying is tiring, but if you could explain—"

"Oh yes! She thinks you are her sire, and that you sent one of your little toys after her. But, of course, that is not true. Something is toying with her. Luring her. They knew she would be scried, and they planted seeds to sow doubt. They want her isolated. I can't explain it all just yet—but I feel it in my bones. There is chaos brewing. Oh, my dear, Altaris, what a fascinating mess."

"Damn." The vamryre hisses, and real concern breaks through his facade. For once he sounds tired—exhausted, and every bit his incalculable age. "How interesting indeed— Really, Caspian! Can you be still?"

Because I'm straining to reach that goddamn window despite the weight of what feels like a million iron chains fighting to restrain me.

"She thinks you sent him to control her," the grimoirer adds with a delicate laugh. "How devious. What on earth have you gotten up to now?"

"A lie," Altaris says. "Caspian, if you do not calm yourself, we will not be able to devote our attention to finding your—"

"You lied to her." I whirl on him and realize that the 'chains' holding me back were his arms. He watches me, his suit wrinkled, eyes more shrouded than ever. Niamh's thoughts are sealed off once again but one realization is crystal clear. "A monster told her I am your pet on a leash. So, was it you? Were you the one who gave me to Cassius?"

"Not quite," he says in a hard, flat tone. "Honestly, Caspian, now really isn't the time to—"

"Tell me! Were you the one who coaxed me into this life? Was I your pet?"

"Of course not," he says, his fangs bared. "Caspian, you were the only person in this world to ever trust me with something truly valuable. Something I have worked like hell to maintain."

"What?"

"Your soul," he says. "And though I wanted to refuse, I have upheld my end of the bargain. For I was not the one who sold you to Cassius. And you went through great pains to ensure that, no matter what, I couldn't intervene."

"Lies," I snap. Nothing would be worth choosing this cursed existence. Nothing.

"I believed so as well," he says, as if plucking the thought from my head. "But you were adamant. Insisted. You sacrificed your soul to pursue this path. I played no part in that aspect, I can assure you."

"Why?"

"I won't say," he says. "It isn't my truth to tell. I can only offer you this: you chose this path, knowing the risks. The dangers. You alone made that decision. All I can do, is all I have ever done for you: assist in any way I can, for we have a contract to maintain, and there is no time for this."

"Why not?" His tone conveys more than some ethical aversion alone. He's hiding something.

A cocked eyebrow and wince on his part confirms it. "Because," he says, "it seems that council has decided to forgo politics. They want you back. Badly enough to send their own spies here to do so. We need to find your wayward friend, before they do first. I doubt I need to explain why."

"No," I hiss.

If I don't track her down in time, Niamh's life will be on the line.

And, if Cassius has his way, far more...

The Story Continues...

The Story continues in **book 3, Eternal**.

About Lana Sky

Lana Sky is a reclusive writer in the United States who spends most of her time daydreaming about complex male characters and parenting her Cockapoo Joey. She writes dark, twisted romance across several genres. Her titles include everything from mafia romance to vampires.

facebook.com/AuthorLanaSky

x.com/lanasky101

amazon.com/author/lanasky

pinterest.com/lanasky101

goodreads.com/lanasky

instagram.com/lanasky101

bookbub.com/authors/lana-sky

tiktok.com/@author_lana_sky

Also by Lana Sky

For more titles by Lana Sky, please visit:

https://www.lanaskybooks.com